BLOCKBUSTER REVIEWS FOR
BURNT SIENNA
AND DAVID MORRELL

more . . .

W9-BUL-148

ALSO BY DAVID MORRELL

FICTION

First Blood (1972)

Testament (1975)

Last Reveille (1977)

The Totem (1979)

Blood Oath (1982)

The Brotherhood of the Rose (1984)

The Fraternity of the Stone (1985)

The League of Night and Fog (1987)

The Fifth Profession (1990)

The Covenant of the Flame (1991)

Assumed Identity (1993)

Desperate Measures (1994)

The Totem (Complete and Unaltered) (1994)

Extreme Denial (1996)

Double Image (1998)

Black Evening (1999)

NONFICTION

John Barth: An Introduction (1976)

Fireflies (1988)

DAVID MORRELL

BURNT SIENNA

WARNER
VISION
BOOKS

A Time Warner Company

WARNER BOOKS EDITION

Copyright © 2000 by Morrell Enterprises, Inc.
All rights reserved. No part of this book may be reproduced in any form or by any electronic or mechanical means, including information storage and retrieval systems, without permission in writing from the publisher, except by a reviewer who may quote brief passages in a review.

Cover design by Jesse Sanchez

Warner Vision is a registered trademark of Warner Books, Inc.

Warner Books, Inc.
1271 Avenue of the Americas
New York, NY 10020

Visit our Web site at
www.twbookmark.com

 A Time Warner Company

Printed in the United States of America

Originally published in hardcover by Warner Books.
First International Paperback Printing: March 2001
First U.S. Paperback Printing: May 2001

10 9 8 7 6 5 4 3 2 1

To Danny Baror:
foreign agent *extraordinaire*

That's my last Duchess painted on the wall,
Looking as if she were alive. . . .

—Robert Browning

BURNT
SIENNA

ONE

1

From *Newsweek*

"That was a long time ago. I don't think about it," Malone claims. But if, according to the critics, his paintings celebrate life more than any artist since the Impressionists, one can't help suspecting that the sensuality in his work is a reaction to the nightmare he barely survived on the night of December 20, 1989, during the U.S. invasion of Panama.

A painter who was once a military helicopter pilot—in the cutthroat competition of today's art world, that dramatic juxtaposition between Malone's violent past and artistic present accounts for part of his mystique. But while his Marine background is exotic to some patrons, it also initially made critics skeptical that his work had merit. As Douglas Fennerman, Malone's art representative, points out, "Chase had to work twice as hard to earn his reputation. From that point of view, it doesn't hurt to have

a soldier's background if you want to survive on the bat-
tlefield of the galleries in Manhattan."

Certainly Malone looks more like a soldier than any
stereotype of an artist. Six feet tall, sinewy more than muscular, he has a sun-bronzed face and ruggedly attractive
features. Interviewed on the beach near his home on the
Mexican resort of Cozumel, he had just completed his
daily exercise of a five-mile jog coupled with an hour of
calisthenics. His sandy hair, bleached by the Caribbean
sun, matches the color of the beard stubble that adds to
his rugged handsomeness. Apart from the paint smears on
his T-shirt and shorts, there is no hint of his place in the
art world.

He is thirty-seven, but it isn't hard to imagine that he
didn't look much different in his lieutenant's uniform ten
years earlier when his helicopter gunship was shot down
by a Panamanian rocket. That happened at 2:00 A.M. on
December 20, and while Malone refuses to talk about the
incident, Jeb Wainright, the copilot who was shot down
with him, remembers it vividly.

"In the night, there were so many tracers and rockets
flying around, not to mention flames shooting up from explosions on the ground, it looked like the Fourth of July. In
hell. To soften everything up, we hit first from the air:
285 fixed-wing aircraft and 110 helicopters. Like a swarm
of gigantic mosquitoes, with damned big stingers. Forty-
millimeter Vulcan cannons, 105-millimeter howitzers,
laser-guided antitank missiles. The works."

One of the principal targets was the headquarters of
the Panamanian Defense Forces, a factorylike building
in a shanty section of Panama City, called El Chorrillo,

"the little stream." The enemy put its headquarters there, U.S. military planners theorized, so that Panamanian troops could use the twenty thousand people in El Chorrillo as a shield.

"And something like that happened," Wainright continues. "When our choppers attacked the headquarters, the enemy ran for cover in the surrounding area. But we kept after them, and that's when Chase started shouting into the radio to tell our command post that civilians were under fire. They sure were. Almost at once, five square blocks burst into flames. Command Central didn't have a chance to respond before we were hit. I still remember my teeth snapping together from the explosion. Chase fought to keep control of the gunship. It was full of smoke, spinning and veering, all the while dropping. Chase is the best chopper pilot I ever saw, but I still don't know how he managed to get us safely on the ground."

The nightmare was only beginning. In the darkness, with the fire spreading from shack to shack, Malone and Wainright struggled to escape. As the twenty thousand residents of El Chorrillo swarmed in panic through a maze of alleys, Malone and his copilot were shot at by Panamanian forces as well as by U.S. gunships whose crews didn't realize American fliers were on the ground.

"Then a bullet hit me in the leg," Wainright says. "I have no idea from which side. While the civilians rushed past us, Chase rigged a pressure bandage on my leg, heaved me over his shoulder, and tried to get away from the fires. At one point, he had to use his service pistol against Panamanian soldiers holed up in a building. I later realized it took him until after dawn to get us out of there.

We were slumped against a wall, soot falling all around us, when American tanks and flamethrowers showed up to level what was left of El Chorrillo. Two thousand civilians died that night. God knows how many were wounded. All twenty thousand lost their homes."

Shortly afterward, Malone left the Marine Corps.

"Chase had always been drawing stuff when we weren't training," Wainright recalls. "Sometimes, instead of going on leave, he stayed in the barracks and worked on his sketches. It was obvious he had talent, but I had no idea how much until after he committed himself to trying to earn a living at it. That night in El Chorrillo, he made up his mind, and he never looked back."

A viewer will find no hint of violence in Malone's paintings. They are mostly colorful landscapes. Their vibrant details, which are reminiscent of van Gogh and yet distinctly his own, communicate a passionate joy in the senses, a thrill of sensual appreciation for the natural world that perhaps only someone who has survived a face-to-face encounter with apocalyptic violence and death could be moved to depict. . . .

2

As waves lapped at Malone's sneakers, the sunset reflected off the Caribbean, creating a hue that seemed never to have existed before. He was conscious of the gritty sand beneath his shoes, of the balmy breeze against his thick, curly hair, and of the plaintive *cree-*

cree-cree of seagulls overhead. Raising his brush to the half-finished canvas, he concentrated to get it all in—not just the shapes and colors but also the sounds, the fragrances, and even the taste of the salt air: to attempt the impossible and embed those other senses in a visual medium so that the painting would make a viewer feel what it had been like to stand in this spot at this magical moment, experiencing the wonder of this sunset as if there had never been another.

Abruptly something distracted him. When Malone had been in the military, his ability to register several details at once had been a survival skill, but it was as an artist and not a soldier that he now noticed movement at the edge of his vision.

It came from his right, from a stand of palm trees a hundred yards along the deserted beach, near where the unseen dirt road ended. A shifting shadow became a squat man stepping onto the sand. The intruder raised a hand to shield his spectacles from the sunset's brilliance and peered in Malone's direction. As the man approached, his dark suit revealed itself to be royal blue. The black of his shoes was soon covered with the white of the sand that he walked across. His briefcase, a chalk gray that matched his hair, had bumps on it—ostrich skin.

Malone wasn't puzzled that he had failed to hear the man's car. After all, the roar of the surf on the shore was so strong that it obscured distant sounds. Nor was he puzzled by the intruder's joyless clothing; even an island paradise couldn't relax some harried business travelers. What did puzzle him, however, was that the man approached with a resolve that suggested he had come specifically because of Malone, but Malone had not told anyone where he would be.

He took all this in while appearing not to do so, using the need of tilting his head toward his palette to disguise his periodic glances in the man's direction. As he intensified the scarlet on his canvas, he heard the intruder come so close that the crunch of his shoes was distinct.

Then the crunch stopped an arm's length from Malone's right. "Mr. Malone?"

Malone ignored him.

"I'm Alexander Potter."

Malone continued to ignore him.

"I spoke to you on the phone yesterday. I told you I was flying in this afternoon."

"You wasted your time. I thought I made it clear: I'm not interested."

"*Very* clear. It's just that my employer doesn't take no for an answer."

"He'd better get used to it." Malone applied more color to the canvas. Seagulls screeched. A minute passed.

Potter broke the stalemate. "Perhaps it's a matter of your fee not being sufficient. On the phone, I mentioned two hundred thousand dollars. My employer authorized me to double it."

"This isn't about money." Malone finally turned to him.

"What *is* it about?"

"I was once in a position where I had to follow a lot of orders."

Potter nodded. "Your experience in the Marines."

"After I got out, I promised myself that from then on I was going to do only what I wanted."

"A half million."

"I'd been obeying commands for too long. Many of them didn't make sense, but it was my job to follow them anyhow. Finally I was determined to be my own boss. The trouble is, I needed money and I broke my promise to myself. The man who hired me saw things differently than I did. He kept finding fault with my work and refused to pay me."

"That wouldn't happen this time." Potter's tie had red, blue, and green stripes, the banner for an Ivy League club that would never have asked Malone to join and to which he would never have wanted to belong.

"It didn't happen then, either," Malone said. "Believe me, I convinced the man to pay."

"I meant that this time no one would find fault with your work. You're too famous now. Six hundred thousand."

"That's more than any of my paintings has ever sold for."

"My employer knows that."

"Why? Why is it worth so much to him?"

"He values the unique."

"Just for me to do a private portrait?"

"No. This commission involves *two* portraits. One of the subject's face. The other full length. Nude."

"Nude? Can I assume your employer is not the subject of the portraits?"

Malone was making a joke, but Potter evidently didn't have a sense of humor. "His wife. Mr. Bellasar doesn't allow even his photograph to be taken."

"Bellasar?"

"Derek Bellasar. Is the name familiar to you?"

"Not at all. Should it be?"

"Mr. Bellasar is very powerful."

"Yes, I'm sure he reminds himself of that every morning."

"I beg your pardon?"

"How did you know I was here?"

The abrupt change of subject caused a shadow of confusion to glide behind Potter's glasses. He raised his brow in what passed for a frown. "It's hardly a secret. The Manhattan gallery that represents you confirmed what was in the recent *Newsweek* article. You live here on Cozumel."

"That's not what I meant."

"How did I know where to phone you?" Potter's expression displayed total confidence again. "There's no mystery. The article mentioned your passion for privacy, that you don't have a telephone and you live in a sparsely inhabited part of the island. The article also mentioned that the only building near you is a restaurant called the Coral Reef, where you receive your mail and take your business calls. It was simply a matter of my being persistent, of phoning that restaurant until I happened to catch you."

"That's still not what I meant."

"Then I'm afraid I don't understand."

"How did you know I was *here*." Malone pointed toward the sand at his feet.

"Ah. I see. Someone at the restaurant told me where you'd gone."

"No. This afternoon, I came here on the spur of the moment. I didn't tell anyone. There's only one way you could have known—you had someone following me."

Potter's expression didn't change. He didn't even blink.

"You're trouble," Malone said. "Leave."

"Perhaps we can discuss this over dinner."

"Hey, what part of *no* don't you understand?"

3

Potter was sitting at a table directly across from the entrance, staring as Malone stepped into the Coral Reef. The man's solemn business suit contrasted with the colorful tops and shorts of the many tourists who had made the ten-kilometer drive from Cozumel's only town, San Miguel, to visit this locally famous restaurant. Years ago, it had been no more than a beer and snack shop for divers attracted to the clear water of the nearby reef. But over time, the building and the menu had expanded, until the restaurant was now listed among the must-sees in every Cozumel travel guide. Potter had every right to be a customer, of course, but although the place was usually busy, Malone considered the Coral Reef to be his private refuge, and he resented that Potter had contaminated it.

Pausing, he gave Potter a long, hard look, then turned to Yat-Balam, the round-headed, broad-faced, high-cheeked Mayan proprietor. Softening his features, Malone said hello. He had never needed a lot of friends in order to be happy. An only child who had been raised by a single mother and who had been left alone a great deal as a child, he had learned to feel comfortable being alone, to be a good companion to himself. He didn't feel isolated living away from the only town on this small island off the eastern coast of Mexico's Yucatán Peninsula. Nonetheless, the restaurant had become important to him. He visited it every day. He had established a warm rapport not only with Yat but also with Yat's wife, who was the cook, and Yat's three teenage children, who were the waiters. Along with occasional visitors from the art world and Malone's former Marine unit, not to mention divers who returned to the area often enough to be regulars, they fulfilled his social needs. Until three months ago, there had also been a woman, but that had ended unhappily, for she had definitely not enjoyed an isolated life, even if it was on a Caribbean paradise, and had returned to Manhattan's art galleries and receptions.

After a few pleasantries, Yat said, "There is a man who has been sitting all evening but refuses to order anything except iced tea. He keeps staring at the entrance. He says he is waiting for you." Yat directed his almond-shaped eyes in Potter's direction.

"Yes, I saw him when I came in."

"He is a friend?"

"A nuisance."

"There will be a problem?"

"No. But I'd better get this settled so I can enjoy my meal. What's the special for tonight?"

"*Huachinango* Veracruz."

Malone's mouth watered in anticipation of the red snapper prepared with green peppers, onions, tomatoes, olives, and spices. "Bring him one and put it on my bill. I'll have the same."

"I'll get another place setting."

"No need. I won't be eating with him. Better bring us each a margarita also. I have a feeling he's going to want a drink after I've finished talking to him."

As Malone started past the busy tables toward Potter, Yat put a cautionary hand on his arm.

Malone gave him a reassuring smile. "It's okay. I promise, there won't be trouble."

The restaurant had an octagonal design, with thatched walls that stopped at waist level, allowing a view of the ocean. A full moon illuminated the surf. Over the bar next to the restaurant's entrance hung a painting Malone had given to Yat, depicting the beach. Here and there, posts supported beams that spread out like spindles on a wheel and held up the round, tent-shaped thatched roof. The effect was spacious and airy, no matter how crowded the room was.

Potter hadn't taken his gaze off Malone. Approaching, Malone decided that, on the beach, the sunset had made Potter look healthier than he now appeared. The pallor of his skin suggested that he was seldom out of doors. Behind his spectacles, his eyes had a grave expression.

"Join me." Potter gestured toward the chair across from him.

"Afraid not. But I've taken the liberty of ordering for you. A specialty of the house. You'll find it one of the most delicious meals you've ever eaten. This way, you won't go back without getting something out of the trip."

Continuing to fix his gaze on Malone, Potter tapped his fingers on the table. "I'm afraid I haven't made it clear that failure to convince you to accept the commission is not an option. I cannot go back to Mr. Bellasar and tell him you refused his offer."

"Then don't go back. Tell him you quit."

Potter tapped his fingers harder. "That is not an option, either."

"Hey, everybody's got job problems. It doesn't matter how much he pays you. If you don't like what you're doing—"

"You're mistaken. I enjoy my employment very much."

"Fine. Then deal with his reaction."

"It's my own reaction I care about. I am not accustomed to lack of results. You must understand how serious this matter is. What can I give you to convince you to agree?"

"It's the other way around," Malone said. "If I took

the assignment, I'd be losing the one thing that matters the most to me."

"And what is that?" Potter's gaze intensified.

"My independence. Look, I've got more than enough money. I don't have to be at the beck and call of any son of a bitch who thinks he's rich enough to tell me what and how to paint."

Malone didn't realize he had raised his voice until he noticed a silence around him. Turning, he discovered that the diners had stopped eating and were frowning at him, as was Yat, who stood in the background. "Sorry." Malone made a calming gesture.

He turned back to Potter. "This is an extension of my home. Don't make me lose my temper here."

"Your refusal to take the assignment is absolute?"

"Have you got a hearing problem?"

"There's nothing I can do or say to change your mind?"

"Jesus, isn't it obvious?"

"Fine." Potter stood. "I'll make my report to Mr. Bellasar."

"What's your hurry? Enjoy your meal first."

Potter picked up his briefcase. "Mr. Bellasar will want to know your decision as soon as possible."

4

A quarter mile offshore, the occupants of a forty-foot sailboat anchored near the reef were more interested in the lights of the restaurant than they were in the moon's reflection off the sea. While the four men studied the beach, they listened to a radio receiver in the main cabin. The transmitted voices were clear, despite the murmur of people talking and eating in the restaurant.

"I'm not close enough to hear what Malone told him," a male voice said from the radio, "but Potter sure looks pissed."

"He's standing," a female voice said. "He's grabbing his briefcase. He's in a hurry to get out of here."

"Back to the airport would be my guess," the thin-haired senior member of the team on the sailboat said. "We know how suspicious Bellasar is about telephones. He'll want Potter to use the scrambler-equipped radio on the plane to get in touch with him."

The female voice continued from the radio. "Rodriguez is posing as a cabdriver. He'll follow the car Potter rented and find out what he's up to."

"In the meantime, Malone's gone over to the guy who owns the restaurant," the male voice said. "He seems to be apologizing. He looks annoyed with himself, but more annoyed with Potter." For a moment, only the drone of the restaurant came from the radio. Then the male voice said, "He's sitting down to eat."

On the sailboat, the senior member of the team sighed in frustration. The bobbing of the craft in the water made him queasy. Or perhaps he was queasy from what he'd just heard. "That's it for tonight, I'm afraid. The show's over."

"And Malone didn't accept the offer," the heavyset man next to him said.

"Just as you predicted."

"Well, I was his copilot. I've kept in touch with him since we got out of the Marines. I know how he thinks."

"He's determined to be his own man? We might never have as good a chance as this. You're the expert on him. How the hell do we get him to be *our* man?"

5

Tensing, Malone heard the roar before he veered his Jeep around palm trees and came within sight of his house, or what under usual circumstances would have been within sight of his house. The dust cloud that confronted him and the mechanical chaos within it were so startling that he braked abruptly to a stop, staring paralyzed at the haze-concealed dinosaurlike shapes of rumbling machines—bulldozers, one, two, three, Jesus Christ, half a dozen of them—tearing up the sand dunes and palm trees around his home.

When he had first seen this isolated cove on the eastern shore of Cozumel, he had known immediately that this was where he wanted to live. The calm waters on the opposite side of the island made that area more attractive for tourists and developers,

which was fine with Malone, who wanted to be away
from crowds. But the dramatic surf on this unpro-
tected side, not to mention the remote intimacy of
this rugged cove with its stretches of white sand
punctuated by craggy black limestone, was irre-
sistible to him. According to Mexican law, a for-
eigner could purchase land only after he or she
obtained a permit from the Ministry of Foreign Affairs. In the case of beach property, however, the
situation was more complicated because the govern-
ment needed to make certain that so precious a resource would be respected. Thus it had been
necessary for Malone to purchase the property
through a fifty-year trust agreement with a local
bank, which retained the title and acted as a guardian
of the beach. He had then hired a prizewinning Mexican architect to design the house. The attractive
sprawling one-story structure was made from a normally unattractive substance, concrete, which was
less affected by the region's humidity than the upright wooden poles lashed together that formed the
walls of many homes on the island. Every corner
and edge of the concrete was contoured, eliminating
sharp angles, softening its appearance. It was stuc-
coed a dazzling white, enhanced by numerous colorful flowering shrubs, and topped with a roof of
thatched palm fronds, providing a traditional look.
Several arches and courtyards allowed breezes to
circulate freely, reducing the need for air condition-
ing.

But everything was changed now. The house was

coated with a thick layer of grit thrown up by the bull-dozers. A normally benevolent breeze was carrying the grit into the house. The sand dunes among which his home had nestled were flattened, carcasses of palm trees lying everywhere. And still the relentless bulldozers kept gouging and tearing, savaging the cove.

As Malone stared at the desecration, his paralysis broke. Furious, he leapt from his Jeep and stormed toward the nearest bulldozer, motioning urgently for the driver to stop. Either the driver didn't see him, or else the driver didn't care, for the bulldozer rumbled past Malone, ramming down another palm tree. With greater outrage, Malone charged after the bulldozer, grabbed a handhold on the side, pulled himself up, reached for the ignition key, and turned off the engine.

"Damn it, I told you to stop," Malone shouted in Spanish.

The driver muttered an obscenity and grabbed Malone's hand to try to get the key back.

"What the hell do you think you're doing here?" Malone demanded.

Cursing, the driver grabbed harder for the key.

Malone threw it into the sand.

At once the cove became silent as the other drivers, having seen what was happening, turned off their machines and jumped to the ground, racing to help their compatriot.

"Answer me!" Malone said. "What do you think you're doing? This is my home! You don't have a right!"

The other drivers flanked the bulldozer, two on one side, three on the other.

"Leave my brother alone," one of them warned.

"You're at the wrong place! I live here, for God's sake. You've made a mistake!"

"The mistake is yours if you don't get away from my brother." The man scrambled onto the bulldozer.

"Listen to me."

No. Spinning, the driver from whom he had taken the key aimed a fist at Malone's stomach. With only slightly less speed than when he'd been in the military, Malone grabbed the man's arm, yanked him from his seat, and hurled him off the bulldozer into the sand. In the same fluid motion, he ducked, avoiding the punch that the driver's brother directed toward his face. Surging upward, he plunged his fist into his attacker's solar plexus and flipped him after his brother. With a painful wheeze, the second man landed next to the first.

The remaining four drivers gaped, no longer certain how far they wanted to push this.

"Nobody has to get hurt!"

"Except you." The first man struggled to catch his breath and stand.

"I'm telling you I don't want to fight! Just stop while we figure this out! You're not supposed to be here with this equipment!"

"The man who hired us was very specific," one of the other drivers said angrily. "He led us to this property. We asked him about the house. He said the land belonged to him. He told us to level everything for a new hotel."

"*What* man? Whoever it was didn't know what the hell he was talking about. Did he give you his name?"

When Malone heard who it was, his chest heaved with greater rage.

6

ROBERTO RIVERA. BANK OFFICER.

Malone shoved the door open with such force, the frosted glass almost shattered.

Rivera, a lean man with dark hair and a thin mustached face, jerked his head up. The elderly client on the opposite side of his desk stopped in surprised midsentence and inhaled, making a strangling sound, as if he'd swallowed a peach pit.

"Señor Rivera, I tried to stop him," the secretary insisted from the doorway behind Malone.

Malone fixed his gaze on Rivera. "My business couldn't wait."

"I'm calling the police." The secretary swung toward the phone on her desk.

"Not just yet." Rivera faced his client, who had recovered his breath but continued to look startled. "Señor Valdez, I apologize for the interruption. Would you please wait outside for a moment while I take care of this unpleasantness?"

As soon as the client left and the door was closed,

Malone stalked toward Rivera. "You son of a bitch, why did you send those bulldozers to wreck my property?"

"Obviously there's been a misunderstanding."

"Not according to the guys driving the bulldozers." Malone's muscles compacted with fury. "They were very clear—you sent them."

"Oh, there's no misunderstanding about that," Rivera said.

"What?"

"I sent them all right."

"You actually admit it?" About to drag Rivera from his chair, Malone stopped in amazement.

"Totally. The misunderstanding I referred to was your reference to the bulldozers being on your property. That section of land isn't yours any longer."

"You bastard, I paid for it."

"In a trust agreement with this bank, which kept the title in its name. But we've had too many complaints about your eyesore of a house."

"What?"

"And the rumors about drugs being smuggled ashore there can't be ignored any longer. I spoke to the Ministry of Foreign Affairs. The trust agreement was revoked. I purchased the property."

"Jesus Christ, you can't do that."

"But it's already happened," Rivera said. "Obviously, you haven't picked up your mail yet, or you would have found the bank's notice of termination."

"I *paid* for that land!"

"You would also have found a check for the amount

that you invested. I added—although I didn't have to—a modest profit to compensate you for the increased market value of the property."

"Compensate? You prick, you're destroying my home." Suddenly something one of the drivers had said struck him. "A hotel."

"What?"

"You sold the property to a developer."

"It was too good an offer to pass up."

"It certainly must have been." Malone grabbed him. "Well, it's going to be awfully hard to spend the money when you're in a wheelchair."

"Call the police now," Rivera shouted to his secretary in the other room.

Malone dragged him to his feet.

"Think twice," Rivera warned. "In Mexico, there aren't any prisoner rights. You'll spend a long time in jail waiting for your assault case to go to trial."

Malone drew back a fist. "It'll be worth it."

"And when you finally do go to trial, I assure you that Mexican judges take a harsh view of foreigners attacking respected members of the community."

The secretary opened the door. "The police are on their way."

"Thank you. Now it's up to Señor Malone to decide whether they're needed." Rivera's gaze was defiant.

"A respected member of the community." Malone wanted to spit. In disgust, he lowered his fist. "Yeah, it must have been a damned good offer."

"Blame the man who negotiated with me. He knows you. He insisted that I pass along his respects."

"His respects? I don't . . . What's his name?"

"Alexander Potter."

"Potter?"

"He said to tell you that his employer also sends his regards."

7

The Coral Reef's parking lot was empty. A taxi headed away, its passengers looking disappointed. Malone got out of his Jeep, crossed the sand toward the restaurant's front door, and found a sign that read CLOSED. All the shutters were down.

He frowned. The silence from inside made the roar of the surf seem extra loud as he told himself that Yat had such a strong work ethic, the only reason he would close without warning would be that something had happened to him or his family.

He tried the door. It was locked. He pounded on it. No one answered. With long, urgent strides, he rounded the building and reached a back door that led to the kitchen. This door, when he tried it, budged open, leading him into the shadows of the cooking area, where the previous night's savory odors still lingered. *From last night,* he emphasized to himself, for the several stoves were cold. There was no sign of any meal in preparation.

Beyond swinging doors, a troubled voice asked, "Who's there?"

"Yat?"

"*Who is it?*" the voice demanded uneasily.

"Me, Yat. It's Chase."

"Oh." One of the swinging doors came open, Yat's round, pensive face peering through. "I thought it was another customer."

Malone felt his chest turn warm from the compliment of being considered more than a customer. "What's happened? What's wrong?"

"Wrong?" Yat assessed the word. "Everything."

Beyond him, in the murky dining area, someone knocked on the front door. A second sequence of knocking, louder, ended with disappointed voices and the sound of a car driving away.

"At first, I explained to everyone who came that we were closed, but finally there were too many. It became too much." Weary, Yat gestured for Malone to join him in the dining area.

To the right, on the bar, Malone saw a tequila bottle and a half-empty glass. "What's the matter? Tell me."

Yat stared toward the front door. "They kept wanting to know when the restaurant would be open again, and I couldn't bear repeating so many times that I didn't know. In the end, I finally just sat here and listened to them bang on the door."

"You've got to tell me," Malone said.

"A man came here this morning and offered to buy the Coral Reef for more money than I ever expected to see in a lifetime."

Malone had a sick sinking feeling.

"I spoke to my wife and children about it. They work so hard. We all work so hard." Yat shook his head, depressed. "It was too much to resist."

"Potter," Malone said.

"Yes, Alexander Potter—the same man who was here the other night. He said to tell you he sends his regards."

"And those of a man named Derek Bellasar?"

"Yes. The Coral Reef is to remain closed indefinitely until Señor Bellasar decides what to do with the property." Yat stared at his glass, picked it up, and took a deep swallow. "I should have thought about it longer. I should have waited before I signed the papers. Now I understand that the money means nothing if I don't know what to do with my time. I didn't realize until now how important coming here was to me."

Yat's use of the past tense was so poignant that Malone poured tequila into a glass. "I know how important it was to *me*." When Malone swallowed the clear, sharp, slightly oily liquid, his eyes watered, but not just from the alcohol. He felt as if someone had died. Bellasar, you son of a bitch, I'm going to get you for this, he thought.

"I almost forgot," Yat said. "You had a phone call."

"What?" Malone wrinkled his brow. "From whom?"

"A man at the gallery in New York that sells your paintings. He said he had something important to talk to you about."

With an even sicker feeling, Malone reached for the phone.

8

"You sold the gallery?" Malone dismally repeated what he had just heard.

"Hey, I'm as surprised as anybody." Douglas Fennerman's voice was faint, the telephone connection a hiss. "Believe me, it was the last thing on my mind. But out of the blue, this absolutely fantastic offer came in."

"From a man named Alexander Potter, negotiating for someone called Derek Bellasar."

"That's a funny thing, Chase. Potter said you'd know who bought the gallery even before I told you the name. But just in case you didn't, he said to make sure I passed along—"

"His regards."

"Are you clairvoyant?"

"And Bellasar's regards, also."

"Amazing. Do you know these people well?"

"No, but believe me, I intend to."

"Then everything's going to work out. You and I go back so far, you'd have been the first person I called, even if Potter hadn't suggested it. I want to tell you how honored I feel to have represented you."

Malone felt a tightness in his throat. "If you hadn't

promoted me so tirelessly, I never would have had any breaks."

"Hey, you're the one with the talent. I'm just the messenger. But just because we're not in business together any longer, that doesn't mean we won't still be friends."

"Sure," Malone managed to say.

"We'll still get together from time to time."

". . . Sure."

Doug sounded melancholy. "You bet." He tried to muster his former enthusiasm. "And at least it won't be like you're in business with strangers. Since you and Potter and Bellasar are acquainted with one another, it's something to build on. After you've worked with them for a while, you might even get to be friends."

"I don't think so."

"You never know."

"I *do* know." Malone's jaw muscles hardened.

"Well, you won't be in business with them anytime soon," Doug said.

"I don't understand."

"Bellasar plans a complete renovation of the gallery. All your paintings are being put in storage until the job's completed."

"*What?*"

"You're going to be off the market temporarily. Could be a wise move. My guess is, once the gallery reopens, your work will increase in value because it's been unavailable."

Malone tightened his grip on the phone. "And *my*

guess is, Bellasar will guarantee those paintings are unavailable for a very long time."

"What are you talking about?"

"Making Bellasar and Potter wish they'd never heard of me."

"Wait a minute, Chase. Obviously, I haven't been clear. There's no reason to feel threatened. If there's something you're worried about, if you need to be reassured about something, just tell me. I'm meeting them Wednesday morning at an auction at Sotheby's. I'll pass your message along."

Sotheby's? Malone quickly calculated: Wednesday morning's thirty-six hours from now. He gripped the phone so hard that his hand cramped.

9

"Chase?"

The husky shout made Malone turn from the suitcase he was furiously packing.

"Are you in there, Chase?"

Peering through a bedroom window, Malone saw a tall, heavy-chested man with short blond hair and a sunburned, big-boned face standing on the devastated beach.

"Jeb?" he yelled.

The big man chuckled.

"Jeb! My God, why didn't you let me know you were coming?"

"I can hear you, but I can't see you, buddy. Where *are* you?"

"I'll be right out!"

When Malone hurried from the house onto the back patio, Jeb Wainright broke into a grin. Thirty-seven, the same age as Malone, he wore sandals, baggy brown shorts, and a garish flower-patterned short-sleeved shirt that had its three top buttons open and showed the curly blond hair on his chest. His shorts revealed the bullet scar on his left thigh from the night Malone had saved his life after they'd been shot down during the Panama invasion. Even after ten years, he still had his military physique: broad shoulders, well-developed muscles.

"I knocked, but I didn't get an answer." Jeb grinned more broadly as Malone came toward him. His face was as craggy as the exposed limestone around him. "I started to worry that you didn't live here anymore, especially after I saw all this." He gestured toward the torn-up beach and the toppled palm trees. "What the hell happened? It looks like a hurricane hit this place."

"It's a land developer's idea of civic improvements."

"These aren't the only changes. I drove past that fantastic restaurant we went to the last time. I figured we'd have dinner there, but it's closed."

"Courtesy of the same land developer. I don't want to ruin my mood by talking about it." Malone gripped Jeb's shoulders. "It's good to see you. How long has it been? At least a year?"

Jeb nodded. "And now I'm back for another diving vacation. Maybe a little windsurfing."

"Where's your stuff?"

"In a rented car out front."

"I'll help you carry it in. You'll stay here, of course." A troubled thought made Malone hesitate. "But you'll have the place to yourself. You caught me at a bad time. I have to fly to New York tomorrow."

"What? But I just got here. Can't you put off the trip for a couple of days?"

Malone shook his head no. Anger quickened his pulse. "I need to settle a score with the guy who's responsible for all this. You'll understand when those bulldozers get cranked up again. You might even find yourself sleeping on the beach if they get orders to push these walls down."

"As bad as that?"

"Worse."

"Tell me about it." Jeb pointed toward the beach. "Let's take a walk."

10

As they reached the pounding surf, Jeb scanned the horizon, making sure there weren't any boats in view. After the demolition job the bulldozers had done, there weren't any nearby places where someone could hide and aim a shotgun microphone at them. All the same, Jeb had to be cautious.

"It started with a guy named Potter," Malone said.

"Yeah, I know about him."

Malone turned to him in surprise.

"And I also know about Bellasar," Jeb said. "The reason I wanted to come down to the water is, your house is probably bugged, but this surf is loud enough, it's all anybody will hear if a mike is trained on us from a distance."

"My house is bugged?" Malone looked as if Jeb spoke gibberish. "Why would—"

"Bellasar's thorough. He would have checked you out before Potter approached you. And he would have kept the surveillance in place to monitor your reaction to what he's done to you."

"How do you—" Malone's features hardened. "So. You didn't just happen to show up for a vacation."

"That's right."

"Then maybe you should tell *me* a couple of things, old buddy. Like, for starters, what in Christ are you really doing here?"

"I switched jobs since I saw you last."

Malone stared and waited.

"I'm not in corporate security anymore. I work for a different kind of company."

The word had implications. "Surely you're not talking about—"

"The Agency." Jeb held his breath, waiting for a reaction. This was the moment he'd been dreading. After his years in the military, Malone's aversion to authority was such that if he thought he was being ma-

nipulated, friendship wouldn't matter—he'd force Jeb
to leave.

"Oh, that's just swell," Malone said. "Great. Fuck-
ing fabulous."

"Now before you get yourself worked up, let me
explain. How much do you know about Bellasar?"

Malone's mouth twisted. "He's a bully with too
much money."

"And do you know how he got that money?"

"Oil. Shipping. Widgets. What difference does it
make?"

"Black-market weapons."

Malone's gaze intensified, his blue eyes becoming
like lasers.

"Bellasar's one of the three biggest arms dealers in
the world," Jeb said. "Name any civil war going on
right now—they're using Bellasar's weapons to destroy each other. But he's not just satisfied to wait for
an opportunity to knock. If a country's on the brink,
he likes to send agitators in to bomb buildings, assassinate politicians, pin the blame on rival factions, and
make the civil war happen. Thanks to him, Iraq got the
technology to build a nuclear reactor capable of man-
ufacturing weapons-grade plutonium. Ditto Pakistan
and India. Ditto North Korea. He sold sarin nerve gas
to that cult in Japan that let it loose in the subways as
a dress rehearsal for taking out Tokyo. He's rumored
to be peddling nuclear weapons he got his hands on
when the Soviet Union collapsed. He's my personal
candidate for world's scariest guy, and if you think
you can just fly to New York and 'settle a score' with

him, as you put it, you're going to find out what a hornet feels like when it gets splattered on the windshield of a car going a hundred miles an hour."

Malone's voice sounded like two pieces of flint being scraped together. "I guess you don't know me as well as I thought."

Jeb frowned. "What do you mean?"

"Have you ever known me to back off?"

"Never," Jeb said.

"It isn't going to happen this time, either. I don't care how powerful Bellasar is. He isn't going to get away with what he's done to me. I had a good life here. I took a lot of effort to build it. And now the son of a bitch is destroying it, no matter what it costs him, just because he can't stand anybody to say no. Well, he's going to find out what no sounds like in thunder."

"Hey, I'm not saying don't get even. I'm on your side. Make him pay. What I *am* saying is, be smart about how you do it. Stick it to him where it really hurts."

"And where would *that* be?"

"Accept the commission he offered you."

11

The surf pounded. Nonetheless, a silence seemed to gather around them.

"Accept the . . ." Malone gestured as if the idea was outrageous.

"The Agency's been wanting to get close to Bellasar for a long time," Jeb said. "If we can find out what his plans are, we might be able to stop them. There's no telling how many lives we could save. But Bellasar comes from a family of experts in survival. His father was an arms merchant. So was his grandfather and his great-grandfather, all the way back to the Napoleonic Wars. It's not just his family's business. It's in his genes. He's got an incredible sixth sense about avoiding traps and sniffing out surveillance. Every time we've tried to get somebody near him, we've failed. But now he's handing us a chance."

"This is a joke, right? You can't seriously be suggesting that I cooperate with him."

"With *us.*"

"And if Bellasar still has people watching me, he now knows someone from the CIA is trying to recruit me."

"An old friend who showed up unexpectedly for a week of diving and windsurfing. As far as anybody can tell, I'm still in corporate security. When Bellasar checks me out, he won't find any tie between me and the Agency. This conversation hasn't tainted you."

"I'm an artist, not a spy."

"The thing is, I was hoping you're still a soldier," Jeb said.

"That was a long time ago."

"You were too good at being a soldier ever to stop."

"But I did stop, remember?" Malone stepped closer. *"You should have been able to predict I wouldn't ever let anybody tell me what to do again."*

The surf seemed to pound louder. Spray drifted over them as they stared at each other.

"Do you want me to leave?" Jeb massaged the bullet scar on his thigh.

"What?"

"Are we still friends, or should I find a place in town to spend the night?"

"What are you talking about? Of course we're still friends."

"Then hear me out."

Malone raised his hands in exasperation.

"Please." Jeb put a wealth of meaning into the word. "There's something I have to show you."

12

As the rented Ford jounced along a potholed road that led past vine-covered mahogany trees, Jeb checked his rearview mirror to make sure they weren't being followed. He took his right hand from the steering wheel and gestured toward his suitcase on the backseat. "Look in the side flap."

Despite his annoyance, Malone pivoted in the passenger seat and leaned back to unzip the flap. But what he found puzzled him. "The only thing in here is a magazine. *Glamour*? What does a fashion magazine have to do with anything?"

"Check the date."

"Six years ago?"

"Now take a good look at the woman on the cover."

More puzzled, Malone studied her. She was dressed in a black evening gown, only the top of which was visible. Its tastefully revealing bustline was highlighted by a perfect string of pearls, matching earrings, and an intriguing black hat with a wide, slightly drooping brim that reminded Malone of the sophisticated look costume designers had given movie actresses in the fifties.

"I didn't know women wore hats anymore," Malone said.

"It was a retro issue. Keep looking at her."

The woman on the cover was a fiery brunette. She had a strong, well-toned presence that suggested she'd been swimming or jogging before she got dressed and made up. Even though she had been photographed only from the waist up, Malone had the feeling that she was tall and that her figure, when seen from feet to head, would be athletic and alluring.

He was reminded of Sophia Loren, and not just because she, too, was a voluptuous brunette with full lips and arousingly dusky eyes, but also because their skin color was the same, a smoldering earth color to which Malone had always been attracted. It made him suspect that the woman had something else in common with Sophia Loren—both were Italian.

The car hit another pothole.

"She's Bellasar's wife," Jeb said.

Malone looked up in surprise.

"The woman whose portrait Bellasar wants you to paint," Jeb said.

"I feel as if I've seen her before."

"Because she was featured on about a hundred magazine covers, not to mention thousands of ads for lipstick, shampoo, eyeliner, you name it. *Newsweek, Time,* and *People* did articles about her. She had a best-selling bathing-suit calendar. She had a once-a-week fashion-tip segment on the *Today* show. She was so famous, all you had to do was mention her first name and people in the fashion industry knew who you were talking about. Sienna."

"The color of her skin."

"The first thing *I* thought of was the city in Italy," Jeb said.

"You're not an artist. Burnt sienna's the most brilliant earth color, reddish brown and fiery."

"Fiery. Yeah, that describes the impression she creates all right," Jeb said. "She was as super as supermodels get. Five years ago, she gave it all up."

"Why?"

"Who knows? She was twenty-five, almost past the prime age for a model. Maybe she thought she'd get out while she was ahead. Or maybe she fell in love."

"With Mr. I Won't Take No For An Answer?"

"That could be exactly what happened. Maybe Bellasar wouldn't take no for an answer."

"But now he wants me to paint two portraits of her, one of her face, the other full length? Nude? I get the feeling I'm missing something."

"Yes."

The way Jeb said it made Malone shift his gaze from the magazine's cover.

"Bellasar was married three times before."

Malone frowned.

"All of his wives were gorgeous, and all of them died young."

"What?"

"The first lost control of her sports car and went over a cliff. The second broke her neck while skiing. The third drowned in a diving accident."

"It sounds like it's bad for a woman's health to be Bellasar's wife," Malone said. "With a track record like that, who'd be foolish enough to marry him?"

"You're assuming the other marriages were publicized. Bellasar's a hundred times more sensitive about his privacy than you are about yours. In his case, it's a survival trait. Believe me, the facts about his marriages and the subsequent quiet funerals are hard to come by." Jeb paused to emphasize what he was about to say. "Before each wife died, Bellasar hired a noted painter to do a portrait of her."

Malone felt a cold ripple along his skin.

"The paintings hang in a secluded room in Bellasar's mansion in southern France. They're a private collection of his trophies. He can't stand imperfection. When his wives get to be about thirty, when they start to lose the bloom of youth and show the slightest blemish, a faint wrinkle around the eyes or an isolated gray hair that hints of aging, he wants nothing more to do with them. But his suspicious nature prevents him from merely divorcing them. After all, they've been around him too long. They've seen and heard too much. They could be a threat."

"I don't understand. If he knows he's going to get rid of them, why does he take the trouble of marrying them? Why doesn't he just ask them to be his mistresses?"

"Because he's a collector."

"I still don't—"

"The way he looks at it, if he didn't marry them, he wouldn't own them."

"Jesus." Malone glanced down at the magazine cover. "And after they're dead, he still owns them as portraits."

"Painted by masters, their beauty immortalized, never aging," Jeb said.

Malone kept staring at the magazine cover. "So now he's getting ready to have *this* wife killed."

"Sure looks that way to us." Jeb let Malone think about it. "But if you go in and paint her, you might be able to figure a way for us to rescue her. The things she knows, she could be very helpful to us."

Dusk cast shadows. The car's headlights illuminated the vine-covered trees.

"No."

"*No?*"

"I'm sorry this woman has a problem, but I don't know her," Malone said. "She's a face on a magazine cover. She doesn't have any connection with me."

"But you can't let her—"

"I don't want to get mixed up with you guys."

"Even if it's a way to get even with Bellasar?"

"I can do that myself. I don't need to let anybody use me."

"I can't believe your attitude. You're just going to stand back and let her die?"

"Seems to me that's what *you're* doing," Malone said. "Don't push the responsibility onto me. I didn't know anything about this woman until a few minutes ago. If you think she's in that much danger, send in a team right now and grab her."

"Can't. The timing's wrong. The moment we play our hand, Bellasar will tighten his security even more. We'll lose our chance to get someone close to him."

"So when it comes right down to it, *you* don't care about the woman, either."

Jeb didn't respond.

"She's only a device you're using to try to recruit me," Malone said. "Getting me in there to look around is more important than saving her."

"The two go together."

"Not as far as I'm concerned. I won't be manipulated. I'll get even with him on my own."

"If you'd just listen to reason for a—"

"Damn it, you and Bellasar have something in common. You won't take no for an answer."

Jeb assessed him a moment. "So that's how it's going to be?"

"That's how it's going to be."

"Fine." Jeb's voice was flat. He frowned toward the lights of San Miguel ahead of them. His voice became flatter. "I need a drink."

"No hard feelings?"

"It takes more than an argument to end a friendship."

But Malone couldn't help feeling that the end of a friendship was precisely what had happened.

13

They headed along the main street of the picturesque town and stopped at a restaurant called Costa Brava across from the waterfront. All the while Malone drank a beer with Jeb, he barely tasted it. They both had trouble making small talk. The specialty of the house, a lobster dinner, was everything it should have been, but Malone couldn't help wishing he was back at the Coral Reef. He was only now beginning to realize the full force of what he had lost.

They returned home earlier than they usually would have. Malone offered a nightcap, but Jeb excused himself, claiming travel fatigue. Malone went out to his shadowy courtyard and stared at the savaged dunes and palm trees. He slumped on a hammock, closed his eyes to the stars, and brooded about Bellasar, about the woman called Sienna and the death sentence she didn't know had been given to her.

When he had first seen the magazine's cover, the face on it had struck him as being commercially beautiful, no more than that. But as he had looked harder, he had begun to notice the subtlety around the lips, the nuance of the way she cocked her head and positioned her eyes. Her eyes. There was something about them—something *in* them—that spoke of a deeper beauty.

Now that face and those eyes hovered in his memory. He kept thinking about her fiery brown skin: burnt sienna, his favorite color. He dozed and woke several times, continuing to brood about the beautiful doomed woman he'd been asked to paint. In an uneasy state between sleeping and waking, he imagined her perfect sensuous features—imagined, not remembered, for it wasn't the face on the magazine cover that occupied him. Instead, it was his conception of that face, his depiction of the beauty behind it, a beauty that would be destroyed if he didn't help her.

And in the process, he'd be getting even with Bellasar.

At dawn, he was waiting outside when Jeb carried his suitcase from the house.

"I'll do it," Malone said.

TWO

1

Sotheby's was on Manhattan's exclusive Upper East Side, where York Avenue intersected with Seventy-second Street. The February sky was a gunmetal gray that threatened flurries. Ignoring a cold wind, Malone kept his hands in the pockets of a fleece-lined leather bomber jacket and watched the entrance to the block-long auction house from a bus stop on the opposite side of the street. A succession of taxis and limousines halted in front, their well-dressed passengers entering the building.

The time was shortly after 10:00 A.M. When Malone had arrived at Kennedy Airport late the previous afternoon, there had been just enough time to phone Sotheby's before it closed and find out the subject of its auction today—Expressionist paintings—as well as the time the auction began—10:15. He had spent a restless night at the Parker Meridian.

Doug Fennerman had said that he'd be meeting Bellasar and Potter here this morning. Malone hoped that the plan hadn't changed. His own plan depended on it. Having agreed to cooperate with Jeb, he had tried to think of a way to accept Bellasar's commission without arousing suspicion. After all, he had been adamant in his refusal to do the portraits. Now that Bellasar had gone to considerable expense to punish Malone by tearing apart his life, would Bellasar believe it likely that Malone would simply throw up his hands in surrender, admit the error of his ways, and agree to do the portraits? Wouldn't Bellasar question this reaction? Wasn't it more in character for Malone to respond with rage?

Do what I intended to do before Jeb showed up, Malone had decided. The only thing that's changed is, I'm getting even in a different way than I imagined. His face felt burned by anger as much as the cold. He checked his watch again—10:08—returned his gaze to Sotheby's entrance, and saw two muscular men get out of a limousine. Their cropped hair and rigid bearing suggested they had recently been in the military. Their slightly too-large suits allowed for concealed firearms while giving their bodies room to maneuver if they needed to act in a hurry. After scanning the area, they nodded toward the limo to indicate it was safe to get out.

Malone felt a spark shoot through his nervous system when Potter stepped into view. The short, somber man wore a funereal overcoat that emphasized the pallor of his skin. His thinning hair was tugged by the wind as he stepped back to allow another man to emerge from the limo. Malone stiffened.

From a dossier Jeb had shown him, Malone knew that the second man was sixty-one, but amazingly he seemed only in his late forties. He was tall but had a presence that made him appear to have even more stature. He had thick, wavy dark hair and broad, handsome features that Malone associated with Mediterranean countries. He had a solid-looking physique. He wore a white silk scarf over a superbly cut dark brown blazer and light brown slacks. No overcoat—he was oblivious to the weather. The impressiveness of the man's separate parts was heightened by their totality, producing a sense of power and strength that made those around him seem insubstantial.

Derek Bellasar. Potter had said Bellasar didn't allow his photograph to be taken, but Jeb had shown Malone photos taken secretly from a distance. There was no mistaking him.

Immediately, another man appeared, rushing out of Sotheby's revolving door, smiling broadly, extending his right hand in welcome. He was Malone's art dealer, Doug Fennerman, his red hair matched by his flushed face. Bellasar responded with only a cursory greeting. The gang's all here, Malone thought, crossing the street, walking quickly closer but unable to reach the group before all of them disappeared into Sotheby's.

He entered the reception area about fifteen seconds after they did. Making his way through the crowd, he saw Doug give Bellasar a catalog of the auction, retaining one for himself along with a small numbered paddle that was used for bidding. Evidently, Doug was here to act as an adviser to Bellasar and do the bidding for him. Bellasar must have thought it demeaning to raise his own hand. The group, including the bodyguards, went up a marble staircase with brass railings and turned to the left toward a spacious auction room.

Upstairs, Malone reached a desk where a Sotheby's employee was registering anyone who intended to bid on the paintings. This close to the start of the auction, most of the attendees had already put in their names, so it took only a minute for Malone to present his driver's license, give his name and address, and provide a signature.

"Chase Malone?" the man asked in surprise. "Are you the—"

Before the man could say anything about his work, Malone went into the brightly lit, green-carpeted auction room.

2

The murmurs of several hundred people filled it. Scanning the crowd, Malone spotted Bellasar, Potter, and Doug halfway down the middle aisle. The bodyguards stood at each side of the room, studying everyone. As the only voice became that of the auctioneer, Malone leaned against a stone pillar at the back and waited.

The first piece, a not-bad Kandinsky, went for $600,000. Watching the price displayed in various currencies on an electronic board at the front of the auction room, Malone couldn't help remembering that, ten years earlier, his own work had been priced at a hundred dollars. Now it went for hundreds of *thousands*. Given the poverty in the world, was any painting, no matter who created it, worth these exorbitant amounts? His complaint was hypocritical, he knew, for until now, he hadn't refused any money. Most of his earnings had been saved to protect his independence. A good thing, he mentally added, for if the gamble he was about to take failed, he was going to need all his financial resources.

The next item, a better-than-average Klee, went for $850,000. But it wasn't until the auctioneer introduced the third painting, a starkly bleak Munch in the style of his famous *The Scream*, that a whisper went through the room. In the catalog, the item had a minimum estimated value of $1.2 million. As was customary, the auctioneer began the bidding at 50 percent of that figure: $600,000.

Malone noticed a shift in the way Bellasar sat, a compacting of muscles, a gathering of energy. Doug made a slight gesture with his paddle, indicating to the auctioneer that he would open the bid at the requested amount. The auctioneer automatically raised the bid to $650,000, which someone else took and which Doug capped as soon as the auctioneer went to $700,000. That was the pattern. With barely a motion of his paddle, Doug outdid every offer. The signal was clear. Others in the room could bid all they wanted, but Doug would always go higher.

The bidding languished at $1 million.

"Going once," the auctioneer said. "Going twice."

"One point one," Malone said.

The auctioneer steadied his gaze toward the back of the room, seeming to ask for confirmation.

"One point one," Malone repeated.

Puzzled, Doug turned to see who was bidding against him and blinked in surprise when he saw Malone. Something he said made Bellasar and Potter spin.

"One point one million," the auctioneer said. "The bid is one point one. Do I have—"

"Two," Doug said.

"Three," Malone said.

"Four."

"Five."

Even from a distance, it was obvious that the auctioneer was sizing up Malone, troubled by his sneakers, jeans, and leather jacket, wondering if he had the money to back up his bid. "Sir, if—"

An assistant approached the auctioneer and whispered into his ear. What he said was presumably what several members of the audience were already telling one another. They had recognized Malone. His name was being murmured.

"Very well," the auctioneer said. "One point five million. Do I have—"

"Six." The voice was no longer Doug's, but Bellasar's: a baritone with a hint of an Italian accent and more than a hint of annoyance.

"Eight," Malone said.

"Two million," Bellasar said defiantly.

"It's yours." Malone shrugged. "I guess you just can't take no for an answer."

The fury in Bellasar's eyes was palpable.

"A black-market arms dealer's money is as good as anybody's, right?" Malone asked the auctioneer.

Bellasar stood.

"Of course, there's blood all over the money," Malone said. "But who says blood and art don't go together?"

The bodyguards approached from the sides.

Avoiding them, Malone walked down the aisle toward Bellasar.

"Chase, what are you doing?" Doug asked in alarm.

Murmurs in the room grew louder.

Bellasar's face was rigid with anger. "You just forced me to pay a million more than I had to for that painting."

"I don't recall twisting your arm. Maybe it's God's way of letting you know you have too much money. Why don't you add that amount to what it cost you to tear apart my life? You're interested in my paintings? I've decided to change my style. I'm now into performance art."

Reaching into the pockets of his bomber jacket, Malone came out with a tube of oil paint in each hand. The caps had already been removed. Squeezing hard, he shot two streams of scarlet paint over Bellasar's dark brown blazer.

Bellasar jerked his head back in shock.

"The color of blood," Malone said. "You could call it a metaphor."

He reached back to drive a fist into Bellasar's stomach but changed position as one of the bodyguards lunged. Pivoting, Malone grabbed the man's arm, swung, and sent him flying into a row of chairs emptied by members of the audience anxious to get away from the commotion. "Call the police!" someone yelled. As the chairs crashed and the bodyguard rolled, Malone prepared a second time to hit Bellasar, but the other bodyguard rushed him. Malone knocked the man to the floor, felt something sting his neck, and spun to thrust the sharp object away, realizing with alarm that Bellasar had pricked him with something on a ring he wore. Something *inside* the ring. As Bellasar swiveled the ring's crested top back into place, Malone's neck felt on fire. The heat rushed through his body. He had time to punch the first bodyguard before his mind swirled. Frantic, he struggled, but somebody hit him, and the floor became rubbery, his knees collapsing. As out-of-focus hands grabbed him, dragging him along the blurry aisle, his hearing lasted slightly longer than his fading vision. He tried to thrash but was powerless. The last thing he remembered was the scrape of his shoes on carpet.

3

He awoke to a raging headache, finding himself strapped to a chair in a large, dark, echoing area. The only light was from a harsh unshielded bulb above his head. Two men, a different pair than the first two, played cards at a nearby table.

"Need to go to the bathroom?" one of them asked.

"Yes."

"Too bad. Besides, you already did."

Malone's jeans were wet where he'd urinated on himself. His stomach was queasy. The back of his neck ached where Bellasar's ring had jabbed him.

In the distance, a door opened and closed with a metallic thump. Two pairs of footsteps scraped on concrete, approaching through the darkness. Bellasar and Potter stepped into view. Bellasar now wore a navy blazer and gray slacks; Potter looked even more somber than usual.

Bellasar studied him. "You're a fool."

"I'm not the one who paid a million more than he had to for a painting."

Bellasar spread his hands. "Money can be replaced. I was referring to your refusal to cooperate with me. If you'd accepted my commission, your life wouldn't be in such disarray at the moment."

"Yeah, but I didn't and it is."

Bellasar studied him harder, then shook his head. "What did you hope to accomplish with that incident at Sotheby's?"

"I sure as hell wasn't going to try to get my hands on you when nobody else was around. Enough important people saw us together at Sotheby's that if my body gets fished out of the East River, you'll be the first man the police want to talk to."

Bellasar, whose tan was enhanced by his brilliant smile, chuckled. "I assure you, if I wanted something to happen to you, your body wouldn't be found in the

East River or anywhere else, for that matter." He let the threat sink in. "You have only yourself to blame. I made a fair offer. You chose to insult me by refusing. But I'm a reasonable man. I'll give you a second chance. I'll arrange for your life to be put back the way it was. I'll even raise my offer to seven hundred thousand dollars. But I warn you—I am not known for my patience. There won't be a *third* chance." He let that threat sink in also.

"Why are you so fixated on me? I can name a dozen artists with bigger reputations. Get one of *them* to do the portraits." Malone mentioned the name of the most famous realist currently working.

"I already own a portrait by him. You underestimate yourself. I'm confident that one day your reputation will be bigger than his. I'm a collector. It's well known that you never accept commissions. If I could persuade you to accept a commission from me after you've turned down so many others, I'd be receiving something unique."

Malone didn't respond.

"Pride's a wonderful thing." Bellasar sighed. "But bear in mind, *I* have pride as much as *you* do. This stalemate can't go on forever. One of us has to relent. But I can't be the one who does. In my business, it's crucial that I never show weakness, that I get what I want. If *you* relent, you receive an honest wage for honest work. If *I* relent, I tempt dangerous men to test me. Given those alternatives, you have the most to gain and the least to lose by forgoing your pride for a time."

"Honest work? Painting a likeness of your wife? You could get any competent sketch artist to do it."

"I didn't say anything about a likeness."

"What?"

"I wouldn't hire a world-class artist and expect him to accept a preconceived notion of what a portrait is," Bellasar said. "That would be absurd. Your style is representational rather than abstract, so I assumed the portraits would be in that manner. But I wouldn't hold you to that approach. Inspiration mustn't be constrained. All I ask is that you be totally honest to yourself and to the subject."

Malone pretended to debate with himself. His objection to accepting the commission had been that he had to maintain his independence, but Bellasar had just given him all the independence an artist could want. Bellasar had also given him a reason to accept without making Bellasar suspicious.

"Honesty to myself and to the subject?"

"That's all."

"And when I finished, that would be the end of it? You'd put my life back the way it was? I could walk away, and I'd never hear from you again?"

"You have my word. Of course, if you do decide to accept my offer, I hope that the drama you arranged at Sotheby's gave you enough emotional satisfaction that we can be civil to each other."

Malone couldn't help thinking that the drama had been arranged by both of them. Bellasar wouldn't have made the appointment to meet Doug at Sotheby's if he hadn't assumed Doug would tell Malone. Bellasar had expected Malone to show up.

"You've got a deal," Malone said.

4

Bellasar's Gulfstream 5 took off from Kennedy Airport at midnight. With modifications for a shower and a galley, the luxurious coporate jet had twenty seats, fifteen of which were occupied. Excluding Bellasar, Potter, Malone, and the two pairs of guards whom Malone had seen, there were eight passengers whose function Malone tried to figure out. Three broad-shouldered men might have been further bodyguards. Four attractive young women spent a lot of time working on laptop computers. The final passenger, a statuesque blonde with a crisp white silk blouse and a Scandinavian accent, turned out to be a flight attendant.

"May I get you anything?"

"Orange juice."

"Shall I add some champagne?"

"No thanks." The tranquilizer Bellasar had injected him with made him feel dehydrated. Alcohol would make him feel even more parched. Besides, he needed to be alert.

As the jet streaked through the darkness, he peered out his window, trying to see lights below him.

"I don't approve of this," Potter said, standing beside him.

Malone turned toward the aisle.

"You had your chance. You didn't want it." The harsh cabin lights reflected off Potter's glasses. "You were punished for not cooperating. That should have been the end of it. We shouldn't have anything more to do with you."

"I'm not exactly eager to be here, either. Did you really expect me to do nothing after those bulldozers showed up at my house?"

"That would have been the smart reaction."

"The smart thing would have been to leave me alone."

"How did you describe me the first time we met? I was trouble, you said." Potter's expression became more pinched. "We have something in common."

As Potter stepped away, the flight attendant came back with Malone's orange juice.

"We'll be serving a choice of entrées," she said. "Which would you prefer: London broil, Cornish hen, or *risotto alla milanese*?"

Malone wasn't hungry, but knew he had to keep up his strength. "Risotto."

"We also have an excellent selection of wines."

"All the pleasures."

"More than you can imagine." The attractive flight attendant gave him an encouraging look, then proceeded to another passenger.

"Comfortable?" Bellasar came along the aisle.

"Potter isn't."

"It's his job to be unhappy. Do the fresh clothes my men bought you fit?"

Malone barely nodded.

"One of them also went to the Parker Meridian, collected your luggage, and paid your bill."

Malone reached for his wallet. "I always pay my own way. How much was it?"

Bellasar spread his hands in amusement. "Until the portraits are completed, all of your expenses are *my* expenses. You'll find I'm extremely generous to those who cooperate with me. I meant what I said. I hope we can put our disagreement behind us."

"Believe me, it's my goal to get through this with as little friction as possible." Malone glanced toward the darkness beyond the window. "Do you mind telling me where we're headed?"

"Southern France. I have a villa near Nice."

"That's where your wife is?"

"Yes. Patiently waiting." Belassar's dark brown eyes changed focus. "Is the fact that I'm in the arms business the reason you didn't want to accept my offer?"

"At the time, I didn't know what your business was."

"But at Sotheby's, you announced it to the world. How did you find out?"

The question sounded casual, but Malone had no doubt he was being tested. "A friend of mine came to visit me on Cozumel. He's a security expert. I told him what had happened. When I mentioned your name, he said he'd heard of you. He said to stay away from you. He said you're a very scary guy."

"That would be Mr. Wainright."

"You were having me watched?"

"I like to stay informed. He seems to be enjoying his vacation."

"You mean the bulldozers haven't pushed down my house yet?"

"They've been called off. As I promised, I'm going to reassemble your life. You do object to my business."

"I guess I keep thinking of all the children who've been killed by the land mines you sell to whatever Third World dictator is in power this month."

"Most of those children would eventually have starved to death." Bellasar's gaze drifted toward Potter coming along the aisle.

"A phone call."

"It can't wait?"

Potter's silence said everything.

Bellasar turned to Malone. "Next time, let's discuss *your* business instead of mine."

5

A little after ten in the morning, Bellasar's jet approached Nice's airport. The blue of the Mediterranean reminded Malone of the Caribbean. The palm trees, too, reminded him of home. But the overbuilt coastline and the exhaust haze were nothing like the clear solitary splendor he had enjoyed on Cozumel. Bitter, he looked away from the view. Some chablis he had drunk with dinner, much of which he hadn't eaten, had helped to relax him enough to sleep, although his dreams had been fitful, interspersed with images of children being blown up by land mines and a beautiful woman's face rotting in a coffin.

He never got into the airport terminal. Officers from customs and immigration came out to the jet, where they stood on the tarmac and spoke to Potter, who apparently had an understanding with them, for they looked briefly into the aircraft, nodded to its occupants, then stamped the passports Potter handed them. Presumably, their expeditious attitude would be rewarded under less public circumstances. Letting Potter handle the details, Bellasar had gone to a cabin in the rear before the authorities arrived; he hadn't given Potter his passport; there was no proof that he had entered the country. Or that *I* did, either, Malone thought. When Potter had gone along the aisle collecting passports, he had taken Malone's, but instead of showing it to the authorities, Potter had kept it in his pocket. Malone was reminded of how easy it was to disappear from the face of the earth.

They got off the plane and broke into two groups, most of them remaining to transfer luggage to a waiting helicopter while Bellasar, Potter, three bodyguards, and Malone walked to a second helicopter. The familiar *whump-whump-whump* of the rotors wasn't reassuring. Feeling the weight of liftoff, seeing the airport get smaller beneath him, Malone pretended that it was ten years earlier, that he was on a military mission. Put yourself in that mind-set. Start thinking like a soldier again. More important, start *feeling* like one.

He glanced toward the front of the chopper, comparing its levers, pedals, and other controls to those he had been familiar with. There were several advances in design, particularly a group of switches that the pilot didn't use and whose purpose Malone didn't understand, but at heart, the principle of flying this craft was the same, and he was able to detach his mind from the tension around him and imagine that he was behind the controls, guiding the chopper.

Bellasar said something.

"What?" Malone turned. "I can't hear you. The noise of the rotors."

Bellasar spoke louder. "I said I've purchased the contents of the best art-supply shop in Nice. The materials are at my villa, at your disposal."

"You were that certain I'd eventually agree?"

"The point is, *this* way you won't have any delay in getting started."

"I won't be able to start right away anyhow."

"What do you mean?"

"I can't just jump in. I have to study the subject first."

Bellasar didn't reply for a moment. "Of course."

Potter kept concentrating on Malone's eyes.

"But don't study too long," Bellasar said.

"You didn't mention there was a time limit. You

told me I could do this the way I needed to. If I'd known there were conditions, I wouldn't have—"

"No conditions. But my wife and I might soon have to travel on business. If you can get your preparations concluded before then, perhaps you can work without her. From a sketch perhaps."

"That's not how I do things. You wanted an honest portrait. Working from a sketch is bullshit. If I can't do this right, I won't do it at all. You're buying more than just my autograph on a canvas."

"You didn't want to accept the commission, but now you're determined to take the time to do it properly." Belassar turned toward Potter. "Impressive."

"Very." Potter kept his eyes on Malone.

"There." Bellasar pointed through the Plexiglas.

Malone followed his gesture. Ahead, to the right, nestled among rocky, wooded hills, a three-story château made of huge stone blocks glinted in the morning sun. If Malone had been painting it, he would have made it impressionistic, its numerous balconies, gables, and chimneys blending, framed by a swirl of elaborate flower gardens, sculpted shrubs, and sheltering cypresses.

The pilot spoke French into a small micophone attached to his helmet, presumably identifying himself to his security controller on the ground. As the helicopter descended, Malone saw stables, tennis courts, a swimming pool, and another large stone building that had a bell tower and reminded Malone of a monastery. Beyond high walls, farmland spread out, vineyards, cattle. He could discern small figures working, and as the helicopter settled lower toward a landing pad near the château, the figures became large enough for Malone to see that many were guards carrying weapons.

"Can you tolerate it here?" Belassar sounded ironic.

"It's beautiful," Malone acknowledged, "if you ignore the guards."

"It belonged to my father and grandfather and great-grandfather, all the way back to the Napoleonic Wars."

Thanks to arms sales, Malone thought.

The chopper set down, the roar of the motors diminishing to a whine.

"These men will show you to your room," Bellasar said. "I'll expect you for cocktails in the library at seven. I'm sure you're looking forward to meeting my wife."

"Yes," Malone said. "For seven hundred thousand dollars, I'm curious what my subject looks like."

6

The spacious bedroom had oak paneling and a four-poster bed. After showering, Malone found a plush white robe laid out for him. He also found that his bag had been unpacked and was on the floor next to the armoire. Opening the armoire, he saw that his socks and underwear had been placed in a drawer, his turtlenecks and a pair of chino slacks in another. He had used a packaged toothbrush and razor he had found on a ledge above the marble sink. Now he carried his toilet kit into the bathroom and arranged its various items on that shelf, throwing out the designer shampoo and shaving soap Bellasar had provided. The small gesture of rebellion gratified him. He put on the chinos and a forest green turtleneck. Looking for the tan loafers that had been in his bag, he found them in the walk-in closet, along with the sneakers he'd been wearing, and paused in surprise at the unfamiliar sport coats, dress slacks, and tuxedo hanging next to his leather jacket. Before he tried on one of the sport coats, he already knew it would fit him perfectly. Yes, there was little about him Bellasar didn't know, Malone realized warily. Except the most important thing: Bellasar didn't know about his deal with Jeb. Malone took that for granted, because if Bellasar *had* known, Malone would have been dead by now.

From his years in the military, Malone had learned that no matter how tired he was after a long flight, it was a mistake to take a nap. The nap would only confuse his already-confused internal clock. The thing to do was push through the day and go to sleep when everybody else normally went to sleep. The next morning, he'd be back on schedule.

Opening the bedroom door, he found a man in the hallway. The man wore a Beretta 9-mm pistol and carried a two-way radio. With a slight French accent and in perfect English, the man said, "Mr. Bellasar asked me to be at your disposal in case you wanted a tour of the grounds."

"He certainly pays attention to his guests."

Proceeding along the corridor, Malone listened to his escort point out the various paintings, tables, and vases, all from the French Regency period. Other corridors had their own themes, he learned, and every piece was museum quality.

They went down a curving stairway to a foyer topped by the most intricate crystal chandelier Malone had ever seen. "It's five hundred years old," the escort explained. "From a Venetian palazzo. The marble on this floor came from the same palazzo."

Malone nodded. Yes, Bellasar was definitely a collector.

Outside, the sun felt pleasant, but Malone ignored it, concentrating only on his surroundings as he strolled with his escort through gardens, past topiaries and ponds, toward the swimming pool.

Abruptly he whirled. Gunfire crackled.

"From the testing range," the escort explained, gesturing toward an area beyond an orchard. Several assault rifles made it sound as if a small war were taking place over there. The escort avoided going in that direction, just as he avoided going toward the large stone building whose bell tower had made Malone think of a monastery and which was in the same direction.

"It's called the Cloister," the escort said. "Before the French Revolution, monks lived there, but after the Church's lands were confiscated, one of Mr. Bellasar's ancestors acquired the property. Not before a mob destroyed all the religious symbols, though. There's still a room that you could tell was a chapel—if you were allowed over there. Which you're not."

Malone shrugged, pretending to be interested only in what the escort showed him and in nothing that the escort avoided. For now, what he was mainly interested in were the high stone walls that enclosed the grounds and were topped by security cameras. The entrances at the back and front had sturdy metal barriers and were watched by guards with automatic weapons. Getting out wouldn't be easy.

When something blew up past the orchard, the explosion rumbling, none of the guards reacted. Malone's escort didn't even bother looking in that direction. "I'll show you where your painting supplies are. Mr. Bellasar suggests that you work in a sunroom off the terrace. It has the best light."

7

When Malone returned to his room, a thick pamphlet lay on his bedside table. Its paper was brown with age. Carefully, he picked it up and turned the stiff, brittle pages. The text was in English, the author Thomas Malthus, the title *An Essay on the Principle of Population*. A handwritten note accompanied it. "I thought you'd enjoy some leisure reading." Leisure? Malone thought. With a title like that? On an inside page, he read that the pamphlet had been published and printed in London in 1798. A priceless first edition. The note concluded, "Cocktails and dinner are formal." To reinforce the point, the tuxedo that Malone had noticed in the closet was now laid out on the bed, along with a pleated white shirt, black pearl cuff links and studs, a black silk cummerbund, and a black bow tie.

The last time Malone had worn formal clothes had been eight years earlier at his art dealer's wedding. He hadn't enjoyed it, had felt constricted. But he was damned if he was going to let Bellasar sense his discomfort. When he entered the library two hours later, he looked as if he wore a tuxedo every day of his life.

The large two-story area had shelves from floor to ceiling on all four sides, every space filled with books except where there were doors and windows. Ladders on rollers allowed access to the highest shelves on the main level. Similar ladders on rollers were on a walkway on the second level. The glow from colored-glass lamps reflected off leather reading chairs and well-oiled side tables.

Next to a larger table in the middle, Bellasar—commanding in his tuxedo, his dark hair and Italian features made more dramatic by his formal clothes—raised a glass of red liquid to his lips. A male servant stood discreetly in the background.

"Feeling rested?" Bellasar asked.

"Fine." Malone held up the pamphlet. "I'm returning this. I hate to think something might happen to it in my room."

"Just because it's a first edition?"

"It's awfully expensive bedside reading."

"All of these are rare first editions. I wouldn't read the texts in any other form. What's the point of collecting things if you don't use them?"

"What's the point of collecting things in the first place?"

"Pride of ownership."

Malone set the pamphlet on a table. "Perhaps a paperback is more my style."

"Did you get a chance to look through it?"

"It's a classic discussion of the causes of overpopulation and of ways to control it. I'd heard of Malthus before. I'd just never looked at his actual words."

Bellasar sipped more of the red liquid. "What would you like to drink? I'm told you like tequila."

"You don't miss much."

"I was raised to believe it's a sin to be uninformed. May I recommend a brand from a private estate in Mexico's Jalisco region? The agave juice is distilled three times and aged twenty years. The family makes only limited quantities that it sells to preferred customers. This particular lot had a quantity of only two hundred bottles. I purchased them all."

"It'll be interesting to find out what the rest of the world is missing."

In the background, the servant poured the drink.

"And make me another of these," Bellasar said.

The servant nodded.

"Since you're a connoisseur, what special vodka do you prefer in your Bloody Mary?" Malone asked.

"Vodka? Good heavens, no. This isn't a Bloody Mary. It's a blend of fresh vegetable juices. I never drink alcohol. It damages brain and liver cells."

"But you're not bothered if the rest of us drink it?"

"As Malthus might have said, alcohol is a way of reducing the population." It wasn't clear if Bellasar was joking.

To the left, a door opened, and the most beautiful woman Malone had ever seen stepped into the room.

8

Malone had to remind himself to breathe.

It was obvious now why Bellasar had insisted that cocktails and dinner be formal. Bellasar wanted a stage in which to present another of his possessions.

The woman's evening dress was black but caught the lamp glow around her in a way that made it shimmer. It was strapless, leaving the elegant curve of her tan shoulders unbroken. It was low-cut, revealing the smooth tops of her breasts. Its waist left no doubt how firm her stomach was. Its sensuous line flowed over her hips and down to her ankles, emphasizing how long and statuesque her legs were.

But the ultimate effect was to focus attention on her face. The magazine cover hadn't done justice to the burnt sienna color of her skin. Her features were in perfect proportion. The curve of her chin paralleled the opposite curve of her eyebrows, which further paralleled the way she had twisted her long, lush fiery brunette hair into a swirl. But the grace of symmetry was only a partial explanation for her beauty. Her eyes were the key—and the captivating spirit behind them.

Captivating even though she was troubled. "The others are late?" Her voice made Malone think of grapes and hot summer afternoons.

"There won't be any others," Bellasar said.

"But when you told me the evening was formal, I thought . . ."

"It'll be just the three of us. I want you to meet Chase Malone. He's an artist. Perhaps you've heard of him."

Malone felt his cheeks turn warm with self-consciousness as she looked at him.

"I recognize the name." Her accent was American. She sounded hesitant.

"There's no reason you should know my work," Malone said. "The art world's too preoccupied with itself."

"But you *will* know his work," Bellasar said.

She looked puzzled.

"He's going to paint you. Mr. Malone, allow me to introduce my wife, Sienna."

"You never mentioned anything about this," Sienna said.

"It's an idea I've been considering. When I had the good fortune to cross paths with Mr. Malone, I offered a commission. He graciously accepted."

"But why would—"

"To immortalize you, my dear."

Throughout the afternoon, Malone had begun to wonder if Jeb had been telling the truth about the danger Sienna was in. After all, Jeb might have been willing to say anything to get Malone to accept the assignment. But a darkness in Bellasar's tone now convinced him. For her part, Sienna seemed to have no idea how close she was to dying.

"Can you start tomorrow morning?" Bellasar asked her.

"If that's what you want." She sounded confused.

"If *you* want. You're not being forced," Bellasar said.

But that was exactly how Sienna looked—forced—when she turned toward Malone. "What time?"

"Is nine o'clock too early?"

"No, I'm usually up by six."

"Sienna's an avid horsewoman," Bellasar explained. "Early every morning, she rides."

Bellasar's pride in Sienna's riding seemed artificial, Malone thought. He sensed another dark undertone and couldn't help recalling that Bellasar's three previous wives had died in accidents. Was that how Bellasar planned for Sienna to be killed—in a faked riding accident? He nodded. "I used to ride when I was a kid. Nine o'clock, then. In the sunroom off the terrace."

"Good." As Bellasar leaned close to kiss Sienna's right cheek, he was distracted by something at the edge of her eye.

"What's the matter?" she asked.

"Nothing." He turned toward Malone. "You haven't tasted your tequila."

9

The dining room had logs blazing in a huge fireplace. The table was long enough to seat forty and looked even longer with just the three of them. Bellasar took the end, while Malone and Sienna sat on each side of him, facing each other. As candlelight flickered, the movements of servants echoed in the cavernous space.

"Food and sex," Bellasar said.

Malone shook his head in puzzlement. He noticed that Sienna kept her eyes down, concentrating on her meal. Or was she trying to avoid attracting Bellasar's attention?

"Food and sex?" Malone asked.

"Two of the four foundations of Malthus's argument." Bellasar looked at a plate of poached trout being set before him. "Humans need food. Their sexual attraction is powerful."

"And the other two?"

"Population grows at a geometric rate: one, two, four, eight, sixteen, thirty-two. In contrast, food production grows at a mathematical rate: one, two, three, four, five, six. Our ability to reproduce always outreaches our ability to feed the population. As a consequence, a considerable part of society is doomed to live in misery."

Bellasar paused to savor the trout. "Of course, we can try to check the growth of population by contraception, chastity, and limiting the number of children a woman may have. Some societies recommend abortion. But the power of the sex drive being what it is, the population continues to grow. This year alone, the world's population has swelled with the equivalent of everyone living in Scandinavia and the United Kingdom. We're approaching the six billion mark, with ten billion estimated by the middle of the twenty-first century. There won't—there can't—be enough food to sustain them all. But other factors come into play, for God's merciful plan arranges that whenever there's a drastic imbalance between population and food supply, pestilence and war reduce it."

" 'God's merciful plan'?" Malone asked in disbelief.

"According to Malthus. But I agree with him. He was an Anglican minister, by the way. He believed that God allowed misery to be part of His plan in order to test us, to make us try to rise to the occasion and strengthen our characters by overcoming adversity. When those who have been sufficiently challenged and bettered die, they go on to their eternal reward."

"In the meantime, because of starvation, pestilence, and war, they've endured hell on earth," Sienna said.

"Obviously, you haven't been listening closely, my dear. Otherwise, you wouldn't have missed the point."

Sienna concentrated on her plate.

"So war's a good thing," Malone said acidly. "And so are weapons merchants."

"It's easy to condemn what you don't understand. Incidentally, my great-great-great-grandfather had a friendship with Malthus."

"What?"

"After the first edition of his essay was published, Malthus traveled from England to the Continent. My ancestor had the good fortune to meet him at a dinner party in Rome. They spent many evenings together, exchanging ideas. That pamphlet I lent to you was given to my ancestor by Malthus himself."

"You're telling me that because of Malthus's ideas, your ancestor became an arms dealer?"

"He considered it a vocation." Bellasar looked with concern toward Sienna. "My dear, you don't seem to be enjoying the trout. Perhaps the rabbit in the next course will be more to your liking."

10

Malone lay in his dark bedroom, staring, troubled, at the ceiling. The evening had been one of the strangest he had ever experienced, the conversation on such a surreal level that he felt disoriented, his mind swirling worse than when he'd been tranquilized.

Jet lag insisted. His eyelids fluttered shut. He

dreamed of two men wearing wigs and frilly long jackets from 1798, huddled by a fire in a smoky tavern, pointedly discussing the fate of the multitudes. He dreamed of Sienna on horseback, galloping through cypresses, never seeing the trip wire that jerked up, toppled her horse, and snapped her neck. He dreamed of the roar of a helicopter coming in for a landing, barely pausing before it lifted off, the rumble of its engine receding into the distance. His eyes jerked open as he realized that the helicopter had not been a dream.

Getting out of bed, he approached the large windows opposite him. Peering out, he saw the shadows of trees across gardens and moonlight reflecting off ponds. Floodlights illuminated courtyards and lanes. A guard stepped into view, throwing away a cigarette, shifting his rifle from his left shoulder to his right. Far off, the angry voices of two men were so muffled that Malone couldn't tell what they shouted at each other. The guard paid them no attention. The argument stopped. As silence drifted over the compound, Malone wiped a hand across his weary face and returned to bed, about to sink back into sleep when he heard a distant gunshot. He was willing to bet that the guard didn't pay attention to that, either.

THREE

1

Startled by the sudden approach of the helicopter, Sienna's Arabian stallion faltered at the jump, nearly throwing her into the stream. Momentarily off balance, she tightened her thighs against the horse's flanks. As the stallion threatened to lurch down the stream's bank, she eased the pressure from her right thigh, applied more pressure to the left, and simultaneously did the same with her hands on the reins. Turning the horse away from the stream, she pressed down on her heels while expertly easing back on the reins, then came to a stop just as the helicopter thundered past overhead. An opening in the trees allowed her to glimpse it while only someone peering directly down would have been able to spot her. Then the helicopter was gone, approaching the hills.

Patting the Arabian's neck, whispering assurances, Sienna waited for the roar to recede completely. The time was a little before eight. The estate had two helicopters, and at dawn, as she had reached the stable, the first one had taken off. She couldn't help wondering if Derek was aboard either of them. In fact, she hoped he was. She dreaded going back to the château, finding him there, and straining to adjust to whatever mood he was in this morning. He'd been gone for six days, and it had taken her three of those days to recover from his icy attitude before he left. During the past few months, no matter how she had tried to relate to him, she hadn't been successful. Interpreting his thoughts had become impossible.

Sometimes she wondered what would happen if she just kept riding, taking a cross-country route, avoiding roads and lanes, heading up into the hills. How far could she get? And what would she be able to do once she was far from the estate? She had no food or water. Certainly she'd arouse suspicion if she packed saddlebags with provisions before she set out for her daily ride. She had never been able to prove it, but she suspected that Derek had men watching her from a distance as she rode through the outreaches of the estate. If she did manage to prove she was being watched, Derek would no doubt shrug and say he wanted to make certain she was protected. She had no money, had no access to it. Derek kept strict control of that. She could have pocketed some of her jewels, but where was she going to find anyone in the countryside who could pay her what they were worth? Without money, she couldn't feed herself, get a hotel room, or even buy a bus ticket if she tried to get away from Derek. However she looked at it, she was trapped. Perhaps that was why the helicopter had thundered in this direction—to remind her that she was never really alone, that she had no hope of leaving.

Riding back toward the compound, she barely noticed the sunbathed scenery around her. She was too preoccupied, knowing that in less than an hour she would have to deal with the new complication that Derek had introduced: the artist he had hired to paint her. Artist? She didn't understand. Derek never did anything on a whim. What was he thinking? Rubbing her left arm where he had twisted it sharply before he left the previous week, she told herself that, regrettably, she would soon find out.

2

When the stables came into view, she dismounted, took off her helmet, and shook her head, letting her lush hair fall loose. As she led the Arabian along a lane bordered by cypresses, she knew she could have asked one of the stable men to walk the horse and cool it down, but she enjoyed the intimacy of taking care of her horse as much as she did the exertion of riding it. She turned to pat the horse's neck and murmur endearments, looked ahead, and faltered at the sight of the artist coming out of the stables and leaning against a rail.

The formal dress of last night's dinner had made it difficult for her to assess his bearing. A tuxedo always gave a man more presence than he normally had. Now the artist's casual clothes—sneakers, jeans, and a blue chambray shirt, the cuffs of which were folded up— made it easier to assess him. He was tall—six feet or so—trim yet muscular, obviously accustomed to exercise. His tan face was attractive in a rugged fashion, his sand-colored hair slightly long, curling at the back of his neck. The way he crossed his arms made him seem comfortable with himself.

"Good morning." His smile was engaging. "Did you have a good ride?"

"Very," she lied. "But I must have lost track of the time. I was supposed to meet you in the sunroom at nine. Am I late?"

"No, I'm early. Getting to know you where we'll be working seemed limited. I thought it would be helpful if I met you at a place where you feel at ease."

"I feel at ease everywhere, Mr. Malone."

"Please call me Chase."

"My husband didn't mention it last night, but I used to be a model. I'll feel at ease wherever you pose me."

"But posing isn't what I want from you."

Sienna shook her head in confusion. "Then how are you going to do the portrait?"

"We'll figure that out together."

Her puzzlement was interrupted when a sudden nudge from behind nearly pushed her off balance. It came from her horse. "Excuse me," she said. "He feels ignored."

"Sure. Finish cooling him down."

"You know about horses?" At once she remembered. "That's right. Last night, you said you rode when you were a boy."

"At my grandfather's farm. Do you want me to get a halter?"

"Why not? You'll find one in—"

"The tack room in the stable. First door on the right. I saw it when I was looking around."

When he came back with the halter, Sienna switched it for the bit and bridle on the stallion, then led the horse to a rail. She raised the left stirrup and unbuckled the saddle. "What did you mean, we'll figure out together how to do the portrait?"

"I'm not a portrait artist. My specialty is landscapes."

"What?" Sienna straightened. "Then why did my husband hire you?"

"Actually, it's called 'offer a commission.' I'm sensitive about the word *hire*. Basically, your husband likes my work, and he's awfully hard to turn down."

"That's my husband all right."

"But I do know how to paint, Mrs. Bellasar."

"I don't doubt it. Call me Sienna."

"Have you eaten yet?"

"Just a couple of apples I shared with my friend here."

"Then maybe we could have breakfast."

3

While a guard watched from a side of the terrace, they sat at a wrought-iron table, an umbrella sheltering them from the sun, which was warm for February.

"Chase?" She sipped her coffee. "That's an unusual first name."

"Actually, it's a nickname. My first name is Charles, but at one of the grade schools I went to—"

"*One* of them?"

"I went to a lot. It's a long story. The teacher put a list of our names on a bulletin board to make it easier for us to get to know one another. To save time, she used abbreviations. Richard was Rich. Daniel was Dan. Charles was Chas. She put a period after it, but the period had a little curlicue that made it look like an *e*, so the kids started making fun of me, calling me Chase. It didn't bother me, though. In fact, I thought it sounded kind of cool, so I kept it."

"Nothing metaphysical about being chased or chasing your destiny?" Sienna picked up a croissant.

"There were plenty of instances, especially in the military, when chasing was going on. As far as being an artist goes, I think I did find my destiny. But *you're* not doing a portrait of *me*. I need to learn about *you*."

"I thought you'd be working by now," a voice interrupted.

When Sienna turned and saw her husband standing at an open door that led to the terrace, her stomach contracted. No longer hungry, she set down her croissant.

But Chase took a bite from his own, responding calmly, "We've already started."

"You have a strange way of painting."

"Painting's the easy part. It's the thought that goes into it that's hard. I'm being efficient, eating breakfast while I study my subject."

Chase made it sound like a joke, but when he glanced at her, his gaze assuring, Sienna suddenly realized how attentive his blue eyes were. Despite the casual way he'd been looking at her, she had the sense that she'd never been looked at so totally, not even when she'd been a model.

A burst of machine-gun fire broke the stillness. From the range beyond the Cloister. On edge, Sienna jerked her head in that direction. Managing to calm herself, she returned her attention to her husband, noticing that neither he nor Chase had been distracted.

"Sounds like a .50-caliber," Chase said.

"You have a good ear."

"Well, I've been shot at by them often enough."

"One of my engineers is working on a modification, a faster feeding mechanism."

"How are they compensating for the increase in heat?"

"That's the problem."

The subject infuriated her. No. Inwardly shaking her head, she corrected herself. What infuriated her was that the man with whom she had been talking, an *artist* who had seemed to display sensitivity during the conversation, was as comfortable talking about guns as was her husband. The two were no different.

She stood. "If you'll excuse me, I'll go shower, fix my hair, and get ready for the session." She made herself look indifferently down at Chase. "What would you like me to wear?"

"Those boots, jodhpurs, and leather jacket you've got on are fine. And if you wouldn't usually shower right now, I wish you wouldn't. I want to get an idea of what *you* are, not what you'd like me to *think* you are. Don't fix your hair or freshen your makeup. Don't do anything special. Just let me look at you."

His gaze was once again total. It made her shiver.

Whump-whump-whump. With an increasing roar, one of the helicopters returned, a distant speck that enlarged into a grotesque dragonfly and set down on the compound's landing pad, halfway between the château and the Cloister.

"I look forward to seeing the progress you make," her husband said, a vague warning in his voice. But it was obvious that his attention was elsewhere as he stepped from the terrace and walked with anticipation along a stone path near a rose garden and a fountain, approaching a man stepping down from the helicopter.

4

The man was too far away for Malone to get more than a general look at him. The hearty way he and Bellasar shook hands, then gripped each other's arms, it was clear the two knew each other well and hadn't seen each other for a while. Wider at the hips and waist than at his chest, the newcomer had rounded, forward-leaning shoulders, which suggested he spent a lot of time hunched over a desk. He wore a suit and tie, was Caucasian, and had hair only at the sides of his head. At a distance, his age was hard to tell, maybe mid-forties. He turned with concern toward several large wooden crates being unloaded from the helicopter.

Each crate was heavy enough to require two men to lift it, and as one of the men stumbled, almost losing his grip on his end of the crate, the newcomer stepped frantically backward, gesturing in alarm, his barked command to be careful echoing the hundred yards to the terrace.

"Ah, the artist's life," a caustic voice said.

Reluctantly, Malone switched his attention from the helicopter toward Potter, who stepped from the château.

"A pleasant chat over a late breakfast. No schedule to worry about."

"I've already had this conversation with your boss," Malone said.

"Then there's no point in being repetitive." Potter took off his glasses and polished them. "I never question methods of working as long as they get results. Good morning, Sienna."

"Good morning, Alex."

"Did you enjoy your ride?" He didn't wait for an answer. "Are you getting along with Mr. Malone? He has a tendency to be abrasive."

"I haven't noticed."

"Then perhaps it's only to me." Potter put his glasses back on and stepped from the terrace. His squat figure got smaller, as he followed the same route past the rose garden and fountain that Bellasar had, joining the group as they entered the Cloister.

"He obviously doesn't like me," Malone said, "but am I wrong, or did he seem a little distant to *you*?"

"There's only one person he gets along with, and that's my husband."

"A first-class guard dog."

5

The sunroom smelled musty. It was a single-story extension of the château, built onto the terrace, the floor made of the same flagstones that led into it. With a southern exposure, it had a wall of windows and several skylights.

"It must be ten degrees warmer than outside," Malone said. "I imagine you eat breakfast in here on chilly days."

"No, the room hasn't been used since I've lived here."

"With a view like this . . ."

"Derek isn't fond of the place."

It was spacious, with a high ceiling. Except for several wooden tables along the left side, it was so empty, their footsteps echoed.

"Are you sure you don't want me to change my clothes?" Sienna asked.

"I don't want anything except for you to do what you'd normally do." Malone sat on one of the tables, his legs dangling. "See, my problem is how to do this portrait so it captures you, so someone who knows you will say, 'Yes, that's Sienna there all right. That's not only how she looks but what she is.' "

"Whatever *that* is."

Malone chuckled. "There's nothing like a heavy conversation to put you at ease."

"You don't need to entertain me."

"After all the weeks I spent learning to play the banjo."

Sienna half-smiled.

The next few seconds stretched on and on as Malone studied the curve of her slightly parted lips, the unique combination of brightness and vulnerability in that half smile.

"What are you doing?"

"Doing?"

"The way you're . . . Even when I was a model, no one ever stared that hard at me."

"Sorry." Malone felt his cheeks turn warm with self-consciousness. "I don't mean to seem rude. I *have* to look at you that way. By the time this project is finished, I'll know your face better than I've known anyone else's in my life. Can I ask you a question?"

She looked unsure.

"I told you how I got mine. How did you get yours?"

"I don't—"

"Your first name."

"Oh." She seemed relieved. "There's not much to tell. My parents were Italian-Americans. From a little town in Illinois. But *their* parents had come from Italy, from Siena, and all the old folks ever talked about was how wonderful that part of Italy was, so when my parents went on their honeymoon, that's the place they chose. They couldn't think of a more loving first name to give me."

"Your parents *were* Italian-Americans?"

"They died when I was twelve."

". . . I'm sorry," Malone said.

"My mother was killed in a car accident. My father had a heart attack two months later, but I always thought it was literally a broken heart."

"You loved them."

"Very much. The way you said that, did you really think I might say no?"

"Everybody's situation is different."

"You didn't get along with your parents?"

Malone was surprised that he'd opened the subject. "I never had any arguments with my father." He surprised himself further. "It's hard to fight with somebody you've never met."

A burst of machine-gun fire broke the moment. Malone turned toward the sunroom's open door. The stuttering blast echoed from behind the Cloister. "Doesn't that get on your nerves?"

"Actually, the pauses are what bother me," she said. "It's like when I lived in Manhattan. I got so used to the noise of traffic, even in the middle of the night, that I felt something was wrong if I was somewhere quiet."

"Well, this sunroom's about as quiet as it's going to get."

6

Malone brought a chair from a corner and set it in the light. It was wooden, with a slotted back. "This doesn't look very comfortable. We should bring a cushion from—"

"It's not a problem." But when Sienna lowered herself onto the chair, she did look uncomfortable. "What do you want me to do?"

"Do? Nothing. Just sit there."

"But how do you want me? Head tilted to the right or left? Eyes up or down?"

"Whatever way you feel natural." Malone picked up a large sketch pad and a box of charcoal crayons. "This is very preliminary."

"Do you mind if I stand?"

"So long as you keep your face in my direction."

The charcoal scratched on the pad.

She looked more uneasy. "Photographers hated it if I stood still. I had to keep moving. Often, there was rock music. When the film in one camera was exposed, they'd quickly hand it to an assistant, then switch to another camera and never miss a shot. They'd have a fan pointed at my hair so when I spun, my hair twirled. They'd tell me to keep fluffing it with my hands."

Malone's charcoal crayon stopped scratching.

"What's the matter?" she asked.

"You're going to have to keep still for *me*. Don't exaggerate. But I do need you a little less animated if I'm going to make a good likeness."

"Can I talk at least? Photographers also hated it when I talked."

"Be my guest." Malone made a few more scratches with the charcoal, then tore the sheet from the pad and set it on a table.

"That one didn't turn out? Did I move too much?"

"No, it's fine for what it is." Malone resumed scratching on the pad. "It's just a study. I'll do hundreds before I try anything permanent."

"Hundreds?"

"To get a feel for your face."

"The photographers I worked with sometimes took hundreds of exposures in a session."

"Well, this is going to take longer."

Sienna raised her eyebrows.

The expression was marvelous. "Good."

7

"Madame, will you be wanting lunch?"

Confused, Malone turned toward an aproned servant standing in the doorway. "So early?"

"It's almost two, monsieur."

Malone's confusion changed to amazement when he looked at the table behind him. A chaos of sketches littered it. "My God," he told Sienna, "you must be exhausted."

She was sitting on the chair by now. "A little. But

you were so engrossed, I didn't want to say anything. Besides, it's been interesting." She thanked the servant.

"Interesting?" Malone followed Sienna onto the terrace. His eyes adjusted to the increased brightness. "Watching me draw?"

"No, talking with you."

Malone tried to remember their conversation. He'd been so absorbed in working while glancing surreptitiously outside toward the helicopter area and the Cloister that the things they'd talked about were a blur.

"I haven't had a long conversation with anybody in quite a while." Sienna sat at a table and told the servant, "Just a salad and iced tea, please."

Malone ordered the same. "Yes, your husband's so busy, you must be alone a lot."

Sienna didn't respond, but something in her eyes made Malone suspect that even when she and Bellasar were together, they didn't talk.

"You never met your father?"

The question caught him by surprise. It took him a moment to recall their unfinished topic from when they'd entered the sunroom.

Sienna looked apologetic. "Don't answer if I'm being too personal."

"No, that's all right. I don't mind talking about it. My mother was a drunk." Malone tried to sound matter-of-fact, but he couldn't stop bitterness from creeping into his voice. "She had a string of boyfriends I was supposed to call Dad, but I never did."

"At the stables, you mentioned something about a grandfather."

"My mother's father. He took care of me on his farm when my mother wasn't dragging me from state to state with whatever boyfriend she had at the time. I spent a lot of time by myself. That's when I started to draw."

"It just goes to show—sometimes good can come out of bad." She sounded as if she wanted to believe it.

"Excellent," Bellasar said, approaching from the sunroom. "You've begun."

Sienna stiffened.

"You saw the sketches?" Malone asked.

"They're very promising. Any of them could be the basis for a splendid portrait," Bellasar said.

"They probably won't be. I've got a long way to go."

"But sometimes first instincts are best. It's possible to overthink something."

"True."

"I'm glad we agree. Not every task has to be difficult and take forever. My wife is an uncommonly beautiful woman. All you have to do is portray her beauty."

"But she's beautiful in a hundred different ways," Malone said. "Since I'm not going to do a hundred portraits, I need to figure out which way most reflects her nature."

Sienna glanced down at her hands.

"Forgive us, my dear," Bellasar said.

"For what?"

"Speaking about you as if you're not here. Going back to work wasn't too tedious?"

"Not at all. I found it interesting."

"Well then," Bellasar said, "let's hope it continues that way."

8

It certainly continued that way for Malone. He couldn't help thinking about the proverb that equated hell with interesting times. The days assumed a pattern. Each morning before work, he did calisthenics by the pool. He would have preferred to jog but needed to be stationary at a location that allowed him to keep watch on the helicopter pad and the Cloister. After Sienna returned from horseback riding, he joined her for breakfast, then went to work with her, trying to conceal his interest in what was going on outside. As the afternoon progressed, he offered to quit early in case she was tired. Always, she told him she wanted to continue. When they separated at five, he knew that he would see her again for cocktails at seven.

That was Bellasar's evening routine—cocktails (although Bellasar kept to his vegetable juice) and dinner (the dress always formal). Malone hoped someone else would be invited: the man who had arrived on the chopper that first morning and who had been so nervous about the rough way the crates he had brought were being unloaded. Malone wanted a closer look at him. Perhaps the man would reveal something about his relationship with Bellasar. But as far as Malone could tell, the man remained in the Cloister.

Sometimes, Malone found another centuries-old first edition on his bedside table, to be analyzed by Bellasar during dinner. Hobbes's *Leviathan* was one, a 1651 treatise maintaining that warfare was the natural state of humans and that the only way to achieve peace was by the force of a dictator. Bellasar's implication was that supplying arms to repressive regimes wasn't the evil it was made out to be. By preventing the masses from following their natural instincts and lunging for one another's throats, dictatorships saved lives—so did arms dealers.

After conversations of this sort, during which Sienna remained silent, Malone climbed the curving staircase to his second-story room, more on guard than he'd been since he'd left the military. No matter his tense sleep, he awoke the next morning with greater concentration, more committed to the dangerous balance he had to maintain. If he focused his attention too much on Sienna, he risked failing to notice something important at the Cloister. But if he *didn't* focus on her, he wouldn't accomplish the quality of work that he wanted, and that could be equally dangerous, for Bellasar might think that he wasn't making an effort.

9

"You won't be working today."

Sienna looked disappointed. "Why?"

"We're ready to begin the next stage. I have to get the surface ready." Malone showed her a large piece of plywood on a table.

"I thought painters use canvas."

"The kind of paint I'm going to use is called tempera. It needs a more rigid surface than canvas. This piece of plywood is old enough that it won't warp anymore. The chemicals in it have evaporated, so they won't affect the paint. But just in case, I'm going to seal it with this glue." He pointed toward a pot of white viscous liquid on a hot plate.

"It smells chalky."

"That's what's in it." Malone dipped a brush into the pot and applied the mixture to the board.

As soon as the board was covered, he set down the brush and rubbed his fingers over the warm glue.

"Why are you doing *that*?"

"To get rid of the air bubbles."

Sienna looked intrigued.

"Care to try?" he asked.

"You're serious?"

"If you don't mind getting your hands sticky."

She hesitated. Her cinnamon eyes brightened when she ran her fingers through the glue. "It reminds me of when I was in kindergarten, doing finger painting."

"Except that in this case, we don't want to leave a pattern." Malone brushed the layer smooth.

"It never occurred to me that painting involved more than drawing shapes and using color."

"If you want it to last, it involves a lot of other things." Malone handed her the brush. "Why don't *you* put on the next coat?"

"But what if I make a mistake?"

"I'll fix it."

She dipped the brush into the pot. "Not very much, right?"

"That's the idea."

"Is there any special way to do this?"

"Pick a corner."

She chose the upper right.

"Now brush to the left. You can use short back-and-forth strokes, but when it comes to the finishing strokes, brush only to the left. Go down a little, and move to the left again. Excellent. Make sure everything's smooth. Are you feeling any drag on the brush?"

"A little resistance."

"Good. Stop a minute. We want it to start drying but not get hard."

"Since you're moving to the next stage, you must have decided how you want to pose me."

Malone nodded.

"What pose is it? How am I going to look?"

"See for yourself." He pointed toward a sketch on another table.

She approached it uncertainly, peering down. For long seconds, she didn't say anything. "I'm smiling, but I look sad."

"And vulnerable, but determined not to get hurt anymore."

Sienna's voice was almost a whisper. "That's how I seem to you?"

"*One* of the ways. Do you object?"

She kept staring at the sketch. "No. I don't object."

"You have all kinds of expressions, but most of them don't show what's going on behind your eyes. At first, I assumed it was a habit from when you were a model. After all, the company that hired you to pose in whatever dress they were selling couldn't have cared less if you happened to be feeling glum when you did the sitting. They just wanted you to make the damned dress look good. So I imagine you did your job, turned on your smile, put a glint in your eyes, and lowered a shield *behind* those eyes."

"A lot of days, it *was* like that."

"But every once in a while, when I was studying you—"

"Which I don't mind any longer, by the way. I'm amazed that I've gotten used to it. When I was a model, the looks I got were usually predatory. But yours don't threaten me. They make me feel good about myself."

"You don't normally feel good about yourself?"

"The man who drew that sketch knows the answer."

"Every once in a while, when I was studying you, the shield behind your eyes would disappear, and this is how you seemed to me. Your sadness and vulnerability are what make you beautiful. Or maybe it's the reverse."

"The reverse?"

"I wonder if it's your beauty that makes you sad and vulnerable."

Sienna's throat sounded dry. "In the sketch, I'm looking to my right. At what?"

"Whatever's important to you."

"A breeze from that direction is blowing my hair. Somehow you've created the illusion that whatever I'm looking at is passing me."

"The important things are passing all of us."

10

Sienna hurried up the steps to the sunbathed terrace and tried not to falter when she didn't see Chase at the wrought-iron table, where they usually met before going to work. I'm a little early, she told herself. He'll be here shortly. But before she could sit down, she saw a servant carry a large bowl of something into the sunroom.

Puzzled, she followed. The servant came out as Sienna entered. She saw Chase peering down at what was now visible to her in the bowl. Eggs.

"Good morning." He smiled.

"Good morning. You're going to have breakfast in here?"

"I might not have breakfast at all. I'm too eager to get started." Chase picked up an egg, cracked it, divided its shell, and poured the yolk from one half to the other, making the white drop into a bowl.

Still thinking he intended to eat the eggs for breakfast, Sienna asked, "How are you going to cook them?"

"I'm not. I'm going to make paint with them."

"What?"

Chase eased the yolk from the half shell and placed it on a paper towel, where he rolled it gently, blotting off the remainder of the white.

"You're gentle," Sienna said. "I'd have broken the yolk by now."

"Believe me, years ago, I broke plenty when I was learning." With a thumb and forefinger, Chase picked up the yolk by the edge of its sack and dangled it over a clean jar. "Feel like helping?"

"I'd break it."

"At this point, we want to. Use that knife to puncture the bottom of the yolk. Carefully. Good." Chase let the yolk drip from its sack, then delicately squeezed the remainder out.

"Here." He handed her an egg.

"What?"

"Help me prepare more yolks."

"But . . ."

"You saw how it's done. The worst that can happen is we have to get more eggs."

She chuckled. "Yesterday I was finger painting. Today you've got me playing with food." But after she cracked the egg and separated the white from the yolk, she wasn't prepared for how sensual it felt to roll the intact yolk in a paper towel and blot off the remainder of the white. The soft pouch felt extremely vulnerable through the paper towel, needing to be handled with the utmost care. When she transferred it to the palm of her hand, the yolk felt surprisingly dry, delicately quivering, the tactile sensation intensifying.

"Thank you," she said.

"Why?"

"I can't remember the last time I had a pleasurable new experience."

"If separating eggs is your idea of a good time . . ." Now it was Chase's turn to chuckle.

She enjoyed the sound of it. "How many do you need?"

"Eight." He lanced the yolk he held.

"What do you want with them?"

"After dinner last night, I came back here and ground the pigments you see in those other jars."

Sienna studied them. White, black, red, blue, green, yellow, violet, and brown. Except for one, they were common colors, and yet she didn't think she'd ever seen any so pure and lustrous. "That shade of brown is unusual."

"Burnt sienna."

She felt a shock of recognition.

"The shade of your skin," Chase said. "Your parents named you well. It happens to be my favorite color."

She looked in amazement from the jar to her arm.

"It's distinguished by a brilliant, transparent, fiery undertone that's especially suited for a medium as brilliant and luminous as tempera," Chase said.

After adding one pigment to each of the yolks, he blended the mixtures with distilled water until they were fluid enough to be applied to a surface. "And now we're ready to rock and roll."

11

The plywood was on an easel, its chalk surface covered with a version of the sketch that Chase had selected.

"So now you color the sketch?" Sienna asked.

"No, it's more complicated than that." He guided

her toward her chair, which he had placed in front of the easel. "The sketch is only a blueprint."

Until that moment, she had thought that he'd stared at her as intensely as anyone possibly could, but now she realized that he hadn't really stared at her at all. The power of the concentration he now directed toward her was eerie. From five feet away, his gaze seemed to touch her. Along her neck, her lips, her eyelids, her brow. She felt invisible fingers caress her skin, making it tingle. She felt something from him sink beneath her, warming her, becoming one with her.

"Are you all right?"

"What?" She straightened in the chair.

"You look like you're falling asleep. If you want to get some rest, we can try again later."

"No," she said quickly. "I'm fine. Keep going."

Chase managed to keep his intense gaze focused on her all the while he dipped his brush into a jar of paint, used his left thumb and forefinger to squeeze some of the paint from the brush, and applied the paint to the rigid surface. Sometimes, his hand went to the surface automatically, as if he knew how the image he was creating appeared without needing to look at it except for quick glances while he concentrated on her.

Overwhelmed, needing to talk but not knowing what about, she said the first thing that came into her mind. "I can feel you painting me."

"If this makes you uncomfortable . . ."

"No. I don't mind it at all. How long will the portrait take?"

"As long as it needs. That's one of the advantages

of tempera. I can add layer after layer for weeks before the yolk finally becomes so inert it refuses to accept another level. Don't worry, though. This isn't going to take weeks."

Sienna surprised herself by thinking that she wouldn't mind if it did.

A muffled explosion rattled the windows.

"What are they doing over there?" Chase asked.

"I have no idea. I've never seen that part of the estate."

Chase looked surprised.

"When Derek and I were married, he told me I wasn't allowed over there. I didn't know how serious he was until curiosity got the better of me and I tried to get a look. A guard stopped me before I was halfway there. That night, the discussion at dinner wasn't pleasant. I never tried again."

"You didn't know how he earned his money when you married him?"

Sienna rubbed her forehead.

"Sorry. That's a question I have no business asking."

"No, it's all right." She exhaled wearily. "I should have asked more questions of my own. I had a vague idea of what he did, but I didn't make certain connections. What is it they say? The devil's in the details. Once I began to understand the specifics, I wished I were still naïve."

The next thing, Chase was standing over her. "Are you okay?"

Her shoulder tingled from the touch of his hand. "It's nothing. A headache."

"Maybe we should stop until after lunch."

"No, we had a rhythm going."

12

"It's exquisite." Bellasar's smile was as bright as Malone had ever seen it, emphasizing the tan of his broad, handsome face. "Better than I dared hope. More imaginative than I dreamed a portrait could be. Isn't it, Alex?"

"Yes," Potter said without enthusiasm.

It was eight days later. They were in the library, where Bellasar had insisted on a special unveiling, champagne for everyone, except, of course, Bellasar.

"There's something dark and unsettling about it. At the same time, it's bright with celebration," Bellasar said. "A study in contrasts. The paradox of beauty."

"That was the idea," Malone said.

"Then I understand it." Bellasar was pleased. "You see, whatever your opinion of me, I do have an appreciation of art. There was a moment, I confess, when your attitude made me wonder if I'd chosen the right artist."

Potter nodded, his spectacled eyes fixed not on the portrait but on Malone.

"What do *you* think, my dear?" Bellasar turned toward where Sienna stood uncomfortably in the background. "How does it feel to have your beauty immortalized? The glory of beauty—the sadness that it doesn't last. But here in this painting, it's preserved forever." Bellasar looked at Malone for reassurance. "You did say the materials were chosen to last an unusually long time."

"Oil on canvas tends to crack after several hundred years," Malone said. "But tempera on wood . . . with six layers of foundation beneath the paint and the glaze I put over it . . ."

"Yes?" Bellasar's eyes were intense.

"I don't see why, in a thousand years, it'll look any different."

"A thousand years. Imagine." Bellasar was spellbound. "Impermanent beauty made permanent. Dante's Beatrice."

Although Malone understood the reference, Bellasar felt the need to explain. "When Dante was nine, he saw a girl a few months younger than himself. Her beauty so struck him that he worshiped her from afar until her death sixteen years later. Her name was Beatrice, and she so inspired Dante to meditate about ideal beauty that the *Divine Comedy* was the consequence. Sienna's beauty inspired you in a similar way. And of course the inspiration will become greater as you work on the second portrait."

"Second portrait?" Sienna sounded puzzled. "But this one turned out so well, why would you want—"

"Because the second will emphasize your body as much as this does your face."

"My body?"

"Nude."

"*Nude?*" Sienna turned toward Malone. "Did you know about this?"

Reluctantly, awkwardly, he said, "Yes."

She spun toward Bellasar. "I won't have anything to do with this."

"Of course you will. We'll talk about it upstairs." Bellasar gripped her arm, the force of his hand whitening her dark skin as he led her across the library. At the door, he glanced back at Malone. "If you're curious about Dante and Beatrice, Rossetti translated Dante's autobiography." He gestured proprietarially toward the far wall. "You'll find an 1861 edition of *Dante and His Circle* over there, although naturally, my own preference is to read the original Italian."

Then Bellasar and Sienna were gone, leaving Malone with Potter and the servant who had poured the champagne.

Potter stopped scowling at Malone and addressed his attention to the portrait. His slight nod might have been in approval, but the sarcasm in his voice was unmistakable. "A career-defining work. It's too bad no outsider will ever see it." He gestured to the servant, who set down the Dom Pérignon and draped a dust cloth over the portrait.

"Coming?" Potter asked Malone. "You'll want to get ready for dinner."

"I think I'll stay here a moment and find that book."

With a gaze that made clear nothing Malone did would ever be good enough, Potter left the room.

Malone turned toward the bookshelves, making a pretense of searching for the book. Behind him, he heard the servant lift the portrait off the easel and take it from the library.

Malone waited ten seconds, then followed. He reached the vestibule in time to see the servant carrying the portrait up the curving staircase. Keeping a careful distance, Malone started up as the servant passed the next level and proceeded toward the top.

A carpet on the stairs muffled Malone's footsteps. The servant couldn't hear him climb higher. Peering beyond the final steps, Malone watched the servant carry the portrait to a door halfway along the middle corridor.

As the servant knocked on the door, Malone eased back down the stairs.

FOUR

FOUR

1

A chopper took off and roared away, its blades glinting in the morning sunlight, but as far as Malone could tell, the man he had seen arrive the first day wasn't aboard. Finishing his calisthenics by the pool, scanning the estate, he couldn't think of a way to get Sienna out. As soon as he finished the portraits and left—*if* he was allowed to leave—he was supposed to tell Jeb how to rescue her. But now that he had studied the compound's defenses, it was obvious that even the best extraction team would have trouble.

To add to his apprehension, this was the first morning he hadn't seen her ride from the stable. It was so important a part of her routine that he could imagine only the worst reasons for her to have abandoned it. Had Bellasar decided that one portrait of her was enough and it was finally time to rid himself of an unwanted spouse?

Making his way to his room to shower and dress, he tried to convince himself that there might be an innocent reason for Sienna to have failed to go out for her ride. She might not be feeling well, for example, in which case she would send word via a servant while he was having breakfast. But all the while he sat alone on the terrace, no messenger arrived.

"I wonder," he asked the servant who brought his coffee, "if you know why madame isn't joining me this morning? Have you heard if she's ill?"

"No, monsieur, I haven't heard anything."

A half hour later, Sienna still hadn't arrived, and Malone was forced to admit she wasn't coming. His stomach uneasy, he decided that his only option was to ask a servant to knock on her door and try to find out what had happened. He felt his pulse speed with the premonition that she was in trouble, perhaps unconscious from a drug Bellasar had given her. On edge, he rose to tell a servant to check on her—and froze with relief when Sienna stepped onto the terrace.

2

She wore dusty boots, faded jeans, and a denim work shirt, as if she had dressed to go riding but had been detained. Her long hair was tied back in a ponytail, emphasizing the classic contour of her chin and jaw. But her pulled-back hair also emphasized a severity in her eyes that Malone hadn't seen before. An anger. Something had happened. Whatever vulnerability hid behind her beauty was definitely not in evidence this morning.

"I'm glad to see you," Malone said. "When you didn't show up for breakfast, I got worried."

Without a word, Sienna walked resolutely toward him, her boots and jeans emphasizing her long legs and tightly belted waist.

"What's wrong?" Malone asked. "You look as if—"

"I'm late." Her words were clipped. "We're wasting time."

"Wasting time? What are you talking about?"

"Let's get to work."

"But what's the matter? Tell me what—"

Sienna pivoted and crossed the terrace, marching toward the sunroom.

Malone followed, mystified, noting her resolute stride and rigid posture. Although the sunroom was bright, it was less so than outdoors, and his eyes needed a moment to adjust to the difference.

He was twice as mystified and suddenly alarmed as she angrily unbuttoned her shirt and threw it onto the floor.

"Wait a minute," Malone said. "Why are—"

She jerked off her bra and hurled it past the shirt.

"Would you *please* tell me what's going on?" Malone said. "I don't—"

"I'm getting ready for work!" She yanked off her boots and socks.

"For God sake, stop! What's happened? Tell me why you're—"

"I'm doing what my husband wants!" She savagely opened her belt, took off her jeans, and threw them, the buckle clattering across the floor. Her white bikini panties went after the jeans. In a final defiant gesture, she untwisted the clasp that bound her ponytail, freeing her hair so it hung to her shoulders. Outraged, she stood before him, her burnt sienna skin uniform from head to toe.

"What are you waiting for?" she asked. "Get your damned sketch pad! Get started!"

Malone found it nearly impossible to speak. He took a deep breath and forced out the words. "This isn't what I want."

"I'm supposed to assume a provocative pose, is that it?"

"No."

"Then what the hell *do* you want? Stop confusing me! Tell me what I'm supposed to do!"

"Put on your shirt." He picked it up, offering it to her.

She glared.

"I mean it," Malone said.

"You accepted the commission, didn't you?"

"Obviously."

"And you knew the second portrait was supposed to be nude."

"Yes."

"Don't you think it would have been polite to tell *me*? All the time you were staring at me, I was flattered. Because it wasn't like you were staring." She struggled to order her thoughts. "You were . . . admiring. Without being predatory. Making me feel good about myself. I thought, Finally here's somebody who understands me as a person, not an object. And now I find out this was just a job for you. Make the bitch feel at ease, and do what you're paid for."

"No," Malone said. "This wasn't just a job. Please." He continued to hold out her shirt.

She grabbed it. Her harsh gaze remained fixed on him, but he never looked away from her eyes, never let his own gaze waver, lest he unwittingly suggest he wasn't being truthful.

She put on the shirt.

"Listen to me," Malone said. "At the start, this was just a job, yes. I didn't know you. The first time we met was uncomfortable. It looked like we might not get along. I figured this was going to be the hardest work I'd ever attempted, and I wished I'd never gotten involved."

She glared.

"But day by day, we got to know each other," Malone said. "More important, we seemed to enjoy each other's conversation. I looked forward to getting up in the morning, to meeting you at breakfast and going to work each day. The project became important to me. I realized that I'd never done better work in my life— because I'd never had a better subject."

She glared harder.

"And each day, as the first portrait came closer to completion," Malone said, "I felt increasingly tense because I knew that I'd soon have to do the second portrait. But I didn't want the *first* one to be completed. Talking with you, identifying with you, transmitting my imagination through you, had become so meaningful to me that I didn't want it to end. I knew, of course, it was going to *have* to end. I couldn't postpone completing it forever. But I couldn't adjust to the thought of what it was going to be like painting you under different circumstances, with everything strained and me having to stare at you all over again, getting to know your body as well as I know your face. I can paint whatever I set my mind to. But if it's going to be the best work I can do, I can't be objective. What I'm going to say is probably the strangest thing you've ever heard a man tell you. Given the relationship we've established, the last thing I wanted was to see you naked. I'd have been content just to study your face, and I had no idea how I was going to deal with the problem when I couldn't avoid it any longer."

The last of Malone's words echoed into nothingness. Silence gathered, finally broken by the scrape of his shoes on the flagstones as he walked to her jeans, picked them up, and returned them to her. The shirt, which she had rebutttoned, was long enough to cover her. Even so, he wanted her to feel totally at ease.

A tear trickled from her left eye. "Why does Derek want these portraits in the first place? I don't understand any of this."

"The only reason I know is what he told you," Malone lied. "He wants to preserve your beauty, to make it permanent."

"Including my body."

"Including your body."

"The next thing he'll have me shot and stuffed," she said.

Her statement was so close to the truth that Malone fought hard not to react.

"If I'm so beautiful, why won't he look at me?" Sienna's voice quavered. "Everything I do is wrong, as far as he's concerned. The disapproving way he treats me. Not just disapproving. He's contemptuous. Why would he want portraits of someone who disgusts him?"

Tears streamed down her face now, reddening her eyes, bringing out the fire beneath her tan skin. Before Malone realized, she was leaning against him, holding him with a desperation that made him think of someone struggling not to drown. Her shoulders heaved, her deep sobs racking them. He smelled apricots in her hair, nutmeg on her skin. He felt her tears drip onto his shirt. They soaked through, burning his chest. At the same time, he felt her breasts beneath her shirt. They pressed against him, making him terribly aware of the jeans she hadn't put on. Her legs were bare. So were her hips beneath her shirt. So was—

"Is this a technique they teach in art school?" Bellasar asked from the doorway.

3

With a frightened gasp, Sienna jerked away from Malone and spun toward her husband.

"Some kind of artistic encouragement?" Bellasar

asked. "But is the artist encouraging the model, or the model encouraging the artist?"

"This isn't what you're thinking," Sienna said.

"How do you know what I'm thinking? You were expected to take your clothes off, after all. If you're afraid I'll think I've caught you having an affair, don't worry. I've never once doubted that you'd remain faithful to me. You wouldn't have the nerve to do otherwise."

Sienna flinched.

"And I've never yet heard of a tryst in which the woman made herself sexually attractive by sobbing all over her lover." Bellasar approached and drew a hand along the tears that trickled down her cheeks. "You're a mess, my dear. You look the way you did when I first saw you in Milan. You weren't photographable then, and you're certainly not anything I'd like to see a portrait of now."

Sienna's sobs came from deep within her.

"Your nose is running. Your mouth is . . . How on earth is this man supposed to do his work?"

Malone couldn't help noticing that Bellasar never once looked at him.

"Go to your room and clean yourself up," Bellasar said. "When you return after lunch, I expect you to have repaired the damage you've done to yourself and be ready to pose."

Sienna's lips trembled.

"Damn it, what are you waiting for?" Bellasar asked. "*Move.* For once in your life, do something right."

Through tear-blurred eyes, she looked at Bellasar, then switched her emotion-ravaged features toward Malone. Abruptly she ran from the room.

It had taken all of Malone's willpower not to stop Bellasar from humiliating her. The rage that had prompted him to accept Bellasar's commission seethed twice as strongly in him. More than anything, he wanted to get even. But not here, not now, he kept telling himself. Attacking Bellasar for what he'd just done, breaking his arms and legs and as many other bones as Malone could before the guards rushed in, wasn't the punishment Bellasar deserved. It wouldn't help Sienna. It wouldn't get her safely off the estate. Keep control, Malone urged himself.

As Sienna disappeared beyond the wall of windows, silence gathered. The sunroom seemed to shrink.

"I want to ask your professional opinion about something," Bellasar said.

"Anything you want to know about painting, I'll do my best to answer."

"This isn't about painting."

4

The stutter of a machine gun grew louder. As Malone aproached the shooting range, he noted that the shrub-lined path Bellasar had chosen avoided the Cloister. He also noted an increase in guards and remembered that Sienna had told him she had never been allowed to enter this section of the estate.

So why is Bellasar bringing me here? Malone thought. Does he feel free to show me the shooting range because he knows I'll never live to tell anyone what I see?

The machine gun stopped, then started again. From the force of its bursts, Malone identified the weapon as a .50-caliber one, and its astonishingly rapid rate of fire made him conclude that the problem Bellasar had mentioned weeks earlier—how to compensate for the heat that a faster feeding mechanism generated—had been solved.

The shrubs gave way to an open area in which there were several wooden shooting stalls that resembled roadside vending stands, with the difference that, although each had a roof, there wasn't a back wall. Where fruits and vegetables would normally be on display, there were spotting scopes and clamps for bracing weapons whose sighting mechanisms needed calibration.

Between two of these stations, a machine gun had been mounted on a tripod. A man in gray coveralls pulled plugs from his ears, leaned over to examine the weapon, then reached for a tool in a box next to it. An ammunition belt, its rounds as thick and long as a finger, fed into the weapon from a large metal bin on the right. Expended brass casings littered the ground, glinting in the sun.

But Malone gave these details only passing notice, too preoccupied by where the machine gun was aimed. That area was spacious: several hundred yards square. It contained a village in which everything had been devastated by explosions and bullets. Huge jagged holes gaped in concrete-block buildings. Walls had toppled, ceilings collapsed. The scorched frames of cars and trucks littered what had once been streets but were now wastelands of rubble and craters.

Movement attracted Malone's attention back to the man in coveralls, who, at the sound of approaching footsteps, straightened from the machine gun. Behind drab spectacles, Potter's eyes hardened when he saw Malone.

"You're more versatile than I thought," Malone said.

"Oh, you'd be surprised what I can do." Potter turned toward Bellasar. "He shouldn't be here."

"I want to show him something."

"It's against your rules."

"And since they're *my* rules, I can break them." Bellasar pointed toward the machine gun. "If you've finished adjusting it, put up some targets."

"But—"

"Do what you're told. I don't pay you to argue."

Potter's cheek muscles twitched. With a glance toward Malone that left no doubt whom he blamed for the reprimand he had just received, he went over to one of the shooter's stations and flicked a switch. Malone momentarily thought his eyes were deceiving him. The ravaged village came to life. Soldiers ran from one building to another. Civilians scurried for cover. Jeeps bumped along the wreckage-scattered streets. To the right, an armored personnel carrier lumbered into view, turning to cross in front of the village. Two large tarpaulin-covered trucks hurried after it.

None of this was what it seemed. The soldiers and civilians were lifelike mannequins dressed for their various roles. They moved in a way that suggested they were attached to a motorized track below ground level. The personnel carrier and the trucks moved on motorized tracks also.

"Impressive," Malone said.

Bellasar nodded, as if he took for granted that the setup was exceptional. "My clients want weapons demonstrated under as close to lifelike conditions as possible."

"It's sort of like your own huge electric train set."

Bellasar looked puzzled.

"I once went to school with a kid who built electric train sets so he could put firecrackers under the bridges and in the water towers and the boxcars and blow them all up," Malone said. "I'd never met anybody who liked to destroy things so much."

"Let's see how much *you* like to destroy things."

"What do you mean?"

"Get over here, and test-fire this weapon. You were in the Marines. Give me your expert opinion on what a .50-caliber gun feels like with a faster feeding mechanism."

"I'm afraid my opinion wouldn't be worth much. It's been ten years since I handled a weapon."

"A weapon's like a bicycle." The statement was a command. "You never forget."

"Derek," Potter cautioned.

"Stay out of this." Bellasar kept his gaze rigidly on Malone.

"Fine." Malone held up his hands in mock surrender. "I'm not sure what point you want to make, but I'll go along."

As Malone approached the machine gun, Potter put his earplugs back in, then reached his right hand beneath the bib of his coveralls—to draw a handgun if the situation got out of control, Malone assumed. Guards unslung their rifles.

"You'll want these," Bellasar said, throwing him a set of earplugs, then putting in his own.

Malone pushed the earplugs into place. Noting how wary Potter looked, he made an exaggerated show of keeping the machine gun aimed toward the devastated village. He looked at Bellasar. "Anything special you want me to blow apart?"

"The truck on the right." Because of Malone's earplugs, Bellasar's voice was muffled.

When Malone aimed and squeezed the trigger, the sudden roaring assault made Malone feel as if he were trying to control a powerful living thing. He had expected an upward kick. He had braced his arms to compensate. But the force of what he held was far beyond his expectation. The recoil from an unimaginable rate of fire thrust the barrel violently into the air. As Malone shoved it back down, he aimed at the truck on the right, and if he hadn't been concentrating so hard to control the weapon, he would have gaped at the damage it did, its massive spray of bullets disintegrating the back of the truck, reaching the front and blasting the entire vehicle into pieces. When Malone released the trigger, his hands and arms vibrated. Anyone unfamiliar with a .50-caliber weapon would have dislocated both shoulders, he was certain.

"Have you got extrapowerful loads in these rounds?"

Bellasar shrugged. "What's your opinion of the modifications?"

"If you don't find a way to stabilize the recoil, nobody's going to be able to handle this thing."

"I don't know what recoil you're talking about." Bellasar stepped to the weapon, aimed, and pressed the trigger.

Malone wasn't prepared.

As the machine gun roared, making a rhythm like a locomotive at full speed, Bellasar controlled it with seeming effortlessness, his arms dominating the weapon's powerful inclination to jerk upward. Empty shell casings flew through the air with a velocity that made them look blurred. Bellasar's broad shoulders, muscular chest, and ramrod-straight posture had made Malone suspect that the man exercised frequently, probably with weights, and was in exceptional condition, especially for a man in his early sixties. But what Malone saw now was a bravado demonstration of strength far beyond anything he would have believed. The ease with which Bellasar handled the bucking recoil was awesome. He blew the second truck apart, switched his aim to the Jeeps in the village, blew *them* apart . . . and the soldiers . . . and the civilians . . . and finally swung the barrel toward the personnel carrier, inflicting what Malone would have considered impossible damage to the armored vehicle, its treads bursting loose, a hatch blowing open, smoke and flames spewing out. Jesus, this ammunition has armor-piercing heads and explosive charges, Malone thought as Bellasar released the trigger and swung the machine gun in Malone's direction.

Malone's heartbeat lurched. Apparently, his wasn't the only one. Seeing the barrel being swung past him, Potter stumbled to keep out of its way. In the background, the guards rushed toward the cover of trees.

Bellasar peered along the barrel toward Malone's chest. Despite the effort it must have taken to control the weapon during the damage he had inflicted on the village, Bellasar looked as if he had expended no more energy than steering a car.

"I'll show you what it feels like on the opposite end of the recoil," Bellasar said. "How would you like a couple of hundred rounds through your chest?"

"I think I'm missing something here."

"No, I don't believe you are. I think you know exactly what's going on."

Christ, does he know I'm working with Jeb? Malone wondered. Bluff, he warned himself. He couldn't assume anything. He didn't dare risk showing even the slightest sign of having been caught at anything. "Just so there's no confusion, why don't you be explicit?"

"Do you think I'm a fool?"

"Never."

"Did you think I wouldn't know the effect it would have on you to be with my wife all day every day? Did you think I wouldn't expect you to be attracted to her when she took her clothes off? I knew you wouldn't be able to keep from imagining what it would be like to make love to her."

Malone's heart pounded less violently. So this wasn't about Jeb. "You've got the wrong idea about—"

"Shut up. I want you to understand something very clearly. I can't control what you feel when you're with my wife. But if you ever act on those feelings, if you ever touch her in a way that's more than what I saw a while ago, if you ever react to her more than an artist merely giving comfort to his model, I'll drag you back here and . . . My wife belongs to *me*. I don't like people touching what I own. Is that clear?"

"Very."

"You're certain you understand?"

"Absolutely."

Bellasar swung the barrel back toward the village and squeezed the trigger, atomizing the walls of several buildings, until the last round fed through the firing mechanism and the gun became lifeless. He glared toward the ruins, a tremble working through him, but not from the effect of the massive recoil. When he finally spoke, his voice was tight. "Now get the hell back to work."

5

"I'm sorry."

Malone looked up from a sketch he was doing from

memory. Sienna stood at the entrance to the sunroom. He wouldn't have thought it possible for someone whose face had been so ravaged by tears to repair the damage in such a short time. She wore a loose pullover and a similar ankle-length skirt, both of them a blue that reminded him of the jade of the Caribbean that he had loved to look at from the beach of his home on Cozumel. *Had* loved, he emphasized to himself. Even though Bellasar had promised to return the property to its original condition, Malone would never go near it again.

"What are you sorry about?" he asked.

"Making a scene."

"*You* didn't make a scene. Your husband did."

"No. I apologize for being unprofessional. We both had jobs to do. I didn't approach mine very well."

"It's not a big deal. We had some issues to work out."

"And now that they've been settled . . ." Sienna gripped the bottom of her pullover and started to raise it over her head.

"Stop."

"I don't want to make Derek any angrier than he is. You've never seen him when he's truly upset. We have to do this second portrait. The sooner the better."

"Sit down."

"Is that how you want to pose me?"

"It's where I want you to relax a minute while I talk to you."

"No, please, we have to work. If Derek thinks we're wasting time, he'll—"

Malone's muscles tightened. "I'm the one doing the portrait. Let *me* worry about your husband. I want you to sit down. Please."

Sienna peered nervously toward the door. Hesitant, she did what she was asked.

Malone brought over a second chair. Straddling it, resting his arms on its back, he hoped that his casual movements would put her at ease. He spoke softly. "When your husband came in this morning, he said you looked the way you did when he first saw you in Milan. He said you weren't photographable then."

Sienna peered down at her hands.

"What was he talking about?" Malone asked.

Something in her eyes went somewhere else. She was silent for so long that Malone didn't think she was going to answer.

"That was a bad time for me," she said.

"When was this?"

"Five years ago."

Malone waited.

"I . . ."

Malone gave her an encouraging look.

"You have to understand . . ." She took a deep breath. "Models are the most insecure women you'll ever meet."

Malone didn't respond, afraid that if he said anything, he might make her too self-conscious to keep talking.

"We keep trying to assure ourselves that we're more than just a beautiful package. We worry about aging. We're always afraid that our best days are behind us."

Malone forced himself to remain silent.

"Oh, there are exceptions. But I wasn't one of them. Imagine what it's like to have to stay so thin that if you eat even a small amount, the camera shows the bulge in your stomach. To go as long as you can without eating. Or to eat and then make yourself throw up. Along the way, you try a little cocaine. It doesn't put on any weight, and for a while, it makes you feel better about yourself, so you try a little more, and meanwhile, with so many people trying to manipulate you, you hope for a man, stronger than the others, to help you get your life together. But when you think you've found him, he turns out to be a son of a bitch who wants to control everything you do, and . . ."

Sienna had spoken faster and faster, and now all of a sudden she seemed to realize that Malone was before her.

He took the risk of saying something. "Tell me what your husband meant about your face not being photographable back then."

"I'd been eating so little, I finally got too thin even for the camera. Worse, the cocaine had put a permanent glaze in my eyes. Worse than that, the man I was living with had split my lip and given me two black eyes."

Malone felt sick.

Her hands fidgeted. "This happened in Milan. I was there for the fall shows, but after I got beaten up, I obviously couldn't work. I stayed in my hotel room while the guy I was with went out to screw everything in sight, and the next thing I knew, there was a knock at the door. When I opened it, Derek was standing there. I'll never forget it. He was wearing a tuxedo and holding red roses. In my blur from the cocaine, I frowned at that handsome tan face, and I swear, for a moment I thought he was Rossano Brazzi, that Italian actor. I have no idea how he knew where I was or what had been done to me. He put a hand under my chin and said, 'I've come to take care of you. Don't bother packing. Just get your coat and come with me.' I blinked. I nodded. I didn't even bother with the coat. I just shut the door behind me and went down to his limousine."

"But you told me you had a loving family. Why would you have been insecure?"

"I didn't say I had a loving family, only loving parents."

"I don't understand."

Sienna swallowed. "After my parents died when I was twelve, I was sent to live with my uncle. He couldn't keep his hands off me. Whenever his wife wasn't around, he'd try to . . ."

Malone tasted bile.

"A couple of times he forced me to . . ."

"Jesus."

"He warned me that if I told anybody, he'd throw me out. I'd be sleeping in the gutter, he said. I couldn't concentrate. I did poorly in school. I cried myself to sleep. Finally, I retreated into a fantasy world. All I did was read fashion magazines and fantasize about being a model and having a glamorous life. This went on until my sixteenth birthday. When he snuck into my room again, I screamed that I wasn't going to do it anymore. I woke up his wife and kids. My aunt wouldn't believe what I said had been happening. *He* beat me black-and-blue for telling what he claimed were lies about him. I hurt so much, I had to stay in bed for two days. The third day, while they were at work, I stole money from under the flour jar, where I knew my aunt hid it from him. I hoped she'd think he'd found it and taken it to buy booze. I packed a bag and took a bus to Chicago, where I lived in a boardinghouse and worked at every rotten job you can imagine. But I never stopped dreaming about becoming one of those women in the fashion magazines. I found a company that gave modeling classes at night. I worked as hard as anybody can imagine to make good on my dream. And by God, from modeling for underwear ads in the newspaper, to doing swimsuit ads in catalogs, to appearing in *Vogue,* to doing covers for it and *Cosmopolitan* and every other major fashion magazine you can think of, I finally got what I wanted. The only trouble was, it wasn't what I'd dreamed of. It wasn't glamorous. It was a meat market."

"What happened when you went away with Bellasar?"

"In the limousine, as we drove to the airport, he looked at the bruises on my face. He told me he couldn't let beauty be destroyed. He said he was going to make sure no one ever harmed my face again and that *I* never harmed myself, either. He brought me here. He had a plastic surgeon waiting to make sure the injuries to my face wouldn't leave scars. He had a medical team detoxify me. He had a psychologist who specialized in eating disorders cure me of thinking food was my enemy. It took six months before the results met with Derek's approval. He was so proud. He'd created me, he said. He'd walk around me, study me from all angles, beam, and say that my beauty wouldn't have existed without him." She shrugged wearily. "He was right. At the downward rate I was going, I'd have been dead in the time he took to resurrect me."

"So he gave you what you needed. Finally, you had someone to take care of you."

"Until three months ago."

Malone frowned. "What happened then?"

"He came back from a business trip, and all of a sudden he'd changed. He complained about the start of wrinkles at the corners of my eyes. He claimed he saw a strand of gray in my hair. He warned me to stop being expressive with my face—the movement was starting to cause furrows in my brow, he said. I kept asking myself what had happened on that business trip to make him change. Had he fallen in love with another woman? When I raised the issue with him, it made him furious. He told me I was imagining things, that I had to get control of myself. I had my hair dyed, had facial scrubs, did whatever I thought would please him. But he only became more impatient with me. Nothing I did was good enough. I began to look forward to his trips away. They gave me a measure of peace. But each time he came back, he was even more critical."

Malone opened his mouth to reassure her and abruptly stopped as something behind him made Sienna stiffen.

She jerked to her feet. "Honestly, Derek, we're just talking about how to pose me. We're just about to start working. I swear it."

Bellasar stood in the doorway. "We're flying to Istanbul. Be ready at five." He narrowed his gaze toward Malone. "You have two weeks to finish your work."

"That might not be enough time."

"*Make* it enough."

"When I agreed to do the portraits, I told you I had to do them on my terms. You accepted those conditions."

"The conditions have changed."

"How am I supposed to work without a model? How long will Sienna be away?"

"As long as necessary."

"Well, the longer she's gone, the longer it'll take me to finish."

Bellasar's eyes darkened. "I'm beginning to agree with Alex. It was a mistake to get involved with you. Five o'clock." He turned angrily and left the room.

Watching him cross the terrace, Sienna shivered. "What time is it?"

"A little after three."

"God, that doesn't give me enough time."

As she stood, Malone asked, "What's in Istanbul? What's so important?"

Her voice was tight. "Whenever this happens, it's business. Several of Derek's clients enjoy spending time with me. Derek has an easier time negotiating with them because I'm around."

Malone nodded. Sure, Bellasar would be a bigger man in their eyes because he was married to a woman so beautiful.

"I can't talk any longer."

As she hurried away, Malone continued his thought. Yes, so much beauty might dazzle a client, might subtly affect his judgment. But what about when that beauty developed flaws? Bad for business. Bad for the rigid standards of a husband who couldn't settle for less than perfection. Bad all the way around. When someone stopped fulfilling a necessary function, a replacement had to be found.

6

The sun was low enough to throw the terrace into shadow, but not enough that it didn't cause a reflection off the spinning blades of a helicopter. Malone watched as Sienna, Bellasar, Potter, and three bodyguards got into it. She wore an elegant suit, her hair impeccably arranged. Even from a distance, her beauty was overwhelming, but also from that distance, Malone was able to tell how reluctantly she got into the chopper. In fact, she had the manner of a well-dressed prisoner being taken to a trial. Or to a funeral.

The metaphor made him uneasy. As the helicopter roared away, he felt a stab of separation.

FIVE

1

Accustomed to cocktails with Sienna each evening at seven, Malone was more uneasy as that hour approached. I would have started down to the library by now, he thought. Instead, he roamed those sections of the grounds permitted to him, a frustrated animal trying to relieve tension. When sunset finally tinted the shrubs, statues, and ponds of the estate, he decided that he ought to try to eat something, but sitting alone at the long candlelit table, he only poked at the veal cutlets that had been prepared for him. He couldn't stop wondering where Sienna was and what she was doing.

If she was still alive.

He had a sudden harrowing image of Bellasar hurling her from the chopper, of her body crashing onto rocks, or of Potter blowing her brains out and dumping her into the sea. No! he kept telling himself. Bellasar's manner suggested that he needs her. For now at least. The crisis won't come until after Istanbul.

He slept fitfully. In the morning, trying to subdue his mind, he extended his calisthenics from one to two hours, but his fear for Sienna intensified. He went to the sunroom and spread out his sketches, gazing at her features. Drawing her from memory, he imagined that she was seated before him, talking to him.

He went to the library. Smelling the must of its ancient volumes, he crossed the carpet to the far wall and climbed a ladder to the middle shelves. It was toward them that Bellasar had gestured the evening the portrait had been unveiled, the evening Bellasar had compared Sienna to Dante's Beatrice, the inspiration for the *Divine Comedy*. "If you're curious about Dante and Beatrice, Rossetti translated Dante's autobiography," Bellasar had said. "You'll find an 1861 edition of *Dante and His Circle* over there . . ."

Bellasar had said something else: that Beatrice had died young and that Dante had obsessed about her ever after. Malone couldn't avoid the insistent comparison: Is *Sienna* going to die young?

I've got to stop thinking about death.

Because the books were arranged alphabetically by author, he had no trouble finding the volume he wanted. In the process, he thought it curious that Rossetti's first name was Dante, the same as the poet whose autobiography he had translated. He sat in a leather chair, opened the book, and came to the first time Dante had seen Beatrice.

> Her dress, on that day, was of a most noble colour, a subdued and goodly crimson. . . . At that moment, I say most truly that the spirit of life, which hath its dwelling in the secretest

chamber of the heart, began to tremble so violently that the least pulses of my body shook.

Yes, Malone thought.

2

Two nights later, Sienna still hadn't returned.

Malone lay tensely on his bed, listening to the
sounds of guards patrolling in the darkness beyond his
window. The intervening slow passage of time had
been agonizing, but it had given him a chance to plan.
Rosetti's translation of Dante lay open before him.

The same wonderful lady appeared to me
dressed all in pure white. . . . Because it was the
first time that any words from her reached mine
ears, I came into such sweetness that I parted
thence as one intoxicated.

Sweat beaded his brow. He went into the bathroom,
rinsed his face with cold water, then shut off the lights
in his room and went over to the window across from
his bed, watching the shadows and floodlights on the
gardens and paths.

A glance at his watch showed that the time was almost midnight. In a few moments, a guard would appear on the right and walk along a white-pebbled path
in the middle, his boots making crunching sounds.

Malone shifted next to the window, where not even his shadow would be seen. He waited.

There. The sound of boot steps preceding him, the guard came into view. Malone nodded. Ten minutes later, another guard would appear, this one on the left. Five minutes after that, a third guard would become visible from beyond the changing rooms at the swimming pool, heading toward the chopper pads. The schedule hadn't varied in the weeks since Malone had noted it.

He picked up the book and left his room. The dimly lit corridor was deserted. His footsteps made no sound on the runner that covered the floor. He reached the top of the curving staircase, started down, and heard boot steps on the marble floor below as a guard emerged from a room on the right, watching him descend.

"Couldn't sleep." Malone showed the guard the book. "I came to get another."

The guard looked puzzled by the notion of finishing one book and wanting to read more.

Malone didn't linger to talk about it. He went along the corridor on the left and opened the library door. In the darkness that faced him, the room had a smothering staleness that reminded him of the funeral parlor in which his grandfather's body had lain. The only thing missing was the cloying scent of too many flowers.

Stop thinking that way, Malone warned himself.

He flicked a switch on his left, blinked from the glare of the overhead light, and closed the door behind him. The books were arranged not only by author but in categories: fiction, nonfiction, and reference, the latter on the right.

As Malone headed in that direction, he heard the door open behind him. Turning, he saw the guard. With a nod, Malone resumed his search. The encyclopedia was easily located. *Britannica.* He didn't know anything about rare books, but he did know about Bellasar's tastes, and he would have bet anything that this particular edition—1911, the copyright page on the volume he selected showed—was the classic version preferred by collectors.

The guard kept watching. Malone nodded to him again, but this time with a slight impatience, as if saying, Fine, you've made your point. You've been a good watchdog. Now get on with your rounds and let me read in peace. The guard's puzzled gaze wavered. After he stepped back into the corridor, his steps receding along the marble floor, Malone went over and shut the door, being sure that the latch made a noise to let the guard know he didn't want to be disturbed again.

He carried the volume he had chosen—for subjects that began with *R* —to an easy chair, and as he turned the heavy book's brittle pages, smelling its must, he tried to stifle his apprehension. Everything's going to be okay, he assured himself. Just keep following the plan.

He found the article he wanted.

"Rossetti, Dante Gabriel: English painter and poet, a founder of the Pre-Raphaelite movement, born in

1828, died in 1882." Stop thinking about death! he told himself.

Rossetti's original first names had been Gabriel Charles Dante, but his obsession with the Italian poet from the Middle Ages had prompted him to insist on being called Dante. The obsession had taken another form when he identified his beautiful wife, Elizabeth, with Dante's Beatrice and dedicated himself to a passionate translation of Dante's devotion to that woman, in effect describing the love he himself felt for Elizabeth. After Elizabeth's death early in their marriage, Rossetti had buried the manuscripts of all his poems with her and had painted a symbolic portrait of his idealized love for her, calling it *Beata Beatrix—Blessed Beatrice*.

Again, the subject was death. Struggling to distract himself, Malone found significance in the parallel he shared with Rossetti—they were both painters, and their lives had been changed because of a woman each had fallen in love with while doing a portrait of her.

Love. For the first time, Malone realized that he had consciously used the word in connection with what he was feeling.

3

A half hour later, when the guard again looked in, Malone pretended to be asleep in the chair, his eyes closed, his head drooping, the encyclopedia open on his lap. This time, the guard shut the door when he went away. Immediately, Malone stood, turned off the lights, and went over to a casement window. Seeing no one outside, he opened the window, eased down to the murky ground, shut the window behind him, and sank behind a shrub. If the guard returned to the library, he would decide that Malone had wakened and gone back to his room.

Staying low, Malone assessed the spotlights in the darkness. After assuring himself that no one was in this area, he crossed a path, reached shrubs, and crept behind them in the direction of the Cloister, its bell tower silhouetted against the starry sky. Moving cautiously, working to blend with shadows, he took a half hour to cover a distance that would normally have been a five-minute stroll.

His palms sweated. Having been away from the military for a decade, he had to work to shut down his emotions. His heart pounded. His lungs couldn't seem to get enough air. Leaving the cover of a fountain and reaching a clump of sculpted evergreen shrubs, he sank to the ground and stared at the arched windows of the Cloister. Although most were in darkness, it puzzled him that all of the basement windows were brightly lit. As he debated whether to risk crawling closer, he was startled by an outside door that opened, revealing a man's shadow against an interior light. A guard with a rifle stepped out, closed the door, stared up at the starry sky, and lit a cigarette. Malone silently gave thanks that he had hesitated to crawl toward the basement windows.

No problem. I'll just wait until he goes back inside or moves on. But with Bellasar and Potter away, the guard wasn't in a hurry. Indeed, after finally finishing the cigarette, then stubbing it out with his boot, the guard continued to remain where he was. Only when the door opened and another man came out, this one wearing a knee-length white coat, did the guard assume a professional stance, as if he'd been standing at attention, watching the door.

The second man, tall, with dark hair, blocky features, and a husky build, wasn't anyone Malone had seen before. With help from the hallway light spilling from the open door, Malone studied him, trying to memorize his broad lips, thick eyebrows, and square face. There was little time. The white-coated man pointed toward the crushed cigarette at the guard's feet and said something curt, with the immediate result that the guard came to greater attention. A further disapproving remark caused the guard to follow the man back into the building. The door banged shut, blocking the interior light. But there was still ample illumination from the security lights in the area, and Malone took a long, careful time to watch for other guards before he reconsidered approaching the basement windows.

Why had the man been wearing a knee-length white coat? he wondered. It looked like the kind of coat a doctor would wear in a hospital. Or a technician in a laboratory. What was behind those basement windows? Ignoring a metal band that seemed to tighten around his chest, he stayed low and darted toward shrubs at the side of the Cloister. No sooner had he disappeared behind one than boot steps rounded a corner, passing close enough to Malone for him to hear a scrape of metal against metal, perhaps from a rifle against an equipment belt.

Other sounds attracted Malone's attention—muffled voices, the rasp of what sounded like wood against stone. Wary, he peered through a window, staying to the side so he wouldn't be seen. Not that it did him any good—the illumination through the glass was filtered by a blind. The voices seemed to come from farther along, however, and when he crawled to the next window, reaching the cover of another shrub, he discovered that instead of a blind, this window had an inside shutter, the slats of which had not been completely closed.

He was able to see part of a room—segments of a stone floor, tables, cabinets, laboratory instruments, computers, and various electronic devices. Two large appliances against the far wall looked like an industrial-grade freezer and refrigerator. The voices became more distinct as the guard and the white-coated man stepped into view. The man spoke what sounded like Russian, which the guard didn't seem to understand and Malone certainly didn't, but the gist was clear—the man wanted the guard to open a wooden crate.

Nails screeched as a crowbar pried them free. When the guard rammed so hard that a board shattered, Malone heard another voice cry out in protest. A third man stepped into view. He, too, wore a knee-length white coat. He gestured in alarm, speaking in agitated Russian, the frantic point of which was obvious: *Be careful.* Malone had seen those gestures before. In fact, he had seen this *man* before, the same balding, stoop-shouldered man he had watched get out of the helicopter the first morning he had been on the estate. The man had been dismayed by the rough way Bellasar's men had handled the crates he had brought, just as he was dismayed now.

Finally getting a closer look at him, Malone focused all his concentration, straining to fix the man's features in his memory: the deep eyes, the high forehead, the oval face, the—

A distant rumble made Malone flinch. As it rapidly swelled to a whumping roar, an icy hand seemed to squeeze his heart. A helicopter. Jesus. Is Bellasar returning? Is Sienna with him?

The roar became loud enough that the men in the basement heard it and turned toward the window. Malone jerked to the side. Nothing in the way they spoke made him suspect that they had noticed him, but in the heightened security that would result from Bellasar's return, a guard was bound to see him. There'd be so much activity at the château, Malone wouldn't be able to sneak back inside.

His only chance was to take advantage of the brief distraction the chopper's arrival would create. Blinding lights came on between the château and the Cloister, illuminating the helicopter pad. Almost at once, another glaring light illuminated the area, but this one blazed from the sky, from the nose of the swiftly approaching helicopter.

The guards will be looking from one light to the other, Malone thought urgently. But the moment the chopper sets down, everything'll be back to business as usual. This is my only chance. Move.

But even as he braced himself to run from the shrubs at the side of the Cloister toward the greater number of shrubs across from him, a guard charged past. Malone barely checked his impulse in time. He looked to make sure that another guard wasn't hurrying after the first one. Yes, they're temporarily distracted, he fought to assure himself. I can do this.

The moment the chopper roared overhead, its spotlight flashing past, Malone sprinted from the side of the building. He reached the opposite shrubs at the same time he heard Russian voices as the door to the Cloister banged open behind him. It sounded as if they were headed toward the landing pad, but he didn't look behind him. He didn't stop. It had taken him thirty minutes to get here, creeping from statue to fountain to hedge to whatever other murky cover he'd been able to find. But now he had to cover the same distance quicker than it would take to walk it.

Staying low, moving with furtive speed, trying to blend with shadows, he heard the chopper set down to his right, its rotors slowing. Any moment now, Bellasar or whoever was in the chopper—Please, God, let Sienna be all right—would get out and proceed toward the château. Bellasar would ask the guards about Malone's activities while he had been gone. The guard who'd seen Malone go into the library would report that the last time he'd checked, Malone was still in the library, asleep in a chair. Bellasar would want to see for himself. And if I'm not in that chair when Bellasar looks in, Malone thought, he might get suspicious enough to check if I'm in my room.

As a guard loomed into view, Malone dropped to a crouch beside another statue and froze, praying that the guard wouldn't look in his direction. On the right, through a gap in some bushes, Malone saw the starkly illuminated landing pad. Angrily, Bellasar got out of the helicopter. Before the white-coated men could reach him, he turned away. Followed by his bodyguards, he took long strides toward the château. But there wasn't any sign of Potter. Far more important, where was Sienna? My God, has something happened to her? The next instant, someone shifted within the helicopter. A figure came slowly into view. But Malone's relief when the figure turned out to be Sienna was immediately replaced by worry when he saw how hesitantly she got down from the helicopter. Even at a distance, she looked dazed.

Move! Malone warned himself. There's nothing you can do for her now, and if you don't get back to the library before Bellasar looks in on you, you won't be able to help her *anytime*. Hell, you won't even be able to help yourself.

As the guard that blocked his way moved on, Malone looked once more at Sienna, noted how unsteadily she walked across the landing pad, and urged himself past the statue, then toward the château. Lights came on in several upper windows—presumably Bellasar's suite. Maybe Bellasar intends to go directly to bed,

Malone thought hopefully. Maybe he won't check on me until the morning.

Malone's chest heaved as he reached the final protective section of shrubs. He peered urgently around to make certain there weren't any guards in the immediate area, that no one would see him dart across the white-pebbled walkway, open the library window, and crawl back inside. As assured as he could be under the circumstances, knowing that he had to commit to taking the risk, he braced himself for a final effort and felt a cold paralysis seize his muscles as the library windows suddenly blazed with light.

4

"You told me he was in here!" Bellasar shouted, squinting from the bright overhead light.

"He was," the guard insisted. "I saw him asleep in that chair an hour ago."

"Then where the hell is he *now*?"

"He must have wakened and gone to his room."

"Suddenly he has an interest in old books? Suddenly he's hanging around the library at midnight? You never saw him go back to his room?"

The guard spread his hands guiltily. "No."

Bellasar stormed toward the casement windows, scowled at each of them, and noted that one was open a crack—enough space for fingers to pry in and open it farther if someone had gone out that way, closed it, and wanted to reopen it easily. "Damn it, find him. Go to his room! I want to know where he is!"

As the guard hurried into the hallway, Bellasar went after him. In the vestibule, he yelled for the three bodyguards who'd been with him to follow. Taking the curving staircase three steps at a time, he rushed up, passing the guard he had sent ahead of him. At the top, he slowed just enough for the group to catch up to him, then charged along the corridor, reached the door to Malone's room, thrust it open, turned on the light, and blinked at the empty bed, the covers of which weren't turned back.

"Search the grounds! Search *everywhere*!"

The guards scrambled to obey.

Following, Bellasar encountered Sienna as she wearily reached the top of the staircase.

"He's missing," Bellasar said. "If I find him where he shouldn't be, you won't need to worry about posing for the second portrait. He'll be dead."

Brushing past her, Bellasar charged down the stairs. "Check every room!" he ordered a group of guards who had heard the commotion and run into the vestibule. Seeing the Russians and another group of guards at the open doorway, he told them, "Search the Cloister! Give me your pistol!" he ordered a guard who raced past. He worked the 9-mm Sig-Sauer's injection slide to make sure a round was in the firing chamber, paused long enough to be satisfied that his commands were being obeyed, then rushed outside to join the search.

Flashlights zigzagged as guards searched under bushes and among trees.

To Bellasar's left, glass crashed. Voices shouted. One, louder than the rest, was terribly clear.

"We've found him! Here! Over here!"

5

Pretending to have been shocked awake, Malone jerked up from the settee on which he lay in the darkness. Men barged into the sunroom with such force that the glass door slammed against the huge window next to it, shattering both panes. Shards of glass hit the stone floor, exploding into smaller pieces, crushed by the boots of the men who charged in, aimed pistols and flashlights, and yanked him to his feet.

"What the—" Malone tried to sound disoriented.

A man rushed outside. "We've found him! Here! Over here!"

"What the hell's going on?" Malone murmured. "Why are you . . ." The lights still hadn't been turned on. The flashlights were aimed at his eyes, one of the beams so blindingly close that he raised his left arm to brush it away, only to have his arm thrust down and the flashlight whacked across the side of his face.

The impact sent a burst of colors through his mind. For a moment, those colors swirled. His legs bent. He started to fall, but the men jerked him to his feet, and the flashlight was cocked back to strike him once again when several more people rushed into the room.

Bellasar demanded, "Where *is* he? Show me the son of a bitch!"

The overhead lights came on. The blow to Malone's face had blurred his vision, but now he managed to focus it, seeing Bellasar stalk through the guards.

Bellasar's normally handsome features were twisted with rage. "The first time we met, you were tied to a chair. You'd pissed your pants." Bellasar's chest heaved, driven by the force of his emotions as he put on leather gloves.

"I don't understand," Malone said. "Why—"

"Shut your mouth!" Bellasar punched it.

Malone's head jerked back. For a moment, he saw more colors flash. His ears rang. As his disorientation cleared, he became aware of blood trickling down his chin from his split lips, joined by blood from a throbbing gash on his left cheekbone where the flashlight had struck him.

"That first time I saw you, as I looked at the piss beneath your chair, I said you were a fool for refusing to cooperate with me." Bellasar's voice trembled. "But I also said that I was reasonable, that I was willing to give you a second chance. I warned you, though." He punched Malone again, mangling his lips further. "I never give *third* chances."

The men holding Malone were jolted back by the strength of the blow.

Malone needed a few seconds longer before his

mind stopped spinning. "I don't give third chances, either. You've hit me twice. Try doing it again."

"What?"

"Without your guards hanging on to me."

"This close to dying, you have the nerve to talk to me like that?"

"Why in Christ's name are you threatening me?"

"You actually think you can bluff your way out of this?"

"Out of *what*?"

"You deny sneaking out of the library window?"

"Sneaking out of the library window? Do you have any idea how crazy that sounds?"

"You deny you were in there?"

"Of course I was in there! You made such a big deal about Dante and Beatrice, I read the book you suggested! You want a question and answer session? You want me to tell you what Beatrice was wearing when Dante first saw her? A red dress! Do you want to know the color of her dress the *next* time he saw her? White! The time after that, he saw her in church! The time after that, she was at a—"

"Why was the library window open a crack?"

"Beats the shit out of me! I didn't know it was!"

"The guard didn't see you leave the library."

"That makes us even, because when I left, I didn't see him, either." Malone wiped blood from his face. "Reading about Beatrice got me thinking about sketching Sienna without her being in front of me. So I came over here and tried something new, but I was sleepier than I thought, and I took a nap on that settee.

The next thing I knew, your storm troopers were barging in."

"Prove it! Where's the new sketch?"

"On the floor next to the settee. One of your guards is standing on it. I'm afraid it got a little smeared from my blood spattering over it."

The guard who was standing on the sketch stepped away. Frowning at the blood and boot marks on it, Bellasar picked up the wrinkled page. "I've seen all the sketches you did of her. If this is the same as . . ." His voice faltered when he looked at it.

Malone had sketched it two days previously, when his obsession with Sienna had compelled him to depict an idealized version of her beauty.

Bellasar's mouth opened as if he wanted to say something. When he finally managed to get the words out, his voice was a whisper. "It's stunning."

"Yeah, with the boot marks and the blood. I can't wait to see it framed."

Bellasar gazed at it, awestruck. "Breathtaking." At last, he lowered it. ". . . Apparently, I was mistaken."

"That makes my face feel a whole lot better."

"I'll send for a doctor."

"While you're being so kindhearted, how about telling your goons to take their hands off me?"

Bellasar gave him a warning look. When he nodded to his men, it was as if he had pressed a switch—they instantly let Malone go.

Malone wiped more blood from his mouth. Glancing past Bellasar, he saw Sienna in the doorway. She seemed even more dazed.

Bellasar noticed her. "There's nothing to worry about, my dear. You'll be able to pose tomorrow."

Sienna didn't respond. The dark of her eyes was huge, her expression listless. Malone wondered if she'd been drugged.

6

Outside on the harshly lit terrace, the two Russians waited. As Bellasar went to speak to them, Malone made another attempt to memorize their faces. Then, knowing he couldn't keep staring at them, he did what he wanted to do more than anything—to look at Sienna, to try to get a sense of what had happened in Istanbul, of what she was thinking and feeling. Something sank within him when she turned away. He couldn't tell if it was from fear or because she was horrified by the injuries to his face. But in that case, if she had any regard for him, wouldn't she have given him a look of sympathy?

Not if she was afraid of Bellasar's reaction.

When Bellasar came back from speaking to the Russians, he, Sienna, and Malone went through the terrace doors into the château. They were followed by three bodyguards.

As the group climbed the curving staircase, Bellasar said, "From now on, if you intend to work at night, ask a guard to escort you."

"You make it sound like I'm a prisoner."

With no reply, Bellasar led Sienna up to the final level. Two of the bodyguards went with them. A third stayed with Malone.

Bellasar's voice echoed faintly from above. "No, my dear, I'm not finished talking with you."

Malone's stomach squirmed, but with the guard watching him, he forced himself to look as if he didn't care about what he'd heard. Then a heavyset man holding a medical bag came up the stairs, and Malone had something to distract him.

The doctor made the repairs in Malone's room, washing off the blood, then applying sharp-smelling disinfectant to the gashes. The one caused by the flashlight blow to Malone's cheek required five stitches. The mangled lips, the doctor concluded, would mend on their own. "Keep the stitches dry." The doctor's English was heavily accented. "Take two of these pills every six hours. They'll relieve the pain. I'll come back to examine you tomorrow."

A guard was in the hallway when the doctor left. Malone closed and locked the door, yanked off his bloody clothes, and threw them into a hamper. Mindful of what the doctor had said about keeping the stitches dry, he leaned his head back from the shower spray when he turned on the faucets. The steaming water rinsed the blood from his chest, arms, and hands, but no matter how hard he scoured his body, he couldn't feel clean.

The bastard, he kept saying to himself. His anger was balanced by apprehension. The situation was out of control.

Toweling himself roughly, he risked a glance at the bathroom mirror and was startled by how ravaged his mouth and cheek were. Initially, trauma had numbed the injuries, but now pain overtook them. Even so, he couldn't risk swallowing the pills the doctor had given him. He had no idea what they were or how strong. Bellasar might have told the doctor to drug him. I've got to think clearly.

After putting on boxer shorts and a T-shirt, Malone picked up a small sketch pad he always kept on his bedside table. He sat against the headboard, closed his eyes to focus his memory, then opened them and started drawing the face of the Russian he had seen the morning he'd arrived and again tonight. Oval face, deep eyes, high forehead. Concentrating to remember whether the man's jaw was pronounced or shallow, whether his eyebrows were arched or straight, Malone drew hurriedly. As the likeness took shape, he refined it, recalling more details, making it more vivid. Finally satisfied after twenty minutes and three attempts, he set the drawing aside and began to sketch the other Russian, the tall, stocky man with thick eyebrows and blocky features. This one took longer. It wasn't until a half hour later that Malone was satisfied.

Immediately he turned it and the first sketch upside down so he wouldn't be tempted to look at them. Beginning the process anew, searching his memory, using shortcuts that the process of doing the first sketch had taught him, he was able to produce another likeness of the first Russian much quicker, in less than ten minutes. He did the same with a new sketch of the second Russian. He compared these sketches with the previous ones and assured himself that they were more or less identical, that his memory wasn't straying. He went through the process again. And again. Each version took less time, and each was the same as the others.

When he was confident that his memory had been so reinforced that he'd be able to produce a sketch of either man at will, he folded each eight-by-ten-inch piece of paper into one-inch strips so the sheets resembled accordions. He opened each accordion enough so it could stand upright in the bathroom sink. He struck a match and lit the top of each accordion, watching the flame burn down to the bottom. The accordion shape caused the page to burn evenly and completely. Equally important, it resulted in almost no smoke. The trick was something he had learned in an otherwise-long-forgotten high school physics class. Who says education's wasted on the young? he thought as he washed the ashes down the sink. He would have torn the pages into small pieces and flushed them down the toilet, but he couldn't be sure that some of the pieces wouldn't drift back up later, as toilet paper sometimes did, and be discovered when the maid came in to clean the room. She might have instructions to tell Bellasar about anything unusual that she found, and if Bellasar ever learned that Malone had sketched the Russians, that would be all the evidence Bellasar would need.

His lips and cheekbone throbbed as he opened the

window to make sure every slight trace of smoke dispersed. Satisfying himself that everything was in order, he shut off the light and crawled into bed. The time was almost 5:00 A.M.

But he didn't sleep.

SIX

1

"Good morning."

"Good morning."

"I missed you at breakfast," Malone said.

At the entrance to the sunroom, Sienna looked down at her feet. "I wasn't hungry."

Although her movements weren't as listless as the night before, she still didn't seem alert. Her face was puffy. Her skin was pale. Her eyes had slight hollows beneath them. Perhaps because she knew she didn't appear at her best, she kept her gaze slightly away from him. Or perhaps she wanted to avoid seeing what had been done to him.

"How bad does it hurt?" She still didn't look at his face.

"I'd give you a stiff-upper-lip attitude, but my upper lip is too mashed." It was a weak attempt at humor, but at the moment, weary from a sleepless night and afraid of how she was going to react to what he planned to tell her, he couldn't think of anything else. Worse, how was he going to appeal to her if she wouldn't even look at him? The gash on his cheek had swollen. His mouth was scabbed. It was a wonder she didn't run from him in horror.

"And you?" he asked softly. "How are you?"

"I've been better."

"How was Istanbul?"

"Humid. Crowded."

"What I meant was—"

"I know what you meant. I think we should talk about something else." She wore sandals and a loose ankle-length skirt of beige linen. The pullover top was ecru. Her hands fidgeted with its hem, then suddenly let go as footsteps outside made her spin. She didn't relax when she saw that it was only a servant going past. "We have to get started."

Something in her eyes reminded him of an animal that had been disciplined so much its spirit was broken. "Derek changed his mind," she said. "He wants me to pose only partially nude."

Bellasar's sudden change in plans puzzled Malone, but he was too preoccupied to consider the implications. It was as if he and Sienna hadn't spent weeks together, as if there were a million miles between them.

"Where do you want me?" she asked.

This wasn't how he had imagined their reunion. He had assumed that she would be communicative, that she would leave him an opening. Instead, he had the nervous feeling that they were opposed. "Over there. Against the wall. With the sunlight on you."

She did what she was told.

But something about the way she moved made him straighten. "Wait a second. Are you limping?"

"What?" She sounded as if she'd been caught doing something wrong.

"You're limping."

"No."

"Sure you are. You look like you're in pain."

"It's nothing. My legs got cramped from sitting too long on the plane yesterday."

"I don't believe you. Come back this way. Walk toward me."

"I'm telling you, it's just a—"

"Walk toward me."

She didn't move.

Malone approached her, studying her. "What's happened?"

She looked away.

"What did he do?"

"Nothing. I don't understand what you're talking about."

Malone felt a terrible urgency. He had always been careful about what he said in the sunroom, assuming that Bellasar had microphones hidden there. A couple of times, he had pushed the boundary, hence Bellasar's sudden appearances to assert his authority. But now as events spiraled out of control, Malone knew that no matter how guarded Sienna was being with him, he had to take the risk.

"Okay," he said.

She looked puzzled, as if she had braced herself to keep resisting and hadn't expected him to back off.

"If you're not hurt, we can get to work. Your husband won't like it if we waste time. In fact, I've already decided on the pose I want. We can skip doing further sketches. I'm going to start painting right away."

As he spoke, he took her arm and guided her toward the back of the sunroom.

"What are you—"

But he cut her off. "I need to get some supplies from the storage room. Wait out here. I'll just be a minute."

In contradiction to what he said, however, he took Sienna with him.

Through a door in back—into the storage room.

2

It was small, damp, and faintly lit, crammed with painting supplies. There weren't any windows.

"What are you doing?"

"Keep your voice down." Malone shut the door, then guided her past easels and boxes toward a sink. He couldn't be sure that the storage room wasn't bugged. Given how cramped it was, Bellasar would probably have dismissed it as a place where conversations would be held. But just to make sure, Malone turned on the faucets, hoping that the sound of running water would obscure their voices. "I'm afraid there are microphones where we work."

"Microphones?" As the idea struck her, Sienna gripped the sink.

"Tell me what he did to you."

"*No.* We have to get out of here. If Derek—"

"I can help you."

"*No one* can help me."

"Please, let me try."

They stood frozen, staring at each other. Slowly, she raised a finger toward his ravaged face. She almost touched his mangled lips. She traced an imaginary line around the stitches on his swollen cheek.

"I'm so sorry," she whispered. "Last night, when I saw what he'd done to you, I wanted to cry."

"But what did he do to *you?*"

Her eyes misted. She shook her head from side to side. "You've seen what Derek can be like. Don't get involved in this."

"I have to."

After the most poignant look anyone had ever given him, Sienna bent slowly. Her hands trembled as she raised her skirt, first past her ankles, then past her shins.

Malone gaped at the bruises above her knees. Her thighs were a purple mass of them; they looked like beefsteak.

"Jesus," he murmured.

In pain, she lowered the hem of her skirt back down to her ankles. Straightening, pulling the waistband slightly away from her body, she showed him where the angry-looking bruises continued to the top of her hips.

"What the hell did he—"

"The man Derek was meeting barely noticed me."

Sienna shuddered. "In fact, he couldn't wait for me to leave. It was the first time that had ever happened. When Derek came back to our suite at three in the morning, he was furious. It was my fault, he said, that the negotiation had almost fallen through. He told me I was useless to him, that he could barely stand to look at me, that . . ."

Malone touched her arm. "Easy. You don't have to put yourself through it again."

"For the first time since I've known him, he made a fist to hit me. It was like I was back in Milan five years ago with the boyfriend who beat me up." She flinched, as if seeing the fist again. "Then he looked shocked, realizing what he was doing. The one thing I thought I could always count on was that he'd never hurt me. All of a sudden, he started kicking me, the way he'd kick a football, the tips of his shoes coming at me. He chose a spot where the bruises wouldn't show—above the hem of my dress. I tried to defend myself, to get behind a table, but he kept coming at me, kicking, and the next thing I knew, I was on the floor. He wouldn't stop. If it hadn't been for Alex coming in, I'm afraid he might have—"

"Where *is* Alex? Why didn't he return with you and Derek?"

"He stayed in Istanbul. Something to do with the negotiations. Some trick Derek has him up to as a way of putting pressure on the man he's dealing with. He's coming back this afternoon."

"This afternoon?"

Sienna frowned. "You make it sound important. Why?"

"I have to explain something."

"No. If Derek doesn't see some progress . . . I realize I look like hell, but this isn't a photograph—it's a portrait. You can fake it. You can make me look as beautiful as—"

"Listen to me."

"*Please.* I don't want to be kicked again. I don't want—"

"Don't worry." Malone's voice hardened. "If I have anything to do about it, your husband's never going to kick you again. No one is."

"What do you mean?"

"If I can get you out of here, will you go with me? Will you take the chance to escape?"

And there it was. The words, so long restrained, were finally free. He couldn't turn back. He held his breath, fearing her reaction. If he'd misjudged her, if she was uncontrollably dominated by Bellasar to the point where she could never imagine going against him, he had just guaranteed that he'd soon be dead. She would look at him in dismay. She would accuse him of having misjudged her. She would tell Bellasar.

"Escape?" Sienna made the word sound like nonsense. "Have you lost your mind?"

Jesus, I made the wrong choice, Malone thought. I just threw my life away.

"It isn't *possible* to escape," she said.

"What?" Malone shook his head in confusion. If

she was going to turn against him, this wasn't what he had expected.

"Don't you think I've considered it? Don't you think I would have done it if I could have found a way?"

"You'll come with me?"

"*How? Where?* Even if we *could* get out of here, Derek would never rest until he found us. He'd use all his power and money, every resource at his disposal, to track us down."

But we wouldn't be alone, Malone wanted to tell her. If we can get out of here, we'll have all the help we could ever want. He didn't dare say it. If she thought he was a spy, if she thought he had come here to use her . . .

"We have to take the chance," he said.

"We can't! Look, you don't have to do this. You don't have to risk your life for me. Complete the portrait and leave."

"And what about *you*?"

"I've been taking care of myself since I was twelve. I survived what Derek did to me in Istanbul, and I'll survive worse as long as he tolerates me. But I'll never survive if he finds out I've betrayed him."

"Listen to me." Malone hesitated. There wasn't an easy way to say this. "He's planning to have you killed."

"What?"

"He's been married three times before."

"*What are you talking about?*"

"All of his wives were beautiful. But when they got

to be around thirty and started to show signs of aging, they died in various accidents."

Sienna's mouth opened, but she seemed to have lost the power of speech.

"Before each accident, your husband hired a prominent artist to do a portrait of each woman—to memorialize her after death, to have a trophy, to make her beauty permanent. Now it's *your* turn."

"I don't . . . How on earth do you know this?"

"Some of it I heard from the other artists," Malone lied. "The rest of it . . . We don't have time for me to explain. There's a room on the third level. In the middle hallway. About halfway along on the left."

Sienna concentrated, trying to get over her shock. "Yes, where Derek keeps his business documents."

"You've been in the room? You've seen the documents?"

"No, it's always locked. When I first came here, I asked what was in there, and that's what he told me."

"That's where the portraits of the other wives are."

"This can't—"

"There's one way to prove it."

3

Trying to hide her fear, Sienna reached the top floor. Her legs in pain, she walked along the middle corridor and almost flinched when the door to Derek's bedroom opened. But it wasn't Derek who came out, only a servant. After a cursory nod, Sienna continued toward her own room, entered, left a slight gap when she shut the door, and listened for the servant to go away.

The moment the receding footsteps became so soft that they couldn't be heard, she eased the door open, peered out, and assured herself that the corridor was deserted. Immediately, she went back down the hall and tried the door Chase had mentioned. As she expected, it was locked, but she had needed to make the attempt on the chance that it might not have been. She went one door farther along, to the one from which the servant had just left, slipped inside, and shut the door.

She had been in Derek's room only once before, five years earlier. Repressing her memories of that night, she saw that nothing seemed to have changed. The place was still decorated with antiques from the Italian Renaissance, including a canopied bed, its four posts intricately carved. The sight of the bed increased her anxiety. She shifted her attention to a door on the right, which led to the room she was interested in. Although it, too, was probably locked, she allowed herself to hope when she tried it, only to lower her head in discouragement when the door didn't budge. I need a key, she thought.

Derek was scrupulously thorough. Anything important had to have a backup, sometimes more than one. Didn't it make sense that he'd want to have a spare key hidden within easy reach?

Allowing herself to hope again, she turned to face the room. Across from her, a five-hundred-year-old

Medici bureau brought back more memories of the only other time she had been in this room. Derek had waited to marry her until the bandages had come off her face and her beauty had been re-created, as he phrased it. The wedding had occurred in a rose garden on the property, just the two of them, a minister, and Potter as the witness. She had been so grateful to have been rescued from her former life that she hadn't regretted not having a bigger celebration. In the dining hall, a string quartet had played waltzes. She and Derek had danced. They had cut the wedding cake and given pieces of it to the staff. Her wedding gift had been a diamond necklace. She remembered how heavy it had felt as Derek had escorted her up to his room.

There, the loneliness of her marriage had begun. Wanting more than anything to make love to the man she had married three hours previously, she had reached for him, then became dismayed when his ardor changed to hesitancy, then to frustration, and then to anger. She had tried everything to arouse him. Her final attempt had made him push her to the floor.

"Derek, it's okay," she had tried to assure him. "These things happen. It's the excitement of the wedding. All we need is a little time."

"Get out of here."

She'd been sure she hadn't heard correctly. "What?"

"Get out. There's a room at the end of the hall. Take it. Sleep there."

"But aren't we going to share—"

"Damn it, I told you to get out!"

He had thrown a robe at her, barely giving her a chance to put it on before he shoved her into the corridor. In her room, she had wept, trying to understand what had happened. She had hoped to sleep, but her turmoil had kept her awake, until finally she had walked down the hall and opened his door, saying, "Derek, if there's a problem, let's talk about it. Whatever it is, we can—"

Slamming a drawer shut, he had spun toward her, his face twisted with more fury than she had ever seen. *"Don't ever come in this room again!"*

Stunned by the emotion of his outburst, she had retreated into the corridor. He had slammed the door, making her realize that she had exchanged one hell for another. The next morning, wary about what would happen next, she had waited a long time before going downstairs, only to be surprised by the gracious way Derek greeted her, as if the previous night had been a fabulous beginning to their marriage. They never discussed what had come between them. They never again tried to have sex. And she never again went into his room. It was so much wiser not to, so much better when Derek wasn't displeased.

But she never forgot the abrupt way Derek had slammed the drawer.

As if he had been hiding something.

Now she crossed the room toward the Medici bureau. She opened its hinged panels and pulled out the middle drawer. It revealed cashmere sweaters. Nothing else.

I was wrong.

Disheartened, she turned to leave the room. *But he looked like he was hiding something,* she insisted to herself. *Where?*

Maybe it isn't something *in* the drawer.

Maybe . . .

She knocked on the drawer's bottom. It sounded hollow. She ran her fingers along the inside, did the same thing underneath, and tensed when she felt a catch at the back. When she pushed it, the inside bottom of the drawer came loose. Hand trembling, she tilted it up. A shallow compartment contained passports for various countries, a pistol, and a single key on a gold chain.

Reaching for the key, she frowned at how the trembling in her hand increased. She pressed down on the bottom, shut the drawer, closed the bureau, and whirled toward the sound of someone approaching along the hallway. As the doorknob turned, she hurriedly crouched behind a large upholstered chair. She held her breath. If Derek came in . . . If he found her . . .

The door opened. Whoever it was crossed the room and entered the bathroom. A moment later, the person came out, passed the chair, and left, shutting the door.

Sienna exhaled. It was probably a servant putting fresh towels or something in the bathroom, she thought. Her crouched position aggravated the pain from her bruises. Straightening stiffly, she listened for more movement in the hallway. When she heard nothing, she moved quickly toward the door, tried the key, and felt her breathing quicken when it worked. With a harrowing sense that this was the most significant threshold she would ever cross, she eased the door open, stepped inside, closed the door, and found herself staring at what seemed like ghosts.

4

The murkiness of the room enhanced the illusion. Thick draperies filtered most of the outdoor light. Across from her, the faces of several women seemed to float in dense twilight. More disturbing, while Sienna recognized the portrait Chase had done of her, she had the sensation of seeing herself reflected in mirrors, so closely did the other portraits resemble her. But how could that be if she had never sat for them? She flicked an electrical switch on her left, blinked from the assault of light, and stared with growing shock at the wall of portraits.

There were seven—the one devoted to her, and three sets of two, each composed of a face and a full-length nude. Each set had the style of a different artist. But the faces were unnervingly similar, sharing the same shape and proportion. Definitely, the flowing hairstyle was the same; it was one that Derek had always insisted on. From a distance or in shadow, the other women could have been mistaken for Sienna. Sienna could have been mistaken for the other women. My God, she thought. Shivering, she approached the paintings. Some had been done in oil, others in watercolor. The signatures on them confirmed that each of the three sets had been done by a different artist. Their names were in the pantheon of late-twentieth-century artists, so famous that even people unfamiliar with art would recognize them.

The dates next to the signatures had unnerving implications. The first was fifteen years previously, the second seven years later, the third three years after that. But the faces in the portraits remained the same age—thirty or so—proving that unless the portraits weren't true likenesses, a different model had been used for each set. More unnerved, Sienna noticed that the date on the third set was the same year Derek had rescued her in Milan. Jesus, she thought. He got tired of the woman before me when she started showing the slightest signs of age. He got rid of her and chose someone younger who looked like her, like *all* of them—*me*.

But when Derek had come to her hotel five years ago, why hadn't he been turned off by her haggard look and the bruises on her face? She shivered as she remembered the plastic surgeon who had been waiting at the estate. He had said that he was going to hide the scars from the beating she had received. After the bandages had been removed, she had noticed that she looked slightly different—not better or worse, just different, her cheekbones slightly more pronounced, for example—but she had attributed that to an unavoidable consequence of hiding the scars. Now she realized, My God, Derek told the surgeon to make me look more like those other women.

In dismay, she peered around the room, so cold now that her teeth chattered when she saw photographs on the other walls. Some were in black and white, others in color. Some were close-ups, others group shots. Some were taken in outdoor settings, others in palatial interiors. But they all had one common denominator: The same woman was in all of them. Although the younger shots of her made her somewhat hard to identify, there was no mistaking her features as she became a teenager and then a young adult.

She looks like *me,* Sienna thought. Like the other women in the portraits. No, that's wrong. I've got it backward. *We* look like her. That's why Derek chose us.

But who in God's name was she? Women's shoes had been arranged on shelves. *Her* shoes, Sienna thought. Mannequins supported festive dresses. *Her* dresses, Sienna thought. She reached for a leatherbound scrapbook, opened it, and shuddered when she stared at a birth certificate for Christina Gabriela Bellasar. Derek's sister?

Born in Rome on May 14, 1939.

One year after Derek was born.

Glancing with greater distress toward the photographs on the wall, Sienna confirmed another common factor—in none of the photos was the woman ever seen as old. Pulse rushing, Sienna flipped to the back of the scrapbook and found the document that would logically end a scrapbook that began with a birth certificate: a death certificate. On the final page, there was a yellowed clipping from a Rome newspaper. Her parents had insisted that Sienna learn Italian. She had no trouble reading the small item.

Christina Gabriela Bellasar (the last name suggested she had never married) had died in Rome on June 10, 1969, as a consequence of a fall from a balcony on the twentieth floor of a hotel. Sienna subtracted 1939 from 1969. Christina had been thirty.

As old as *I* am, Sienna thought. As old as the women in the portraits seemed. With soul-numbing dread, she felt compelled to turn toward a corner of the room, where she saw an antique table, upon which sat an urn. The urn seemed centuries old, its faded paint showing maidens lying beside a stream in an idyllic forest. Sienna had no doubt whose ashes were in that urn, just as she had no doubt what Derek would do to her if he discovered that she had violated this shrine. He wouldn't wait for the second portrait to be completed. He would kill her now.

5

Descending the stairs, she was certain that every servant and guard she passed must be sensing the fear she struggled to conceal. Despite the pain in her thighs, she felt a panicked need to run, but no one looked at her strangely, and her body obeyed her fierce will, maintaining an apparently untroubled pace.

When she entered the sunroom, she saw that Chase had rejected tempera paint in favor of oil. Having attached a canvas to a frame, he was sketching on it. Her angle of approach prevented her from seeing the image.

She didn't care. All that mattered was getting him where they could talk without fear of microphones.

Chase looked at her, troubled by the stark expression on her face.

"I've been thinking this should be set outdoors," Sienna said for the benefit of anyone who might be eavesdropping.

"Oh?"

"The first portrait was inside. The second ought to have a different setting. There's a place on the terrace I think might work."

"Why don't you show me."

When she took his arm, leading him, her trembling fingers made him frown.

They emerged onto the sun-bright terrace, Sienna guiding him toward a corner of its stone railing. "Here," she said. "Like this." She pretended to show him a pose, at the same time lowering her voice. "Do you think we can be overheard?"

A machine gun rattled in the distance.

"No. But if we stay outside too long, we might attract suspicion. What did you find?"

"Were you serious about taking me out of here?"

"Absolutely."

"You honestly think there's a chance?"

"I wouldn't try it otherwise. But if you stay here, there's *no* chance."

The words rushed out of her. "Do it."

"What you saw was that bad?"

"As soon as possible."

"This afternoon," Chase said.

The sense that everything was speeding up made her light-headed. "How?"

When he told her and explained what she was going to need, her dizziness intensified.

6

Time had never seemed so swift and yet so slow. She felt pushed forward and shoved back. Suddenly it was lunch hour, but as quickly as the morning had passed, the meal itself seemed to last forever. Derek stopped by to express his enthusiasm for how much work had been accomplished that morning, and Sienna tried not to look puzzled, wondering what on earth he was talking about. Work? No work had been done. But when she and Chase returned to the sunroom, she realized she had been too preoccupied all morning to pay attention to how much Chase had accomplished.

The sketch had been completed. It showed her only from the waist up, naked, standing against a blank background, her back straight, her arms behind her, a defiant gaze directed toward anyone viewing the canvas. The lack of detail in the background gave the impression that she was so furious about being forced on display that she had detached herself from her surroundings, her body here but her mind miles away.

That wasn't an exaggeration. She felt so apprehensive about what they would soon try that everything around her was a haze. Even Chase seemed as insubstantial as smoke, and as for her half-naked body before him, she was hardly conscious of it. The only reality was in her imagination as she brooded about the future. She shivered, but not at all because her skin was uncovered.

Maybe this isn't a good idea, she thought. Maybe we shouldn't try it.

But I have to. It's my only chance.

But maybe we should think about it more. Maybe this isn't the right time. Maybe we should wait for a better—

From the testing range, a burst of machine-gun fire brought her back to the moment. The sunroom seemed to materialize before her. The haze dispersed. She became aware of Chase studying her, darting his brush toward the canvas.

A distant explosion rattled windows. Immediately another sound rattled windows, the din of an approaching helicopter.

7

Pressing the bridge of his spectacles against his nose, Potter stared down toward the estate's walls, trees, ponds, and gardens. They seemed to enlarge as the helicopter descended. Specks of figures became distinct, guards watching the entrances, others patrolling, gardeners tending the grounds, servants going about their business. Smoke from an explosion rose from the testing area.

But there was no sign of activity at the landing area. No guards converged; no one waited in greeting. Derek would long ago have heard the helicopter approaching. He would have had ample time to stop what he was doing and walk to the landing area to welcome him. But that isn't Derek's way, Potter thought, burning with resentment. No, Derek likes others to come to *him*. No matter how interested he was in what Potter had to report, he would never stoop to do anything that implied how dependent he was on Potter's help. He had to treat everyone as inferior.

Except for the artist, Potter thought angrily. Oh, Derek was eager enough to make allowances for Malone all right. Potter had seen Derek order men shot for showing half the insolence that Malone did, and still Derek put up with Malone's behavior because he wanted the portraits. *Why* Derek wanted the portraits so badly, Potter had no idea. If Derek felt like getting rid of his wives, fine. Take some snapshots for old times' sake, then arrange an accident. But his obsession about the portraits was puzzling and dangerous. This morning, when Potter had made a preliminary report to Derek on a scrambler-protected phone, he had learned about the incident the previous night, about Malone's disappearance and Derek's suspicion that Malone had tried to find out what was in the Cloister. A false alarm, Derek had said.

Wrong, Potter thought. The incident had happened too conveniently while they were away. The explanation had been too complicated. Potter intended to conduct a painstaking investigation and trap Malone in inconsistencies. For example, if the artist had been suddenly inspired to do some late-night sketching in his workroom, he would have had to turn on a light, but had the guards been asked if any of them had seen that light?

I'll expose the flaws in his story, Potter vowed. We should never have gotten involved with him. After we punished him for refusing to accept the commission, that should have been the end. I haven't forgotten how he manipulated Derek into criticizing me at the shooting range. I've been made to look like a fool a dozen times over. Well, not any longer. Now it's my turn.

As the helicopter set down, Potter released his seat belt and shoved the hatch open, eagerly waiting for the speed of the rotors to reduce so he could get out and find Derek. The whine from the spinning blades hurt his ears. The wind they created stung his eyes and ruffled his thinning hair. Then he couldn't force himself to wait any longer. His short stature made it difficult for him to climb down, requiring a slight jump to the concrete pad. Clutching his briefcase, he bent his knees on impact. Despite his shortness, he took care to stoop as he ran beneath the spinning blades. Pressed down by the gust of the blades, he hurried toward the weapons-testing area.

But a noise behind him made him stop. A shout? Surely that isn't possible, he told himself. As close as he was to the helicopter, the shriek from the rotors would have overwhelmed other sounds. And yet he was certain he'd heard a muffled outcry. Puzzled, he turned to look back toward the helicopter, and if he couldn't have heard the shout, he was equally positive that he couldn't be seeing the commotion behind him.

8

When Malone heard the approaching helicopter, his hand and the paintbrush it held froze over the canvas. A startled portion of his mind wondered if he'd had a stroke. Then his heartbeat lurched, jump-starting his body. He turned toward Sienna, who stared toward the windows and the increasing roar of the chopper.

"This is it," he said.

She seemed not to have heard him. Mechanically, she put on her top but continued to stare distractedly toward the windows.

"Are you ready?"

She still didn't respond.

With growing unease, Malone set down his brush and walked toward her.

"Look at me." He put his hand on her face, turning it toward him. "If we're going to do this, we have to move *now*." He no longer worried about hidden microphones. If this effort failed, eavesdroppers would be the least of his problems.

"I didn't expect to be so afraid."

"If you stay here, you'll die. We can't wait any longer. We have to move."

The chopper sounded closer.

She studied him with an intensity that rivaled the

way he had studied *her* for weeks now. Her eyes blazed with resolution. "Yes."

She had followed Malone's instruction and exchanged her sandals for walking shoes. Now she went with him to the doorway, watching the chopper approach the landing pad. Despite the distance, Potter's pinched features were distinct behind the hatch's Plexiglas. He seemed to be the only passenger. No one gathered at the landing pad. A few patrolling guards glanced in the chopper's direction. Most went about their business.

Malone grabbed a sketch pad so the reason he and Sienna were outdoors would appear to be related to work.

The chopper set down.

They left the sunroom, crossed the terrace, and descended the stone steps toward the path to the Cloister.

Malone heard Sienna's fast breathing. Then the rapid rise and fall of his own chest warned him that she wasn't the only one in danger of hyperventilating.

A guard blocked their way. "You can't go near the Cloister."

"We need to speak to Mr. Potter." Sienna motioned toward the helicopter, where Potter jumped to the landing pad and turned toward the Cloister and the weapons-testing area. "Alex!" The noise from the chopper would prevent Potter from hearing her, but the guard would think she was making an honest attempt to get his attention.

"We'll lose the rest of the day if . . ." Sienna moved forward. "Alex!"

But Potter was hurrying toward the Cloister.

"Alex!" Sienna called again, moving more quickly forward.

Malone noted that the other guards, sporadically placed, weren't paying attention.

"Alex!" Sienna ran now, Malone with her.

The chopper was only fifty yards ahead of them. The pilot had not yet turned off the engines. The blades continued to spin.

The guard behind them yelled something, his gruff voice obscured by the whine of the chopper's blades.

Malone imagined him frowning, then unslinging his rifle from his shoulder. But would he dare to shoot? The chopper was in his line of fire. One of his targets was his boss's wife. That would make him think twice. In the meantime, the chopper was closer, thirty yards now, but if Sienna was a target who would make the guard hesitate, Malone was another matter. He felt a spot between his shoulders get colder and tighter in anticipation of a bullet that would shatter his spine.

Racing to his limit, he strained to convince himself that his apprehension was baseless. The guard didn't have a reason to assume the helicopter was their objective. Had any of them even been told that Malone had once been a chopper pilot? As far as the guard was concerned, the problem was to keep them out of a restricted area.

"Alex!" Sienna shouted again.

Another guard yelled a warning.

Twenty yards.

Amazingly, despite the noise from the helicopter, Potter heard the commotion and turned.

Despite his frantic emotions, Malone enjoyed a microsecond of satisfaction from the way Potter gaped. Then he and Sienna reached the helicopter. A guard raced toward them. As Malone grappled with the man, knocking him to the ground, Sienna did what she had been told. Never looking back, never faltering, she scrambled up through the open hatch. Immediately Malone lost sight of her as he raced around to the pilot's side, caught the surprised man looking the other way toward Sienna, pulled his harness free, and yanked him out. He had a sense of guards racing in his direction as he surged up behind the controls, secured the harness, and increased power to the idling rotors. Seeing how the extra noise and wind sent Potter staggering back, Malone felt another microsecond of enjoyment, but then as he worked the controls, his sense of near victory turned sour when the helicopter struggled five feet into the air, sank back to the landing pad, rose awkwardly again, and veered, as if obeying its own impulses toward the château.

9

"Get your safety harness fastened!" Malone yelled. Sienna fumbled to snap it into place. Adrenaline and the roar through the open hatches made her shout. "I was afraid we were going to crash!"

"Everything's fine! There's nothing to—"

"Watch out! We're—"

Speeding toward the château at a height of about twenty feet, Malone urged the helicopter into a steep ascent that pressed his stomach against his spine.

Sienna moaned.

Fighting for altitude, Malone saw the château's upper stories seem to rush toward him. Then only the *third* story. Then only the hazy sky was before him as he felt a jolt that made the helicopter shudder.

"What was—"

"Something hit the rudder!"

"Something?"

"They're shooting!"

Another impact shook the controls. As the chopper twisted to the left and tilted, Sienna was thrust halfway out the open hatch, dangling, her harness straining to hold her.

"Shut the hatch!" Malone yelled.

". . . Trying!"

Despite his fear for her, he couldn't risk looking at her; he was too busy fighting the controls. *"Can you reach it?"*

"Think I . . . got it!"

From the corner of his eye, he saw the desperate effort she put into tugging the hatch shut. The noise suddenly lessened. With equal suddenness, he brought the helicopter back to a level position. Slamming his own hatch shut, he took a momentary delight in the relative silence, the roar from the engines muffled enough that he and Sienna didn't need to shout anymore.

He studied the panel of unfamiliar switches that had puzzled him when he'd been flown to Bellasar's estate. The pilot hadn't used them, so Malone had no idea what purpose they served, but this wasn't the time to experiment—the chopper was close to stalling. As it passed over fields and stone fences, Malone felt the controls buck. Ahead, a cypress-studded hill blocked the way. He urged the chopper higher, but the response was sluggish.

"What's wrong?"

Malone glanced urgently toward the control panel. "The oil pressure's dropping. A bullet must have hit—" He angled toward the lowest section of the hill. Barely cresting it, he winced from another jolt as one of the landing skids brushed a cypress top.

"Are we going to—" Sienna sounded terrified.

"No! If I think we're even close to crashing, I'll set us down first!"

"But we won't get far enough away! We're still over Derek's property! He'll—" She stared out the hatch. "Smoke!"

Black clouds of it spewed from the engine.

"If we can just stay in the air a little longer . . ." Malone checked the compass on the control panel. "There's a small airfield ahead of us."

"Where? I don't see it."

"In the next valley."

"How do you know?"

Back on Cozumel, when Malone had agreed to work with Jeb, they had calculated several rescue plans if Malone had a chance to get Sienna away from Bellasar. One had involved reaching a café in Nice, where the proprietor was on the CIA's payroll and would hide Malone and Sienna until Jeb's team arrived. Another plan had involved going to Cannes and contacting a pleasure-boat operator who sometimes worked for the Agency. But those areas were in the opposite direction. Malone was heading inland, not toward the sea, and that left him with a remaining option, an airfield that Jeb had told him about, the compass bearings for which Malone had memorized. Jeb had promised to have a pilot and a small plane waiting for them. "If you can reach that airfield," Jeb had said, "you're as good as out of the country."

"I don't understand," Sienna said. "How do you know about the airfield?"

"I don't have time to explain."

"You knew about the portraits of Derek's other wives." The chopper dipped, making her gasp. "How did you learn so much about—"

Malone struggled with the controls. "I'll tell you the first chance I—"

"My God, are you a—"

"What?"

"A spy?"

10

As an engineer aimed another missile at a tank in the weapons-testing area, Bellasar tensed at the sound of shots from the château. He grabbed a pistol from one of the guards and raced along a hedge-lined path toward the Cloister. Assuring himself that the area wasn't under attack, he charged down another path, this one toward the château, and stopped abruptly, surprised to see the helicopter veer over the building, its landing skids barely missing the roof, guards firing at it.

"What the hell happened?"

Seeing Potter to his right, he rushed toward him.

Potter's face was livid as he stared toward the retreating helicopter. "They stole it!"

"What are you talking about?"

"Malone and your wife! They're in that helicopter!"

"Sienna?"

"They waited for me to land! Before the pilot shut off the engine, they tricked a guard into believing they needed to talk to me! The next thing, they took off!"

Bellasar was so stunned, he couldn't speak.

"I warned you!" Potter said. "I told you he couldn't be trusted!"

Briefly, the helicopter was out of sight behind the château. It reappeared on the right, receding into the distance. It sputtered and lurched. Black smoke trailed from it.

"We hit it!" a guard said.

"He made a fool of you!" Potter said. "What do you suppose has been going on all the time they've been together?"

"Don't call me a fool!" Bellasar drove a fist into Potter's stomach, doubling him over, sending him to his knees.

Gasping for air, Potter peered up, his spectacles

askew, his features contorted with pain. "Maybe you'd better figure out"—he managed a breath—"who's your friend and who's your enemy."

In the distance, the helicopter kept sputtering.

Bellasar pivoted toward the guards. The second chopper was due to return with a load of lab equipment in thirty minutes. Until then, the only way to go after Malone and Sienna was in vehicles. Bellasar shouted orders.

As the guards rushed to obey, Potter groaned. Holding his stomach, he tried to straighten. "If I'm right"—he squeezed the words out—"this isn't just about Malone and your wife. It's about what he might have seen at the Cloister last night."

Bellasar squinted toward the smoke trailing from the receding helicopter. The damage to it reduced its speed enough that the vehicles wouldn't be outdistanced. The smoke would make it easy to follow. "Help me catch them!"

11

The controls had become so stiff that Malone could hardly move them. The chopper twisted sickeningly. At once, it dropped ten feet, with such force that Malone's lungs seemed to soar into his throat. He needed all his strength to stop it from plummeting farther. But no matter how hard he tried, he couldn't keep it steady. For a moment, he was back in Panama, struggling to control his gunship after it had been shot. "Brace yourself! Find a place that's flat where we can land!"

"I don't see any!"

Staring down, Malone didn't see any, either. They were over a rocky, shrub-dotted slope. There was no way the chopper would ever clear the top. The controls shuddered violently. If he didn't land now, the chopper was going to make the decision for him. Using every skill he could remember, he forced the chopper out of a dizzying spiral, wobbled along the side of the slope, glimpsed a space between boulders, gave one last determined command to the resisting controls, and slammed down.

The impact rammed his teeth together. Ignoring the pain that shot along his jaw, he shut off the engines, unsnapped his safety harness, and spun toward Sienna. Her head was drooped. My God, is she—

But before the thought could be completed, she raised her hand toward the back of her neck and rubbed it, shaking her head in a daze.

"Are you okay?" he blurted.

". . . Head hurts."

"We have to get out of here." He coughed from the black smoke that swirled around him, stinging his throat. "This thing might explode."

That caught her attention. After one more dazed look at him, she was suddenly animated, freeing her harness, shoving at the hatch on her side of the chopper. "It's stuck! It won't—"

Malone desperately tried his own side and groaned

when he found that it, too, was stuck, the impact having twisted it. Sweat stung his eyes as he strained to his limit, his nerves quickening when the hatch reluctantly creaked open. One of the blades had been bent down by the force of the landing. Rotating, it had struck a boulder and frozen, jamming the rotor so that the other blades were frozen also.

At least, I don't have to worry about one of them spinning out of control and chopping my head off, he thought.

He had plenty to worry about as it was. When he jumped free, then turned to grab Sienna's hand and help her out, he saw flickers of crimson in the swirling black smoke on top of the chopper. The engine wasn't just overheated; it was on fire. Jesus, if the flames reach the fuel tank . . .

Leaping down, Sienna saw the flames, too, her panicked look communicating that he didn't have to tell her to run as far and fast as she could. They raced, dodging boulders, sprinting past bushes, charging along the slope. Malone's throat, already irritated by the oily smoke, was made more raw by his quick, deep, strident breathing. His legs stretched to their maximum. Beside him, Sienna strained to run faster.

Hearing a *whoosh* behind him, Malone recognized the distinctive sound of flames reaching spilled fuel. He barely saw a gully suddenly appear before he had time to jump instead of stumble into it. He landed and rolled, Sienna tumbling next to him, the shock wave from an explosion striking his eardrums. It was far more powerful than the blast from a burning gas tank.

Numerous secondary explosions were almost as strong, punctuated by the crackle of bullets. Jesus, had there been munitions aboard? Malone wondered in dismay as something else exploded. Chunks of smoking metal clanged off boulders and rebounded down the gully. Then the afternoon was silent, except for Malone's and Sienna's gasping attempt to catch their breath and the muted rumble of the unseen flames.

They stared apprehensively at each other, their eyes asking if either was hurt, each quietly responding, *I'm all right, but what about you*? Tasting sweat, smoke, and dust, Malone tried his arms and legs. After Sienna did the same and nodded in assurance, they rose cautiously to peer over the rim toward the blazing hulk of the chopper.

"How far is that airfield?" Sienna's face was smeared with soot.

"Maybe a half mile."

"We're wasting time." She climbed painfully out of the gully. "But if we ever get away, you're going to tell me how you learned about this place."

He didn't know how to respond. Not that it mattered. As they climbed the rocky slope, another sound intruded. Malone now had an added taste in his mouth—coppery, that of fear—as he turned toward approaching engines and saw three four-wheel-drive vehicles speed past trees on a road below him. They swerved into the bumpy field that led in this direction.

People from a nearby farm? Malone wondered. Did they see the chopper go down and come to help? The state-of-the-art vehicles, almost military in design,

made his heart sink with doubt. So did the relentless-
ness with which their occupants ignored the jostling
punishment of the uneven terrain.

"It's Derek," Sienna said.

Despite her bruised legs, she spun toward the crest
and ran.

12

As his vehicle jolted across the field, Bellasar
gripped the steering wheel harder and glared through
the windshield toward the smoke and flames billowing
from the wreckage. *"Does anybody see survivors?"*

Increasing speed despite the shocks to the vehicle,
he scanned the rocky slope. The spreading haze made
it difficult to distinguish shapes. His vision was unsteady because of the jouncing shudder of the vehicle.
Even so, he thought he saw figures moving to the right
of the blazing wreckage. He shoved his foot harder
onto the accelerator, stiffening his neck to keep his
head from jerking back.

There damned well had *better* be survivors, he
thought, steering sharply toward the right. It no longer
mattered to him that he had been making arrangements for Sienna's death. Now, more than anything,
he wanted her alive. And Malone. He wanted to see
their faces. He needed to study the fear in their eyes
when he made them pay.

"I see movement!" The guard next to Bellasar

pointed toward the right, toward where Bellasar steered.

Even the toughest civilian four-wheel-drive vehicle would have long since broken its suspension, so punishing was the rocky terrain. But one of Bellasar's engineering teams had developed a military version that had civilian styling, rode well, was heavily armed, and would survive just about any hardship demanded of it. A number of drug lords and dictators had ordered the armor-plated model, but before making delivery, Bellasar had wanted to test it further. It gave him great satisfaction that its performance this afternoon left no doubt that it was ready.

You think you can get away from me? he mentally shouted toward the two partially glimpsed figures who scrambled up the slope. You think you have even the slightest chance?

Reaching the bottom of the slope, not bothering to reduce speed as he jolted upward, he saw the smoke disperse enough to verify that the scurrying figures were in fact Sienna and Malone. He raised the lid on a console next to him, exposing a button and two small joysticks. The button he pressed opened a port beneath each headlight, exposing the muzzle of a .30-caliber machine gun built into each wheel well.

Each weapon was capable of swiveling within a thirty-degree radius, of being raised and lowered within a similar range, and of firing independently. Bellasar didn't worry that shots would bring the police. This was still his property; he sometimes tested weapons here. Farmers in the area would think it was business as usual. Judging the distance and angle, he used his right hand to maneuver the right stick, pressed a button on top of it, and heard a *brrrrp*, its vibration negligible as a stream of bullets tore up the slope to the right of his targets. He didn't want to hit them. God no. He wanted to scare them and convince them that running any farther was futile. He wanted them alive, to make them suffer.

Sienna and Malone frantically changed direction, angling to the left as they charged up the slope. Bellasar switched to the other stick, maneuvered it, pressed the button on it, and sent a burst of bullets into the slope above them, spraying dirt, shattering rocks, and disintegrating bushes. He redirected the stick, curving the bullets downward to the right, then up again, blocking the next route they tried. Sienna and Malone flinched, bent low, and reversed their direction, sprinting again to the left, heading back toward the wreckage.

Bellasar tracked them with the left machine gun. About to press its button and tear up the slope farther to their left, he had to jerk his hand from the stick and grip the steering wheel, needing both hands to veer around a boulder that loomed ahead of him. The instant he was safely around it, he gripped the stick again and refocused his gaze on the running figures.

Or tried to. In the few seconds it had taken him to avoid the boulder, Sienna and Malone had reached the smoke from the wreckage. His vision obscured, Bellasar steered to the left now, following them, speeding farther up the hill. Without warning, a gully blocked his way. He stomped on the brakes so hard that he lurched painfully forward, his shoulder harness cutting into him. The guards in the back slammed forward. As the brakes gripped, tires skidding, the gully got closer, wider, deeper. Bellasar didn't realize he was holding his breath until the vehicle stopped, its front end tilting downward. He exhaled.

Immediately he grabbed the microphone from the dashboard's two-way radio. "Keep after them! Block their route!"

The machine guns in the other vehicles began shooting into the smoke.

"Damn it, don't shoot to kill! I want them alive! Use your bullets to block their route!" Instantly he changed to another frequency, contacting Potter at the château.

Potter's voice crackled from the radio. "The second helicopter has arrived."

"Bring it. I've found them." Bellasar blurted directions to where he was. "I'm activating a homing signal. Follow it."

Dropping the microphone, Bellasar drew his pistol and hurried from the vehicle. "Spread out!" he ordered the guards. "They're hiding up there in the smoke! As far as I know, Malone isn't armed! You don't need to shoot to kill! Find them! Bring them to me!"

Preparing to hurry down into the gully and up the other side, Bellasar took a second to admire the two vehicles beyond it as they sped up the slope on his left, veering among bushes and boulders, easily handling the rough landscape. The sound of their engines was solid and powerful. Five minutes from now, Alex and the second helicopter would arrive. Bellasar would order the pilot to hover over the wreckage. The downdraft from its whirling blades would disperse the smoke, making it easy to find where Sienna and Malone were trying to hide among the rocks. It's only a matter of time, Bellasar assured himself. Soon I'll have them. In fact, for a moment a deep sound blended with that of the vehicles and made him think that the second helicopter had arrived more quickly than he expected. As the deep sound became a rumble, he realized how wrong he was.

13

Coughing so hard that he feared he might vomit, his eyes watering from the smoke that swirled around him, Malone heard the vehicles roaring up the slope toward Sienna and him. The burning wreckage and the smoke from it temporarily shielded them, but the relentless vehicles would soon burst into view.

Hunched next to him behind a boulder, Sienna coughed as hard as he did. "Let's see if we can move this thing," she said.

"What?"

"This boulder."

As the vehicles charged closer up the hill, Malone suddenly understood. The smoke thinned enough for him to see a glint of hope in her raw, red, irritated eyes. They rose to a crouch and pressed both hands against the boulder, shoving against it.

Harder! Groaning with effort, Malone felt something in him thrill as the boulder shifted.

More! The boulder tilted, rolling, gaining momentum, rumbling out of sight through the smoke.

They raced toward another. Desperation fueling their strength, they got it rolling faster than the first one and immediately rushed to another and then another, crisscrossing the slope, protecting both sides of the flaming wreckage.

The combined rumble reminded Malone of thunder. But the thunder became distant. The boulders were taking too long. They must have passed the vehicles and continued toward the bottom. At once, a crash of rock, glass, and metal echoed from below. A second crash was even more violent. Before the engines died, Sienna was already in motion. She ran up the slope, coughing, straining to break free of the smoke. A third crash made Malone's spirits soar as he hurried after her.

Gagging, he left the smoke, but he was too distracted to enjoy the sweet, clean air he sucked into his lungs. The crest of the slope was only thirty yards ahead, but it might as well have been a mile. He had no way of telling how damaged the vehicles were. He didn't dare waste time looking behind him to check. If the machine guns haven't been disabled, we don't have a chance, he thought.

Indeed, he did hear gunshots, but they were single fire, not from automatic weapons, and the bullets were ricocheting off rocks below him. That meant the gunmen were aiming as if they were on level ground. To hit a target moving uphill, they had to aim slightly above what they were shooting at, letting the target rise into their sights. But they would soon make that adjustment. Of that, Malone had no doubt.

Sienna was so propelled by fear that he had trouble keeping up with her. The top of the slope seemed as far away as when he had started. The single-fire bullets whacked closer behind him, and he realized with alarm that the gunmen weren't making a mistake. They're aiming low on purpose, he thought. They don't want to kill us. They're shooting toward our legs. They want to cripple us so Bellasar can take us alive.

What sounded like superfast bumblebees sped past his legs. One of them nicked his jeans and stung his left calf. Racing harder, he stared toward the top. He swore his eyes were playing tricks. Everything seemed to become magnified, the crest suddenly close before him. He saw Sienna disappear over it, and a moment later, chased by bullets, he joined her, lurching onto a flat ridge that led to a gradual descent to olive trees in a valley. In the distance was a gray ribbon of concrete flanked by a handful of matchbox-looking buildings: the airfield.

14

The crunch of metal and the shatter of glass sent a wave of nausea through Bellasar. His sick feeling quickly changed to the most intense fury he had ever known. His engineers had assured him that these vehicles could withstand an attack from assault rifles, grenades, and even a glancing hit from a rocket. But the boulders had crushed the front of the cars and bounced up to strike the bullet-resistant windshields, smashing through and crushing the men in the front seats.

Bellasar screamed in outrage. With the men from his car and the survivors who lurched from the other cars, he fired toward Sienna and Malone. Determined more than ever to take them alive, aiming at their legs, he emptied his pistol, but before he could eject its magazine and shove in a new one, they disappeared over the crest.

Cursing, Bellasar leapt back into his vehicle. The men with him barely had a chance to jump in before he rammed the gearshift into reverse, tore up dirt backing away from the gully, spun the steering wheel, and sped up the slope.

But the incline steepened, and the ground became more uneven. The engine, strained to its limit, could no longer propel the weight of the reinforced body. The more it slowed, the more Bellasar pressed the accelerator, until, with a bang that shook the vehicle, the transmission failed, the vehicle rolling backward. Bellasar stomped the brake pedal, twisted the steering wheel, and yanked the lever of the emergency brake. Slamming a fresh magazine into his pistol, he charged out and ran for the top.

15

As Malone reached the cover of the olive trees at the bottom of the slope, he risked a precious few seconds to catch his breath and check behind him. But any hope that Bellasar might have been left back there was destroyed when he saw the tiny figures of men hurry over the crest. At their lead, his suit and tie somehow more threatening than the rugged clothes of the guards, his broad shoulders and strong chest unmistakable, was Bellasar.

Malone raced on. The olive trees were dense enough that he couldn't see Sienna, but the snap of branches and the crunch of footsteps ahead told him where to run to catch up to her. Despite his excellent physical condition, he had trouble narrowing the distance between them. At once he glimpsed her, the earth colors of her skirt and top helping her blend with the trees as she fled through them. He managed to join her as the trees gave way to a field, a fence, Quonset huts, and the airstrip.

All the while he and Sienna raced across the field, Malone was intensely aware of the cold spot on his back where he expected to be shot. Sienna got to the fence first, dropped to her back, pushed up the lowest strand of wire, and squirmed under. Shouts from the trees behind Malone added to his speed when he gripped a post and vaulted the fence to catch up to her.

The Quonset huts were rusted, he saw when he reached them. Cracks in the airstrip were choked with grass. Christ, it's abandoned, he thought. Jeb, what have you sent me to? But even as unnerving doubts seized him, he and Sienna rounded a corner and almost bumped into a pickup truck. Past it were an old Renault sedan and a beat-up station wagon. Three single-propeller planes stood at the side of the runway.

About to hurry into the largest building, Malone bumped into a bearded man coming out dressed in mechanic's coveralls and carrying a greasy rag.

With his limited French, Malone tried to blurt his apologies, quickly adding, "I'm looking for a man named Harry Lockhart."

The man raised his eyebrows and hands in confusion.

"Harry Lockhart." Malone couldn't help noticing the frown Sienna gave him. "Do you know a man named . . ."

The mystified expression on the Frenchman's face made Malone give up.

"Speak English, monsieur. I don't understand your French. I've never heard of anyone named Harry Lockhart."

"But he's supposed to meet me here!"

Sienna's frown became more severe.

"Are you certain you came to the right airfield?" the Frenchman asked.

"Is there another one around here?"

"No."

"Then I'm in the right place."

"You're bleeding, monsieur."

"What?"

"Your face. You're bleeding."

Malone had assumed the moisture he felt was

sweat. For a moment, he feared he'd been shot. Then he realized that the blood came from the scabs on his cheek and mouth. The exertion had opened them.

Two other men stepped from the building. They, too, wore coveralls, and although one was a little heavier than the other, they looked like brothers.

The first man turned to them and asked something in French.

At the mention of the name Harry Lockhart, they shook their heads no, then looked puzzled at the blood on Malone's face.

Damn it, Jeb, you promised he'd be here! Malone thought.

"What happened to you?" the first man asked in English. "Were you in those explosions we heard?"

Sienna kept glancing nervously back toward the field they had run across. "We can't wait any longer. If this guy Lockhart isn't here to help us . . ." She started to run.

Malone spoke more frantically to the Frenchmen. "Did anybody show up here in the past couple of weeks and say he was waiting for Chase Malone."

"No, monsieur. The only people who come here are the three of us and a few others in the area who like to fly old planes."

You bastard, Jeb. You swore you'd back me up.

The Frenchman's gaze drifted toward the sky and the swiftly approaching sound of a helicopter.

Oh shit, Malone thought. He pulled his steel and gold Rolex from his wrist and put it in the man's hand. "This is worth six thousand dollars. Show me how fast you can get your plane in the air."

16

Halfway across the field, Bellasar faltered at the sound of a small plane sputtering, then droning. The engine gained more power, sounding as if it was about to take off. No! he raged, charging forward again, faster. If Sienna and Malone are in that plane . . .

The engine reached full power, the distinctive thrust of a plane speeding along a runway. I've lost them! Bellasar thought. He came to a breathless stop. His sweat-drenched suit and white shirt clinging to him, he stared at the sky above the metal buildings. Raising his pistol, his men doing the same, he got ready to fire the instant the plane soared into view. His intentions were rash, he knew, given that there would probably be witnesses at the airfield. The imprecision bothered him also, the risk of stray bullets killing Sienna and Malone rather than merely forcing the plane down. But, by God, he had to do something. He wasn't just going to stand there and watch Malone fly away with his wife.

17

When Potter saw the smoking wreckage of the helicopter and then the three abandoned vehicles, two of them crushed, the doors of the third one open, as if its occupants had left in a hurry, he was reminded of the aftermath of an ambush he'd seen in the Balkans a month earlier. Except, in this case, there weren't any bodies. Where was . . . About to tell the pilot to keep a distance until he figured out what was going on, he heard his cell phone ring, and he answered it.

"I'm in the next valley!" Bellasar shouted. "There's an airstrip! Sienna and Malone are in a plane, about to take off!"

As Bellasar told him what to do, Potter felt uncustomarily euphoric. The helicopter increased speed, clearing the top of the hill. Immediately the airfield was in view. So was the tiny outline of the single-prop airplane taking off. Although the airplane rapidly gained altitude, the turbo-charged helicopter climbed much faster, making Potter feel energized, pressing his stomach pleasantly against his back.

The airplane leveled off, speeding toward rugged hills to the west. The helicopter raced after it, gaining, quickly coming abreast of it on the left.

Potter studied the shapes of passengers in the backseat and motioned for the plane's pilot to set down.

The pilot ignored him.

The plane dipped sharply.

So did the helicopter.

The plane veered more sharply to the right.

So did the helicopter.

"Get ahead of him," Potter said. "Keep cutting him off. Force him to go back to the airfield."

But before the helicopter's pilot could do what he was told, the plane soared.

So did the helicopter.

Unexpectedly, the plane swooped toward the countryside and banked beneath the helicopter, speeding in the opposite direction.

The pilot muttered, chasing the plane, narrowing the distance between them. Now he matched everything the airplane did, dipping, banking, soaring. Each maneuver bringing him closer, the pilot took the offensive and cut ahead of the plane, compelling it to turn. When it dipped, he anticipated which side the plane's pilot was going to choose and was waiting for him, forcing him to turn again. When the plane soared, the helicopter pilot again anticipated which side he would bank to and waited to block his way.

As the helicopter nudged closer, the bearded face of the plane's pilot became distinct. Although his Plexiglas window was scratched and dusty, there was no mistaking his alarm. Potter's French was excellent, and so was his ability to read lips. The pilot was cursing.

The man grabbed his radio microphone. The chopper's pilot found the frequency he was using. "What the hell do you think you're doing?" the Frenchman demanded.

"Go back to the airfield. Set down," Potter said.

"You don't have a right."

"Your passengers give me the right."

"What passengers are you talking about?"

A suspicion struck Potter so hard that he felt punched. "In the seat behind you!"

"Those are duffel bags!"

"Get closer!" Potter ordered his pilot. When the pilot started to object that it was too dangerous, Potter shouted, "Do it!" Staring as the plane seemed to enlarge next to him, he strained to see past the dusty rear Plexiglas and decipher the dark forms that he had taken for granted were Malone and Sienna. No! he thought, distinguishing the torso-shaped outlines of what were indeed duffel bags.

"Go back!" he yelled to his pilot.

18

"How much did they pay you?" Bellasar demanded.

The overweight man in coveralls looked baffled. "Me? They didn't pay me anything. I don't know what's going on! They gave Pierre an expensive watch for doing what he was going to do anyhow—take off and fly to Marseilles!"

"Where *are* they?"

The man pointed toward a path that went through trees on the opposite side of the airfield. "They stole two bicycles."

Right, Bellasar thought. Or maybe you *sold* the bicycles for one of Sienna's bracelets. "Then it isn't too late. They can't go far." He pulled out a money clip and peeled off several large-domination bills. "Give me the key to the station wagon."

"It won't do any good."

"What are you talking about?"

The man pointed toward the front right tire.

It was flat. So was a tire on the pickup truck and the Renault. "Before the man left, he did that."

"Fix them!" Furious about the waste of time, Bellasar didn't wait for Potter to return. He ran toward the path. Potter will scan the countryside from above, he promised himself. A man and a woman on bicycles won't be hard to see. We'll keep going. We'll catch them. I'll never stop.

19

Pedaling as hard as he could, Malone steered around a wooded bend. The trees opened up. Facing a paved road, he squeezed the brake levers on the handlebars. To his right, from beyond a curve, he heard a truck approaching.

Sienna stopped beside him.

"Quickly," Malone said. "We have to get to the other side."

He dismounted and hurried with the bicycle, laying it on the pavement in front of the yet-unseen truck. After wiping his hand across his face, smearing the blood over a wider area, he lay on the road and pulled the bicycle over him.

"Look panicked," he told Sienna. "Wave for the driver to stop."

The truck sped into view. Sprawled on the ground, gripping his leg, allowing himself to show pain, Malone suddenly worried that the truck was approaching too fast for it to be able to stop in time. Tangled with the bicycle, he wouldn't be able to crawl free and roll to the side of the road fast enough.

"Jesus"—Sienna waved frantically—"he's going to hit us!"

As she lunged to pull Malone's bicycle off him, brakes squealed. But they didn't seem to do any good. The truck kept hurtling toward them. She threw the bicycle to the side and dragged Malone off the road as the truck's brakes squealed louder and smoke came from the tires. On an angle, the truck skidded to a stop twenty yards beyond where Malone had been lying.

The truck, larger than a pickup, had wooden sides, across which a tarpaulin was stretched. The inside was filled with ladders, sawhorses, and lumber. The driver's door banged open. A sunburned man wearing sawdust-spotted clothes ran around the back and shouted angrily. The man's French was far too rapid for Malone to understand, but Sienna answered him as rapidly, gesturing toward the blood on Malone's face.

The man's anger turned to surprise and then shock. Paralyzed for a moment, he broke into motion, rushing to help Malone toward the truck.

"I told him you were hit by a car! He's taking you to a doctor!" Sienna said.

"Ask him if there's room in the back for the bicycles."

As the man helped Sienna set the bikes out of sight under the tarpaulin, Malone climbed into the front and leaned his head back as if in pain. The next moment, the driver hurried behind the steering wheel, Sienna getting in the other side. Putting the truck into gear, the driver sped along the road.

"He says the nearest hospital is ten minutes away," Sienna explained.

"That might not be soon enough." Malone tried to sound in agony. Despite the rattle of the truck, he heard the helicopter in the distance. Hoping the driver would go faster, he made himself wince and moan.

The man came out with another torrent of French.

Malone barely listened, too busy concentrating on the approaching sound of the helicopter. He assumed that the truck would soon attract its attention. After all, he hadn't seen any other vehicles on this road. How long would it take Bellasar to conclude that they had reached the road and caught a ride?

Isolated houses appeared. As the truck sped around another curve, Malone saw cars, trucks, bicycles, and people walking. The driver had reached a town, its speed-zone sign forcing him to slow. Imagining the view from the chopper, Malone had a mental overhead image of the speck of a truck blending with other specks. At a four-way stop, he noticed vehicles heading away in each direction and finally relaxed, deciding that for now there was no way Bellasar could track them.

For now, but Bellasar wouldn't stop searching, and plenty of other problems remained, Malone knew. He needed to convince the truck driver not to go into the hospital with him. He needed to find a place where he could clean himself up. A men's room near the emergency ward perhaps. Then he had to find a way out of town before Bellasar's men converged on it. The first chance he got, he would use the emergency phone number Jeb had given him. But that was another problem. Why hadn't Jeb followed through on the rescue plan they'd arranged? And that question, in turn, made Malone dread an even more immediate problem, the hard look in Sienna's eyes as she studied him, impatient to ask how he'd known about the airfield and what the hell this was all about.

SEVEN

1

"Who's Harry Lockhart?" Sienna's tone was subdued, presumably to avoid alarming passengers near them on the bus, but her question was obviously a demand.

"I don't know. I've never laid eyes on him. A pilot with that name was supposed to meet us."

They were in the backseat. The ticket seller at the depot had taken so long agreeing to accept some of the dollars Malone had brought with him from the United States that they had barely gotten to the bus before it moved out. As they left the outskirts of town, dusk thickened, lights coming on in houses. Malone glanced out the rear window to see if any cars seemed to be following them.

Sienna continued to press him. "Who was supposed to arrange for Lockhart to be there?"

"A friend of mine."

"Except he didn't. Is he the same friend who told you about what happened to Derek's other wives?" Her voice was sharper.

"Yes."

"You planned to get me out of there from the first day you arrived?"

"Yes."

"Which means you intended to use me against Derek from the start."

"No," Malone said. "It wasn't like that."

The bus's motor was beneath them, its raucous vibration muffling their voices.

"Who do you work for?"

"Nobody."

The back of the bus was cast in shadows.

"You just admitted that you have people providing you with information. You have a group that was supposed to give you backup."

"It isn't what you . . . I'm working *with* some people, yes, but I don't work *for* them."

"The CIA?"

"Yes," he said reluctantly.

"Jesus." Sienna threw up her hands. "If Derek finds out, if he thinks I'm cooperating with—"

"I'm not a spy."

"Damn it, what do you call it, then?"

Their voices had become louder, causing people in the seats ahead of them to look back.

"Calm down. If you'll let me explain . . ." Malone said softly.

"That's what I've been *waiting* for." The strain of lowering her emotion-laden voice tightened the sinews in Sienna's neck.

"All right." Malone took a deep breath, then told her what had happened on Cozumel. "Your husband destroyed most of what was important to me. When my friend turned up and offered me a way to get even, I took it."

"And used me to pay Derek back."

"That isn't why—"

"I trusted you! I thought you were my friend. But all this time, you've been lying to me, playing up to me to—"

"I never lied."

"You sure as hell never told me the truth."

"Not all of it. But what would you have done if I *had* told you?"

She opened her mouth but seemed not to know what to say.

"Your husband really was planning to kill you. But if I'd told you how I knew, would you have believed me? Would you have gone with me, or would you have suspected I was trying to trick you?"

She still didn't know what to say.

"I *am* your friend." Malone held out his hand.

She didn't take it.

"I never used you," Malone said. "I don't care if you never tell the Agency a thing. All that matters to me is that I got you out of there."

Sienna was so motionless, she didn't seem to be breathing. "I don't know what to believe."

She looked at him for the longest time. When she finally gripped his hand, it was as if she were on the brink of a cliff, depending upon him to keep her from falling.

2

The bus pulled into Nice around midnight. Given the combination of darkness and glaring lights, Malone wasn't able to get an impression of the city. Even the salt smell from the sea didn't register on him, so desensitized were his nostrils by the diesel smell of the bus.

To guard against the risk that Bellasar's men might be waiting at the bus depot, Malone chose a busy intersection at random and asked the driver to stop. The instant they stepped off, Malone led Sienna into a crowd. "I don't know what went wrong at the airfield," he said, "but Jeb and I had a backup plan."

They went into a late-night convenience store, where Malone used nearly all of his few remaining dollars to buy sandwiches, fruit, bottled water, and a telephone card.

"Now let's find a pay phone."

There was one around the corner, and as Sienna anxiously watched, Malone inserted the phone card, then pressed the numbers Jeb had given him to memorize. It won't be long now, he thought. We'll soon be out of here.

On the other end, the phone rang twice before it was answered. Pulse rushing, Malone started to use the identification phrase he'd been given—"the painter"—when a computerized voice cut him off. Its French was too hurried for him to understand. The connection was broken. "What the . . ."

Sienna stepped closer. "Is something wrong?"

"I must have pressed the wrong numbers."

He tried again, but the same computerized voice cut him off.

"I don't understand what it's saying. *You* try." He told her the numbers and watched her press them.

Nervous, she listened. Seconds later, she frowned and lowered the phone. "That number's been disconnected."

"What?"

"Maybe the CIA doesn't pay its phone bills," she said bitterly. "The line's no longer in service."

Jeb, you son of a bitch, Malone thought. What are you doing to me? What's gone wrong?

3

It was almost 1:00 A.M. as they walked wearily at random along narrow, shadowy side streets.

"That hotel up ahead looks good," Sienna said.

"It sure does."

But they passed the welcoming entrance, knowing that they didn't dare check in. Without enough cash to rent a room, Malone would need to use a credit card, but by now, Bellasar would have ordered his computer experts to access the databases of every credit-card company, looking for any transactions in Malone's name. If Malone used a credit card, Bellasar and his men would storm into the hotel room before morning.

"I brought some jewelry," Sienna said, "but we won't be able to sell it until the secondhand stores open tomorrow morning."

"We might have to wait longer."

"What do you mean?"

"Your husband will check to see if any of your jewelry is missing. He'll anticipate that you'll try to sell it. We might walk into a trap."

"*Everything* seems a trap."

The fear on her face made him touch it. "Keep remembering you're not alone."

"Not alone."

Around the next corner, they discovered that their aimless path had brought them to a park overlooking the harbor. Between palm trees, a bench invited them. In the distance, yachts gleamed. Faint music drifted from one, a piano playing "I Concentrate on You"; men and women in evening clothes were chatting and drinking.

"Cocktail?" Malone opened one of the bottles of water and handed it to her.

"I could use one."

"Hors d'oeuvres?" Malone set out the choices of sandwiches: egg salad, tuna salad, and chicken salad.

"That's quite a selection."

"The best in town."

"The service is awfully good. We'll have to recommend it to all our friends."

"And leave a generous tip."

"Absolutely. A generous tip."

Sienna's willingness to go along with his attempt at humor encouraged him. As long as their spirit persisted, they weren't defeated. But as a breeze scraped palm leaves above them, he noticed that she hugged her arms, shivering.

"Take my sport coat."

"Then *you'll* be the one who's cold."

"I'll sit close to you." He stood and put the coat around her, his hands lingering on her shoulders. Then he realized how tired he was and eased back onto the bench. He was so thirsty, it took him only a few deep swallows to drink a quarter of a liter of water. The egg salad tasted like the waxed paper it had been wrapped in. The bread was stale. He didn't care. Under the circumstances, it was the most delicious meal he had ever eaten. On the yacht below them, the piano player shifted to "The Days of Wine and Roses."

"Care to dance?" he asked.

Sienna looked at him, bewildered.

"I couldn't help thinking about the lyrics to that song," he said. "About regret and time passing. If we were another couple sitting here, this would be a beautiful night. A moment's what we make of it, I guess."

". . . Yes, I'd like to dance."

As they stood and faced each other, Malone felt pressure in his chest. He tried to keep his right hand steady when he put it around her waist. Her left hand trembled a little when she put it on his shoulder. They turned slowly to the distant mournful music that evoked children running through a meadow, never to reach a door to infinite possibilities. Barely able to breathe, Malone drew her closer to him, certain he was going to pass out if he didn't get more air into his lungs. He felt her breasts rising and falling as she, too, tried to get enough air. Pivoting tenderly with her, he saw the shadowy path behind them, where an elderly man and woman were walking their poodle through the park and had stopped to watch them dancing. The couple looked at each other, then back at Malone and Sienna. Smiling, the man took the woman's hand and continued walking through the park. Then Malone was aware of nothing around him, only of Sienna in his arms. As the piano brought the haunting melody to a close, Malone recalled the lonely nights of the lyrics. When he and Sienna kissed, he felt as if he were a youngster, light-headed: his first time.

4

They spent the night sitting on the bench. She slept with her head on his shoulder. He kept an arm around her, not sleeping as much as dozing, his troubled thoughts often waking him. Below, the lights on the various yachts gradually went out. The traffic sounds from the city lessened. In a while, he was able to pretend that he and Sienna were in a private universe. But the real world would intrude all too soon, he knew. Bellasar would relentlessly hunt them, and the moment they sold Sienna's jewelry or Malone was forced to use his credit card, the focus of the hunt would narrow. We have to get out of Nice, he thought. Hell, we have to get out of the country. Out of Europe. But even if they had money, they still couldn't leave—Bellasar had their passports. Without Jeb's help, Malone reluctantly confessed to himself, we don't have a chance.

5

In misty morning sunlight, the thin-faced waiter narrowed his disapproving eyes as Malone and Sienna made their way among the sidewalk tables toward him. Early customers peered up from their coffee and frowned. Malone imagined what he looked like, his clothes rumpled, his cheeks unshaven, his lips and upper left cheek scabbed and swollen. Some homeless people look better than I do, he thought. I bet that's what the waiter thinks I am. He probably figures I want a handout. Although Malone's nostrils were too accustomed to the smell for him to notice it, he was also sure that he reeked of smoke from the helicopter crash, and sweat, and fear.

Thank God, Sienna looks better, he thought. In fact, even though her clothes, too, were rumpled and her makeup had worn off, she looked terrific. A few strokes from a comb she'd borrowed from him had given her hair a sheen. Her tan skin glowed. No matter how bad she felt, Malone sensed it was impossible for her to *look* bad.

"Monsieur." The waiter raised his hands to keep Malone at a distance. Although his French was too quick for Malone to understand it, the gist was clear.

The café had standards. It would be better if Malone
went somewhere else.

Sienna didn't give him a chance to finish. Her hurried question to him included a word that sounded like
proprietor. The waiter's reply, accompanied by gestures, suggested that the proprietor wasn't necessary
to deal with this problem.

Sienna turned to Malone. "Do you remember the
owner's name?"

"Pierre Benét."

The boss's name made the waiter pay closer attention. Then Sienna told the waiter Malone's name,
pointing at him as she did, adding something in French
that might have been "Your boss is expecting us."

The effect was immediate. The waiter jerked his
head back. A torrent of words from him left Sienna
looking shocked.

"What is it?" Malone asked. "What's he saying?"

"They know who you are, but they weren't expecting us."

"What?"

"The operation was canceled."

"Jesus, not another screwup."

"Worse than that. They think you're dead."

6

"Chase, this is terrible! I can't tell you how rotten I
feel about this!" Jeb said. It was twelve hours later.

They were in an apartment above the café, where Jeb, out of breath from having charged up the stairs, looked heavier than the last time Malone had seen him, his blocky face redder than usual. "I was in Washington when I heard. I got here as soon as possible. I don't want you to think I left you hanging."

"It occurred to me."

"Christ." Jeb slammed his hands against his legs. "Buddy, we've been through a lot together. You saved my life. I swear to you—I'd never knowingly fail to back you up. Have they been taking care of you?"

Malone pointed toward a stack of used cups, glasses, and plates on a counter. "Whatever you said to them on the phone, they've been coming up every hour, it seems, with food and coffee."

"My God, your face. What happened to it?"

"You should have seen how bad it looked before I got cleaned up." Malone explained how he'd received the injuries.

"The bastard."

"I can think of stronger ways to say that."

"And what about . . ." Jeb turned toward Sienna. Malone had introduced her as soon as Jeb had entered the room, but since then, Jeb's apologies had taken up most of the conversation. He seemed self-conscious, as if trying not to stare at her beauty. "Are you hurt?"

"No." Sienna assessed him. "But after what happened, I'm not exactly filled with confidence."

"I don't blame you for thinking I don't know my job. Please, listen to me for a minute." Jeb ran a flustered hand through his short blond hair. "Chase, after you picked that fight with Bellasar at Sotheby's, you disappeared from the face of the earth. The last time anybody saw you was when Bellasar jabbed you with his ring and his men dragged you out of Sotheby's."

Sienna hadn't heard the details of the confrontation. She leaned forward, troubled.

"We know you were driven away in Bellasar's limo. And after that—poof. Two days later, a body too mangled to identify—I'm talking no fingers and no teeth—was found floating in the East River. The face had been burned with a blowtorch."

Sienna paled.

"It was dressed like you. It had your height and weight. It had a Parker Meridian room key in its bomber jacket pocket, the same hotel where you were staying. You can understand why we made assumptions."

"Except Bellasar's men had already picked up my luggage and checked me out," Malone said. "When you learned I wasn't registered there any longer, it should have been obvious the body wasn't mine."

"The problem is, nobody checked you out of your room."

"What?"

"You were still listed as a guest. Your clothes and things were still in your room when we went there."

"Somebody's, but not mine. My bag was on Bellasar's jet. Did you bother to compare the hair samples on those clothes with ones at my home on Cozumel? Did you try to match DNA samples from the body—"

"With *what*? Chase, your home doesn't exist anymore! After you left, the bulldozers leveled it. Trucks hauled the pieces away."

For a moment, Malone was speechless. "But Bellasar told me the bulldozers had stopped. He told me he was going to restore . . ." His voice became hoarse. "Just like he told me his men checked me out of my hotel room."

"Even then, I didn't give up," Jeb said. "I tried to find out if anybody had seen you get on Bellasar's jet. No luck. I checked with the airport authorities at Nice to see if they had any record that you'd entered the country. No luck there, either. I waited for a signal from you. Nothing. It's been five weeks, Chase. For God's sake, we had a wake for you. I never expected to see you again. I did my best to convince my supervisor not to do it, but he finally pulled the plug."

Malone peered down at his hands.

"I can understand if you're pissed at me," Jeb said, "but what would you have done that I didn't? I swear to you—it wasn't anybody's fault."

Jeb's suit was rumpled from the long flight. His eyes were swollen from lack of sleep. His burly frame looked puffy from sitting too long.

"It's okay," Malone said.

"Really, I want to put this behind us, Chase. I don't want you thinking I let you down."

"I'm not. Everything's fine. We're back on track."

"You're positive? No hard feelings?"

"None."

"But in the meantime, my husband's still looking for me." Sienna's stark tone made clear that whatever Malone felt, she herself was not reassured. "I keep worrying that he and his men are going to smash through that door any minute. How are you going to help us?"

For the first time, Jeb looked directly at her. "It'll be my pleasure to show you I can do my job."

7

After nightfall, twenty miles east of Nice, a van stopped along the narrow coastal road. Malone and Sienna got out, accompanied by Jeb and three other armed men. As the van drove away, they clambered down a rocky slope to where a motorized rubber raft waited in a cove. A half mile offshore, they boarded a small freighter and set out for Corsica.

"Two days from now, you'll be transferred to a U.S. aircraft carrier on maneuvers in the region," Jeb said after using a scrambler-equipped radio to verify the schedule. "From there, you'll be flown to a base in Italy, and from there"—he spread his hands—"home."

"Wherever *that* is," Sienna murmured.

The three of them sat in the dimly lit galley while their escorts and the crew remained on deck, watching for any approaching lights.

"Can I get you anything?" Jeb asked. "Coffee? Hot chocolate? Something stronger?"

"The hot chocolate sounds good," Sienna said.

"Same here," Malone said.

"Coming up," Jeb said. "And after that—given all

you've been through, I'm sure you're exhausted—there are bunks in the stern."

"I'm too on edge to sleep," she said.

"Then why don't we talk about why we're here."

"Can't this wait until tomorrow?" Malone asked.

"I'm not trying to force anything." Jeb tore open an envelope of hot-chocolate mix. "Whatever Sienna wants."

The smell of diesel fumes hung in the air.

"It's okay." She exhaled wearily. "Let's get it over with."

"This is going to take a lot longer than you think," Malone told her.

The freighter rocked as it passed through waves.

"Chase, I'm trying to make this as pleasant as possible," Jeb said. "We'll move at whatever pace she wants."

"Then I'll go first," Malone said, giving her a chance to rest. "I saw two men at the estate."

Jeb paused in the midst of pouring the hot-chocolate mix into a cup.

"They were Russians," Malone went on. "One of them brought in several crates of equipment via chopper. When the guards mishandled the crates, the Russian got very nervous, as if he was afraid of what might happen if something inside broke. I managed to get over to the building where the Russians were staying. I got a look through a window. The crates contained lab equipment."

Sienna frowned, realizing how little she had known about what Malone had been doing at the estate.

"Lab equipment?" Jeb asked. "What for?"

"Beats the hell out of me."

"Describe the Russians."

"I can do better than that."

"What do you mean?" Jeb's look of curiosity was matched by Sienna's.

"Have you got any sheets of paper around here?"

Jeb freed the latches on several drawers and peered inside, finally locating a pencil and a pad of eight-by-ten yellow paper.

Malone ordered his thoughts, then began to draw, calling not so much on his memory of the men's faces as on his memory of the numerous drawings he had done of them two nights previously. He had reproduced the faces enough times that he had little trouble replicating the strokes that filled in their features. On occasion, when the freighter shuddered from the impact of a wave, his pencil missed its mark, but he quickly erased the errors and added more details.

Time seemed to stop. Only later, when his pencil quit moving and the faces were complete, did he realize twenty minutes had gone by. Silence had seemed to envelope him. Now he shoved the sketches across the table to Jeb. "Look familiar?"

"Afraid not." Jeb held them closer to the light. "But these are vivid enough, I'm sure somebody in the Agency will be able to identify them. Vivid? Hell, they're close to being photographs. What you just did—I've never seen anything like it."

Malone turned toward Sienna. "If you're not tired, I'd like to try something."

"What is it?"

"I think it'll save time in your debriefing. But we can wait until tomorrow if . . ."

"No, you've got me curious."

"Did the man your husband met in Istanbul ever give his name?"

The reference caught Jeb by surprise. He leaned forward. "What man?"

"I never knew the names of anybody Derek did business with," Sienna said. "Whenever he used me as window dressing, the people he met avoided referring to one another even by their first names."

"Istanbul?" Jeb asked. "When was this?"

Sienna gave him the details. "It was an important meeting. Derek was very tense about it."

"We've been trying to keep track of your husband's activities," Jeb said, "but I had no idea about this meeting."

"That's not a confidence booster," Sienna said.

Jeb looked down at his cup.

Malone readied his pencil. "Describe the man."

Sienna nodded, understanding. "He was Middle Eastern."

"Describe the shape of his face."

She looked across the galley, focusing her memory. "Rectangular."

"How narrow?"

"Very."

"Any facial hair?"

"A thin mustache."

"Curved or straight?"

As Jeb watched, Malone began putting a face to Sienna's description. Most of his questions were based on geometry—the shape of the man's lips, his nose, and his eyes. High or low forehead? How old was he? Late forties? Malone put crow's-feet around the eyes and added wrinkles to the forehead.

"Is this starting to resemble him?"

"The lips were fuller."

Malone made the correction.

"The eyes looked harsher."

"Good."

Malone tore off the page and started a new one, copying details from the first rough sketch, leaving out smudges from erasures and the clutter of needless lines. He went to work on the eyes, adding the harshness that Sienna had mentioned. "What about his cheekbones?"

"He often looked like he'd tasted something sour. His cheeks were sucked in."

Malone's pencil moved faster.

Jeb peered over Malone's shoulder. "Jesus, I recognize this guy."

"What?"

"When I was assigned against Bellasar, I had to familiarize myself with other black-market arms dealers. This is Tariq Ahmed, his main competitor. A couple of years ago, they agreed on which territories each could have without interference from the other. Bellasar took Africa, Europe, and South America. Ahmed took the Mideast and Asia. Bellasar cheated when it came to Iraq. Ahmed cheated in Ethiopia. But basically they got along, especially when they had problems with other arms dealers trying to take some of their territories. So what did they need to meet about? Is their truce falling apart?"

"I haven't the faintest idea," Sienna answered. "My husband never talked about business in my presence. It was only indirectly that I learned how he made his fortune."

"You're telling me he never once mentioned a name or a detail about a transaction?"

"That's right."

"What *did* you talk about?"

"Very little. Once Derek married me, I was just another possession."

Jeb looked frustrated. Obviously, he'd expected more.

"That's why I wanted to give you these drawings right away," Malone said. "They're the only things of substance you're going to get out of this."

"Maybe not. Once we debrief the two of you, it's hard to say what might turn up—something you remember, some reference you overheard but didn't understand or think was important."

"The sooner I do it, the sooner I'm free. First thing in the morning?" Sienna asked.

Jeb nodded.

As Sienna and Malone stood, moving toward bunks in the stern, Jeb added, "Uh, Chase, I wonder if I could talk to you a minute."

"Sure."

"On deck."

"Sure," Malone repeated, puzzled. He touched Sienna's shoulder. "See you later."

She returned his touch, then disappeared into the shadows of the stern.

Malone followed Jeb up the steps to the murky deck. The canopy of stars was brilliant. He couldn't recall ever having seen so many. A cool breeze ruffled his hair.

"I need a little clarification," Jeb said.

"About?"

"I just wanted to make sure it wasn't my imagination. The way you're so concerned about her . . . the way you touched her shoulder just now . . . Do you and she have something going?"

"Excuse me?"

"It's not a hard question to understand. Are the two of you emotionally involved?"

"What the hell business is it of yours?"

"Look, as your case officer—"

"Case officer?"

"You haven't had the psychological training, so let me just tell you it gets messy when an operative becomes emotionally involved with an informant. Among other things, you lose your objectivity. There's a risk you'll miss something we need to know."

"You're talking as if I work for you," Malone said.

"Well, isn't that what we're doing here?"

"When I went into this, I told you it was personal. It had nothing to do with the Agency."

"Well, you sure need us now," Jeb said, "so maybe

you'd better rethink your position. She's the most beautiful woman I've ever seen. It's understandable you're attracted to her. But *she's* Bellasar's target more than you are. If you stay with her, you're doubling the chances he'll catch up to you."

"Not if you do your job."

Jeb looked toward the pitch-black sea, working to calm himself. "I'm just trying to be your friend. You're making a mistake."

"The mistake would be to pass up the chance to be with her."

"Hey, I'm doing my best to be tactful about this," Jeb said. "This isn't the first time this kind of situation's come up. Nine times out of ten, when an operative gets romantically involved with an informant, the romance collapses as soon as the pressure of the assignment passes. Buddy, you're setting yourself up for a fall."

"I think, from now on"—Malone's voice became severe—"you'd better assume I'm not one of your operatives."

"Whatever you want."

"That's right," Malone said. "Whatever I want."

8

The debriefing began the next morning. It continued into the next day, until they were transferred to the aircraft carrier. They had a rest while they were flown to the base in Italy, but as soon as a U.S. Air Force C-130 transport plane took off from there, carrying them toward the United States, Jeb resumed the debriefing. One of the armed escorts assisted him, sometimes questioning Malone, sometimes Sienna, always in separate areas where they couldn't be overheard. Jeb and the escort sometimes changed places; the idea was that the person being debriefed shouldn't get accustomed to a particular style of questioning and that one debriefer might take a question the other had already asked and rephrase it in a way that opened the memory of the person being questioned.

It wasn't an interrogation, although the polite but insistent, seemingly inexhaustible sequence of questions had aspects of one. For Sienna, the daunting task was to reconstruct the five years of her marriage. For Malone, there were only five weeks to account for, but the more he was asked to reexamine, a weariness set in that made him sympathize with how exhausted Sienna, with so much more to try to remember, had to be feeling.

From the start of the debriefing, Malone and Sienna were never allowed to meet with each other. The theory was that they might compare what each had said and inadvertently contaminate each other's memories, making the two versions conform. Jeb and his associate were the only ones allowed to compare, eager to find inconsistencies and use them to ask more refined questions that would perhaps open new memories.

After the transport plane landed at Andrews Air Force Base, the group was flown by helicopter to a clearing in a wooded estate in the Virginia hills.

There, to Malone's displeasure, he and Sienna were kept apart again, driven in separate cars to a low, sprawling modernistic house made of metal and glass. The house was smaller than Bellasar's. Its materials and design were not at all similar. But he couldn't suppress the disturbing sense that little had changed, that he was back where he had started. The gardeners who showed no interest in gardening and who seemed out of place in late March reinforced that conviction—they were guards.

Sienna's car arrived first. As Malone got out of his, three men were already taking her through the double-doored entrance to the house. She had a chance to look back only briefly, her unhappy gaze fixed on him, reminding him of an anxious animal being put in a cage, and then she was gone. Jeb was nowhere to be seen. Without anyone in authority to object to, Malone allowed himself to be taken inside.

The house had slate floors and beamed ceilings. There were corridors to the right, left, and straight ahead. Malone had no way of telling where Sienna had been put, but he himself was taken to the left, to a bedroom at the far end. The room was spacious, with institutional furnishings. But what Malone paid most attention to was the large single window, which couldn't be opened and which was unusually thick, suggesting it was bullet-resistant. He looked out toward a swimming pool that still had its winter cover on, leafless treed hills beyond it. He saw a tennis court, a stable, and a riding area, all of which looked as if they hadn't been used in a long time. He doubted that they'd be used while he and Sienna were there, either. He saw a "gardener" peering up at him. Turning, he studied what might have been a hole for a needle-nose camera lens in the opposite top corner of the room.

His legs ached from having been on too many aircraft. His head pounded from jet lag. His eyes burned from lack of sleep. He hadn't had a chance to talk to Sienna in two days. Where *was* she? What were they doing to her? He kept feeling he was back on Bellasar's estate. "This is bullshit," he said, directing his remark to where he assumed the hidden camera and microphone were.

He walked to the door through which he had entered, tried to open it, and found it locked. A number pad on the right seemed the only way to disengage the lock.

"Hey!" He pounded on the door. "Whoever's out there, open up."

No response.

He pounded louder. "Open the damn door!"

Nothing.

"Fine." He picked up a bedside lamp and hurled it against the window, shattering the lamp but having no effect on the glass. He grabbed the lamp on the other side of the bed and threw it against the mirror above the bureau, protecting his face as chunks of glass flew. He pulled out a dresser drawer and heaved it down through a glass-topped table in a corner. He hurled a second drawer toward an overhead light fixture, disintegrating it. He yanked out a third drawer and was about to head toward the mirror in the bathroom when a metallic sound directed his attention toward the door.

Someone was turning the knob.

The door swung open.

Jeb stepped into view, shaking his head in displeasure. His suit seemed to constrict his large frame. "What do you think you're doing?"

"Where's Sienna?"

"When we're finished, you can see her."

"No, I'll see her *now*." Malone started past him.

Jeb put a restraining hand on his shoulder. "This isn't the time."

"Get out of my way."

"Look, we have procedures that need to be followed."

"Not anymore. Where *is* she?"

"Chase, you're making a—"

Malone pushed him aside.

"Stop!"

Malone stalked from the bedroom.

An armed man appeared before him, holding up his hand. "Sir, you're going to have to go back to—"

"Go to hell." Malone shoved past him. "Sienna!"

"Stop!" Jeb repeated.

At the foyer, a guard blocked Malone's way, shoving him back. Malone pretended to lose his balance. When the overconfident guard came forward to shove him again, Malone stiffened the fingers of his right hand and drove them into the man's diaphragm. Wheezing, suddenly pale, the man sank to his knees. Malone whirled and used the heel of his palm to stiff-arm the other guard, who rushed toward him. Struck in the chest, the man jerked back as if yanked by a rope, then slammed onto the floor.

Malone braced himself, raising his hands offensively against Jeb. "You want some of this?"

"Mr. Malone."

Malone turned toward a bureaucratic-looking man in his late fifties.

"I think we should talk," the man said.

9

The man had thinning gray hair and was of average height and weight, but his rigidly straight posture and commanding eyes, seemingly magnified by his metal-rimmed spectacles, gave him a presence out of proportion to his size. Accompanied by two assistants, he had just emerged from a room farther along the hallway. The door remained open.

"Is Sienna in there?"

The man spread his hands. "See for yourself."

Malone passed the first guard, ignoring the injured man's attempt to stand. Rapidly, he also passed the bureaucrat and entered the room, which was an office with glass bookshelves, a computer on a desk, and several closed-circuit TV monitors, one of which showed the wreckage in Malone's room. He didn't find Sienna in the office, and he didn't see her on any of the screens.

"I've told you what I know," Malone said as the man entered with his assistants, followed by Jeb, who shut the door. "I didn't get involved in this to be treated like a prisoner. Where's Sienna? I want to see her."

"Yes, your file made clear you have a problem dealing with authority."

"You want to see a problem?" Malone picked up the computer's monitor and hurled it onto the floor. The screen shattered. "You want to see *another* problem?"

"*You're* a problem. You've made your point. Now let me make mine."

"Why do I get the feeling we're still not communicating?"

"Ten minutes."

"What?"

"You need to understand some things."

Malone tensed, studying the man, suspicious.

"You've had a long journey. Take a seat. Would you like something to eat or drink?"

"You're wasting your ten minutes."

"My name is Jeremy Laster."

"I doubt you'd give me your real name, but if that's how you want it, fine, you're Jeremy Laster."

Laster sighed. "Considering your relationship with Mrs. Bellasar"—he put a slight emphasis on *Mrs.*, as if he felt Malone needed to be reminded—"I can understand why you're impatient to see her, but that can't be permitted for a while."

"How long?"

"It's impossible to say."

"That's what *you* think." Malone started toward the door.

Laster's two assistants blocked it.

"I still have nine minutes," Laster said.

Malone debated whether to try to force his way out, then told Laster, "Use them."

"You've insisted you're not associated with us. That makes it difficult to confide in you. Within the Agency, we operate on a need-to-know basis. But someone on the *outside* . . ." Laster made a gesture of futility.

"Join the Agency and you'll tell me what's going on, is that it?"

"Hardly. I've seen enough to be sure we don't want you."

"I'm glad we agree about something."

"What I'm trying to do is make clear how unusual the circumstances are that would lead me to explain *anything* to you." Laster went over to the desk and picked up a one-page document. "This is a confidentiality statement. It forbids you to disclose what I'm about to tell you. The penalty for violating it is severe."

"Like an unmarked grave in the woods?"

"Be serious."

"Who's joking?" Malone took the document and read it. "So I'm supposed to sign this, and then you'll tell me what's going on?"

Laster handed him a pen.

Malone impatiently used it. "Fine. Now talk."

"At last we're making progress." Laster put the document in his briefcase and pulled out a black-and-white photograph of the man Sienna had met in Istanbul. It was similar to Malone's sketch. "As Mr. Wainright told you, he recognized this man. Tariq Ahmed. Another black-market arms dealer. We're extremely curious about the purpose for their meeting. And we think the answer involves the two men you saw at Bellasar's estate." Laster pulled out two other black-and-white photographs. "Thanks to your accurate sketches, a team from our Russian desk was able to identify them as Vasili Gribanov and Sergei Bulganin." Laster paused. "They're specialists in biowarfare."

"Bio . . ."

"In 1973, the Soviets established a biological weapons research and production system called Biopreparat. Gribanov and Bulganin came on board in 1983. Various scientists had their specialties. Marburg, anthrax, pneumonic plague. Gribanov and Bulganin chose smallpox."

Malone felt cold. "But I thought smallpox had been destroyed."

"Eradicated from the general population, yes. The last known case was in 1977. But if it ever came back, the World Health Organization decided that a small amount of the virus ought to be kept frozen for research purposes. The United States has some. So do the Russians. Scientists being what they are, they love to tinker. Gribanov and Bulganin decided that smallpox in its natural form wasn't deadly enough. They altered its genetic makeup to make it more aggressive."

"But that's insane." Malone's skin itched as if he'd been infected.

"For eight years, Gribanov and Bulganin worked happily, running their experiments and performing tests. But in 1991, the Soviet Union collapsed, and the research money stopped. They found themselves out of a job. So they offered their skills to another employer."

"Bellasar."

Laster nodded. "As it turns out, Ahmed is less thorough in his security arrangements than Bellasar. By intensifying our electronic surveillance on his associates, we've been able to learn about the meeting in Istanbul. It seems Bellasar has no qualms about selling a biological weapon to anyone prepared to meet his price, but he doesn't want to be linked directly to the weapon. What he'd prefer is to sell it to Ahmed and then let Ahmed dispose of it as he wishes. That's why the meeting didn't go as smoothly as Bellasar hoped. Ahmed figures that if he's going to take the heat for making the weapon available, he wants better financial terms than Bellasar is offering. Bellasar's argument is that Ahmed shouldn't be greedy, that Ahmed's already guaranteed a hefty profit when he sells it."

"To whom?"

"That's one of various things we're hoping Mrs. Bellasar will tell us."

"She doesn't know."

Laster only stared at him.

Malone shook his head in disgust. "What's the weapon's delivery system?"

"Microscopic powder released via aerosol containers. The best method is to have an aircraft open the containers while flying over a city. Our experts calculate that a half dozen aerosol containers opened on a windy day could contaminate several square miles."

"But the thing's uncontrollable," Malone said. "Before victims start showing symptoms, some of them could get on planes and fly to major cities all over the world. It could cause a global epidemic."

"Not in this case," Laster said. "The weapon has a fail-safe feature that prevents it from spreading beyond its target."

"Fail-safe?"

"What makes the weapon so unique is that Gribanov and Bulganin genetically engineered the smallpox virus so it can't infect anyone unless it combines with another virus, a benign but rare one."

"Why? What purpose would that serve?"

"You release the benign virus first. As soon as the target population is infected, the lethal virus is then released. But anyone who hasn't been infected with the benign virus can't be infected by the lethal one, which means that even if someone who's infected with the lethal virus gets on a plane before the symptoms show up, that person isn't going to start an epidemic in another country, because that other population hasn't previously been exposed to the companion virus."

"Unless someone exposed to the benign virus has already traveled to that country."

"Can't happen."

"Why not?"

"The benign virus has a six-hour life span when it isn't combined with the lethal one. It doesn't travel well. By the time someone flew from Tel Aviv to Rome, Paris, or New York, say, it would have died. Anyone arriving with the lethal virus couldn't pass it on."

"Jesus."

"This is a quantum leap in the notion of what a weapon can be," Laster said. "Controlled massive destruction of human life without any destruction to property."

"Why would anybody want to develop a weapon like that?" Jeb interrupted. "How the hell rich does Bellasar need to be?"

"It's not about money. It's about power," Malone said.

Laster nodded. "So our profilers suggested, but their conclusion is theoretical. We've never had access to anyone who spent as much time with him as you did. Except for—"

"Sienna."

"She knows the mechanisms that trigger his emotions. In our efforts to put him out of business, no observation from his wife is too small not to be of value to us."

"So basically the debriefing could go on forever?"

Laster spread his hands fatalistically.

"You prick."

"Millions of lives are at stake."

"That doesn't mean she has to be a prisoner."

"Bellasar's never going to stop searching for her. Do you honestly believe if we let her out of here—I don't care under what new identity—that he won't eventually find her? This is the safest place in the world for her."

"Then why won't you let me see her?"

"Because, if she feels as powerfully about you as you do about her, the longer she's away from you, the more frustrated she'll become. That'll give us leverage. We're not sure we can trust her. Maybe she's having second thoughts about betraying her husband. Maybe she's withholding crucial information. But if she knows she can't see you until she convinces us she doesn't have anything more to tell us, she'll have greater motivation to confide in us."

"To call you a prick is being generous," Malone said. "You want to put Bellasar out of business? Send in a black-ops team and assassinate him. Bomb the hell out of the place. Scorch it to the ground and pour salt all over it."

"We'd love to."

"So why don't—"

"Because we have to make sure the biological weapon is secure. When our team moves in, it's going to be at the proper time and with the proper information."

"Sienna and I gave you all the information we have."

"That remains to be determined."

"I want to see her."

"By all means." Laster pointed toward one of the closed-circuit television monitors.

Malone walked to it and felt his pulse increase. Seen from the back, Sienna peered out a large window similar to the one in his room. The image was black and white and grainy, from an angle that looked down and across the room at her. The lens had a fish-eye distortion. But nothing could obscure her beauty.

"This evening, we're going to question her again about Bellasar's sister," Laster said. "None of us knew about her. We're eager for more details."

"Knock yourself out."

10

When Malone returned to his room, it had been restored, the light fixture, table, and mirror replaced, the broken glass removed. Noticing that the closet door was ajar, he pulled it open and found clothes on hangers: a sport coat, two shirts, a pair of jeans, and a pair of slacks, all of them in his size and all of them new. Yeah, just like at Bellasar's, he thought.

Through the window, the sky was becoming bleak, a shower approaching, leafless branches wavering in the breeze. He went over and watched specks of rain hit the glass. The room light was off. As the sky became grayer, the late afternoon felt like evening.

I should have made another attempt to reach her.

With those two guards waiting for an excuse to get

even? he thought. One of Laster's assistants had been holding something that looked suspiciously like the kind of flat black case doctors kept syringes in. Malone was certain that if he'd made another attempt to get to Sienna, he'd have been sedated.

The way Bellasar had jabbed him with his ring at Sotheby's.

Calm down, he thought. Get control. Think this through.

Right, he thought. Even if he and Sienna had the freedom to leave this place, what were they going to do about it? Malone had counted on the Agency to solve the problem for them, but Laster had as much as admitted that the Agency didn't have a solution. Bellasar would keep coming and coming, and a man with his resources would eventually find a lead. In the meantime, every shadow would make them flinch. Even on the most basic level, they needed the Agency to supply them with new identities and documentation. How were they going to keep on the move without new credit cards, driver's licenses, and passports?

The rain pelted the window. It was gloomy enough outside that Malone could see his troubled reflection in the glass.

Someone knocked on his door. Turning, he saw it opening and noted that the hand coming into view didn't have a key. He couldn't help concluding that even though a combination of numbers had to be pressed on the pad next to the door to unlock it from the inside, the door could be unlocked from the outside merely by turning the knob.

Jeb appeared, looking sheepish, holding a six-pack of Budweiser in one hand and a bottle of Jack Daniel's in the other. "Peace offering?"

"You really let me down."

"The assignment was taken from my control."

"Was it ever *in* your control?"

"I thought so. I was wrong. Can I come in?"

"Since when does anybody around here ask permission of the prisoners?"

"Since now."

Malone exhaled and waved him forward.

"What would you like?" Jeb set the whiskey and the beer on the bureau.

"Some passports would be nice."

Jeb frowned.

"A set of new IDs. Just to give me the illusion there's a future."

Jeb opened his mouth, closed it, thought a moment, and finally said, "I'll see what I can do."

"I sort of hoped they were already in the works."

Jeb avoided the subject. "What would you like for dinner?"

"You're the food director now?"

"Just trying to make you happy."

"Next thing, you'll be leaving chocolates on the bed."

"Hey, this is a shitty deal, I admit. But it's like what they say about a real prison: You can do easy time or hard time. Why don't the two of us get loaded, eat a steak dinner, and watch the Lakers game tonight? Things could be worse."

". . . I want to see her."

"I know, pal."

"Take me to her."

"I'm sorry. I really am. For what it's worth, she's been insisting to see you, too."

Malone's chest ached.

"That's all she wants. Listen, if the decision was up to me . . ." Jeb twisted the cap off the liquor bottle. "But Laster's determined to give her a reason to remember harder. He figures if she has everything she wants, why should she help us?"

"One day, he and I are going to have a long talk about this."

The rain lanced harder against the window.

"Have you got any glasses?" Jeb asked.

"Maybe in the bathroom."

Thunder rumbled.

"I'll go look," Jeb said.

The next rumble shook the building. The thickness of the window wasn't enough to shut out a muffled scream.

Jeb froze on his way to the bathroom.

"That wasn't thunder," Malone said.

11

"Christ." Jeb rushed toward the door and jabbed numbers on the pad. When he yanked the door open, Malone was immediately behind him, hearing a commotion down the hallway, urgent footsteps, frantic voices.

"—in back!"

"Breached the—"

Outside, a burst from an assault rifle was followed by a scream and another explosion. Jeb ran along the corridor, yelling to Malone, "Stay here!"

Like hell, Malone thought, then charged after him. In the foyer, the two guards he had struggled with earlier had drawn their pistols, aiming toward the front entrance. Other guards raced along corridors.

Louder gunfire, a third explosion.

I have to find Sienna, Malone thought.

In the foyer, he turned toward the middle corridor, where he saw Laster and his two assistants rush from a room halfway along on the left. Laster's face was pale as he slammed the door shut behind him, grabbed a guard running past, and blurted questions.

Malone whirled toward the guard he had earlier struck in the stomach. "Give me a pistol."

Sweat beading his forehead, the guard stared toward the front entrance and didn't seem to hear him.

"Listen, damn it, I need a pistol!"

"Go back to your room!" Laster shouted, reaching him.

"Where's Sienna?"

An explosion shook the front doors. Smoke appeared at the end of the middle corridor. Although the exterior of the house was made of metal and glass, reinforced to withstand an attack, the interior's wooden walls and beams had caught on fire. Outside, the shots intensified. Then suddenly the shooting wasn't outside any longer. Malone heard an ear-torturing burst from an assault rifle. Rapid single shots from pistols followed. The smoke worsened.

"Go back to your—" Laster started to repeat. Gunfire interrupted him.

"Tell me where Sienna is!"

"I don't understand how they—" Laster spun toward an assistant. "Get the woman."

The assistant stared at the smoke churning toward him and backed away.

"Get her!" Laster repeated.

"Where is she?" Malone demanded. *"In the room you just left?"*

Laster whirled toward the sound of an explosion outside.

"Damn you." Malone took a deep breath and shoved past. As the smoke enveloped him, it stung his eyes and blurred his vision. For all he knew, it was poison gas, but he didn't allow himself to think about it. He had to find Sienna. In the swirling haze, he couldn't tell how far along the corridor he had gone.

He reached a door, turned the knob, and thrust inside. "Sienna!" The room was free of smoke. Sweet air entered his lungs. Then smoke gusted in, but not before he saw that the room was empty. There weren't even any sheets on the bed.

In the last of the unfouled air, he took another deep breath and lunged back into the smoke-filled corridor, rushing farther. "Sienna!" He shoved open the next door and found another empty room.

From down the hallway, he thought he heard a muffled cry. "Chase!" Was he imagining it? Was he making himself hear what he wanted to hear? He ran to the next door, and this time when he charged in, she was there before him, rushing toward him. Coughing, he wanted to slam the door behind him to prevent the smoke from spilling in, but he realized that he'd be locking them in, that he had to keep the door open. He grabbed a chair and braced it between the door and the jamb.

They held each other. He wanted to keep his arms around her forever, but as nearby gunfire made her flinch, the smoke began to fill the room.

"Help me," he said. "We need wet towels."

In the bathroom, he filled the sink with cold water. Sienna grabbed two towels and plunged them in, soaking them.

The gunfire was closer. Smoke reached the bathroom.

Coughing, Malone pressed a dripping towel against his face. Although it was hard to breathe through, the moisture filtered some of the smoke. But that wouldn't last long, he knew. As Sienna covered her face with the other towel, they made their way toward the door.

He shoved the chair aside, grasped Sienna's hand, and entered the chaos of the hallway. Someone ran past, not seeing them in the smoke. Shots at the end of the corridor made Malone crouch, forcing Sienna down with him. He led her to the right, toward the foyer, where he had been with Laster and his assistants. Jeb? Where *was* he?

Unable to see the floor, Malone almost tripped over something. A body. Sienna make a choking sound. He released her hand and stooped toward the corpse. His hand touched warm, sticky liquid on the unmoving chest. He felt a suit and wondered if the body belonged to Laster or one of his assistants. He checked the body's right hand, found a pistol, and shoved it under his belt. He probed the inside suit pockets and found a wallet, which he also grabbed.

The moment he shoved the wallet into his jeans, he urged Sienna farther along the corridor. The wet towel became harder to breathe through, the smoke too thick. Sienna coughed. But Malone wasn't afraid that the sound would attract attention to them—there were too many other sounds: shots, screams, racing footsteps, the roar of a fire at the end of the corridor behind them.

He kept his shoulder against the wall. Then suddenly the wall was gone. He'd reached the foyer. But the area seemed abandoned. The shots, screams, and footsteps became eerily silent, the only noise the growing *whoosh* of the flames behind him. Is everybody dead? he wondered.

"Chase!" someone called.

Malone spun.

"Chase!"

The hoarse voice was Jeb's. To the right.

Worried that someone might be forcing Jeb, Malone took the towel from his mouth long enough to whisper to Sienna, "Grab the back of my belt. Don't let go." He returned the towel to his mouth. Not that it did much good any longer. The smoke was too strong. As she grabbed his belt, he pulled out the pistol he had taken from the body.

"Chase!" Jeb sounded closer. At once he appeared amid the smoke, his face red from coughing, startled by the weapon Malone pointed at him.

As smoke seared Malone's throat, he could barely say, "Get us out of here!"

Jeb tugged his arm, leading him to the right. Outside, two shots made Sienna tighten her grip on Malone's belt. Abruptly Jeb reached a door and opened it, pulling them into a dimly lit room. The area was comparatively free of smoke, and as Malone and Sienna breathed in, trying to fill their lungs, Jeb quickly closed the door.

But this is a trap, Malone thought. How are we going to leave the building? Immediately he noticed concrete steps leading downward.

"There's a utility tunnel that goes to the pool house," Jeb said.

Malone didn't need to hear any more. He and Sienna ran down. At the bottom, they paused only long enough for Jeb to find a light switch and flick it on. A concrete corridor was lined with doors. Pipes passed along the ceiling, interspersed with glaring bulbs.

As Malone ran, his labored breathing echoed. He and Sienna threw their towels into a laundry area. A door banged open behind them. They raced harder.

The corridor turned sharply to the left, bringing them to an unlit segment of the tunnel. It was cool, damp, and smelled of mold. The instant Malone rushed around the corner, he took cover in the shadows and aimed back along the corridor.

At the far end, footsteps clattered down the stairs. Four men rushed into view. They held assault rifles, one of them shouting, "Check every room!"

As the men split up, Malone held his fire. There were too many men. They were too far away. He glanced toward Jeb, whose strained eyes seemed to be reading his thoughts. Jeb cocked his head toward the continuation of the tunnel, as if to say, Our best chance is to get the hell out of here.

Hoping that the sounds the men made would prevent them from hearing other sounds, Malone, Sienna, and Jeb hurried on. But the farther they went from the lights at the other end of the tunnel, the more darkness gathered around them. They had to slow, feeling ahead of themselves to make sure they didn't bump into something.

The steps caught Malone by surprise, his right shoe striking one. He felt a metal rail to his left and started up, only to stiffen as a furious voice in the other corridor shouted, "I heard something!"

Malone worked higher up the stairs. Sienna rushed next to him. Ahead, Jeb attempted to free something, making a noise as what sounded like a lock was released.

"That way!" the angry voice shouted.

Jesus, Malone thought. As the men's footsteps raced closer, Jeb yanked open a door. Gray light spilled in. The door's hinges grated.

"Around that corner!" one of the men yelled.

Silhouetted against the light in the tunnel behind them, the men rounded the bend and raised their rifles.

Malone fired, hit one of them, and fired again, absorbing the pistol's recoil while the remaining three men scrambled back around the corner. One of them cursed, but Malone barely heard it—his ears rang painfully, as if someone had slammed hands against them.

He whirled and ran the rest of the way up the steps, entering a utility room, where Sienna shifted a table toward him while Jeb slammed the door. Dusky light through an opposite doorway revealed the pump, filter, and water heater for the swimming pool, but Malone paid little attention. Without a key, they couldn't lock this door from the outside. Rushing, he helped Sienna move the table, jamming it against the door a moment before a bullet walloped against it from the other side. The door was metal. The bullet didn't pierce it. But the table wasn't heavy enough to keep three men from forcing the door open.

Jeb hefted a large plastic container marked CHLORINE TABLETS and set it on the table. Malone did the same with a second container. It was heavy, but not enough. Any moment, the men would ram their shoulders against the door.

Malone hurried with Jeb and Sienna to a canopied area next to the pool. In the dimming light, rain pelted a cover stretched over the pool. His pistol ready, Malone scanned the lawn, stable, tennis court, and misted hills. Turning to the left, he saw the house in flames, figures in confusion around it. The roar of the fire must have prevented them from hearing his shots. There was no way to tell whether they were Laster's men or Bellasar's. If the latter, Malone couldn't risk attempting to ambush the men behind him when they charged from the pool house. In the open, the shots would bring more pursuers. The only choice was to keep running.

The stable, Malone thought. He motioned for Jeb and Sienna to run to the right toward a gate that led to a lane. After the heat of his exertions, the rain felt welcomely cool. But as his wet clothes clung to his legs, back, and chest, a shiver swept through him.

His shoes slipped on mud. He fought for traction and ran harder. The rain made the dusk gray enough that he prayed they couldn't be seen from the burning house or from the pool area. The stable loomed closer. They splashed through puddles, reaching a door.

The rectangular building hadn't been used in quite a while. A horse trailer was covered with cobwebs. The ten stalls along each side were empty except for dusty straw and more cobwebs.

Straining to catch his breath, Malone peered out the open door toward the pool area. While he had time, he ejected the magazine from the grip of his pistol and checked to see how many rounds were left. He couldn't assume that it had been full when he picked it up—the man from whom he had taken it might have fired several times before he was shot. He was right. The weapon, a 9-mm Beretta, the same type of pistol Malone had used in the military, could hold as many as sixteen rounds, but only nine were left.

"Do you see anybody?" Jeb asked.

"There." Sienna pointed toward the rain-shrouded lane, where a man with a rifle hurried in their direction.

"But I don't see the others." Malone immediately understood. "Jesus, they've split up. They'll be coming at us from three sides."

Jeb pulled out a pistol. "There aren't any doors along each side. I'll watch the one at the far end."

"How can I help?" Sienna asked.

"We don't have another gun. Take cover."

"I see one of them," Jeb said from the other end. "He's still too far away. I can't get a shot at him."

Malone stared at the man hurrying toward them along the lane. Abruptly the man sank behind the fence that flanked it. "This one's taking cover, sneaking up."

"But where's the *third* one?" Jeb asked.

Straining for a glimpse of a target, Malone told Sienna, "Better get behind those hay bales."

But when he glanced in her direction, he didn't see her. He looked in another direction and saw a ladder that led to a platform above him. She was halfway up.

"What are you—" Immediately he quit talking, his attention totally focused on the gunman in the lane, who suddenly appeared at an open gate and dashed through the rain to the cover of a shed.

Malone aimed, ready for him to emerge on the right or the left.

Above, amid the rain drumming on the corrugated metal roof, Malone heard Sienna on the platform.

"There's a window," she said.

"For God sake, be careful." He kept aiming.

"I'm high enough that I can see him behind the shed. He's—"

Her abrupt silence made Malone tense.

"He's motioning to someone on your right," she said. "He's pointing toward the side of the building. The third man must be heading toward it. He's going to sneak along it on your blind side."

Several rapid *thunks* at Jeb's end of the building sounded like bullets slamming into wood.

"Jesus, are you okay?" Malone asked. "I didn't hear the shots."

"He's using a silencer," Jeb said.

A thought nagged at Malone, but before he could analyze the implications, the man behind the shed fired three rapid shots toward the open door. As Malone pressed himself against the wall next to the door, bullets splintered the slats of a stall behind him. But he didn't hear the shots, and not because of the ringing in his ears. This gunman, too, was using a sound suppressor. *Why?*

"The one behind the shed is looking to your right again," Sienna said from above. "Toward the side of the building. I get the sense that the third man's farther along it."

Malone understood. The gunman behind the shed would keep firing to distract Malone while the third man crept next to the door and waited for Malone to return fire. The moment Malone revealed his position, the third man would make his move.

"The man behind the shed just nodded," Sienna said. "They're ready."

Prepared for the gunman behind the shed to show

himself, Malone pulled the trigger the instant he saw motion, shooting one, two, three times, the pistol bucking in his hands. As the gunman pitched backward, Malone dove forward through the doorway, landing in mud, firing to his right, toward where Sienna had predicted the third gunman would be. The man's face twisted in surprise, unable to redirect his aim before Malone's bullets struck him in the chest, knocking him down.

Malone scrambled back to the cover of the building. Studying the men he had shot to make sure they weren't moving, he realized that Sienna was next to him.

Jeb was next to him also. "The third man took off through the woods. But the ones at the house are running this way."

"They work for Laster," Malone said.

"How do you know?"

The thought that had nagged at Malone became clear. "The men I shot wouldn't have used sound suppressors unless they didn't want the men at the house to hear them. Laster's men managed to fight off the attack."

"Yes," Jeb said. "I see Laster."

"Go out and tell him we're safe," Malone said.

"You're not coming with me?"

"Sienna and I need a minute by ourselves."

Jeb hesitated, massaging his left thigh, where he'd been shot the night Malone had saved his life in Panama City. "Sure." He hesitated longer. "You've earned it."

He stepped into the dusky rain, heading toward the

rapidly approaching men, who were outlined by the smoke of the burning house.

Watching Jeb walk away, Malone led Sienna deeper into the stable. "They had their chance. They can't protect us. Your husband couldn't have found us this fast unless he has an informant in the Agency."

Sienna's eyes darkened at the thought of Bellasar.

"He'll learn about every other place the Agency tries to hide us. The only way we'll be safe is on our own—where we won't be in prison, where nobody'll keep us apart."

"I don't want to be separated from you ever again," she said.

Malone took her hand, leading her toward the back door. The cold rain lessened to a drizzle as they ran out toward murky trees. In a few minutes, it would be too dark for Laster and his men to see to follow. Maybe we can circle around to the front and steal a car, Malone thought. Or maybe we can . . . Vague possibilities encouraged him. He had the wallet from the dead man in the house. He had money, credit cards, a new identity. He knew that Laster would eventually figure out whose identity he was using. Bellasar's spy would pass the word. But that was a problem to be worried about tomorrow. For now, the two of them were free, vanishing into the mist-shrouded woods.

EIGHT

1

The hypnotic *clack-clack-clack* of the train's wheels reinforced Malone's exhaustion. He and Sienna slumped next to each other in a locked compartment, barely noticing the lights of towns that flashed past. It was almost midnight. They had boarded the train an hour earlier at Washington, D.C.'s Union Station, where they had driven after Malone had followed his first impulse and stolen a car from the front of the burning house while Laster and his men searched the woods. Hoping to conceal his trail, Malone had left the car in a restaurant's parking lot and taken a taxi to the train station. There, he had used the credit card in the dead man's wallet to buy two tickets to Dallas. Despite the rain, the burned house wouldn't have cooled enough for Laster's men to search it. They wouldn't find the body for quite a while. Even then, there was a good chance the fire had so charred the corpse's clothes that no one would realize the wallet was missing. When the credit-card charges persisted after the man's death, Laster would understand what had happened, but by then it would be too late. Meanwhile, Malone and Sienna were together. That was all he cared about.

"Hungry?"

Sienna looked at the bag of sandwiches they'd bought. She shook her head no. "Tell me what we're going to do."

"It depends on your expectations. We're not going to be able to live the way you did on your husband's estate."

"I wouldn't want to."

"I don't mean the tension you went through. I'm talking about the absence of luxury. I've got plenty of money in various places, but I can't think of a way to get to it without letting your husband or the CIA know where we are. They'll have computer experts watching for any transactions in my accounts. The instant I order a wire transfer—to a bank in Dallas, say—they'll be after us. The airport, the train station, the car-rental agencies—they'll all be watched."

"You make it sound hopeless."

Even in her damp, rumpled blazer, her hair combed with her hands, Sienna somehow managed to look more beautiful than ever. How do I hide one of the most striking women in the world? he thought. "I promise, there *is* a way out of this, but it's going to be a lot less first-class than you're used to."

"Is that why we're going to Dallas?"

"We're not going there."

"But our tickets—"

"We're getting off before then. At a town called Braddock."

"In case Derek finds out we took the train and he's waiting for us in Dallas?"

Malone nodded. "And because there's someone I have to meet in Braddock."

2

The Texas sky was cobalt blue as they stepped from the train and studied the small depot and waiting area. Beyond were low buildings: a gas station next to a car-repair shop, a hardware store next to a bar. A few trucks moved along the street. Otherwise, the town seemed deserted.

"A place this small, it's a wonder it has its own train station," Sienna said.

"Clint's got the influence to make sure he gets what he wants."

"You're telling me people other than actors actually have names like Clint?"

"Chase, ol' pal, it's been too damn long," a man's voice said in the deepest, twangiest drawl Sienna had ever heard.

She turned toward the open door to the waiting room, from which a man in cowboy boots, jeans with a belt buckle shaped like a saddle, a denim shirt, a leather vest, and a cowboy hat stepped grinning into view, embracing Malone, slapping his back.

"Why didn't you let me send the jet to pick you up?" the man asked. "And how come you phoned collect? All the money I paid you over the years, you can't be short of cash."

"Sort of."

The man looked puzzled.

"A long story."

"Well, I hope you'll be stayin' long enough for me to hear it." Still smiling, the man turned expectantly toward Sienna. "And what a lovely lady you've brought along."

"Clint, this is my friend Beatrice. Beatrice, I want you to meet Clint Braddock."

"I'm one of Chase's biggest fans." Braddock's smile was even broader.

Sienna was tall enough that she wasn't used to looking up at most men, but for Braddock, she had to tilt her head back to look him in the eyes. His cowboy hat made him seem even taller. He had grainy tan skin and a bushy salt-and-pepper Zapata-style mustache.

"Clint, you did what I asked, right?" Malone's tone was serious. "You didn't tell anybody about my phone call. You didn't let anybody know I was coming."

"Hey, this is me, *compadre*, remember? When have I ever let you down? You're the man. What you say goes."

Malone visibly relaxed.

"But what's goin' on? When I offered to send the jet, you said you couldn't go near an airport. I couldn't help wonderin' if you're in trouble."

"You're not far wrong. Where's your car? I don't want to stand around in the open."

"Around the corner, pard. Where're your bags?"

"We don't have any."

The wrinkles around Braddock's eyes deepened. "Yeah, you're in trouble all right."

At the side of the depot, they reached an almost empty gravel parking lot, the prominent vehicle in which was a gleaming red pickup truck with fence posts in the back. As Braddock got in the driver's side, Malone guided Sienna toward the passenger door, whispering to her, "Don't let the drawl and the getup fool you. Clint's real first name is Peter. He was born and raised in Philadelphia."

"What?"

They got into the truck. "Clint, I was just explaining to my friend that you saw a lot of Westerns when you were a kid."

"And grew up to earn the bucks to live 'em." Braddock smiled. "See a movie, *be* a movie."

3

Bucks is right, Sienna thought, watching the grass-land stretch away. Every mile or so, a shade tree punctuated the view, but otherwise, there was only sky and land. And cattle, plenty of cattle. And then an oil pump, then another, and another, until hundreds cluttered the landscape, their armatures bobbing up and down. Braddock had been driving for a half hour before they got to a sprawling two-and-a-half-story white house. With a porch that went along almost the entire front, it made Sienna think she'd seen it before.

Then she realized she had.

"Recognize it?" Braddock asked.

"Wasn't this in that James Dean movie, *Giant*?" she asked in amazement.

"Sort of," Braddock said. "The real house is south of here on somebody else's spread. It's not even a real house. It's just a shell they built for exteriors and then let fall apart when they were done with the movie. So I had this replica built."

They drove through an arched entrance that had the word RIATA written across it, the same name as the ranch in *Giant*.

"With all your interest in the West," Malone said, "I never understood why you collected me instead of Remington or another western painter."

"Variety."

"And all the time I thought it was my genius."

"I didn't want you to get a swelled head." Braddock chuckled. "The truth is, little lady, the first time I saw Chase's work, I knew I had to own it."

Sienna understood after they parked on the curved driveway in front of the house, then crossed the lawn and the echoing porch to go inside. Braddock stayed outside to give instructions to one of his ranch hands, then joined them, enjoying the way Sienna admired the paintings on the walls.

There were at least twenty, all landscapes, all vibrant with color. She saw Chase's signature on the bottom of several and turned toward him in surprise. "How many of these are yours?"

Braddock answered for him. "All of them. I've got some in the dining room, too. How come you're surprised?"

"It's just . . . well, the only work of Chase's I've seen was a portrait of me. And some sketches of me and . . ." She looked at him in amazement. "I had no idea what your real work was like."

"The portrait of you was the best thing I've ever done," Chase said.

Braddock straightened. "Is it for sale?"

"I'm afraid that can't be arranged."

"Money's no object."

"It isn't with the man who owns it, either. Plus, there are"—Malone hesitated—"personal reasons for him to want to keep it."

"I've never seen paintings that make me feel so many other senses. I can almost smell the dew on the grass," Sienna said.

"You should have been an art critic."

"Don't joke."

"He's not," Braddock said. "You got the point right off. Chase's paintings celebrate life. You'd be a better art critic than those SOBs who don't know pretension from piss."

Sienna laughed.

"The two of you had breakfast?" Braddock asked.

"No."

"Why don't I tell the cook to fix you somethin'."

Sienna's stomach rumbled. She laughed again.

"But I warn you," Braddock said. "My cook's not one of those namby-pambies who worries all day about how much cholesterol's in his menus. He'll give you good honest bacon and eggs, hash browns and pancakes, or a breakfast burrito with salsa and refried beans."

"Sounds wonderful," Sienna said.

"Meantime, the biggest guest bedroom's to the left at the top of the stairs. The two of you go get yourselves cleaned up. The closet has extra clothes in various sizes. I like to keep spares for my guests. I'm bettin' you'll find this or that to fit you."

"Thanks," Sienna said.

"Then we'll get down to business"—Braddock directed his gaze firmly at Chase—"and find out what kind of trouble you're in."

4

Sienna bit into a chunk of burrito stuffed with eggs, rice, beans, and sausage. "Great. Especially the sausage. I've never tasted anything like it."

"Chorizo. It's Mexican," Braddock said. "Not too hot for you?"

"I can't get enough of it." She spooned more green chili over the burrito.

"Yeah, you've got fiery skin. A lady after my own heart."

Malone raised his spoon from a bowl of refried

beans topped with red chili and melted cheese. "What I need," he said, "is a patron."

Braddock set down his coffee and waited for him to continue.

"Somebody to subsidize me."

"What are you talkin' about?"

"Somebody to buy my paintings in advance."

Braddock narrowed his grizzled eyebrows. "You need cash that bad?"

"Things are a little tight."

"After everything I bought from you?" Braddock pointed toward the dining room wall across from him, where there were three other of Malone's paintings. "Over the years, I must've paid—what, six million? What on God's earth did you do with the money?"

"I still have it, but I can't get to it. As soon as I try, someone who's looking for us will know where we are."

Braddock squinted at Sienna, then back at Malone. "Somebody like a husband?"

Malone spread his hands.

Braddock's bushy eyebrows narrowed more severely. Then his head started to bob. He laughed. "Shoot, boy, why didn't you just say so? Twenty years ago, I had a situation along husband lines myself. I always had a suspicion you and I were alike. You want some travelin'-around money while he cools off, is that what you're askin'?"

"Maybe more than just traveling-around money. He's not going to cool off for quite a while. In fact, I don't think he's *ever* going to cool off."

Braddock studied Sienna for several seconds, then nodded pensively. "Yeah, I can see why. This husband—you can't use offshore accounts to dodge him?"

"I wouldn't dare try," Malone said, "and I'd never risk getting a friend to do it for me."

"But isn't that what you're doin' right now, askin' a friend?"

"To pay me in advance for paintings I'll deliver."

"Assumin' you live to complete 'em," Braddock said.

Sienna felt the color drain from her face.

"It's that serious, right?" Braddock asked. "Your husband's a player."

"Yes."

"Who doesn't believe in rules."

"Yes."

Braddock thought a moment, then whistled to himself, low and pensively. "How much do you need?"

"A million dollars."

Braddock didn't even blink.

"In cash. Hundreds," Malone said.

"Exactly what am I gonna get for this lavish amount?"

"Ten paintings."

"*Ten.*"

"That's a hundred thousand apiece."

"I never paid less than two hundred thousand for any of your work."

"Call it a fire sale."

"If word gets around, if you do this with any of your other collectors, you'll drive down the market."

"You're the only one I approached," Malone said. "The only one I'll *ever* approach."

"Where do you figure to hide?"

"You don't want to know."

Braddock thought about it. "You're right. And you don't want me to know, either. In case somebody comes around."

Sienna broke her silence. "How can we be sure someone won't?" She looked at Malone. "One of your biggest collectors. Isn't it logical that my husband will make the connection and wonder if we asked for help?"

"Nobody knows I'm one of Chase's biggest collectors," Braddock said. "One of the reasons I'm successful is, I don't let people know my business."

"Then you'll do it?" Malone asked.

Braddock thought about it. "With a condition."

"Name it."

"One of the works has to be of . . ." Braddock looked at Sienna. "I assume your real name isn't Beatrice."

"No." She sounded apologetic.

"I'd like one of the paintings to be of you."

"Don't worry." Malone smiled. "In a way, she *is* Beatrice. From now on, I'll be doing a *lot* of paintings of her."

5

"Thank you." Sienna kissed Braddock's cheek.

It was ten the next morning. The sky was bright. The breeze smelled fresh. Malone, Sienna, and Braddock stood on the front porch.

He rubbed his skin where she'd kissed him, then blushed. "Shoot, that's almost fair-enough payment for what I gave you."

Malone held the money in a brown suitcase that Braddock had supplied. Ten thousand one-hundred-dollar bills took up less room than Malone had expected—and weighed less: only about twenty pounds. To fill out the suitcase, Braddock had added some denim shirts and jeans in Malone's size. Sienna's suitcase contained similar basic articles of clothing.

"As soon as we settle somewhere, I'll get to work," Malone said. "In a month or two, you'll start receiving paintings."

"No rush. Whenever inspiration strikes."

"I've got plenty of that." Malone smiled at Sienna. "By the way, Clint, wherever I ship the paintings from won't be where we're staying."

"I figured. I'm also figurin' I won't see you for a while."

Malone shrugged.

"Maybe a *long* while."

Malone looked away.

"Be careful, my friend," Braddock said.

"Believe me, I'm going to try."

A silent moment lengthened.

"I guess we'd better get moving," Malone finally said. His mouth was dry from emotion. He shook hands with Braddock—firmly.

As he and Sienna got into the car, his chest ached with the regret of severing this connection. It's a good thing I don't have close family, he thought. I'd need to sever those connections, too.

Then he realized he was wrong—he *did* have close family. He studied Sienna as she got into the car, wishing he had the time to sketch how she looked this morning. It wasn't just that the white blouse Braddock had found for her brought out the quality of her skin and the luster in her hair. It was something deeper, something that he knew he would never stop wanting to draw.

6

The car was an eight-year-old Ford Explorer that Braddock had bought from one of his ranch hands for more money than the man had ever seen at one time in his life. It had a dented front fender and spewed foul black smoke, but it would get them where they needed to go.

The wallet Malone had taken from the dead man contained ID for Dale Perry. In Abilene, Malone used it to get a Texas driver's license in Perry's name. He registered the Explorer in Perry's name.

They headed west.

7

Yuma, Arizona. Malone had been there twelve years earlier on a military training exercise at the Marine Corps Air Station on the edge of town. During the summer, the city was small, about fifty thousand people, but during the winter, the population doubled, the area's sunny climate and the Colorado River attracting snowbirds from the north, most of whom stayed in trailer parks. At the end of March, the city was still booming.

Malone and Sienna rented a self-storage unit and stuffed it with old tables and bureaus, the furniture in such poor condition that anyone who broke in would curse and go on to other targets. In back was an old chest, in which Malone hid the suitcase containing the million dollars.

He locked the pull-down metal door, gave Sienna one key, and pocketed the other. With the twenty thousand dollars they kept, they went to various banks, avoiding attention by never exchanging more than two thousand at any one place. Where they were going, twenty thousand in pesos would last them quite a while.

They loaded up on things they might need, then

headed south, reaching the Mexican border in forty minutes. The crossing was at a city called San Luis, where the Mexican guards barely looked at the Explorer. It was the same casual attitude Malone recalled from when he had crossed the border years earlier while on leave from military exercises in Yuma. Normally, visitors driving a vehicle into Mexico needed a tourist card and a temporary vehicle import permit, but Malone's destination was part of an area called the Sonoran Free Trade Zone, and such documents weren't necessary. The length of visits was unrestricted. Even if these guards *had* decided to stop and search the Explorer, Malone wouldn't have cared. He had nothing incriminating. The handgun he had taken from Dale Perry's body was down a sewer in Yuma.

The city gave way to small farms. Then the farms became sporadic until there was only sand and tufts of grass.

"Smell it?" Malone asked.

"What?"

The Gulf of California separated mainland Mexico from its western peninsula, Baja California. In his youth, Malone had been surprised to learn how close the Pacific Ocean was to southern Arizona—less than two hours away—and had never forgotten driving down to it.

"The moist air. The salt smell. We ought to have a glimpse of the sea over the next rise."

Instead, they faced a military roadblock.

Sienna tensed.

"Take it easy," Malone said. "They're looking for drugs smuggled in by boat. They're interested in vehicles coming *from* the sea, not toward it."

Each side of the barricade had three armed soldiers. On the opposite side of the road, a battered pickup truck was being searched. The officer in charge, a mustached, lean-faced captain, watched from behind mirrored sunglasses.

Sienna wore sunglasses also. A droopy straw hat. No makeup. She'd done everything practical to conceal her features without being conspicuous about it. Nonetheless, Malone worried that the guards would sense how attractive she was and want to take a look. His worry turned out to be groundless. The soldiers were so interested in what was going on with the pickup truck that they waved him on.

Looking in the rearview mirror, Malone saw the captain watching the Explorer drive away.

"There," he told Sienna. "No problem."

8

"I see it!" Sienna pointed to the right, where a distant sheet of blue glinted from reflected sunlight.

The road paralleled the water, gradually narrowing the space between. In a couple of miles, buildings appeared, then palm trees, the outskirts of a town. Malone drove past a convenience store and a car-repair shop. A sand-colored two-story house had a red-tiled roof. The house beside it was made from cinder blocks. Next came a refuse-littered lot, and after that, a shack. That was the pattern: expensive houses next to poor ones in a seaside community that didn't have the pretensions of a beach resort. Farther into town, the pavement ended, the wide road turning to sand. On the right was an open square with benches underneath shade trees, flanked by a police station and a small grocery store. On the left, past a chain-link fence, was a row of one-room school buildings, each well maintained, the grounds immaculate, as were the children playing at recess.

"This is Santa Clara," Malone said. "It's a fishing village that got discovered by Americans with motor homes who were looking for a place to take cheap vacations. So many Americans come and go down here, we won't look out of place. In fact, as long as we stay to ourselves and contribute to the local economy, we'll be welcome."

"Staying to ourselves is definitely what I want to do."

A few streets veered to the left, but most led to the right toward palm trees and clapboard bars and restaurants along the sea. Malone ignored these turnoffs, driving straight ahead, passing a row of RV parks, finally stopping when there were no further buildings, only sand. And the sea.

"This is the end of the road," he said.

"So we're going to drive back to town and find a place to stay?" Sienna asked.

"Not exactly. Why don't we get out and stretch our legs."

Baffled, Sienna followed him across the sand until they reached where the waves lapped at their shoes. Seagulls glided overhead. In the distance, the specks of low motorized fishing boats bobbed in the water. The sun was hot, the sky as blue as the sea.

Malone savored the salt smell. "God, I love living near water." For a moment, he was reminded of what Bellasar had done to his home on Cozumel.

He calmed himself. "Up this far, near the tip of the gulf, we're close to Baja California. If you look real hard, you can see the opposite shore. It's kind of hazy today, but you should be able to see the rocky cliffs. They're about five miles away. Farther south, the gulf's a lot wider—as much as a hundred miles."

Malone pivoted to study the northern shoreline, where pickup trucks hooked cables to fishing boats and pulled them onto the sand. "The town's bigger than when I was here twelve years ago. Two of those RV parks weren't here, or that restaurant with the outdoor dining area. But that's to be expected."

What he *hadn't* expected was that the seaside part of town would look run-down. Sun shelters made of poles supporting palm fronds had toppled, as had a concrete retaining wall. Chain-link fences leaned. Carports had collapsed. What on earth had happened? Then he realized. "They had a hurricane last year. I remember how powerful the newspapers said it was. They're still digging out from the wreckage. I imagine it'll take a while."

But Sienna didn't look anywhere he pointed. She just stared at him. "What do you mean we're not going back into town to find a place to stay?"

"We're going somewhere else."

"Didn't you say this was the end of the road?"

"Yes."

"Then . . ."

Malone hesitated. He'd prepared her for everything except this. "We agreed that the only way to get away from your husband and Laster is to go to the end of the earth and pull the edges in after us."

She nodded.

"Down here, American drifters are part of the economy. If somebody wonders where you came from, you can tell whatever lie you want, and nobody'll think twice or be the wiser. The locals don't care where your money comes from, and they don't ask for Social Security numbers. But just to be extra safe . . ." Malone turned toward the southern shore and the widening gulf. "I wonder if there isn't an even better edge of the world. When I was here the last time, a villager was renting out dune buggies. One of my buddies and I drove along this shore. There's nothing for fifteen miles. Then just before the beach runs out, there's a fishing camp."

"You mean a village."

"Smaller. Maybe a dozen trailers. It's simple. The scenery's spectacular. The people who live there are loners. There'll be no one to account to or to bother us."

For a moment, the only sound was the distant drone of a motorboat.

"That's where you'd like to go?" Sienna asked.

Malone couldn't decide if her tone was dismay. "It's as perfect a place to disappear as I can think of. Then we'll figure out our next move."

She seemed lost.

"It's not forever. A man in your husband's line of work, there's a good chance the authorities or one of his competitors will get to him. We just have to survive long enough for that to happen."

"Surviving is Derek's specialty."

A sober moment lengthened. Sienna looked at him. Looked at the sea. Looked east past the sand dunes. "What's on that hill?"

"A lighthouse. The locals told me it was abandoned."

"Can we climb to it?"

"Of course, but it'll take us the rest of the day to get there and back."

"Not today."

It was Malone's turn to look puzzled.

"Later," she said. "After we get settled."

". . . You're willing to stay?"

"My life's been too complicated for a very long time. I kept telling myself I had to simplify." She took his hand.

"It won't be like we're hermits." Malone squeezed her fingers. "If we want some nightlife, we can go into town. The last time I was here, the restaurants were good. The town has fiestas. People do come here for vacations, after all. Let's try it. If it doesn't work out, we'll find somewhere else."

9

The four-wheel-drive Explorer had no trouble on the hard-packed sand. With the windows open and the breeze ruffling her hair, Sienna smiled as they drove along the unmarked beach. "I feel like we're the first ones to do this."

"Lewis and Clark."

She chuckled. "Captain Kirk. 'Where no one has gone before.' "

To keep the tires from digging into the sand, they didn't drive faster than twenty miles an hour. The slow, smooth, almost hypnotic ride took forty minutes before they came around a final dune and stopped where a rocky outcrop blocked the way farther south.

The camp didn't look the way Malone remembered it. The dozen or so trailers he had seen twelve years earlier had been reduced to two, one of which was tilted, partially buried by sand. The other had an awning extending from it. A fishing net hung on a wall, faded shorts, jeans, and other laundry dangling from it. In front, a char-filled fire pit was surrounded by blackened rocks. A motorboat had been hauled up onto the beach. A sun-wizened Mexican man worked on its engine while two children stopped scampering in the waves and looked warily toward Malone and

Sienna as they got out of the Explorer. A pensive woman appeared in the trailer's doorway, assessing the new arrivals.

Malone gestured reassuringly to her and walked with Sienna to the motorboat.

The man's face was so sun-creased, he might have been anywhere from forty to sixty. His hands were gnarled from years of working with fishing lines. The logo on his baseball hat had faded so much, it was impossible to read.

In Spanish, Malone introduced themselves as Dale and Beatrice Perry. He offered his hand.

The man looked suspiciously at it, then shook it, his calluses palpable. His name was Fernando, he said.

"The last time I came here, twelve years ago, there were more people," Malone said. "What happened?"

Malone listened, then told Sienna, "He says the hurricane last summer was very bad. The Americans with trailers got away before it arrived. They never came back. It killed one fisherman and scared the others enough to leave. *They* never came back, either. The hurricane season will soon start again. The other fishermen don't want to be around when it does."

"So we've pretty much got the place to ourselves?"

"Yes, better than we hoped." Malone turned toward Fernando. "My wife and I were thinking about camping here for a while. Would you object?"

Fernando seemed pleased that Malone had used *usted,* the formal word for "you." People could come and go as they liked, he said.

"But we want to be good neighbors. Maybe you

could use some help with the boat. Maybe we could contribute something in exchange for being here." Malone reached into his shirt pocket and removed a pack of cigarettes. Although he didn't smoke, he knew they could be handy as gifts.

As Fernando smoked one, they discussed the weather, the boat, and other seemingly casual subjects.

When Fernando finished the cigarette, he pinched off the end and pocketed the remnant of tobacco. Pointing toward the tilted trailer partially buried in the sand, he explained something.

"What did he tell you?" Sienna asked.

"That the trailer isn't as damaged as it looks. He says that with the four-wheel-drive vehicle we have, we can pull the trailer upright, repair it, and live in it."

"*Gracias,*" she told Fernando.

10

It was as near to paradise as Malone had ever come: swimming, sailing, fishing, hiking, or merely lying in a hammock, reading. But most of all, it was painting, trying to capture something in Sienna's eyes that had become his single goal to depict.

Beatrice indeed.

Sometimes, Fernando's ten-year-old boy came over and looked spellbound at Malone's images of her.

"Would you like to learn to do this?"

The boy nodded solemnly. One lesson turned into several. The boy went around with a sketch pad, drawing everything he saw, as if he'd discovered magic.

At night, as Malone and Sienna lay in bed together, she whispered, "You have a way with children."

"With one child, anyhow," he joked.

"Be serious. It's a nice thing you're doing."

"Well, he's a good kid."

"But what you're teaching him isn't simple. You know how to get a child to listen. You'd make a good father."

"Make a . . . Wait a minute. Are you telling me you want to have a child?"

"The thought crossed my mind."

"With all the trouble we're in . . ."

"I didn't say right now. But if we weren't in trouble, how would you feel about . . ."

"Having a child with you?"

"Yes."

"If it would make you happy."

"Happier."

In the night, they held each other, not doing anything else, just holding.

11

At his table on the château's terrace, his coffee and croissant untasted, Potter listened to the roar of the machine gun. His face felt tight. His eyes were gritty.

To be expected. After all, the machine gun had wakened him before dawn, as it had on the previous morning and the morning before that. On occasion, it was interrupted by explosions and handgun fire, but mostly it was the machine gun. All day. Every day. Potter's nerves weren't the only ones affected. The guards looked on edge, interrupting their patrols to stare toward the shooting range and frown at one another.

Potter didn't understand how Derek's body, his hands, arms, and shoulders, could withstand the relentless punishment he subjected them to. The machine gun itself couldn't sustain it. Derek had already broken one tripod, destroyed two feeding mechanisms, and burned out a dozen barrels. In contrast, Derek's body showed no signs of wearing down, his fury so great that only if he didn't vent it would he suffer physically.

Derek's emotions were another matter. Potter had never seen him so distraught. From the day Sienna had escaped with Malone, Derek had been unable to concentrate on anything except revenge. Important business matters went unattended. He haunted the weapons-testing range, firing every weapon he could get his hands on, reducing the mock village to rubble, ordering his men to rebuild it, then reducing it to rubble again, not a wall or a house remaining. When overuse broke the weapons, he screamed at his engineers to design them better and to bring him others to test. When he tired of firearms, he changed to grenades and rocket launchers, the enraged expression on his face demonstrating the schemes of revenge he imagined.

Potter finally couldn't bear it. He rose from the table and made his way along a path to the testing range. He saw Derek bent over the machine gun, cursing as he yanked at its firing mechanism but couldn't get it to eject a jammed shell. Derek wore earplugs, so he didn't know Potter was in the area until Potter stepped in front of him.

Rage swelled Derek's body, giving him an even more imposing presence than usual. His huge eyes were dark with fury. *"Have you found them?"*

"No. We're still looking. You have to stop this, Derek. You're due in Miami tomorrow."

"Find them, damn it!" Derek freed the jammed cartridge and fired at a mannequin that moved along a track, blowing it to pieces. *"Find them!"*

12

The restaurant was called El Delfin—the Dolphin. It was a couple of blocks from the beach, on a sandy street: a dingy one-story building with an orange shingled roof and an air conditioner braced in a window. An utterly unassuming place, with the exception that it served the best food in Santa Clara.

At dusk, Malone and Sienna opened the restaurant's screen door and stepped onto the faded linoleum floor. For a moment, all the tables seemed occupied. Then Malone noticed an empty one in back on the right-hand side. He noticed something else: a Mexican military captain talking with three male civilians. The captain had a lean, sallow, mustached face that reminded Malone of a hawk. He had a pair of mirrored sunglasses, folded, hanging from a shirt pocket by one of the bows.

"Behind you," Sienna said as she and Malone sat across from each other.

"Yes," Malone said. "The officer from the road-block. No big deal. Everybody's got to eat."

When the waitress came, they each ordered a beer, then studied the wrinkled single-sheet menu.

Malone reached across the table and grasped her hand. "Hungry?"

"Famished. This shrimp dish sounds good."

"I recommend it," a voice said.

They turned.

The captain stood next to their table.

"Then I'll have it," Malone said.

"Captain Ramirez." The man smiled pleasantly as he held out his hand.

Malone shook it. "Dale Perry."

"Beatrice Perry." Sienna shook his hand.

"A pleasure."

Malone noticed that Ramirez looked to see if she wore a wedding ring. They had bought two before they left Yuma.

"I apologize for interrupting, but I like to say hello to our visitors from the United States. It gives me a chance to practice my English."

"Which is very good."

Ramirez made a modest gesture.

"Would you care to join us?" Malone asked.

"Perhaps for a minute or two. *Una otra cerveza*," Ramirez told the waitress, then pulled out a chair and sat next to Malone. "Are you enjoying your visit?"

"Very much."

"You don't find it a little hot this time of year? Most of your countrymen have left by now."

"Actually, we like it hot," Malone said.

"You must have fire in your blood."

"Only when I was a teenager."

"Yes, to be a teenager again." Ramirez chuckled. "Mrs. Perry, most of the Americans who come down here are retired. It's rare to see a woman from the north who's so young." He paused. "And so beautiful."

She looked uncomfortable. "Thank you."

"You're obviously too young to have retired. Perhaps you won the lottery."

"Don't we wish. Dale was a commercial artist in Abilene, Texas." The practiced story accounted for their Texas car plate and driver's license. "But a couple of months ago, the company went out of business."

"Unfortunate," Ramirez said.

"Dale always wanted to be a painter. When the company folded, I told him it was God's way of urging him to follow his heart. We took our life savings and drove across the Southwest, stopping when Dale saw something he wanted to paint. Eventually we headed down here."

"You're an understanding woman—to go along with your husband's dreams."

"All I want is what makes him happy."

"I'm sure you do."

"What?"

"Make him happy."

The waitress brought the beers.

As Ramirez picked his up, an anxious soldier entered the restaurant and motioned for Ramirez to step outside.

Ramirez nodded, then turned to Sienna. "As you can see, I must leave."

"Nice chatting with you," Malone said.

But Ramirez kept his eyes totally on Sienna. "The pleasure was mine. *Nos vemos.*"

As Ramirez walked to the door, Sienna asked, "What did he just say?"

" 'We'll see each other.' "

The screen door banged shut behind Ramirez and the soldier.

Everybody in the place had been watching the conversation. Now they went back to their meals.

Sienna leaned close to Malone, pretending to murmur endearments. "I think I'm going to be sick."

"Take a deep breath."

"All the while he was sitting there, I was sure I was going to throw up." A film of sweat slicked her face. "Did it show? What the hell was he doing?" She kept her voice down, afraid she'd be overheard.

"I have no idea." Doing his best to look relaxed, Malone took a long swallow of beer and wished it were stronger.

"At least, he didn't ask to see your ID."

"Which means he can't have been that interested in us. Maybe he just felt like jerking some gringos' chains. But he certainly had a lot of questions. He knows almost as much as if he *had* looked at my ID."

"You're not reassuring me," Sienna said.

"I'm not reassuring myself."

"I'm not kidding. I'm sick. Let's get out of here."

"We can't."

"What?"

"Suppose he sees us come out. He'll wonder why he upset us so much that we didn't stay for dinner."

"Jesus."

"We don't have a choice," Malone said.

When the waitress returned, they ordered the shrimp. Malone gave Sienna credit. She did what was necessary and ate what was on her plate. On the way back to the trailer, she had to get out and throw up.

13

She didn't sleep. Lying in the darkness, she stared at the ceiling and hoped that the lapping of the waves would soothe her, but the calm they usually gave wouldn't come. Maybe Ramirez *was* just practicing his English, she tried to assure herself. The area depends on tourism, after all. Why would he bother two of the few visitors still remaining in town? It doesn't make sense. He was just being friendly.

Sure, she thought.

But she couldn't shake the apprehension that what had happened at the restaurant was the same as what had happened at every fashion show and modeling assignment she'd ever been a part of, at every party, at every . . . It didn't matter that she hadn't worn makeup, that she hadn't taken off her hat, and that she had kept her gaze downward. Ramirez had come over to their table because of her looks.

"We have to get out of here," she told Chase in the morning. The haggardness around her eyes showed how little she'd slept, yet she didn't look as plain as she wanted to be.

Outside, as they loaded the Explorer, the sound of an approaching engine made her turn. At first, she thought it was a motorboat. But as she scanned the waves, movement farther along caught her attention. Not on the water—on the shore. A military Jeep. Its top was down, showing that the only person in it was the driver. Her muscles compacted when she saw twin glints of light reflecting off mirrored sunglasses.

14

As Ramirez parked next to the trailer, Fernando's wife urged her children into their trailer. Her panicked reaction gave Ramirez a look of satisfaction as he got out of his vehicle and straightened his sunglasses. His uniform was pressed stiffly, emphasizing his taut stomach and rigid back. His pistol was prominent on his right side. Unsmiling, he approached the trailer. "Good morning."

"*Buenos dias,*" Malone said, trying to sound friendly.

"Please, in English." The contrast between Ramirez's polite words and his stern expression was vivid. "I so enjoyed our conversation yesterday evening that I regretted having to leave. I decided to pay you a visit."

Malone spread his hands in a welcoming gesture.

"You weren't easy to find." Ramirez concentrated on Sienna.

Malone imagined the effect she had on him. Without the hat she had worn in the restaurant, her beauty was striking. Despite her restless sleep, her skin had a smoldering quality.

"You so impressed me with the sacrifice you're willing to make for your husband's artistic career, I thought I'd come and see his paintings," Ramirez said.

"They're not as good as I'd like," Malone said, "but—"

"Nonsense. I'm sure you're being too critical." Ramirez turned toward a canvas leaning against the Explorer, where Malone had been about to load it. "Getting ready to leave?"

"A day trip up the coast. There's an area I want to paint."

"But you said you did landscapes. This is a painting of your wife."

"Every once in a while, I do one of her."

"I've never seen anything so beautiful." From the curve of Sienna's hips, waist, and breasts in the portrait, he turned toward the real thing. "I'm surprised you don't live in town, Mrs. Perry. Aren't you lonely down here?"

"Dale says he doesn't want to be distracted."

"I should think *you* would distract him."

"We enjoy the peace and quiet."

"And to tell the truth," Malone said, "we're trying to save money. In Santa Clara, we'd have to pay rent."

Ramirez kept his attention on Sienna. "What do you do for amusement, Mrs. Perry?"

She looked more puzzled. "Swim. Read. Go sailing."

"And that's enough?"

"In Abilene, we were always worried about Dale's job. Then the worst happened, and we didn't have to worry anymore. A simple life has been very satisfying."

"To make up for my early departure last evening, I'd like you to be my guest for dinner."

"Certainly. Dale and I would be honored."

"Actually, the invitation was only for . . ." Ramirez aimed his mirrored sunglasses at Malone. "May I see your tourist card?"

"Tourist card?" Malone looked baffled. "But we don't need one here. Santa Clara's part of the Sonoran Free Trade Zone."

"That's correct. But this isn't Santa Clara. You don't live in the Free Trade Zone. Your tourist card, please." Ramirez held out his hand.

"We don't have one."

"That presents a problem," Ramirez said.

"It certainly does. We'd better drive back to the border and pick one up."

"That won't be necessary."

"But you just said—"

"I have business at the border. I'll obtain a tourist card for you."

Malone frowned. "But don't they have to be picked up in person?"

"I'll see that an exception is made."

"That's very generous."

"Not at all." Ramirez stared again at Sienna. "It'll give me a chance to visit again. But I have to verify your names. The immigration officer I obtain the card from will need to be assured of your identities. May I see your driver's license, Mr. Perry?"

". . . Of course." Malone pulled out his wallet and handed over the license.

Ramirez looked at the photograph of Malone that the Texas clerk had laminated onto the license. He read the name. "Dale Perry. An excellent likeness." He put the license in his shirt pocket.

"Wait a minute. Why are you—"

"I need to keep this so I can present it as corroboration when I get the tourist card."

"But—"

"It's strictly a formality. I'll return it as soon as possible. You weren't planning to drive out of the area, were you?"

"No."

"Then you won't be needing it."

15

"He wants me," Sienna said.

"Yes."

Numb, they watched Ramirez drive along the shore toward Santa Clara.

"He'll run Dale Perry's name through the computer to see if there's anything he can use against me." Sienna found it impossible to take her gaze from the receding Jeep. "To demand sex from me."

"Yes."

"By now, whoever Perry worked for knows his wallet is missing. Either my husband or Laster will have computer specialists checking for anybody who tries to use Perry's credit cards or his Social Security number."

"Yes."

"We'll soon have company." As Ramirez's Jeep disappeared into the heat haze, Sienna was finally released from staring at it. Her mouth was dry. "So what in God's name are we going to do?"

"You said it earlier—leave."

"But how? There's only one road to the border.

There's a roadblock. Ramirez will have his men watching for us."

Chase turned to the south toward the rocky bluff where the beach ended. "I wasn't thinking of the road."

"You want to go around that and walk to the next town?" She referred to Puerto Peñasco, a hundred miles to the south. "That would take days. In this heat, we might not make it. Besides, by then Ramirez would have figured out what we were doing. He'd have soldiers waiting when we got there."

"I wasn't thinking of walking."

"Then . . ."

Chase stared toward the gulf.

With a tingle, she understood.

"When Fernando comes back from fishing, I'll pay him to take us down to Puerto Peñasco," Chase said. "We'll be there in a couple of hours. Ramirez won't have time to get back here by then and realize what we're doing. We'll find an American. A hard-luck story and a couple of hundred dollars ought to get us a ride to the States."

"But what about Fernando? Ramirez will suspect he helped us. We'll be putting Fernando in danger."

"Not if Fernando claims I made him do it. In fact, I've got a better idea. We'll pay him to let us have the boat. He'll tell Ramirez we stole it and ask a friend to take him down to Puerto Peñasco to get it back."

They studied each other.

"We don't have a choice." Sienna's voice was unsteady.

"It's going to be okay." Chase held her. "By tonight, we'll be back in the States. We'll take a bus to Yuma, get our money out of the storage locker, and find another place as good as this."

She held him tighter, wanting to believe him.

"There are other places at the edge of the earth," Chase said. "By tonight, this will have been just another nightmare we put behind us."

"Sure."

"Don't sound so low. I promise we'll get out of this." He kissed her, his affection flowing into her. "Come on, let's hurry and pack so we're ready when Fernando returns. We don't want to waste time."

Time, she thought.

16

They left most of their things, putting only essential toiletries and a change of clothes in their knapsacks. Sienna set them against the kitchen door. She couldn't repress her wistful feelings as she peered back at the trailer. It had been their home.

They split the pesos they had remaining—sixteen thousand dollars' worth. Sienna shoved some into the jeans she had put on in place of her shorts. She stuffed most of it into her knapsack. Chase stuffed his half into the front pockets of a khaki fisherman's jacket that he had worn on the days he had gone out with Fernando on his boat.

"Any sign of him?" Sienna asked.

"Not yet."

"It's three o'clock. Isn't he usually back by now?"

"Fernando says the early hours are best for fishing."

"Then where *is* he?"

"Having a better day than we are. Relax. It won't be long."

But three o'clock became four, then five. As the sun began its descent, Sienna fidgeted. "Ramirez will be back here soon. Or someone from my husband, or—"

"Maybe Fernando had an accident."

"If he doesn't hurry, *we're* going to have an accident."

She kept staring toward the northern shore, expecting a military Jeep to appear.

Six o'clock. Seven. The sun hung lower.

Smoke made her glance toward Fernando's trailer, where his wife prepared a meal in the charcoal pit. Afraid of the military, she had remained inside for a long time after Ramirez had left. When she finally came out, she had stopped her children from approaching the trailer and had cast suspicious glances toward it.

"She thinks we brought trouble," Chase said.

"We're about to bring more."

"I hear an engine."

A motorboat appeared, getting larger, Fernando working the rudder.

"Thank God," Sienna said.

They ran to the beach as Fernando steered into shore. Chase waded in to help him, dragging the boat onto the sand. By now, Sienna had learned enough Spanish that she understood when Chase told him, "We were worried about you."

But Fernando's reply was too rapid, and she needed Chase to explain that Fernando had been delayed because of a meeting in Santa Clara with the company to which he sold his fish.

As Fernando set an anchor to keep the boat from floating away during high tide, he frowned toward his somber wife, who approached from the shelter. "What's wrong?" he asked in Spanish.

Fernando frowned harder when his wife described the visit from the military. Fernando's confusion became dismay when Chase explained that he and Sienna wanted to rent his boat, take it down to Puerto Peñasco, and leave it there for him to retrieve.

"No." Fernando's wife held up her hands.

"I'll give you five hundred dollars," Chase said.

"No!"

"Seven hundred."

"No!" The woman tugged Fernando toward their trailer.

"A thousand."

It was probably more money than Fernando had ever seen at one time. He blurted something before his wife hustled him inside.

"He says he'll try to talk to her," Chase told Sienna.

"He'd better do more than try." Sienna stared again toward the northern shore. Although the sunset was less brilliant, there was still enough light to see if any vehicles were coming. "If he doesn't want to rent it to us, we'll take the damned thing. I won't spend the night here."

"I'll tempt them with more cash," Malone said.

"Give it *all* to them. Just so we get out of here."

They crossed the sand to the trailer. From outside, they heard Fernando and his wife arguing. When Chase knocked on the door, the wife shouted, "Go away!"

But Chase opened the door anyhow and stepped in, noticing the frightened looks of the children.

"Translate for me," Sienna said.

She tried to explain how afraid she was that her husband would find her.

The wife put her hands over her ears.

"To hell with her," Sienna said. "Distract them while I get the knapsacks and put them in the boat."

She hurried outside. Clouds obscured the sunset as she ran to their trailer, yanked open the screen door, and reached for the knapsacks.

A hand shot from the shadows, grabbing her arm.

17

"Good evening, Mrs. Perry."

Ramirez dragged her into the gloom of the trailer. As tight as his hand was on her arm, she felt a greater tightness in her throat, a sensation of being strangled.

"Or should I call you Mrs. Bellasar?"

"What are you talking about?" she managed to say, her voice hoarse.

Facing her, Ramirez twisted her arm behind her back. Making her wince, he drew her close to him. "You don't need to be afraid. I haven't told anybody about you." He pressed her against him. "I did a computer search. I learned your real names. I learned that the CIA is looking for you. But don't worry. I broke contact. Your secret is mine." He put his other arm around her. "But what *is* the secret? Why is the CIA looking for you? What would you do to reward me for not reporting that I'd found you?"

He brought his mouth toward hers. She turned away and struggled. He redirected his mouth, trying to reach her lips. When she pulled her head back, he squeezed her tighter. She stomped on his boot.

He hit her.

For a moment, she saw blackness. Then he hit her again, and suddenly she was on the floor. Through blurred vision, she saw him reach back his boot to kick her, and for a frenzied moment, she thought he was Derek, that she was back in the hotel room in Istanbul, that Derek was kicking her and—

Something slammed. A figure rushed past. As her mind stopped spinning, she realized that the noise was the trailer's door, that the figure was Chase, that he had collided with Ramirez and knocked him onto the kitchen table.

When the table collapsed, toppling them onto the floor, Sienna looked desperately around, hoping to find something she could use to hit Ramirez. In the gloom, Chase and Ramirez were indistinguishable, rolling one way, then another, striking each other. One of them groaned. Their breathing was forced. They struggled to their feet and slammed against the kitchen counter. A pot clattered into the sink. A dish smashed onto the floor.

Someone lurched back from a blow to the face and punched the other man's stomach. The second man staggered back. At once the man straightened, his silhouette clear against the twilight at the kitchen window. He raised his right hand. Something was in it. A pistol. Ramirez. Sienna opened her mouth to shout a warning. Too late. The gunshot was deafening. Ears ringing, Sienna could barely hear herself scream.

The bullet shattered a window. Chase struggled with Ramirez's gun arm, trying to wrench the weapon away as the pistol went off again, its muzzle flash almost blinding in the gloom. Her ears in greater pain, Sienna felt the bullet pass her, but all she cared about was squirming to the broken table and groping for one of its legs. The wide end had splintered, forming a spear tip. She plunged it into Ramirez's back. He screamed. The two men lost their balance. The pistol went off a third time as they fell to the floor.

Sienna grabbed another table leg, raising it to bash it across Ramirez's head, but away from the twilight at the window, she couldn't tell which man was Ramirez.

"Chase, where are you?"

"Here!"

She slammed the club against Ramirez's head so hard that the weapon split in half.

She picked up another table leg and struck him again, feeling something on his skull go soft, but he showed no reaction, remained motionless, seemed not to have felt it.

18

For long seconds, no one moved. The only sound was Malone's labored breathing. He couldn't stop his heart from racing.

"Is he dead?" Sienna struggled to get the words out.

"Yes."

Hot bile rose in her throat.

"Are you okay?" he asked.

"I think . . ." She wiped blood from her mouth. "I'm all right."

Outside, thunder rumbled in the distance, a storm coming up the gulf.

Malone braced himself against the counter. "Why didn't we hear his Jeep?"

"It isn't outside. He must have parked on the beach and snuck up."

The thunder rumbled louder.

They held each other.

"He called me Mrs. Bellasar."

"Jesus."

"He said he'd done a computer search." Her shoulders heaved. "He knew that the CIA is looking for us."

"If he put Dale Perry's name into the computer, you can bet it set off alarms in the Agency. By now, whoever told your husband we were at that Virginia safe house has passed along the news. Your husband will be coming." When thunder again rumbled, Malone stared toward the window. "We don't have much time."

"But what about . . ." Sickened, she peered down at the body. "We can't just leave him. The Mexican police will connect him to us. The next thing, *they'll* be after us, too."

Malone strained to order his thoughts. "We'll tie something heavy to the body and dump it in the gulf. His Jeep. We've got to find it. I'll drive it to Santa Clara while you follow in the Explorer." His mind raced. "We'll make it seem like he parked on the edge of town. The storm and the tide will wipe out the tire tracks. If we're careful not to leave fingerprints, the police won't be able to prove we had anything to do with this."

"But the shots . . ."

"We're too far from town for anybody to have heard. Yes, Fernando must have, but he's too afraid of the authorities to tell what he knows." Ignoring how quickly Ramirez's body was turning cold, Malone searched the pockets. He found car keys, but they weren't enough. He needed Dale Perry's driver's license. Where *was* it? He *had* to find it. "There. Thank God." He pulled the license from the corpse's trouser pocket. "Hurry. Help me carry him to the boat before that storm comes any closer."

He grabbed the corpse's hands, started to lift, then realized that Sienna hadn't moved.

Spurred by a new burst of thunder, she grabbed the corpse's boots, shuddered, and lifted.

They lugged the body across the trailer. Malone was in the lead, backing toward the screen door. He nudged the door open with his hip. Then he got a better grip on the corpse and backed out, startled by a flash of lightning that revealed a look of terror on Sienna's face.

But not because of Ramirez. Something was behind him.

He turned.

A blaze of lightning revealed Bellasar, Potter, and three bodyguards.

"You should have known I'd find you," Bellasar said.

Sienna gasped.

"Taking out the garbage?" Bellasar asked.

Malone released the body and tried to straighten.

Not fast enough.

Potter slammed the barrel of a pistol across his forehead. "Let's deal with this garbage first."

19

Blood streaming down his face, Malone felt himself being lifted, two men carrying him into the darkness of the trailer. As if from a distance, he heard Bellasar demand something.

Sienna's answer was a murmur. Malone was too dazed to know what it was. At the moment, what he was most aware of was the force with which he was slammed onto a chair.

More indistinct voices. Something flickered. At first, Malone thought it was the lightning outside, his impaired vision barely registering it. But a second flicker and a third spread across the trailer, the darkness dissipating until he realized that what he was seeing were candles that Bellasar had made Sienna take from a drawer. She lit a fourth and a fifth. The trailer glowed.

"More portraits." Bellasar's features were twisted. He rammed a fist through an image of Sienna's face. "I've lost my enthusiasm for your work." Cursing, he threw the ruptured portrait into a corner, the frame shattering as it bounced off the wall. He went over to Malone and punched his face so hard that the chair fell over, sending him sprawling onto the floor. "Do you remember I warned you never to touch my wife?"

Malone was in too much pain to speak.

Thunder shook the trailer.

"Pick him up."

Hands yanked Malone to his feet.

"Hold him steady."

With pain-blurred vision, Malone saw Bellasar put on leather gloves.

"No!" Sienna shouted.

The blow to Malone's stomach would have doubled him over if Bellasar's men hadn't been holding him so rigidly. The next blow was aimed toward his nose, the one after that to his stomach again. His mouth. His—

The last thing he heard, passing out, was Sienna screaming.

20

"You're killing him!"

"That's the point." Derek drew back his fist again.

Sienna broke loose from the man holding her and grabbed Derek's arm before he could launch the blow. "I'm begging you!"

"You'll beg me a lot more when *your* turn comes."

"I don't care what you do to me! Let him live! If you ever had any feelings for me—"

When Derek shoved her across the room, she banged against a small table, knocking a candle onto the floor.

Wind shook the trailer.

"That storm's too close," Potter said.

On the floor, the candle continued to burn.

Chase's swollen face was covered with blood as Derek punched him again.

A few drops of rain pelted the metal roof.

"Get the car where we left it when we followed the Jeep," Potter ordered a guard.

The candle's flame spread to the carpet.

"Hurry," Potter told the guard, "before the storm hits and you can't find the car. I don't want to be stuck here."

The guard ran outside.

"Put out that fire," Potter told another guard.

"No," Derek said. "Let it burn. Let everything burn."

As smoke rose from the burning carpet, Derek hit Chase one more time, frowned at his blood-covered glove, and gestured for the men to let him go.

Chase collapsed on the kitchen floor.

When Sienna tried to run to him, Derek grabbed her.

Lightning cracked. More drops of rain pelted the trailer.

"Sounds like it's going to be bad," a guard said.

The flames spread across the carpet, reaching the portraits.

"Take a last look at him," Derek said, pulling her away.

Sienna shrieked. She couldn't stop shrieking. She felt as if her vocal cords were going to burst, and still she wailed as the flames rose higher and Derek dragged her toward the door.

Headlights glaring, a large four-wheel-drive vehicle pulled up, its windshield wipers flicking away the rain. Derek yanked her outside with a force that jerked her gaze from Chase.

Thrown into the vehicle, she scrambled to look through the rear window toward flames bursting from the smoke. As the vehicle sped away, the trailer disappeared into the darkness and the rain. Only the flames remained. Then they, too, disappeared, obscured by the blur of her tears.

NINE

1

A sharp noise from outside made Fernando swing toward the door.

His wife tensed. *"What was that?"* she asked in Spanish. "It sounded like . . ."

"A shot." Motioning for the children to stay back, Fernando cautiously opened the door. In the deepening twilight, he stared to his right toward Dale's trailer. The shot had been in that direction. But it didn't make sense. Dale and Beatrice wouldn't be shooting at each other. Had the military officer returned? Hearing a second shot and a third, Fernando stiffened.

"They need our help," he told his wife.

But his legs didn't want to move.

Thunder rumbled. To the south, dense black clouds approached.

But Fernando's attention was fixed to the north, where five men in suits walked swiftly through the gray light. They were about fifty yards away, rapidly narrowing the distance. One was short and stocky. Three were tall and heavy-chested. But the other, the one in the lead, although equally tall, radiated far more strength, scarily so. He had dark hair and sharply defined features stark with emotion. His angry march was relentless.

The thunder rumbled more loudly.

"It isn't safe here," Fernando said. "We have to go."

"But where?"

Fernando immediately thought of where they'd survived the previous summer's hurricane. "To the cave. Quickly. Bring the children."

He grabbed his son's hand and urged him from the trailer, hoping they wouldn't be seen as they darted around the side. Ignoring the lightning and the thunder, they raced through the deepening shadows toward a sand dune.

If we can get around it without being seen . . . Fernando prayed. He had never felt a more powerful premonition. Those men seemed enveloped by a greater darkness than the approaching storm. Chilled by more than the suddenly cold wind, he ran harder. Rounding the cover of the dune, he and his family rushed toward a rocky bluff and the small, almost hidden mouth of a cave.

But even after they reached the echoing shelter of its blackness, Fernando didn't feel safe. The cave was hard to see unless you knew where it was, especially with twilight about to turn to dark, but the footprints they'd left in the sand were another matter. If the men had flashlights . . .

Stop thinking like that, Fernando warned himself. Why should those men care about us? It's Dale and

Beatrice they're interested in. We mean nothing to them.

That's just the point. We mean nothing. If they noticed us, if they're worried that we'll be witnesses . . .

We can't just wait here to be killed.

"I have to hide our tracks!"

Rushing from the cave, Fernando reached where the footprints curved around the dune. He yanked off his shirt and dragged it over the footprints, stepping backward, trying to smooth the sand, but the force of the wind almost yanked his shirt away. A few drops of rain struck his bare skin, then *more* drops, their cold force stinging him.

I don't need to cover the tracks, he realized. The rain will do it for me.

But what if the men come before it does?

Lightning cracked, temporarily blinding him, making him feel exposed. As thunder rumbled and darkness again cloaked him, he hurried to the cover of the dune. Then the only sound was the shriek of the wind.

And a vehicle approaching.

Headlights blazed past the dune. Fernando heard the vehicle stop. The trailer's door slammed. Beatrice shrieked. There were sounds of a struggle. Then the doors on the vehicle slammed, and the headlights veered away.

It sounded as if the men had taken Beatrice.

But what about Dale?

Stung by colder rain, Fernando peered around the dune. As the vehicle's taillights disappeared into the darkness, he was startled by flames in the trailer's living room windows. Seeing a body outside the screen door, he scrambled toward the trailer, almost blown off balance by the wind-driven sand. The man was Dale, he was certain, but when he got there, he was surprised to find a man in a military uniform. Where was—

Fernando frowned through the screen door. The flames were on the right, in the living room, spreading to the left toward the kitchen and the bedroom. Raising an arm to shield his face from the heat, he stepped closer, able to see into the kitchen, to see Dale sprawled on the floor. Then the flames blocked the way.

He isn't moving. His face is covered with blood. He's probably dead. I'd be foolish to—

Before Fernando realized what he was doing, he raced to the left, around to the bedroom side of the trailer. When Dale had repaired the damage from last summer's hurricane, he had used a tarpaulin to seal a gap in the back corner of the bedroom. Fernando reached it and tore it free, the wind so fierce that it flipped the tarpaulin into the night. Drenched, Fernando forced himself into the narrow gap. Turning sideways, scraping his bare stomach and back, he squeezed into the bedroom.

Smoke drifted toward him, making him cough as he hurried around the bed. The doorway was filled with rippling, growing light. He felt the heat before he reached it and almost lost his nerve at the sight of the flames entering the kitchen. Jesus, Mary, and Joseph, he prayed, then darted forward. Feeling the fire singe his hair, he grabbed Dale's legs and pulled frantically toward the bedroom. He dragged him over the wreckage of a table, banged against a kitchen counter, and suddenly lost his balance. Falling backward but continuing to keep his grip on Dale's legs, he landed in the shadows of the bedroom, and although the heat was accumulating in there, he had never felt anything so welcomely cool. In a rush, he tugged Dale to the gap and positioned his head toward it. Rain gusted in. The wind shrieked. Heart racing, he squeezed outside, turned, and blanched when he saw that the flames had entered the bedroom.

He grabbed Dale's shoulders and pulled. Dale's head came through. Seeing the flames reach the bed, Fernando pulled harder. The wind filled his mouth, taking his breath away. Harder! he told himself. But Dale's chest was caught on something, the pockets of his fisherman's jacket so full they jammed him. Fernando shoved him back in. Unable to remove the jacket, he yanked its bulging flaps through the gap, then tugged again on Dale's shoulders, exhaling in triumph when Dale came toward him. Dale's chest was through. His stomach. His hips. With one last pull, Fernando fell backward, Dale landing next to him, the wind and rain overwhelming them.

But Fernando couldn't take the time to catch his breath. As the flames reached the gap, he lifted Dale to his feet, doubled him over his right shoulder, and staggered toward the other trailer. When he burst inside, leaving the storm behind, he set Dale on the floor and groped through the darkness to find a candle and light it. What he saw as the tiny flame grew made him moan in sympathy. Dale's face was raw, swollen with bruises. Not even the fierce rain had been able to wash the blood off. Fresh blood seeped from his nose, and Fernando shivered, not because of his wet clothes but because of excitement as he realized, Corpses don't bleed.

"My God, you're alive."

2

Pain roused him. It stabbed. It festered. It ached. His entire face was alive with it, pulsing with agony, about to burst. And his scalp. And his stomach, oh, Jesus, his stomach. And the right side of his chest hurt so . . .

As his nerve ends came back to life, the pain grew and dragged him from his delirium, prodding him into consciousness. His swollen eyelids struggled open, sending the tortured area around them into spasms. Among shadows, he saw a flickering light. The fire. He was lying in the trailer. The flames were about to reach him. Sienna. Where was . . . Moaning, he squirmed to get away from the flames. Hands grabbed him: Bellasar's men. A face appeared before him: Bellasar about to hit him again. He thrashed harder to get away, the effort intensifying his pain.

A distant voice said something he couldn't understand.

He struggled.

"Be still," the voice said.

In Spanish.

"You're safe," the voice said.

Malone opened his eyes a little more, seeing a face with gray beard stubble, wizened from years of working in the sun.

"You're safe," Fernando repeated.

Movement made Malone tense until he realized it was Fernando's wife touching his forehead with a cloth. Other movement made him glance toward a corner, where Fernando's children huddled, afraid.

Having trouble getting air through his nose, he opened his mouth, his jaw hurting, but when he expanded his chest to take a deep breath, the pain in his upper-right ribs was even worse.

Outside, wind shrieked. Rain lanced against the windows.

"Sienna," he managed to say. "Where . . ."

Fernando frowned, as if Malone had spoken gibberish.

Which I did, Malone realized. Not only had he spoken in English, but Fernando had never heard Sienna's name before. He knew her as Beatrice.

"Beatrice," Malone said. *"¿Donde está? ¿Qué pasa?"*

Fernando and Bonita exchanged troubled looks.

"¿Qué pasa?" he demanded.

Fernando sighed and told him what he had heard.

Malone closed his eyes, his emotional pain greater than what his body suffered. He imagined the terror

Sienna must have felt when she was forced into the car. The terror would be worse now, as Bellasar prepared whatever hell he had in mind for her.

If she was still alive.

How long ago had they taken her? Straining to clear his thoughts, Malone checked his watch and saw that the time was almost 10:30. Bellasar and his men had arrived at dusk, around 8:45. He had no idea how long they'd remained after he was knocked unconscious, but he doubted it had been long. That meant they had about a ninety-minute head start.

By now, they're close to the border, he thought sickly. No, I'm wrong. The rain at the window made him realize the storm would have slowed them. They might even have had to take shelter in Santa Clara. There was still a chance.

"Help me stand," he told Fernando.

"No. You mustn't try to move."

"Please." Malone grimaced. "Help me stand."

"But . . ."

Malone shuddered, sitting up. Nausea swept through him as he struggled for the further energy to get on his feet.

"*Loco.*" Fernando lifted him, holding him steady as Malone wavered.

Malone fumbled at the pockets of his jacket. "Help me open these zippers."

Confused, Fernando did, his curiosity turning to amazement when he saw the wad of pesos Malone pulled out.

"Half of this is yours," Malone said.

"What?"

"I'm going to keep some in case I need it on the way to Yuma. Otherwise . . ." Malone waited for a swirl of dizziness to pass. "Your share's about four thousand dollars."

Fernando's wife gasped.

Malone fumbled in his jeans, pulling out the Explorer's keys. "You've been a good friend."

Fernando's voice was tight from emotion. *"De nada."*

"If you'll just do one more thing for me."

Fernando waited to hear what it was.

"Help me to my car."

3

There must have been something in the way Malone said it or in the look he gave. Fernando didn't argue. With a nod, he put an arm around Malone's left side, careful not to aggravate the pain on his right.

When Malone pulled the door open, rain shoved them back. He braced himself and stepped into the raging darkness, Fernando going with him, holding him up. Drenched, they staggered toward the gutted trailer. Despite the storm, a few flames struggled to flicker, guiding the way toward the dark outline of the Explorer next to the trailer.

If only the fire hasn't spread to it . . . Apprehension made Malone's heart pound faster. Despite the cold rain, he sweated. He smelled smoke. Lightning gave him a glimpse of the driver's side. Heat had blistered the car's paint. He felt along the windows, finding them intact. "Fernando, the tires," he fought to say in the wind. "Are they all right?"

"Yes."

"Help me inside."

Fernando eased him behind the steering wheel. The effort increased the pain in Malone's ribs and made him see gray for a moment. He fumbled to put the key in the ignition switch.

"Are you sure you can do this?" Fernando asked.

"I have to."

"We will pray for you."

"I'll need it." Malone turned the key. For a moment, he was afraid water had gotten into the electrical system, but after the briefest hesitation, the engine started. He switched on the headlights. They barely pierced the storm. When he turned on the windshield wipers, he saw Fernando running into the darkness toward his trailer. Then he pressed the accelerator and tore up wet sand, heading toward Santa Clara.

The strength of the wind made the waves higher than usual, thrusting them farther onto the beach. Malone had to steer close to the storm-obscured dunes, forced to reduce his speed so he wouldn't crash into them. It made him furious.

Just remember, Bellasar had to go through this, too. He had to face the same obstacles, Malone thought. I'm not really losing time.

But they're still ninety minutes ahead, and the storm wasn't as bad as this when they left.

He had no doubt that Bellasar's destination was the nearest major airport, which was in Yuma. The only way Bellasar could have arrived so fast (he must have been closer than his estate in France) was by jet.

But he won't be flying anywhere in this storm, Malone thought. Bellasar's ninety-minute head start doesn't mean anything as long as he can't take off.

A gully loomed, water churning through it. Before Malone could hit the brake pedal, the Explorer charged down and up through it, splashing waves on each side and over the windshield. Driving blindly, desperate to control his steering, Malone couldn't understand where the gully had come from. He'd driven along the beach many times and had never encountered the obstacle. Then he remembered there had been numerous wide, shallow dips. Were they the equivalent of dry streambeds? In major storms, did water rage from the bluffs on the right and fill these dips with flash floods?

The wave drained from his windshield. Wind buffeted the car. At once his headlights reflected off another gully, this one wider. Reflexively, he stamped the brakes, instantly realizing it was the wrong decision. As the car's tires dug into the wet sand, he wouldn't be able to stop in time. He would slide into the surging water and be trapped. He needed to go as fast as possible, to force the car through to the other side. Jerking his foot off the brake, he applied gas. He felt the car skid and then gain speed. And more speed.

When the front end hit the water, the impact jolted

his teeth together. Waves sprayed. But the car kept surging forward. *Flying* forward. With a punishing jolt, it landed on the opposite bank and started to climb the crest.

But the back end was in the water. Although the tires dug into sand, they fought the strength of the current. Malone pressed harder on the gas pedal. The car gained traction, but not enough. He felt the back end shifting sideways. Oh, Jesus, the current's pulling me in.

As the Explorer swirled in the raging water, he tried to work the steering wheel. It spun in his hands, the current controlling him. The water drowned the engine. The electrical system shorted out. The headlights darkened. He felt the force of the water beneath the car. Then the Explorer twisted sideways and walloped to a stop. Blocked by the edges of the gully, the car was now a plug, the current roaring against it, rising above the windows on the driver's side and pouring over the roof. Water seeped past the windows. I'm going to drown in here, he thought.

He shifted to the passenger side and pressed the switch to lower the window, belatedly remembering that, with the electrical system dead, the window wouldn't budge. More water seeped in. He pulled the latch on the passenger door and shoved, wincing from the pain the effort caused him.

Nothing happened.

He tried harder.

The door opened slightly.

He rammed his shoulder against it. The force of the water spilling over the roof caught the door and thrust it fully open, yanking him with it. He barely had time to breathe before he was sucked under. The current's turmoil shocked him. He couldn't tell up from down, right from left. He struggled to swim but found it impossible. About to inhale water, he brushed against the side of the channel. The current foamed around a curve and hurled him against a slope, where he gasped for air, clawing. He kicked his feet to propel him, kept clawing, and broke free, flopping onto the top of the sand. A wave crashed into him, almost dragging him back. Another wave followed, this one rolling him onto higher ground.

He struggled upright and staggered onward. But his legs didn't want to support him. Dazed, he sank to his knees. He gulped air and shivered. Despite the pain in his ribs, his chest heaved.

Santa Clara was too far to walk to in the storm. The roiling stream blocked him from going back to Fernando. The odds were he would get hypothermia and die out here.

It didn't matter. What happened to him wasn't important. Getting to Sienna *was,* and now he would never be able to help her.

Lights flashed from farther along the beach. A car.

Help, he thought.

He managed to stand.

It's someone who can help me.

Squinting from the headlights, he waved his arms. An alarming thought made him wave his arms harder. Dear God, the car's coming so fast, the driver won't be able to see the stream in time to stop. He'll do what I did and crash into it.

Stop! he mentally shouted. The headlights sped closer.

Abruptly another alarming thought seized him. Nobody drives along this beach at night in a storm unless . . .

It's the police. Someone saw the fire. They're hurrying out to investigate.

Or it's a friend of Ramirez, wondering where he is.

Assaulted by stronger rain, Malone looked frantically around for a place to hide, but the only place was a dune on his right. His legs were numb with cold. He seemed to take forever as the headlights got larger. With a torturous effort, he rounded the dune and collapsed.

Can't go any farther.

From his vantage point, he saw the headlights glint off the raging stream. They seemed to be slowing. Had the driver seen the stream in time?

Or did the driver see *me*? Malone wondered.

A car stopped just before the stream. Malone couldn't tell if it was the police. He tensed, waiting to see what the driver would do.

Two men got out.

Flashlights gleamed toward the dune.

Shit, Malone thought. What if they work for Bellasar? What if he sent them back to make sure I'm dead.

He struggled toward a farther dune.

But the flashlights kept coming. They checked the

first dune, found where his footprints led to the next, and followed.

Malone didn't have the strength to do anything except crawl. His hands and knees didn't seem to belong to him. He felt skewered in place.

The flashlights centered on him, hurting his swollen eyes as he squinted up. He waited for the bullet that would blow his brains out.

"Jesus, what happened to you?" a familiar voice asked.

Malone frowned up at a burly man beyond one of the flashlights, straining to identify him.

"My God, Chase," Jeb said, hurrying to lift him, "we have to get you to a hospital."

4

"No. Not the hospital."

"What? I can't hear you." Driving as fast as he dared along the stormy beach, Jeb risked a glance toward Malone in the backseat.

"The airport," Malone murmured. "Yuma's airport."

"The poor son of a bitch is delirious," the man next to Jeb said.

"Save your strength," Jeb said.

"Yuma's airport." Malone shivered. "Bellasar's there. He's got Sienna with him."

"*What?*"

Malone tried to explain about Ramirez.

"I know about him," Jeb said. "This morning, Ramirez used a computer at the Mexican immigration office at the border to find out what he could about a couple named Dale and Beatrice Perry. Dale Perry was one of ours."

"I took his wallet."

"We eventually figured that out. A half hour after his name surfaced, I was on an Agency jet to talk to the Mexican immigration official whose computer Ramirez used."

"Bellasar arrived ahead of you," Malone managed to say.

"*How?* Dale Perry was *our* man, not his. Bellasar couldn't have known about him."

"Unless somebody in the Agency is on his payroll." Malone forced out the words. "How else could Bellasar have known we were at that safe house in Virginia?"

A rumble of thunder was followed by a heavy silence in the car.

"Hell," Jeb said.

Malone hugged himself, shivering worse.

"We've got to get him out of those wet clothes." Jeb's stocky companion crawled into the backseat and opened a travel bag on the floor. He pulled out a shirt and a pair of jeans. "Since we're about to get intimate, I might as well introduce myself. Name's Dillon."

"I've got the heater turned as high as it goes," Jeb said. "We'll do everything we can to get you warm, Chase."

The weather was so bad, no matter how fast Jeb tried to drive, it still took four hours—twice as long as usual—to reach the border. Dillon tried to use a cell phone to warn the Yuma authorities not to let Bellasar's jet take off, but the storm was so bad that the call wouldn't go through.

Beyond the border, the weather improved, but it still took an hour to get to Yuma. The cell phone finally worked.

Malone, who'd been drifting in and out of a feverish sleep, barely heard Dillon talking urgently to someone in Yuma. He fought toward consciousness, his chest cramping as he tried to get a sense of what the person on the other end was saying.

"Here!" Jeb swerved into the modest airport and skidded to a stop in front of the single-story terminal. Police cars, their roof lights flashing, waited. Jeb rushed out of the car, hurrying to a group of officers. Malone struggled to get out and join him, but even before he took a step, he saw the bleak look with which Jeb turned to him.

"I'm sorry, Chase. I wish I . . . Bellasar's jet took off forty-five minutes ago."

Malone sank.

5

"Your ribs are bruised but not broken," the doctor said. Windows vibrated from the roar of jets taking off and landing at the Marine Corps Air Station at the edge of Yuma. "Your nose is broken. You've got a concussion."

"Is the concussion going to kill me?"

The tall, thin doctor, a captain, peered over his spectacles. "Not if you take it easy for a while."

"He's talking about R and R," Jeb said.

"I *know* what he's talking about."

"What he's *not* talking about," Jeb said, "is trying to go after Bellasar. *We'll* handle it. You're in no shape to do it."

"How?"

"I don't—"

"How are you planning to go after him? Tell me how you'll get Sienna back."

Jeb looked uncomfortable.

The doctor glanced from one man to the other. "Excuse me, gentlemen. I don't think I should be hearing this."

The door swung shut behind him.

"Do you know where Bellasar went?" Malone asked.

"South over Mexican airspace."

"And then?"

"By the time we alerted the Mexican authorities, he was off their radar."

The painkillers the doctor had given Malone didn't stop his skull from throbbing. "So he probably flew over Baja and reached the Pacific."

"That's the theory."

"He could be going anywhere."

"We've asked Canada and the Central American

countries to alert us about unidentified civilian aircraft."

Malone massaged his forehead. "We can't assume he'll go back to his estate in France. The most I can hope for is, whatever Bellasar plans to do to Sienna, he'll wait until they get off the jet. It gives us a little more time."

"To do what? A man that powerful . . . I'm sorry, Chase."

"I won't give up! Tell me what you learned about Bellasar since we disappeared. Maybe there's something that'll help us."

"The arms dealer Bellasar planned to use to broker the weapon—"

"Tariq Ahmed."

Jeb nodded. "He got word that Bellasar's wife had run away with another man. He doesn't know the Agency's involved. Bellasar's trying to keep that a secret, but the fact that Sienna ran off jeopardized the negotiations. Ahmed's the kind who believes that if a man can't control his wife, he can't be depended upon to control his business. There's a chance Bellasar might keep her alive to show Ahmed that she's back and that he's the boss."

"Maybe."

"You've got a look in your eyes. What?"

"Bellasar might prove what a man he is by inviting Ahmed to watch him kill her."

Another jet roared into the air.

"That's just the sick sort of thing Bellasar would do," Jeb said. "Kill her in front of Ahmed. It would solve a lot of problems. He'd not only get the negotiations back on track; he'd also scare the hell out of anybody tempted to underestimate him."

"If your people keep a closer watch on Ahmed—"

"He might lead us to Bellasar."

"And Sienna."

Jeb pulled out his cell phone.

6

As the fuselage hummed from the Gulfstream 5's powerful engines, Sienna barely looked out at the whitecapped ocean below. She told herself she ought to. This would be the last time she'd see it. But she didn't care. Staring at the back of the seat, she kept remembering what Derek had done to Chase. In her mind, she saw Chase lying on the floor, the flames spreading toward him. He was dead. Nothing else mattered.

Someone stood in the aisle. When she turned, Potter's expression had never been more sullen, the gaze behind his spectacles never more sour.

"That business with the duffel bags in the plane," he said. "Cute. I'm going to enjoy what happens to you."

She returned her mournful stare to the back of the seat. In a moment, Potter's presence was replaced by a darker one, and she didn't need to look to know who took the seat next to her.

"How much did you tell them?" Derek asked.

"Everything I could."

"Which wasn't anything important. You were never present for meetings. I never engaged in pillow talk. You know nothing about my business."

"Then you don't have anything to be afraid of."

"Did you live with me for so long and not learn even the most basic thing about me?" Derek grasped her chin and turned it in his direction. "I'm not afraid of anything."

"I didn't live *with* you, Derek."

"What are you talking about?"

"You would never allow anyone to live *with* you. I just happened to share the same building with you."

"Why did you betray me?"

"You expected me to wait around until you killed me? It was all right for you to plan my murder, but for me to leave was unforgivable? You arrogant . . . Even if you hadn't been planning to kill me, I'd have left you. For the first time in my life, I found a man who cared for me more than he did for himself."

"I gave you the best of everything."

"And treated me like one of those things."

"It's better than dying."

7

"Good!" Jeb pushed the disconnect button on his cell phone and turned to let Dillon know what he'd learned.

Malone interrupted, emerging from a stack of battered furniture in an outdoor storage unit.

"I don't know what we're doing here." Jeb squinted from the morning sun.

"I had to pick up this suitcase."

"What's so important about it? I already got you fresh clothes."

Malone opened it.

Jeb stared at the money.

8

"No, *you* come to *me*," Ahmed said into his scrambler-equipped telephone. Outside, the traffic sounds of Istanbul's evening rush hour grew louder. "I don't see why I should put myself out for you. You're the one whose affairs are out of order. It's your obligation to regain my confidence."

"But you don't have the proper facilities." Bellasar's voice, crackling with static, came from his own scrambler-equipped telephone aboard his jet. He had refueled at a client's airstrip in El Salvador, toward which he'd been flying from Miami when he'd learned where Sienna and Malone were hiding. "My technicians can't guarantee the safety of the demonstration unless it's conducted in a level-four chamber."

"If the weapon is so sensitive, *that* doesn't fill me with confidence, either."

"I guarantee that when I'm finished, I'll definitely have your confidence."

"It'll take a great deal to convince me your personal affairs are back in order."

"Not after tomorrow. I have a special demonstration planned. Believe me, you've never seen anything like it."

9

As the Agency's jet reached its maximum speed, Jeb came back from the cockpit's radio. "We just got a report that Ahmed ordered his pilot to be ready to fly to Nice tomorrow."

"Then the meeting must be at Bellasar's estate," Malone said. "We can intercept Bellasar at Nice's airport. We can get Sienna away from him."

"No. He's too far ahead of us. We'll never get there in time."

"But you can have the French authorities do it."

"On what basis? As far as the French are concerned, he hasn't done anything wrong."

"Then, damn it, order a special ops team to take Sienna away from him."

"Without permission from the French? At a major airport? Bellasar's bodyguards wouldn't just throw down their weapons and surrender. There'd be gunfire. There's too great a risk civilians would be killed."

"Jesus, you're telling me we know where and when he's going to kill her, *but we can't stop it*?"

"If I had the power to make the decision, I would, but the guy dragging his feet is Laster."

"That son of a—"

"Hey, I don't like him any more than you do," Jeb said, "but he's got a point. We can't cause an international incident over what looks like a family fight."

Malone trembled from anger, pain, and exhaustion.

"When was the last time you took your pain pills?" Jeb asked.

"They make me groggy."

"Good. You need some rest."

They studied each other.

Malone mentally resisted, then nodded.

He swallowed two pills and tried to tell himself that things weren't as hopeless as they seemed, that there was something he could think of to save Sienna, but he had the terrible suspicion he was wrong.

Isn't denial the first phase of grief? he asked himself.

Don't give up. She isn't dead yet.

10

No one talked to her again. No one even looked at her. They behaved as if she weren't present. As far as they're concerned, I'm already a corpse, Sienna thought.

Throughout the flight, when meals were served, she

wasn't offered anything, a further example of the contempt with which she was treated. Not that she was hungry. Chase's death had so numbed her that she couldn't care less about food. But that didn't matter—if she was going to starve, by God, she wanted it to be her choice. As everyone else ate, she went to the galley at the rear of the jet. When she brought back crackers and a cup of tea, she got no reaction from anyone. She was like a ghost passing among them. She felt like hurling the steaming tea at Derek, and that was when she realized that despair had given way to fury.

She was determined to survive. To get even. *How* she was going to survive, she had no idea. But she had to think aggressively. Because survival wasn't enough. She had to make Derek pay.

That motivation fiercely possessing her, she forced herself to pick up a cracker. Her emotions were so chaotic that the thought of eating made her nauseous, but she marshaled her strength. She bit into the cracker, chewed tastelessly, swallowed hard, and got it down.

She took another bite, then another.

Still, no one looked at her. Staring at the back of Derek's head, she thought, You bastard, I'm not a thing. You can't just hang me on a wall. Her memory angrily transported her back to the room where she had seen the portraits of her and Derek's other wives.

And the photographs of Derek's sister, whom she and the portraits so closely resembled.

And the clothes on the mannequin, and the shoes neatly arranged, and the scrapbook.

And the urn.

None of this would have happened if I hadn't re-sembled Derek's sister.

Derek's sister, she chillingly realized, was the only chance she had.

11

"I need to wake you, Chase."

Malone felt as if his eyelids had weights on them.

Slowly, Jeb came into focus. "The same drill as before. How many fingers am I holding up?"

". . . Three."

"Seeing double?"

". . . No."

"Feeling sick to your stomach?"

"No." Malone rubbed his hand across his face, regretting the gesture when his injuries protested. He squinted toward the darkness outside the jet's window. "Where are we?"

"Over the Atlantic. Do you remember refueling at Dulles?"

Malone thought a moment. "Yes."

"I think we can stop worrying about your concussion."

"Where are we headed?"

"Southern France."

"Didn't Laster object?"

"He doesn't know about this."

Malone's surprise increased when he noticed Jeb's

partner, Dillon, talking to five stocky men in the forward seats.

"Who . . ."

"I made some calls en route from Yuma. These are guys I've worked with from time to time. They're looking for work. When they came aboard at Dulles, you'd fallen back asleep."

"But you said Laster didn't sanction a mission."

"Affirmative. This isn't official. You're hiring them with what's in your suitcase."

"An unsanctioned mission could cost you your job. Why are you sticking your neck out?"

"Because you saved my life in Panama."

"You already paid that back."

"No. If not for me, you wouldn't be in this mess."

"If not for you, I'd never have met Sienna."

"Then let's see if we can get her back," Jeb said. "This is the latest information we have."

Malone frowned at a dossier Jeb handed him.

Opening it, he found an eight-by-ten-inch photograph. "A picture of Sienna." Then he felt a chill as he realized he was wrong.

The photograph showed a sensuous dark-haired woman sitting with Bellasar, drinking from a champagne glass on a terrace that overlooked a beach.

"It was taken at Puerto Vallarta three months ago," Jeb said. "There were a lot of guards around Bellasar, so our photographer had to work from a distance. The poor angle and the graininess make it seem this woman is Sienna. But the truth is, she's the daughter of a French industrialist who manufactures some of the weapons Bellasar sells. Bellasar met her at a cocktail party the father gave in Paris six months ago."

"About the time Bellasar started rejecting Sienna. Of course. He'd found her replacement." Malone concentrated on the photograph. "With slightly longer hair and some surgery to narrow her chin, she'll look even more like Sienna."

"And like Bellasar's sister. Until Sienna told us about her, we had no idea about the sister's importance." Jeb pointed toward the next photograph.

His skin prickling, Malone studied it. The voluptuous dark-haired woman wasn't Sienna, and yet she had the same body type and facial structure, the same smoldering quality in her eyes. In shadows, the two could have been confused for each other.

"Bellasar and his sister became lovers when he was fourteen and she was a year younger," Jeb said.

"What?"

"By all accounts, the sister—her name was Christina—was remarkably self-indulgent and impetuous. They went everywhere together. *Did* everything together."

"But if it was so obvious, the parents must have known. Didn't they object?"

"They didn't have a chance."

Malone was puzzled.

"The parents died in a fire at their summer home in Switzerland—the same summer Bellasar and his sister became lovers." Jeb let the significance sink in.

"Oh shit," Malone murmured.

"For the next three years, Bellasar and Christina

partied. Rome, London, Rio. Meanwhile, a trust ran the business. But when Bellasar turned eighteen, he and his sister took control. Their tastes were so expensive that, to generate more income, they ran the business more ruthlessly than the trust had. But thirteen years later, the parties ended."

"What do you mean?"

"When Christina was thirty, she died in a fall from a hotel balcony in Rome. It seems Bellasar wasn't enough for her. She had affairs with every man who came along. One night in Rome, Bellasar broke into her room, found her with a woman, and couldn't keep control any longer. They fought. It ended when she went over the balcony."

"He murdered his sister?" Malone tasted bile. "But according to this dossier, he wasn't charged."

"The only witness was the woman Bellasar found her with. Bellasar paid her off. The story was that Christina had been doing drugs, which was true, and that she'd toppled over the railing. The bribed witness died in a hit-and-run accident three months later."

"And ever since, he's been searching for someone to replace his sister."

12

She knew she had to try to sleep. She couldn't risk fatigue dulling her thoughts. More, her plan depended on Derek's knowing she had slept.

At first, she pretended, merely closing her eyes and tilting her seat back. Furious ideas buzzed through her mind, interrupted by bursts of fear that she strained to repress. She had to make rage her solitary emotion. To steady herself, she concentrated on the drone of the jet's engines. The darkness behind her closed eyes deepened.

A hand shook her roughly.

"Uh . . ."

"Wake up." Potter shook her again.

Groggy, she blinked, adjusting her eyes to the harsh lights in the cabin, noting that outside it was dark.

"Get in the rest room."

"What?"

"We're about to land," Potter said. "Get in the rest room. Stay there until I tell you to come out."

As the jet descended, Sienna saw lights below and recognized the glitter of the Promenade des Anglais along Nice's harbor.

"Damn it, do what I tell you." Potter yanked her seat belt open and pulled her upright so hard, her teeth snapped together. He dragged her to the back and shoved her into the rest room.

As the door was slammed in her face, Sienna remembered a time when Derek would have killed Potter for treating her like that, but now Derek hadn't even bothered to glance at the commotion.

Hearing the engines change pitch as the jet descended, she braced her hands against the rest room's walls. Moments later, with the slightest of bumps, the jet landed. Whatever Derek had in mind, it wouldn't be long now. She prayed that he wouldn't keep demonstrating his contempt by staying away from her. Her plan depended on getting close enough to talk to him.

The harsh light in the rest room made her look as sick as she felt. The bruise on her jaw, from when Ramirez had punched her, was alarming. If there's ever been a time when I need to look good, she warned herself, this is it. A sink drawer contained basic cosmetics. Hearing voices in the main cabin (probably immigration officials checking the plane), she hurriedly tried to make herself presentable. Trembling, she washed her face, removing the specks of dried blood. She did the best she could with her hair, applied powder to the bruise on her jaw, and used a little lipstick, her lower lip stinging when she put pressure on it.

The door was yanked open.

Potter glared. "Move."

She didn't give him time to repeat the order. Veering past him, she headed along the aisle. She did her best to hide her nervousness, to look as confident as if she were still in Derek's good graces. But her determination faltered when she saw only bodyguards and not Derek waiting at the exit.

As she went down the steps toward the tarmac, she paid little attention to the sweet smell of the sea, even though she knew she should savor it—she might never experience it again. She couldn't let anything distract her. The helicopter was already warming up. She had a sense of events moving terribly fast. With bodyguards on each side and in back of her, she was herded toward the open hatch, and in another sign of how much had changed, no one offered to help her in. She climbed up, hoping to get Derek to look at her. She failed, but she did manage to take the seat next to him before a bodyguard claimed it.

For a moment, she was afraid that Derek would change seats, but the bodyguards took the others, leaving only one in back, which Potter, his expression more dour, sat in. She fastened her safety harness. The hatch was closed. Aggravating the uneasy sinking feeling in her stomach, the helicopter took off.

Except for the muffled roar of the engines, the compartment was silent.

"I had a strange dream," she said to Derek, not looking at him.

He stared ahead, giving no indication that he had heard.

She waited a moment, trying to seem confused. "I was falling."

Again no response.

As the helicopter rose into the darkness of the hills, she concentrated to remember everything as vividly as she could. The locked room next to Derek's bedroom. The portraits of his other wives. The photographs of Derek's sister. The details in them. The scrapbook.

Derek's sister had died on June 10.

A newspaper on the plane had been dated June 8.

"It wasn't like the usual nightmare about falling," she said. "Where everything's dark and you don't know where you're falling. This was almost like it was really happening."

The muffled rumble of the helicopter's engines filled the silence. Her heart pounded so hard that she thought it would burst. She'd pushed what she needed to say as much as she dared. If Derek didn't respond . . .

"Falling?" Derek's voice was so subdued it took her a moment to realize that he'd spoken and to figure out the word.

"Onto a street." She remembered the death certificate had said that Christina died at 3:00 A.M. "It was night. But I saw streetlights and the headlights of a car and lights in some windows. The reflection on the pavement rushed toward me. Then I hit, and other kinds of lights exploded in my head, and I woke up."

"Falling," Derek said.

"The pain when I hit was . . ." She lapsed into silence.

Thirty seconds.

A minute.

I failed, she thought.

"And where were you falling from?"

She didn't answer.

"Was that not in the dream?" he asked.

"A railing." She paused as if trying to come to terms with the detail. What she said next was full of puzzlement. "On a balcony."

And now, at last, Derek turned and assessed her.

"A balcony," he said.

"Of a hotel." She shuddered and looked at him, searching his eyes, trying to establish emotional contact. "I could feel my insides rush up. It was like it was really happening."

"A balcony."

Lights glowed in a valley ahead.

The pilot identified himself to the compound. He got permission to come in.

The chopper descended.

"Someone called me Christina."

Derek's gaze was more intense.

"A man. I don't understand. Why would I respond to someone calling me Christina?"

"I've had enough of this," Derek said flatly.

"What do you mean?"

"Who told you about her?"

"I still don't—"

"The CIA?"

"You know someone named Christina?" Sienna asked.

"There's one way to end this. Describe the balcony."

"I . . ."

"If the nightmare was so vivid, you ought to have seen what you fell from. You've made such a drama about this. Describe the balcony."

Sienna hesitated. She was going to have to guess, but if she made the wrong choice . . . She remembered the photographs she had seen on the wall of the locked room. One of them had shown a teen-aged Christina on a balcony, leaning against an ornate metal railing, a view of St. Peter's in the distance. Had the hotel been a favorite?

"It was spacious. There was a black metal railing, very ornate. St. Peter's was in the distance."

The helicopter swooped lower, the lights of Derek's estate enlarging, other lights coming on, illuminating the landing pad.

"You're playing a game with me!" he said.

"Game?"

"If you think I'm not going to kill you because of some trick you're—"

"Trick? I don't—"

"Shut up. Don't say another word."

"I dreamed I was on a pony."

"What?"

"I was a little girl on a pony. The Alps were all around me. But I've never been to Switzerland, and I've never owned a pony. How could I have felt I was actually riding that pony? I *loved* that pony. Jesus, am I losing my mind?"

13

"How soon till we get to Nice?" Malone asked.

"An hour."

Malone peered from the Agency's jet. The sky was turning gray. It would soon be dawn. "We're going to need weapons and special equipment."

Jeb nodded. "Back in February, when you agreed to work for us, I made arrangements to have them ready in case we had to go in."

"After we land and the jet's refueled, one of these men will have to fly to Paris."

"What's in Paris?"

"Bellasar's new girlfriend and her father."

"What are you thinking?"

Malone explained.

Jeb raised his eyebrows.

"When does Bellasar expect Ahmed?" Malone asked.

"Two P.M."

"That gives us enough time," Malone said.

"To do what?"

When Malone told him, Jeb raised his eyebrows higher. "Risky."

"Have you got an alternative?"

"You know I don't."

"Then, with or without your help, I intend to try this."

"Hey, who said I wouldn't help?"

"But it isn't going to work if I can't get into France. I need a passport."

Jeb reached into his jacket.

Malone looked in amazement as Jeb handed him a passport. "How . . ."

"It was with the documents I had delivered at Dulles when we refueled."

Malone examined his photograph and the name in the passport. "I'm Thomas Corrigan?"

"A pseudonym will come in handy if this doesn't work."

"But it *is* going to work. It *has* to."

"Maybe this will encourage you."

Malone shook his head, puzzled, when he was handed another passport.

The photograph inside was Sienna's, the name under it Janice Corrigan. "Thank you," Malone said.

It gave him a reason to hope.

TEN

1

"How do you know these things?" Derek insisted.

Sienna was sprawled in a chair in the library, where Derek had pushed her as soon as they entered.

"What things? I don't know what you mean. All I did was tell you about a disturbing dream I had."

"In which you fell from a balcony and you were also riding a pony."

"No. Not in the same . . . I woke and drifted off. Several dreams blurred together."

"What color was the pony?"

Sienna strained to remember the photograph. "It was dark. But it had a white mane."

"In the Alps, you said."

"Yes." Sienna shook her head from side to side. "Why are you doing this? Quit bullying me. If you're going to punish me, do it. But stop this—"

"How old were you when you had the pony?"

"I didn't say I had a pony. I said I dreamed about—"

"Damn it, how old were you?"

There had been a handwritten date on the photograph: 1949.

The date on Christina's birth certificate had been *1939.*

". . . Ten."

"And who gave you the pony?"

This is the end, Sienna thought. If I guess wrong . . . The obvious answer was, "My parents," but something in Derek's insistent gaze told her that the question had a trick, that the pony's relevance was fiercely personal. Why should it matter who gave the pony? Unless . . .

"My brother."

Derek shuddered.

"Why am I having these dreams?" Sienna demanded.

Someone knocked on the door.

"Not now!" Derek shouted.

"Do you want me to meet Ahmed at the airport?" Potter's voice came from behind the door. "Or do you want the guards to bring him?"

"Meet him!"

"But how do you want me to act? Friendly or distant?"

"Whatever you want! Just leave us the hell alone!"

After a pause, footsteps retreated along the outside corridor.

Derek swung toward Sienna. "Who told you about the balcony and the pony?"

"Nobody! They were in my dream!"

"What else did you dream?"

"I was at a carnival."

"What kind of—"

"A fiesta. In a street. People were in costumes."

"Where?"

The crowd in the photograph's background had looked Latin. Sienna remembered another photograph in which a gigantic statue of Christ, His arms outstretched, had loomed on a ridge behind Christina. The only statue like that she knew of was in—

"Rio."

The city was famous for its carnivals, but Derek didn't react.

God help me, I guessed wrong. Sienna tensed.

"Rio." Derek glared.

He's going to kill me now.

"How Christina loved Rio." Derek yanked her up from the chair. "Who told you about my sister?"

"Your sister? I didn't know you have a—"

"Had!"

"Her name was Christina?" Sienna asked.

"She died a long time ago. *Are you trying to convince me you're dreaming about her?"*

"I'm not trying to convince you of anything! I never heard of her until you—"

"Do you think I won't kill you because I'd feel it was like killing my sister?"

"Killing your sister?"

The look in Derek's eyes was terrifying.

"Did Christina fall from a balcony? Did I dream about how she died?"

Derek shook with anger. "As much as I adored her, she had a way of making me furious. Just as *you're* making me furious."

With a chill, Sienna realized what had happened on the balcony that night. "In the dream, I was pushed."

Derek raised his hands.

"Please, don't kill me again," Sienna whispered.

2

Distraught, Potter watched Nice's airport enlarge below him as the helicopter descended. He was intentionally early to meet Ahmed. Anything to get away from Derek. To be shouted at. To be treated no better than a servant. When this is over, I'm leaving, Potter thought.

The helicopter set down in its usual far corner of the airport. After getting Ahmed, Potter would return to the estate, and by this time tomorrow, he thought, when the woman is taken care of, when business is settled and I bring Ahmed back to the airport, I'll keep going. I saved my money. I planned for when Derek would turn against me. Now he'll find out what it's like to be on his own.

"We have plenty of time. Refuel it," Potter told the pilot. He turned to his two guards. "We'll go into the terminal."

But instead of moving, they stared past him toward the open hatch, where three men in mechanic's coveralls leaned in, aiming pistols.

One of the guards almost drew his weapon, but

after a further look at the sound suppressors on the pistols, he remained still.

"Think," one of the armed men said. He was heavy-set, with short blond hair. "Very slowly, using the tips of your fingers, remove your weapons and set them on the floor. Good. If you do this right, nobody's going to die."

"Who . . . ?" Potter started to ask.

The man ignored him. A van pulled up next to the helicopter. "Everybody out. You're taking a ride."

The guards looked apprehensively at each other.

"Hey, if we'd wanted to, we could have killed you," the man said. "Play nice and you'll get out of this alive." He made a sharp gesture toward the van. "Move."

The pilot and the guards reluctantly obeyed, but as Potter started to follow, the man said, "Not you."

"If it's money you want, I—"

"Sit down. We'll soon be taking our own ride."

Seeing the pilot get out of the helicopter and into the van, Potter said, "But who's going to fly the—"

"I am," a voice said.

Disturbed by its familiarity, Potter turned toward the pilot's hatch, where a man with a severely bruised face appeared, but even with the bruises, the face was instantly recognizable. Potter's stomach contracted.

Malone.

3

Ahmed's pilot announced they would soon be landing. *But not soon enough,* Ahmed thought. The four-hour flight from Istanbul had seemed interminable. He didn't like Bellasar. He didn't like to travel. Being away from the sounds and smells of home always put him on edge. Whatever Bellasar's demonstration was, it had better be worth the trouble of coming to see it. If there was one more hint that Bellasar's affairs were out of control . . .

Ahmed's jet set down. Bellasar had promised that passing through customs and immigration would be swift, and encouragingly, that was the case. But when Ahmed emerged from the processing area, neither Bellasar nor Potter was in sight. If this was an indication of how the meeting was going to . . .

"Mr. Ahmed?"

A heavyset man with short blond hair emerged from the crowd. He wore a suit and looked apologetic as he extended his hand. "I'm Raymond Baker. I'm sorry for the slight delay. Mr. Bellasar sent me to get you."

"He couldn't come himself?"

"Unfortunately, he was occupied. He sends his apologies. He's so determined to make your visit successful that he's personally taking care of the final details."

"I've not met you before. Why wasn't Alex Potter sent to meet me?"

"I'm new on the staff. Mr. Potter had some security matters to take care of. He'll meet us at the helicopter. If you and your escorts"—the man nodded toward the two guards Ahmed had brought with him—"will accompany me. It's a short flight to Mr. Bellasar's estate."

Ahmed hesitated, annoyed that Bellasar had sent an underling to greet him but gratified by the man's subservient manner. "The sooner this meeting is over, the sooner I'll be on my way back to Istanbul."

"In that case, you'll be pleased that Mr. Bellasar has made arrangements to be certain there won't be any delays in your return flight. If you'll follow me . . ."

4

Approaching the helicopter, Ahmed couldn't help frowning when he saw Potter waiting stiffly next to the open hatch. Ahmed had never liked the man's perpetual disapproving look. His presence turned everything dark around him. Potter didn't even extend his hand as Ahmed neared him. Typical. I'll rot before I extend *my* hand first, Ahmed thought.

As he started to get in, Ahmed blanched when two men in coveralls turned from the helicopter and put a gun in the small of the back of each guard. A van pulled up. Five seconds later, the guards were in the vehicle, the men in coveralls had gotten in with them, and the van was driving away. The speed with which everything had happened was bewildering.

"I couldn't warn you," Potter said. He tilted his head toward the interior of the helicopter, where two other men in coveralls pointed weapons at them.

"Inside," the man who had met Ahmed in the airport said. His right hand was beneath his suit coat, as if ready to draw a pistol at the slightest provocation.

"Who *are* you? What do you—"

"Shut up and get in the helicopter."

Pushed inside, Ahmed was searched, buckled roughly into a safety harness, then handcuffed along with Potter to a bar on the side of the fuselage. But as dismaying as all this was, nothing prepared him for what he felt when the pilot turned to look back at him, revealing a face swollen and purple with bruises.

"Welcome to Payback Airlines."

5

"Potter's and Ahmed's bodyguards are handcuffed and having a nice morphine sleep in the back of the van," Jeb told Malone as he hurried to fasten his copilot's harness. "Our local contact will drive them to a secluded campground and wait to hear from us."

"And twenty-four hours from now, if he still hasn't heard from us?"

"He'll know everything went to hell and he'll let them go."

"But everything *won't* go to hell." Malone's voice was hoarse with emotion. "Except for Bellasar."

He radioed the control tower, getting clearance for takeoff. Then he flicked some switches. The rotors started to turn.

"When I was taken to Bellasar's estate and later when I stole the chopper to escape, I was puzzled by an extra panel of switches I couldn't account for," Malone said.

The rotors spun faster.

"I've been trying to figure out what they're for," Malone said louder, in order to be heard above the engine's roar. "When the chopper crashed and the gas tank exploded, the blast was greater than it should have been. Finally I think I understand."

"What are you getting at?"

"It's just what you'd expect an arms dealer to do. He went after me with four-wheel-drive cars that were actually assault vehicles equipped with machine guns. Why wouldn't he modify his helicopters the same way?"

"You're telling me—"

"This thing has retractable weapons. It's a gunship."

6

"What else did you dream?"

"I can't concentrate anymore. I need to lie down. I—"

Derek slapped her.

She stumbled back.

"What you need to do is what you're told. *What else did you dream?*"

"I can't remember."

Derek slapped her harder.

"You promised you'd never hurt me!" she shouted.

"That was before you ran off with—"

"I meant Christina! You promised not to hurt her again. Tomorrow."

"What?"

"She died tomorrow."

Derek slapped her a third time. "Tell me how you know so much about—"

"There was a yacht." Sienna strained to remember more of the photograph.

Derek froze, his hand drawn back to strike her again.

The photograph had shown Christina as a voluptuous adult, wearing a bikini, sunbathing on the deck of a yacht. Behind her, the yacht's name had been stenciled on a life preserver.

"The yacht was called *Christina.* There were parties and—"

"Always parties! Christina couldn't get enough parties! Whenever my back was turned . . . *She* betrayed me, the same as *you* did."

"It had nothing to do with betraying you! I had to try to save my life!"

Derek's glare remained riveted on her, then wavered, as if her logic had made an impression on him.

"Why does it have to be this way?" Sienna pleaded. "Why can't we start over?"

Derek studied her.

"Why can't we forgive each other? Five years ago, we loved each other. Why can't we go back?" She took a tentative step toward him, holding out a hand to touch him.

"What else did you dream?"

"What?"

"Tell me how you know so much about my sister."

Sienna's spirit plummeted.

"The balcony, the pony, the carnival, the yacht, the time and date of . . ." Derek's eyes widened. "Jesus, you saw them."

"What?"

"You saw them!"

"I don't know what you're—"

Derek grabbed the hand she'd extended and yanked her viciously toward the doorway. She struggled to resist, but his strength was too powerful. He flung the door open so hard, it slammed against bookshelves.

"Derek, no, what are you—"

He forced her along the corridor, into the vestibule, and up the curving staircase. As she resisted, his next tug made her lose her balance and drop to her knees. He yanked even harder, dragging her.

The first landing.

The second.

"Stop!" Sienna pleaded.

He kept pulling her.

"Where are you taking me?"

The top floor. Jerking her upright, he reached the door next to his bedroom, pulled a key from his pocket, unlocked the door, and shoved it open. Shadows beckoned.

"No, I don't want to—"

He shoved her inside, turned on the lights, ignored the portraits on the wall, and forced her toward the urn. "Christina," he murmured. He spun her toward the wall of photographs. "You have no idea how much I loved her." He stared at the numerous photos, scanning them, finding the ones he wanted. "There. On the balcony, on the pony, at the carnival, and on the yacht." He flipped open the scrapbook, turning to the final page. "The time and date when she died. That's how you knew about my sister! *Somehow, you've been in here before.*"

"No, I swear. I didn't know anything about—"

" 'Five years ago, we loved each other. Why can't we go back?' " Derek mocked.

"I meant it."

"Oh, of course."

"What happened between us?" Sienna asked. "*Why did you turn against me?*"

For a moment, Derek's eyes cleared, as if he finally understood how wrong everything was.

"Christina happened," he said.

His eyes again black with fury, he dragged her out of the room. "Ahmed will soon be here. Finally you're going to be of use to me."

7

The speeding chopper cleared the ridge and came into view of the valley. Bellasar's estate was hunkered in the middle.

"We'd better be right about this," Jeb said. "Back at the airport was risky, but now . . ."

Malone adjusted the microphone on his helmet. "Bellasar's expecting the chopper to come back with Ahmed. Here it is."

"He'll also expect a radio message, some kind of identification before he lets this thing get closer. You don't know what you're supposed to say."

Malone nodded. When he had flown here with Bellasar a lifetime ago, he had heard the pilot speak to the estate, but the pilot had used French, and Malone had no idea what he had said.

He adjusted the radio's frequency until he heard a male voice saying something in French. Even with the accent, some of the words were close enough to English that Malone understood he was being asked to identify himself.

He tapped the microphone a couple of times, then brushed a piece of paper across it, murmuring a few of the French words he had just heard, trying to create the impression that radio problems were breaking up his signal.

He switched off the radio.

The helicopter flew closer to the estate.

"This had better work," Jeb said. "An arms dealer's likely to have missiles down there."

"Probably. But he won't risk killing Ahmed unless he has to. So far, we've done nothing to indicate we're a threat." Malone looked back at Jeb's partner and the others who were helping him. "Ready?"

The tension on Dillon's face was all too familiar from when Malone had prepared for missions in the military. He switched his attention to Ahmed and Potter, handcuffed to the side of the chopper. Their expressions were stark with fear.

"Buckled in nice and tight?" Malone asked.

He jerked on the controls. Abruptly the chopper tilted and spun.

"Jesus!" Jeb had known this was coming, but he hadn't been prepared for how closely Malone's maneuvers would simulate a chopper that was out of control.

"Gas masks." Malone tilted the chopper dizzyingly in the opposite direction.

Each man had one. They slipped them over their heads.

"Might as well let Potter and Ahmed have one also," Malone said. He took off his pilot's helmet, put on his gas mask, then made the helicopter waver so alarmingly that anybody on the ground would assume it was close to crashing.

"Hatches!"

Dillon and the others opened them.

"Smoke grenades!"

"Ready!"

"Do it!"

Two grenades were dropped to the chopper's floor. Muffled *whumps* were followed by sudden gray smoke that filled the chopper. For a moment, Malone feared that he had miscalculated, that the smoke swirling around him would get so thick he wouldn't be able to see to control the unstable maneuvers he was forcing the chopper to perform. If the charade wasn't convincing to the guards on Bellasar's estate . . .

Wind from the open hatches cleared the smoke, allowing him to see the estate as the chopper wavered onward. Most of the smoke now billowed outside, making it seem that an accident had happened on board. Malone imagined the frantic questions the radio controller was trying to send him.

He spun. He tilted. All the while, he moved closer to the buildings and gardens of the estate. He was near enough now to see guards down there. On paths, among trees and shrubs, they stared up in confusion.

At a height of a thousand feet, he wavered over the estate. Some of the guards ran for cover, afraid the chopper was about to crash on them.

"*Ready?*" Malone shouted to the back.

Dillon opened a box.

From the corner of his vision, Malone saw him throw out a quart-sized glass container of a type used in laboratories. It tumbled through the air, easily visible because of the white powder in it. As guards hurried to avoid it, the container shattered on a sidewalk. Malone imagined the noise it made and the consternation on the guards' faces as the powder burst into the air and the day's breeze carried it toward them. A few whose curiosity was stronger than their apprehension came close to investigate. Malone knew that when they saw the sturdy label keeping some of the shattered pieces of glass together, they would stumble back and panic. Even in English, the message was unmistakable. CAUTION: ANTHRAX. BIOLOGICAL HAZARD. The skull and crossbones symbol was equally unmistakable.

Smoke spewing from the chopper, Malone tilted toward other areas of the estate. As more glass containers plummeted, he switched his attention toward the tennis court and the area of the first impact. Amid the drifting white powder, guards raced away. He imagined them holding their breath. A few of them shouted warnings. Guards who weren't near the impact zone put greater distance between them. A container shattered among *those* guards, who raced in a different direction, while another container broke ahead of them.

Five, six, seven. As Malone guided the chopper's erratic path over the property, more and more containers smashed on the grounds, white powder spewing. Twelve, thirteen, fourteen. The mansion, the Cloister, the stable, the swimming pool, and the weapons-testing range had blotches of white on them. Seventeen, eighteen. More guards rushed to escape. Some jumped into vehicles and sped toward the gates.

Until now, Malone had relied on the double distraction of the apparently about-to-crash chopper and the falling containers to keep the guards from firing at him. Believing they were under attack from a biological weapon, few had overcome their primal fear enough to get off a few shots before they ran in panic. But even a few were too many. Malone assumed that the chopper was armored, but he knew from experience that it wasn't invulnerable—when he and Sienna had used the other chopper to escape, a barrage of gunfire from the guards had managed to disable it. Now, as bullets whacked against the fuselage, he needed a reinforcement that the estate was under attack from biological and chemical weapons.

"Kick the smoke grenades out!"

The men got rid of the ones on the floor. As the air in the chopper cleared, they pulled the pins on other grenades and hurled them to the ground. But these were tear-gas grenades, their dense haze blossoming across lawns and gardens, forcing the guards to race even harder.

"Close the hatches!"

Malone sped from the estate, then swung to face it. He flicked four of the switches that had puzzled him earlier. En route from Nice, he had experimented, learning what did what.

Ports opened on each side of the chopper. Machine guns swung out. If they were anything like what Malone had been familiar with in the military, each was capable of firing six thousand 30-mm rounds a minute. Above them, launchers equipped with 2.75-inch folding-fin rockets emerged. Perfect for the dictator who loves to surprise his enemies, Malone thought.

Now it was time for *Bellasar* to get a surprise.

The haze from the tear gas obscured the grounds. It'll also obscure the chopper, Malone thought. Firing both machine guns, he swooped down, unable to see the damage he was causing but knowing he was destroying everything in his path. Careful not to hit the château or the Cloister, where Sienna or the biological weapon might be, he launched a rocket. Another. Even with the roar of the chopper, he heard the rockets explode among the guards. When he turned to face the estate from the opposite direction, he saw flames amid the smoke and the tear gas.

"Potter!"

No answer.

"Damn it, Potter, you know what you're supposed to do! Make the call!"

Malone attacked again. As the machine guns thundered, so many bullets streaked down at once, they became moving columns of devastation. Behind each, a line of dust and shredded wreckage flew into the air, mixing with the smoke and the gas. He must have hit a munitions area. The shock wave from a huge explosion shook the chopper, creating more smoke, a fireball rising from it.

"Potter!"

Still no answer.

"So help me God, Potter, if you don't call him, we'll throw you out!"

Muscles cramping with fury, Malone launched another rocket. It streaked toward an antiaircraft bunker. The fiery blast sent concrete and metal flying. Skirting smoke from the crater, spraying guards who aimed toward the chopper, he reached the far end of the estate, swung, and again faced his target.

Hovering, he glared back at Potter, whose cuffed hands held a cell phone awkwardly to his ear.

"Yes," Potter said into the phone. "Six men, plus Malone and Ahmed." Seeing the rage on Malone's bruised face, Potter flinched, afraid of what Malone would do to him for telling Bellasar who was in the chopper. "Malone wants to talk to you. Derek, this couldn't be helped. I'm sorry." Whatever Bellasar said to him was so insulting that Potter looked like a dog that had been beaten. But humiliation wasn't all his expression communicated as Dillon took the phone from him and gave it to Malone. Potter's anger was unmistakable. His voice was strangled. "He shouldn't talk to me that way. Kill the son of a bitch."

Malone sent another rocket into the smoke, the explosion rumbling. Only then did he press the phone to his ear. "Have I got your attention?"

8

"Totally." In the Cloister, Bellasar stared through a window at the smoke-obscured helicopter. Sienna, too dazed to know what he said, lay in a corner. "You're supposed to be dead," he said into his cell phone.

"Sorry to disappoint you."

"Not at all. It gives me the pleasure of killing you a second time. I assume you've come for my wife?"

"She'd better still be alive."

"Or?"

Through the haze outside, Bellasar saw the blur of a rocket spewing from the helicopter. In a fiery roar, it struck the château's terrace, flagstones erupting.

"I'll have it rebuilt," Bellasar said into the phone. "I'm not over there, by the way. I'm at the Cloister. But think twice about launching another rocket. The love of your life is in here with me."

"She's alive?"

"In a manner of speaking."

As Sienna struggled to her feet, Bellasar punched her, knocking her down. Her groan was loud enough to be heard through the phone.

"I want to talk to her!" Malone said.

"If she can." Bellasar peered down at her. "Guess what, my dear? Your boyfriend's on the phone."

Sienna blinked up, dimly comprehending.

"That's right. Your boyfriend. The famous artist. He's come calling. Isn't that thoughtful of him? Say a few words." He lowered the phone.

Frowning as if afraid she was losing her mind, she took it.

"Hurry, don't keep him waiting. He's come quite a distance."

She blinked in confusion. Apprehensive that this was a trick, she raised the phone to her ear. "Chase?"

"Are you all right?"

"My God, is it really you? I thought you were dead! I thought—"

Bellasar yanked the phone from her hand. "I said 'a

few words,' not a speech. Satisfied?" he asked into the phone.

"Let her go."

"I can't think of a reason why I should."

"I can. Do something for me. Call the following telephone number." Malone recited it.

The number was so familiar, Bellasar felt uneasy. "What are you—"

"Just call that number in Paris. An associate of mine is with your next wife and her father."

"What?"

"Unless you do what I want, my associate is going to show them a dossier about your three previous marriages and how you killed your wives. He's going to tell them how you planned to kill your *present* wife. He's going to tell them that you and your sister were lovers, that you murdered her, and that your wives all looked like her. He has photographs."

Outrage made Bellasar speechless.

"Your fiancé won't be able to bear the sight of you, let alone be married to you. Her father will be so furious about the danger you present to his daughter that he'll stop supplying weapons to you. Of course, he's only one of your manufacturers, but a father whose daughter's honor has been assaulted will spread the word. You're fanatical about your privacy. It'll be destroyed. I'm willing to bet other suppliers will stop doing business with you, especially when they find out you've been compromised by the CIA."

"The CIA?"

"If anything happens to Sienna, I'm going to spread

the word that the CIA knows everything you're doing, that your business is out of control. No one will trust you. If you want to keep being an arms merchant, you'll have to sell cheap handguns to dope dealers on street corners."

Bellasar glared.

"Once you lose your power," Malone said, "everybody you stomped on, everybody who holds a grudge against you, will pay you back. You ruined *my* life. Now you're going to find out what it feels like on the other side."

"And if I do what you want, the conversations you're threatening me with will never happen." Bellasar's voice was contemptuous.

"That's right."

"You expect me to believe you won't tell the woman in Paris? To protect her from me?"

"You'll protect her yourself."

"What do you mean?"

"You'll break off the relationship. I won't need to tell her anything."

"And in exchange, you get Sienna. But how can I trust the men with you to keep the agreement? Since when does the CIA care about private arrangements?"

"This isn't a sanctioned operation. These men work for me. They'll do as I ask."

"And that'll be the end of it?"

"Not quite," Malone said. "You've got a biological weapon. The pressure won't be off you until I make sure it's destroyed."

Bellasar's fury reached a peak. "I'm bringing her out."

He broke the connection and swung toward Sienna. "Get up!" He dragged her to her feet and shoved her from the room. But instead of heading toward the outside door, he forced her downstairs toward the basement.

And the basement below that one.

9

Watching the tear gas disperse, seeing guards regroup, Malone fired a burst from the machine guns. Trees and shrubs blew apart. Bodies flew.

"It's been three minutes! Where *is* he?"

Strafing the grounds, Malone sped to the landing pad, hovered, turned in a circle, and leveled everything around him. The moment he set down the chopper, Jeb, Dillon, and the others charged out, firing. Although the chopper's rotors dispersed the tear gas, the men still wore gas masks, hoping to intimidate their opponents by continuing to pretend that the powder they'd dropped was anthrax.

As Malone hooked tear-gas grenades to his belt, Potter yelled, "What about us? Unlock these handcuffs!"

Malone didn't bother answering, just grabbed an assault rifle, jumped down, and raced toward the Cloister.

Behind him, he heard gunfire, Jeb and his men giving the guards another reason to run from the estate. As a bullet zinged past, Malone ducked to a shattered tree and fired at a guard who showed himself a second too long. Malone's volley hit him in the chest, knocking him into the swimming pool.

He scanned the wreckage, searching for other targets. Statues had been decapitated. Ruptured fountains gushed water. There! He fired at a guard who rose to aim from behind the rubble of a column. As the man fell, Malone spun, saw no other targets, and raced nearer to the Cloister, only to dive behind another shattered tree as the main door swung open.

"Malone!" Bellasar shouted from inside.

"Where *is* she?"

"Have you still got your cell phone?" Staying hidden, Bellasar shouted numbers.

What's he doing? Stomach cramping with apprehension, Malone sank lower behind the shattered tree. He took the phone from his windbreaker and pressed the numbers he'd been given.

"*Chase?*" Sienna answered immediately, frightened.

"Are you okay? Where are you?"

"In the Cloister's basement. Locked in a room."

"*What* room?"

"I don't know! He blindfolded me once he brought me down here!"

Malone tried to keep his voice calm. "Don't be afraid. I'm coming to get you."

He pressed the disconnect button and shouted toward the Cloister's open door, "Bellasar!"

No response.

"Bellasar!"

Silence, except for gunshots in the distance.

Malone pulled a tear-gas grenade from his belt, freed its pin, and hurled it through the open door.

Vapor filled the opening.

He darted toward the side of the Cloister, used the butt of his rifle to smash a basement window, and threw a tear-gas grenade into the opening.

As vapor filled the room below, he raised his gas mask from where it dangled around his neck. He put it on, knocked the remaining shards from the window, and climbed through. At the bottom, he aimed around the haze-filled room, seeing no targets, hearing no coughing. He rushed to the side of an open doorway, tossed his final grenade into a corridor, and followed it, stalking invisibly through the dense gas. He still didn't hear any coughing. Bellasar couldn't have anticipated a tear-gas attack. He wasn't likely to have had a gas mask in easy reach. Was Bellasar using Sienna as a decoy while he ducked out the back of the building?

Bellasar doesn't matter! I have to find Sienna!

He moved along the corridor, checking each room. Empty.

He reached stairs that rose toward the gas-filled entrance.

Other stairs led down. Malone followed them.

The temperature cooled. The rocks that formed the

walls became larger, the construction cruder, older, as if from a thousand years ago.

He came to the brightly lit bottom, where a shiny metal door blocked his way. Silently praying that it wasn't locked, he pulled, exhaled when it budged, and stepped carefully to the side as it swung open.

Was Bellasar hiding on the other side, waiting to shoot him?

Malone took off his gas mask, held it at head level, and inched it around the doorjamb as if peering beyond the door. No bullet struck the mask from his hand. He readied himself, lunged through the doorway, and dropped to a crouch, aiming.

No target presented itself.

Instead, he saw the bright corridor of a laboratory. Along each side, windows showed research rooms. He hurried along, not seeing anyone.

"Sienna!"

She didn't shout back.

"Sienna!"

He came to another steel door. It, too, was unlocked, but this time when he lunged through, aiming, he found the two Russian bioweapons experts, their faces ashen.

As he straightened, they stared from him toward a window, beyond which was another window.

"Sienna!"

She didn't react. Past the first window, a corridor, and a second window, she sat at a table, looking dismally at her hands. Her face was battered.

"Sienna!"

"She can't hear you," said the stoop-shouldered Russian whom Malone had seen arrive by helicopter so long ago. His English was thickly accented, his tone heavy with discouragement. "She can't see you, either. The glass on her window works only one way."

Malone rushed toward a door, tugged, but couldn't budge it. He pulled with all his strength.

"It won't do any good," the Russian said. "Even if you had a key. Not for six hours."

"Six hours?"

Malone pounded the butt of his rifle against the glass. The window trembled. He pounded harder, but the glass wouldn't yield.

"You're wasting your time," the Russian said. "You can't get through that glass with a sledgehammer or a bullet. To be doubly sure, she's in a chamber within a chamber. Anything to prevent a leak."

"Leak?" Malone felt dizzy.

"I never believed he'd do it." The Russian looked dazed. "Bellasar said he was going to make an example to the man he was negotiating with, but I never dreamed . . ."

"An example? Jesus, what did he—"

A phone rang in an office behind him.

Malone stared at it. As it rang again, he suddenly knew whose voice he would hear. Rushing in, he answered it. *"You bastard, how do I get her out of there?"*

"You can't," Bellasar said. "Not for six hours."

"Six hours?" Again that time limit. Malone vaguely remembered having been told about its significance.

When? Who had told him? "What's so damned important about—" His skin turned cold when his memory
cleared. Laster. At the Virginia safe house.

*"What makes the weapon so unique is that Grib-
anov and Bulganin genetically engineered the smallpox virus so it can't infect anyone unless it combines
with another virus, a benign but rare one,"* Laster had
said. *"You release the benign virus first. As soon as
the target population is infected, the lethal virus is
then released."* The benign virus had a six-hour life
span, Laster had continued. After that, even if you had
smallpox, you couldn't spread it to anyone who hadn't
come in contact with the benign virus within the previous six hours. The time limit was a way of controlling the weapon and keeping it from spreading beyond
the target area.

"I promised I'd give her to you," Bellasar said, "but
I didn't guarantee in what condition."

"You released both viruses at once?" Malone's
legs felt weak.

"Tell anyone anything you want about me. It won't
make a difference. When my enemies understand
what I'm capable of, they'll be twice as afraid of me."

"You exposed her to smallpox?" Malone screamed.

10

Raging, he charged up the stairs. I'll catch him! I'll
get my hands on his throat! I'll— But as Malone

neared the top, he heard gunfire, not just the rattle of assault rifles but the roar of the chopper's machine guns. The *whoosh* of a rocket was followed by an explosion. At the top, the gas had dissipated. Rushing from the Cloister, Malone stared to the left, toward where he had last seen Jeb and his men. Dust, flames, and smoke obscured his vision.

The chopper wasn't where he had left it. A rumble cramped his muscles. On his left, the haze dissipated as whirling blades and the chopper appeared. Like malignant growths, a new array of weapons emerged from its belly. It stopped a hundred feet up and a hundred yards away. Even at a distance, Bellasar's stark features were vivid behind the Plexiglas. From a loudspeaker beneath the fuselage, his voice boomed. "I don't sell equipment I can't handle!"

Before Malone could run back to the Cloister, a burst from a machine gun tore a crater behind him. The force of it threw him to the ground as dirt, stones, and redirected bullets flew around him. He rolled to get farther from the crater, only to see the chopper alter its angle of fire, a machine gun tearing up another crater, this one to the right of him, the chaos making his ears ring.

He could have killed me! The son of a bitch is toying with me!

Frantic, Malone pivoted as if to run to the left, but the moment Bellasar guided the chopper that way, Malone changed direction and raced to the right.

Away from the Cloister.

Away from Jeb and his men, if they were still alive.

Toward the weapons-testing range.

Behind him, he heard the chopper's motors change pitch as Bellasar pursued him. Even with the ringing in his ears, he heard it come so close, he had to dive to the ground, the chopper speeding over him, wind from it ruffling his hair. Before Bellasar could turn and come after him again, Malone scrambled to his feet and raced onward.

This part of the estate hadn't been damaged by Malone's attack. He charged closer to the weapons-testing range, using hedges, trees, and bushes to provide cover. The trees to his left disappeared, the machine guns vaporizing them. He dove to the ground an instant before the hedges between which he'd been running burst into pieces, specks of leaves and branches filling the air, the chopper swooping over.

Again, before Bellasar could turn, Malone sprang to his feet and ran. Beyond one last line of shrubs, he rushed into the open, reaching the wooden stalls of the testing area. To his right was the .50-caliber machine gun Bellasar had threatened him with. But as Malone tried to reach it, Bellasar fired, dirt and grass flying, a trough appearing between Malone and the weapon.

Malone tried again, and again Bellasar's bullets cut off his route. The bastard's enjoying himself. Furious, Malone spun in another direction. Beyond the stalls was the mock village Bellasar and his clients used for target practice. It had been rebuilt since Malone had last seen it. He sprinted toward one of the stalls, flicked the switch Potter had used months earlier, and charged toward the suddenly animated village, realistic-looking soldiers, civilians, and vehicles now moving along the streets.

A volley from a machine gun tore up grass on his right. Veering to the left but continuing to race toward the village, Malone tensed in dread of the volley that would be aimed in that direction. Trying to time it, he swung to the right an instant before the next volley devastated the grass to his left, but now the bullets hit closer to him. Bellasar was tiring of the game.

The village loomed. Malone zigzagged across the final twenty yards, dove over a stone wall, landed hard, gasped from the pain in his ribs, then squirmed frantically toward the corner of a stone building, where he pressed himself behind a pile of rubble. Both machine guns firing, the helicopter attacked the village. It blew a gap in the wall, destroyed the corner of the house, and heaved up the cobblestones in a street farther along.

The moment the chopper sped over the tops of the buildings, Malone raced along the street. Before Bellasar could turn and see him, he darted left into a courtyard and sprawled behind another wall. His chest heaved. Sweat dripped from his face. When he wiped it, his hand came away bloody, and he realized the concussion of the near hits from the machine guns had made his nose bleed.

Bellasar skimmed the village, searching. "Don't think you can hide!" his voice boomed from the loudspeaker. "This chopper has night-vision and heat-sensor equipment! As soon as it gets dark, I'll have no trouble picking up your heat signature!"

Malone studied a military Jeep filled with mannequins dressed as soldiers. The Jeep was on a track that moved the vehicle along a street. Other mannequins dressed as villagers were on similar tracks that made them appear to walk.

"And don't think you can wait for me to run out of fuel!" Bellasar's voice thundered. "Before that happens, I'll level this place!"

A flatbed truck filled with mannequins dressed as workers was so realistic that Malone had the start of an idea, interrupted by an explosion as a rocket blew the truck apart. It heaved, chunks flying in all directions. Burning mannequins, many without arms and heads, flipped through the air. A fireball soared. As black smoke drifted over him, Malone's nostrils contracted from the stench of cordite, scorched metal, and burning gasoline.

Burning gasoline? Had Bellasar made the village that realistic?

The chopper crisscrossed the village, continuing to search. As soon as Bellasar faced the opposite direction, Malone rushed from cover and hurried toward another Jeep. Wary of the chopper, he grabbed a rifle from one of the mannequin soldiers and raced back to the cover of a wall.

Breathing heavily, he examined the weapon. An M16. Its magazine was fully loaded. Did that mean the grenades the mannequins carried were real also? Why would . . .

So the sound effects and the visuals will be accurate, Malone understood with a chill. When Bellasar and his clients shoot at this village, it has to seem as realistic as possible. An explosion has to detonate gasoline in vehicles. It has to set off grenades and ammunition as it would when fire engulfed military corpses.

The chopper pivoted, coming in Malone's direction. He'll fly right over me, Malone realized, his heart beating faster. He'll see me behind this wall.

Racing toward an alley, Malone heard the chopper increase speed. He saw me! Entering the alley, charging between houses, he cursed when he saw the alley end at a doorway.

If that door's a fake, if it's jammed . . .

He didn't have an option. He knew what Bellasar would do next. Stretching his legs to their maximum, he reached the dead end. Slamming against the door, pawing at its latch, he thrust it open. His momentum carried him into a house, but instead of stopping, he kept running. He saw an open window, raced toward it, dove through it, and, even as he flew through the air, an explosion behind him thrust him farther, the rocket Bellasar had launched hitting the front of the house. The force of the blast sent walls toppling, rubble flying. When Malone landed in a stone courtyard, the pain in his ribs almost made him pass out. Chunks of rock fell over him. Dust and smoke overwhelmed him.

Smoke. Despite his pain, a thought that had started forming earlier now insisted. *Smoke.* The fires in the ruined buildings had created so much smoke that this section of the village was blanketed with it. Bellasar couldn't see where Malone was sprawled.

Wrong. As the chopper approached, its spinning blades dispersed the smoke, allowing Bellasar a glimpse of the wreckage.

The smoke will work, though, Malone decided. There just has to be enough of it.

Wincing from the pain in his ribs, he forced himself across the courtyard. Gaining speed, he reached a street and saw another Jeep approaching. He took off his windbreaker and formed a sling with it. He darted out, jumped onto the Jeep, grabbed grenades from the equipment belts on the mannequins, stuffed them into the sling, heard the chopper approaching, grabbed two more grenades, and leapt off, taking cover in a doorway as Bellasar flew over.

Straining to get enough air in his lungs, he pulled the pin from a grenade, heaved the grenade toward the receding Jeep, and raced the opposite way along the street. A truck came around a corner. He tossed a grenade into it as well and ran harder. The blast from the first grenade gutted the Jeep, set off a secondary explosion in the gas tank, and detonated the ammunition in the rifles. *Pop, pop, pop,* he heard, then winced from the louder explosion of the second grenade, the truck bursting into flames. Continuing to run, he hurled a third grenade at a pickup truck, a fourth at a bus, a fifth at a station wagon. The chain of explosions behind him was accompanied by rising columns of dense black smoke from burning gasoline and tires.

Bellasar shot into the smoke, but Malone was already in a different sector, blowing up a half-track, another Jeep, and another pickup truck. The secondary explosions added to the chaos, more dense smoke billowing. The stench was so acrid Malone bent over, coughing. The flames spread to buildings. Mannequins dressed as civilians moved on their tracks, continuing to walk even though they were burning.

The smoke drifted from the village, spreading across the field around it. Malone used it for cover, racing toward the weapons-testing stalls. The .50-caliber machine gun, he kept thinking. Bellasar had cut off his route to it earlier. If Malone had persisted, he was certain Bellasar would have decided the threat was sufficiently serious for him to quit toying with Malone and stop the game right then.

A change in the sound of the chopper's motors warned Malone that Bellasar had seen him running across the smoke-obscured field.

No!

He raced as hard as he could.

The chopper sped toward him.

What if the machine gun doesn't have ammunition? What if—

Run!

Bellasar fired, narrowly missing him.

Faster!

Malone's makeshift sling still held a few grenades. His legs pumping, his chest heaving, he grabbed a grenade, pulled its pin, reached the machine gun, then whirled and threw the grenade as far and as high as he could in the chopper's direction. He was too desperate to worry about shrapnel as he swung toward the machine gun on its tripod and shouted in triumph when he saw that an ammunition belt was attached to it.

The grenade exploded in front of the chopper, its shock wave jolting the fuselage, shrapnel whacking against the Plexiglas, the distraction enough to keep Bellasar from firing again.

For an intense moment, Malone saw Bellasar's fury-contorted features. In the back, desperate and frenzied, Potter and Ahmed tugged at the bars to which they were handcuffed. Then Malone yanked back the arming mechanism on the machine gun, tilted the weapon upward, and pulled the trigger. The awesome rate of fire threatened to twist the weapon out of his control. But although he had found the recoil daunting when Bellasar had made him fire the weapon months earlier, he now felt angrily at ease with it. Its repeated shudder, reminiscent of the speed and power of a locomotive, aggravated the pain in his body, but his body transcended his pain. In the next pure timeless moment, he and the weapon were one as he steadied his aim and kept squeezing the trigger. The rounds had extrapowerful loads. The tips were explosive. Bellasar had been so proud of them. Now a steady spray of them struck the chopper, blowing it, along with Bellasar, Potter, and Ahmed, to hell.

The blast was so powerful, it slammed Malone to the ground, and this time he did pass out—but not before he saw the flaming wreckage cascade, slamming, onto the field. How long he was unconscious, a minute or five minutes, he couldn't tell. All he knew was that when he came to, the wreckage was still burning across from him. But he didn't have time to rejoice in his victory. He had no thought of celebration. He hadn't been victorious. There was nothing to celebrate. He was alive, and he had gotten his revenge, but he hadn't won. Wavering to his feet, he stumbled past mutilated trees and hedges toward the Cloister. Sienna! he kept thinking, and then, as he broke from a stumble to a run, he wailed it.

"SIENNA!"

11

Time had deceived him. What had seemed like fifteen minutes had taken an hour. When he reached the Cloister, he found Jeb passed out on its front steps, a pool of blood around him, a bullet hole in his arm. "Now I owe *you*," Malone said. A policeman and a doctor, alarmed by the rumble of the distant explosions, had arrived from the nearest village twenty kilometers away. While the doctor worked on Jeb, the policeman and townspeople summoned by phone were searching the grounds, trying to help the survivors. Three of Jeb's men, including Dillon, had been wounded. Two were dead. Sickened, Malone rushed down the basement stairs to the corridor outside Sienna's chamber.

The Russians had remained, still devastated by the reality that Bellasar had actually used the weapon. Pale, they continued to stare through both windows toward Sienna. After having waited so long, she was pacing, her eyes panicky. Through the one-way glass, Malone watched her tug frantically at the door, then study the ceiling, trying to calculate a way out. The bruises on her face were more pronounced. It broke his heart to see them. But they were the least thing that would mar her beauty.

"How long does the disease take to develop?" he asked the stoop-shouldered Russian.

Downcast, the man replied, "Normally, seven to ten days."

"Normally?"

"We engineered it so the effects are accelerated. But it was all a research experiment. We never dreamed Bellasar would actually use it."

"How long?"

"Three days."

"Does she know she's been exposed?"

Looking more dejected, the Russian shook his head from side to side.

Malone swallowed bile. His ordeal had left him so weak, he could barely stand. But how he felt didn't matter. He went into an office behind him, picked up its phone, and pressed the numbers Bellasar had earlier given him.

Across from him, through the one-way glass, Sienna spun toward the room's table and the phone on it. From Malone's point of view, it rang silently as she picked it up.

"Chase?"

"Right here, sweetheart."

"I got so worried. You said you were coming, and when you didn't—"

"Something held me back."

"You sound . . ." She straightened. "Are you all right?"

"Tired. Banged-up. Otherwise . . . You want to hear some good news?"

"God yes."

"It's over. He's dead. You don't have to be afraid of him ever again."

For a moment, she didn't react. She seemed not to believe what she had heard. Then tears welled from her eyes, streaming down her ravaged face.

With all his heart, Malone wanted to hold her. He imagined how closed in she must feel, not being able to see outside the room.

"Come get me," she said. "Please."

"I can't." Malone's voice didn't want to work. "Not yet. Not for five hours."

"Five hours? Why? I don't understand."

"Some kind of time lock. I won't be able to open the door until then."

"Time lock? Five hours?"

"But you won't be alone. You and I can still keep talking like this. Now that you don't have to fear him, what would you like to do? Where would you like to go?"

"Do? That's easy. I want to spend the rest of my life with you."

Malone's throat tightened. "You've got a deal. And what about where?"

"You'll think this is corny."

"I doubt it. Give it a try."

"I'd like to go where I told you my parents went on their honeymoon."

"To Siena? In Italy?"

"Yes."

"There's nothing corny about that at all."

When policemen streamed into the corridor, Malone refused to interrupt what he and Sienna were talking about: their dreams, regrets, and resolves. He locked the door and motioned vigorously through the window for the policemen to leave him alone. At first, they tried to break in, until the Russians told them what had happened.

Five hours passed.

A lifetime.

Finally the time lock opened.

Malone hung up the phone and stepped out of the office. The policemen had long ago left the building, afraid that the Russians had miscalculated, that the disease would still be contagious. Even the Russians had left, finally losing confidence in the safeguards they had taken.

Only Malone stood in the corridor. It made no difference to him if he caught the disease. Without Sienna, he didn't want to live. Still not knowing how to tell her, he entered the chamber. They hugged as if it had been years since they'd been allowed to see each other. They kissed as if it would be the last time they ever did.

Epilogue

Siena sits on three hills in the rolling countryside of Italy's Tuscany. Its famed cathedral has an intricately textured facade, its white marble offset with green- and rose-colored stone. The city's piazza—sloped like half of a giant shell, paved with fiery bricks in a herringbone pattern—is rimmed by medieval palaces and civic buildings. Much of the old part of the city has survived. Its ancient gates, its narrow, winding up-and-down streets, its stone buildings and sloping rust-colored tile roofs have the effect of obscuring cars, motorbikes, and electrical lines and, like the piazza, taking one back in time.

That was the impression for Jeb Wainright as he made his way along a brown brick lane, opened a gray wooden gate, and entered a brightly colored flower garden, its reds, purples, and greens in contrast with the smoldering earth tones for which the city is famous. He wore sneakers, jeans, and a blue short-sleeved polo shirt. He had a camera bag slung over his left shoulder. Periodically, he rubbed that arm as if troubled by a persistent ache.

An elderly man came out of a doorway into the

sunlight, his straw hat and gardener's coveralls dusty. "May I help you?" he asked in Italian.

Jeb, who had often worked in Italy and knew the language, answered, "I'm looking for someone I'm told is renting some rooms here. An American."

"Signor Malone?"

Jeb tried to appear subdued. "Yes. I haven't seen him in a long time."

The man's troubled expression made *Jeb* feel troubled.

"He is where he always is." The white-bearded man pointed toward an opposite gate, beyond which shrubs blossomed.

"Grazie."

Massaging his left arm again, Jeb walked along a path, heard bees murmuring among the flowers, opened the gate, and entered a different kind of garden, lush grass bordered by ornamental bushes, trees providing shade.

To the left, a man was so rapt in concentration, an artist's brush in his hand, a canvas on an easel before him, that he didn't hear the gate open. The painting depicted the most beautiful woman Jeb had ever seen.

Its subject sat in a wicker chair, a section of the fiery brown city spread out behind her. Jeb remembered a time when he had felt so awkward in the presence of the woman's beauty that he had found it difficult to look at her. As he approached, he fought the urge to look away.

For her part, seeing him, she fidgeted, then crossed the garden and disappeared through a doorway.

Saddened by her departure, Malone turned to see who had interrupted the session. "Jeb?" He blinked as if he thought his eyes were tricking him.

"How are you doing, old buddy? You promised you'd keep in touch. When you didn't, I got worried."

Surprised by Jeb's arrival, Malone didn't answer right away, seeming not to know what to say. "Keep in touch? Yeah, I meant to."

"But things got busy?"

"Something like that."

"You're a hard man to find," Jeb said. "All I had to go on was, the Russian heard you promise Sienna on the phone that the two of you would come here."

"It's a beautiful city."

"So I found out. The next time I have to go to ground, this is where I'll do it." Jeb glanced toward where Sienna had disappeared through the doorway. He returned his attention to Malone. "So, how have you been?"

Malone hesitated. "Good." He thought about it. "Everything considered."

"You're looking well."

"So are you." Malone studied him. For the first time, he spoke directly. "What do you want, Jeb?"

"Just to see my old friend and find out how he's doing. Maybe have a few beers together. Catch up on lost time."

Malone glanced down at his hands. "I guess I'm being rude."

"What gave you that idea?"

The playful sarcasm made Malone smile slightly. Then he sobered. "How's the arm?"

"That damned bullet nicked a nerve or something. The muscle twitches."

"Sorry."

"No big deal."

"But it is. You did a lot for me." Malone glanced toward the doorway. "For both of us. What about your job?"

"Laster was furious that I went behind his back. He assigned me to a desk until he decided whether he could trust me back in the field."

"I know how sitting at a desk would drive you crazy."

"It had its advantages. It gave me a chance to watch Laster."

Malone frowned.

"I couldn't stop wondering who Bellasar's informant was in the Agency," Jeb said. "From the start, it bugged me that Laster had been so ready to believe the body in the East River was yours. As fast as he could, he canceled the backup I'd arranged in case you managed to get Sienna off Bellasar's estate. And there were other things—the way he brought you and Sienna to that safe house in Virginia and prolonged your debriefing, even though it was obvious we'd gotten all the information we were going to. Then Bellasar suddenly knew you were at the safe house, the same way Bellasar suddenly found out you and Sienna were in Mexico after I told Laster."

Malone's gaze hardened.

"So I checked his background. He's got a wife, two kids in college. Manages to live within his means. The first couple of times I followed him, he seemed to have the most boring life in the world. But one weekend, he broke his routine, didn't go home, and drove up to Baltimore instead. It turns out he's got another life up there, another identity, another house, and another woman, this one twenty years younger. Under his other identity, he also has a bank account in the Bahamas that got deposits from one of Bellasar's corporations. He's looking at twenty years in prison."

"Not long enough." Malone's voice hardened. "But when he gets out, he and I are going to have a talk."

"Talk to *me*. I mean it, Chase. Are you all right?"

"Sure."

"And what about . . ." Jeb pointed toward the doorway.

"Fine."

Sunshine through a window revealed numerous paintings on a wall. All of them depicted the same beautiful woman. "You've been busy."

"The two things I don't lack are time to paint and inspiration. When an artist finds his Beatrice . . ." Malone glanced at the portrait he'd been working on, lost in thought.

"Aren't you going to offer me that beer?"

"Sorry." Malone looked displeased with himself. "I guess I'm still being rude. Sit down. I'll be right back."

But Malone didn't return for several minutes. Sitting on a bench, Jeb heard an indistinct conversation.

Finally, Malone came out with the beers.

"Sienna won't be joining us?" Jeb asked.

"She's a little under the weather."

"That's too bad. I was looking forward to talking with her."

"She sends her best."

"Give her mine."

It went on like that for an hour, a strained conversation between friends whom circumstance had parted. Jeb told him about how the CIA and its French equivalent had worked quickly to cover up what had happened at Bellasar's estate, claiming there'd been an industrial accident.

One thing Malone and Jeb *didn't* talk about was what it had been like during the three weeks Malone had struggled to keep Sienna alive. Because no one was certain that the fail-safe feature incorporated into the weapon would prevent it from being contagious after six hours, the Cloister had been quarantined. After teams in biohazard suits had removed the wounded and the dead, a thousand-meter perimeter had been established. No one had been allowed on or off the obliterated estate.

Ghostlike among the rubble, the only building still standing, the Cloister had been the makeshift hospital in which Malone, guided by telephone conversations with physicians, worked to keep Sienna's fever down, to adjust her intravenous lines, give her sponge baths with cool water, and will her to live.

One of the most feared plagues, smallpox had been eradicated in 1977. Because few present-day physicians had ever seen its devastating effects, Malone was asked to make detailed notes about its symptoms, all the more necessary because this was a new form of the disease. The virus's unpredictability was the main reason the authorities had decided not to risk taking Sienna to a hospital. Medicines and food were dropped by parachute. In theory, the disease wasn't contagious; these precautions were needless. But if Malone developed symptoms, plans had been made to use a thermal bomb on the area and destroy every trace of the virus.

Malone hadn't known about that contingency any more than Jeb, recovering from his wound, had known what Malone was going through in the Cloister. Jeb could only imagine and ask doctors what Malone had said and, later, read the notes Malone had made while taking care of her. First had come the fever: 106 degrees. Then vomiting, diarrhea, and delirium. Then a rash of scarlet hemorrhagic blotches beneath the skin. The doctors had told Jeb the risk of death was greatest at this point. Spots had appeared on Sienna's face and neck. The spots grew into blisters. The blisters became cloudy. At last, the eruptions dried into scabs. Throughout, the urge to scratch had been almost uncontrollable. Despite her weakness, Sienna's efforts to claw at her face had been so powerful that Malone had lost strength holding her arms down and at last had been forced to tie them to her sides.

When it appeared that she was going to live and that the virus was not contagious without its companion, the authorities had relented on the quarantine, removing Sienna to a sealed ward in a hospital, keeping a close watch on Malone in case belated symptoms appeared. Meanwhile, Jeb had continued to recuperate. When visitors were finally allowed into the ward, Jeb, his arm in a sling, had been the first to arrive. But Malone and Sienna had been gone. . . .

As the conversation drifted to a halt, Jeb finished his beer. A breeze rustled leaves. A distant drone of traffic blended with the sound of bees in the flowers.

Malone didn't make an offer of a second beer. "How soon are you expected back in Washington?"

"It's kind of open-ended," Jeb said. "Are you up for dinner tonight?"

"We really don't go out much."

"Just the two of us maybe."

"I don't like to leave Sienna alone."

"Sure," Jeb said. "Should I drop around tomorrow?"

Malone didn't say anything.

"Well, this is the name of the hotel where I'm staying." Jeb handed him a card he had taken from the lobby. "If you change your mind . . ."

"Right." Malone put the card in his shirt pocket.

"So . . ." Jeb shook his hand. "Say good-bye to Sienna for me. Make sure you give her my best." Feeling awkward, he turned toward the easel. "It's a masterpiece. You've never done better work."

"Yes."

"And those other paintings . . ." Jeb pointed toward

the ones he had seen through the window. "They're masterpieces, too."

"I've never been this inspired before."

"Take care of yourself," Jeb said. "And of her."

"Believe me, that's the most natural thing in the world."

As Jeb opened the gate, Malone went into the house.

Ahead, in the flower garden, the white-bearded man asked Jeb, "Did you enjoy your visit with your friend?"

"It's complicated."

"His wife," the elderly man said in wonder. "He's so devoted to her. They never go out. They're totally content to be with each other. They've lived here six months, and you're the first visitor they've had."

"They have each other. What more could they want?"

"Have you seen the paintings?"

Jeb nodded.

"They all show his wife," the elderly man said. "He doesn't paint anything else."

"With work that exceptional, he doesn't *need* to paint anything else."

"But I don't understand." The old man hesitated. "Have you seen her?"

"Briefly. When I entered the garden, she went into the house."

"She always does that. She avoids being seen. What happened?"

"A disease."

"And yet in the paintings she's so beautiful."

"She *is* beautiful."

The old man looked puzzled.

"What's on the canvas is what he sees."

Jeb walked past the bright flowers and paused at the gray wooden gate.

He loves her so much, Jeb thought, she'll always be the most beautiful woman in the world.

DAVID MORRELL is one of America's most popular and critically acclaimed storytellers, with more than fifteen million copies of his novels in print. To give his stories a realistic edge, he has been trained in wilderness survival, hostage negotiation, executive protection, antiterrorist driving, assuming identities, electronic surveillance, and weapons. A former professor of American literature at the University of Iowa, Morrell now lives in Santa Fe, New Mexico.